Dedication

Little Ditto, you are our golden boy!!…

D. Turner

Cyber Lovers

Austin Macauley
PUBLISHERS LTD.

A CIP catalogue record for this title is available from the British Library.

ISBN 978 1 78455 246 6

www.austinmacauley.com
First Published (2014)
Austin Macauley Publishers Ltd.
25 Canada Square
Canary Wharf
London
E14 5LB

Printed and bound in Great Britain

Acknowledgments

Thanks to today's modern technology this allows us to stay in touch and communicate in a cyber world.

Preface

Michelle's heart was broken as she sobbed herself to sleep night after night. Her sleep was both restless and distressed. She went to work each day, carried out the duties of a mother at home, but her whole life was on autopilot and she barely know how to drag herself through each day. Somehow or another she had to pull herself together and try to fit back into the life she once knew. She had never felt such pain inside, or so empty and lonely. Her whole life had come crashing down around her. How had she managed to fall so in love with a married man? He was married with a family, and so was she. But, from the moment Mike had kissed her on that Christmas Eve two years ago, she had she had feelings for him that she should not have. Their love affair began. And their love for one another grew stronger and stronger. But when the inevitable happened and they were found out, devastation hit them both as they were clawed back into their family lives. Two marriages to be patched up, but this way their families were not torn apart. In time they would each recover!... Or so they thought!...

For the next twenty years Mike and Michelle did not see one another, although they never completely broke their contact. They would still speak on the telephone from time to time. And never a Christmas or birthday went by that they did not speak to one another, and for all these years their love remained. When it looked as though Mike was to be offered early retirement, this would mean their telephone contact would no longer be able to take place. So for the first time they exchanged e-mail addresses. This book tells the story from their first e-mail. Their relationship took off to a whole new level, as they became 'cyber lovers' through the internet world of Skype and e-mail.

This novel is written in a modern-day format of e-mails and instant interactive texting... as the story unfolds it is full of LOVE, LUST, ROMANCE, SEDUCTION, EMOTION; it is RAUNCHY, PASSIONATE, EROTIC AND SENSUAL. A must-read for anyone who has ever indulged in a forbidden love affair, found love on the Internet, or indulged in cybersex. This is a must-have book to read for lovers and cyber lovers everywhere and you will not be disappointed with this read.

THIS IS AN X-RATED ADULT READ ONLY...

CHAPTER ONE

As she crawled up the bed with the predatory insouciance of a slinky panther, she licked her lips in an outrageously flirtatious manner, she looked straight into the eyes of the man she loved. Their love-making was erotic and passionate, yet always so intimate. For the past five minutes she had been sucking his cock until it was so thick and hard it was ready to blow. Their love for one another was insatiable, and they could never get enough of one another's bodies'. She was completely devoured and absorbed by the powerful feeling that she could make him so hard, and want her so much. She kneeled across his hips now, her legs straddled wide apart, she could feel how wet she was inside and wanting him inside her so badly. She could also feel the pheromones radiating from him as he sent off all the hormones of a wild animal waiting in anticipation. His hands reached up and cupped her breasts, as he pulled her gently towards him. His body beneath her so lustrous, healthy, strong and vigorous. His eyes captured her with their severe intensity... God this man was so horny! She knelt up high, as his fingers and thumbs rolled around her nipples, gently tugging. His eyes were unabashedly drinking her in, as she knelt naked, hovering over him. One of her hands went down and took hold of his cock firmly she stroked it from root to tip... He writhed beneath her in ecstasy. With it firmly in her hand, she lowered herself onto it... Her hand grasping tightly at the shaft, she teased the tip against her sensitive skin, gently stroking it up and down. With his cock she parted the sensitive tissue, now right at the entrance to her womanly world. Mesmerized by the fire in his eyes, she slid right down onto his cock. Taking him right into the centre of her world. He was so thick and hard, and from this angle he stretched her as he penetrated deep within her vagina. She pulled her hands up into her hair and swirled it onto the top of her head; with both of her arms high upon her head her body was fully exposed to him. Her sinuously curvy body writhed on top of his, as she threw her head back, flicking her hair wildly as she began to move up and down on his thick and rigid cock. He thrust into her with a vengeance, he was at the point of no return and she could see this without question. His hands moved round to her buttocks as he grasped one cheek in each hand; his grip was possessive and commanding as he pulled her so hard down onto him. Perspiration glistened over her body as she rode his body frantically up and down; the sensation was phenomenal for her. She looked back down at the man beneath her, his head was pounded tight back into the pillows, his skin aglow from the sensations he was experiencing. His eyes shut tight as he called out, "Christ Michelle, it feels so good inside you... I've never been so hard and thick... I am so deep inside you... ride me baby, ride me hard and fast." An orgasm brewed like a storm inside of her as everything tightened and clenched, squeezing... Her orgasm reverberated right through her as she called out his name, "Oh My God... Mike..." She could feel his hot love juices pumping inside her as he found his release. Sheer ecstasy rippled throughout her body as her own orgasm took over her entire being. Still she moved up and down on him, not wanting to deprive him of one ounce of his pleasure. As she slowed her pace and looked into his eyes once more, he murmured the words, "I love watching you come Michelle, the sounds you make, and the way your body quivers... it really turns me on..." He leaned up and sucked one nipple, and then the other, as she ran her fingers through his damp hair... His arms went around her waist, and still with his cock inside her he rocked her to and fro on him, as he buried his head into her breasts.

She woke up with a jump. Gathered her thoughts... sank into her duvet as one lonely teardrop ran down her face... It was all just a dream... Another dream about her Mike... Still now after all these years she dreamed about him. She lay there thinking. He had phoned her a couple of days before, as he still occasionally did, and given her an e-mail address if she ever wanted to e-mail him... Should she? What harm would it really do? It would only be e-mail, for goodness sake. Surely they could not get found out with this one! An e-mail to and from him occasionally would be lovely... She got up, showered, dressed, made herself a coffee and got her laptop out. Simon, her husband, had got up and gone to work an hour ago. She had half an hour to spare before going to work. She began to type...

E-mail from: Michelle
To: Mike
Date: 16 December 2011
Subject: One, two, three, testing ~ Are you receiving me?

Hi there Mike

I hope this is your e-mail address, as I didn't write it down. So I sincerely hope this finds you.

Love Michelle x

E-mail from: Mike
To: Michelle
Date: 16 December 2011
Subject: It looks like all systems are GO!

Hi Michelle

It is nice to hear from you. I do hope we can stay in touch this way, albeit thanks to the modern technology. They are still developing this new 'touch technology', but they have not quite got it developed enough to enable me to transmit myself down an internet cable and give you a big hug and a kiss! OMG... This brings back memories to a Christmas a long time ago, eh!

If I do not hear from you before Christmas, have a lovely Christmas and best wishes for the New Year.

Love always.
Mike
Xxx

Attachment sent of a kiss popping out of a computer screen.

Date: 17 December 2011

An e-card sent from Mike to Michelle. With the message:

I Love You

E-mail from: Michelle
To: Mike
Date: 19 December 2011
Subject: Mwah

Hi there Mike

I like being in touch with you this way… I'm liking it a lot!! And I loved the 'pop out picture of your computer kiss'. It really made me smile, I almost felt that kiss. I've never forgotten your kisses, warm and sensuous; they always made me tingle from head to toe. Always melted my heart.

And then, an e-card… Thank you so much. I can see I need to up my skills with internet sending. Your other card still hasn't arrived by post. I think you are right, using the internet this way could be much better and certainly much safer than sending cards in the post.

With my love
Michelle x

E-mail from: Michelle
To: Mike
Date: 24 December 2011
Subject: Christmas Eve

Hi Mike

Just to let you know I am thinking of about you today. I am sure you still remember that Christmas Eve all those years ago when we shared our first kiss. When work finished at lunch time we all went to the pub for a few drinks, except you and I had decided to go for a meal together for the very first time. We went to the pub with everyone else, had one drink each, and then separately made our excuses to leave. You went out of one door, I went out of another, so we were not seen to be leaving together, and then we met in the car park of the nicest restaurant in town, where you had reserved a table just for the two of us. We had a drink at the bar, were given menus to choose our meal, and just sat talking and laughing. I brought along photo's from our works night out the week before, and we laughed and laughed at the frivolity. We had both had quite a lot to drink that night, and we were no more than just colleagues on that night out, although I think we did make eyes at one another quite a bit, we had done for quite some time. We danced together, but kept one another at arm's length. We danced all the faster dances with everyone else, but also had a couple of smoochy dances... I remember you smelled so good.

The photos of that night out really made us laugh, but when the waiter came back to take our order we hadn't even looked at the menu. I could not for the life of me tell you what we ate that Christmas Eve, probably you couldn't either, because we were so wrapped up in one another. For three hours we just sat talking, laughing, eating and enjoying one another's company. We talked about our families, I told you what I had bought Simon for Christmas. You told me what you had bought Cheryl. And we each told one another what our Christmas entailed with our families. We shared a bottle of wine, and I still to this day remember your fun-filled, laughing brown eyes that day. Your sexy laugh and smile. When we noticed the time it was after 4pm, and we were the only ones left in the restaurant, with the waiters at a distance clearly waiting for us to ask for our bill. At the time, I thought this would be a one-off event, but OMG I enjoyed it so much there with you. As I know you enjoyed it too. When we left, we went out the back door to the car park. You put my coat on for me, and took just a little longer than you should to adjust the collar for me. Your fingers brushed my neck, and sent goose-bumps all over my body. When you opened the door to let us out, you caught hold of me, looked into my eyes, and kissed me on the lips... I could not believe you had done that... but, my word that kiss swept me clean off my feet. When the kiss ended, you said sorry maybe I shouldn't have done that... I said no... and then I instigated the second kiss... These two kisses turned our worlds upside down, and life was never the same again. We walked to our cars, you opened my door for me, and I slipped into the driver's seat. I thanked you for a wonderful time, and paying for the lunch (which you would not let me pay half towards). I think you were thinking of reaching in my window for another kiss… But this would have been dangerous, maybe someone would see us? So I planted a kiss on one finger, and placed that finger on your lips. We wished one another a Merry Christmas, and I drove off. My head was spinning, no not from the wine… but from the kisses. I spent that whole Christmas with my family, but thinking of you. And I know afterwards you told me you did the same. Yes Mike… That was the day I started to fall in love with you. And, although this seems like a million years ago now, and much happened between us after that day, one thing remains the same: "I will always love you".

So I just wanted to tell you… Even all these years on I remember this day… Every year since, on Christmas Eve, I have thought about it. And wondered if you have too?

Merry Christmas Mike.

I love you ~ I will always love you

Michelle ~X~

Date: 24 December 2011

An e-card sent from Mike to Michelle. A romantic Christmas card, with beautiful words and music. Also with the typed message:

Hi Michelle, Yes, I have thought about this every year since too. This is why I am here today, to send you a message. You are right, that day changed each of our lives, in fact turned our lives upside down! We had more than liked one another for quite some time before that day, but done nothing about it. Well, maybe we had been quite flirtatious with one another at times, but you were married with children and so was I. I also remember your eyes that day, those sparkling blue eyes, flashing in a very sexy manner to me. But I would not change a thing. I have loved everything we have ever shared together. Have a good Christmas. I will be in touch in the New Year.

I will always love you ~ Mike xxx

E-mail from: Mike
To: Michelle
Date: 25 December 2011
Subject: "DITTO"

Hi Michelle.

I have attached a photo I found on the internet, of a house decorated in Christmas lights, spelling out the word "DITTO"... Who on earth would do this? People like us I guess. Ditto has a very special meaning to us, taken from that film *Ghost*, where the word ditto means "I love you"... and we took this on as our own. So here I am on Christmas Day, thinking about you, and sending you my love.

Love always, Mike xxx

E-mail from: Michelle
To: Mike
Date: 28 December 2011
Subject: Christmas Cards & Messages

Hi Mike

OMG!!! Why didn't we do this earlier??? We have made this cyber world our home, where we can share our feelings of love together. Thank you for your lovely messages and e-Christmas card ~ You have always known how to melt my heart!!!

Yes, your Christmas card arrived in the post last Friday (23rd) and I think you are right, this way is safer. So maybe we'll stick to this for the future... I'm liking it. Liking it a lot.

For all the times my heart has ached to see you, or hear from you... Now I can just pick up my laptop, and there you are. I hope you received my e-card about 'Christmas Secrets'. You are my

Christmas Secret, and Christmas has always been a very special time for us, because that is when it all started for us. I couldn't get on my computer over Christmas whilst Simon was home… But I was thinking about you for sure!

I love you now and always

Michelle x x x

E-mail from: Mike
To: Michelle
Date: 31 December 2011
Subject: Happy New Year

Hi Michelle

I will raise a glass to toast the New Year; every year I have this thought of us and I can sometimes just taste your lips on the glass… Do you remember when we used to say at midnight on New Year's Eve, when everyone else is toasting one another, we would each put our lips to the glass in our hand, and on the rim of the glass would be our kiss to one another, wherever we were, and whoever else we were with, we would always think of each other at this special time? I have done this every year since. Have you? I still remember this, and if only people knew what I was thinking in my own mind when everyone around is celebrating… I am thinking of you!

Very best wishes and may you have love, joy, good health and happiness. I still love you, and this will always remain this way.

Love always

Mike xxx

E-mail from: Michelle
To: Mike
Date: 2 January 2012
Subject: Happy New Year

Hi Mike

Midnight New Years Eve, I think I did feel that kiss... Did you have my favourite aftershave on? Yes Mike, for all these years I have always remembered this, and at midnight wherever I have been, as that clock is striking in the New Year, I have thought of you, held my lips to my glass, and hoped you have always remembered it too. So nice now to know we have always both thought about this for all these years.

We also both used to say we hated the winter ~ dark, cold and miserable. But I'm not feeling so bad about it at the moment, as you brighten my days and put sunshine in my heart!!!...

I Love You

Michelle
~ x ~

E-mail from: Mike
To: Michelle:
Date: 5 January 2012
Subject: Happy New Year

Hi Michelle

"Happy New Year." May all your dreams come true. Wishing you love, joy, good health and happiness.

I send to you all my love... 8 letters and 3 simple words... "I LOVE YOU"

Mike xxx

Sent with attachment: a video clip of the song by Celine Dion, "I love you".

E-mail from: Michelle
To: Mike:
Date: 6 January 2012
Subject: I LOVE YOU

Hi Mike

I can't tell you how much I am enjoying these e-cards. The one you sent me yesterday is so beautiful ~ I love roses ~ and the Celine track you chose is one of my all-time favourites. A beautiful track, "I Love You"… she sings it like an angel.

Celine is my absolute favourite these days, and has been for a while, really since she came onto the scene, and Whitney stopped recording. How bizarre that was Whitney's last big hit, and now one of the greatest love songs of our times, is "I will always love you". I think she recorded this one especially for us!!!! Don't you? We used to love to listen to Whitney together, in one of our cars when we met for a quick little kiss and cuddle. Or in bed, when we would spend afternoons together in bed, making love, and listening to our Whitney love songs. And when we could no longer go on seeing one another, she released the song "I will always love you"; I bought it for you, and I know this song has always broken both of our hearts every time we have heard it since, and this has been many many times for each of us. When I have heard it, it has felt like a sledgehammer slamming into my heart, and all that pain came flooding back. How we have both suffered, and how we have both missed one another. I wonder if we had known, all those years ago, just how much pain we would feel for so long, whether we would have made a different decision? Who knows? We made our choices for all the right reasons for everybody else… But look at the price we each paid. Anyway, moving on… I have every CD Whitney or Celine has ever recorded, I play them at full volume in my car, and my home is always filled with music. When the album was released with the track "I Love You", I almost bought this single for you and sent it to you… And now you have sent it to me. That really made me smile, and touches deep into my heart… So what music are you into these days? Who's your favourite, or favourites'?

You didn't answer my question about aftershave on New Year's Eve? Were you wearing my favourite? What is her favourite???? I hear you thinking… It's Calvin Klein of course, because it reminds me of you!!! … and that mixed with the smell of my own favoured perfume reminds me of 'us'!!! Do you still remember my favourite perfume? You bought it for me once!!! …

Against all odds our love has stood the test of time… and …

"I LOVE YOU"

"I WILL ALWAYS LOVE YOU"

Michelle

~ x ~

E-mail from: Mike
To: Michelle
Date: 8 January 2012
Subject: Your perfume

Hi Michelle

Yes I did buy you perfume… 'Georgio Armani'. That was a long time ago and yes you are right about mine being Calvin Klein. OMG… There has been a lot of water going under the bridge since then. I remember this well, because I knew it got me into trouble sometimes, because your perfume could still be detected on me!!! Big trouble!!!

I also recall going on the best employers' training course ever and who would believe that it was to be held in the Cotswolds!!! Well, this is what we told everybody else!!! When we took ourselves off and spent five very special and precious days and nights together… Do you remember all that rain? What an excuse to stay in bed. Do you remember it was so dark with the lights off, so we slept with a light on? It was a long time ago, but I remember our times together very well like they were only yesterday and I will always cherish those good memories and the love that we shared together.

I have had the song "I Love You" on my computer for a long time now and that is why I sent it to you. Funny how we still have the same tastes in so many different things, or perhaps it is something called fate. Whitney Houston "I Will Always Love You" still brings back those memories of all those years ago. It always serves to remind me of you on every occasion I hear it. It must have been recorded especially for us!!!

Do you remember the necklace with the charm that I bought you, the little golden clown, and between us we named it 'Ditto'… Tell me, is 'Our Little Ditto' still alive and kicking? I hope you still keep it warm in a nice place.

Love always…
Mike xxx

E-mail from: Michelle
To: Mike
Date: 9 January 2012
Subject: I WILL ALWAYS LOVE YOU

Hi Mike

I am impressed, and really quite touched that you still remember the name of my perfume all these years on. I'm sorry that it ever caused you problems. Truly I am… I still wear this perfume most of the time. In fact I have it on today. Whenever I smell Calvin Klein on anybody it reminds me of you!!… us!!… It drifts me back to our kissing, cuddling, and our bodies entwined. Making love with you… Ummmmm… Tender loving moments!!! I hope the smell of Georgio Armani evokes such thoughts for you.

Yes, 'Our Little Ditto' is still very much alive and kicking. When you gave him to me, you told me he would be my good luck charm, and that he would keep me safe. Well he always has. He spends much of his time asleep in my jewellery box, and when I need him, I wear him on his long chain around my neck, usually tucked down inside my blouse or jumper, touching my skin, and next to my heart right where he belongs…

I too, remember our time in the Coldswolds very well. Yes, it's quite funny that it was so dark we left a light on at night ~ and the rain was indeed the perfect excuse we needed to stay in bed. Wonderful memories… I especially remember the shower! ~ Do you?… I also remember one odd occasion the sun did come out, and we were sitting outside a pub by the river, you were sitting opposite me with a drink in your hand and the sun dancing on your face, you looked so sexy and handsome, and I said to you I wished I had a camera to take a picture of you ~ and with an imaginary camera in my hands I took a picture of you… Well I obviously could never have this developed, but as it turned out I never needed to, because this picture has been engraved in my mind ever since… And, do you still remember the Swarovski crystal bear we bought my Mum? She treasured that bear!! For obvious reasons he is in my possession now, sitting in a display cabinet, and when he comes out occasionally for a wash and polish I give him a little kiss, as he is my memory of the wonderful days and nights we spent together in the Coldswolds… So indeed, memories we have both treasured, clung onto, and nobody else can ever take them from us… You are right, we are very alike. We share the same mindset. We both enjoy many similar things!!! It must be fate!!!…

I'm off to work now. Think of me Wednesday afternoon, I have my Staff Appraisal at work. But I will be OK because 'Our Little Ditto' will be with me…

My love to you… Always…
Michelle x x x x

13.01.2012: Michelle sent Mike a romantic e-card…

We always said 13 was our lucky number, and the 13th our lucky day… do you still remember this?

E-mail from: Mike
To: Michelle
Date: 13 January 2012
Subject: "I WILL ALWAYS LOVE YOU"

Hi Michelle

Thank you for your e-card. This is a lucky day and it always will be. Yes, I always think of you/us with number 13… always lucky for us in so many ways… 13th always such special days for us. (We spent many of them in bed, making love all day, when we should have been at work, and phoned in sick. And we used to laugh with one another and say, well at least we spent the day in bed when we were meant to be sick.)

Where we would just spend hours in bed together, kissing, cuddling, talking, laughing, drinking champagne, and making love... and making love... and making love again. How I loved to touch your body, cover you in kisses, and enjoy every single little inch of you... I loved your boobs so much, and those very erect long hard nipples, how I used to love to play with them, suck them. MMMmmmm... it makes me hungry for you just thinking about it.

I will always love you... every bit of you!

Mike
Xxx

Sent with a video clip of the song by Whitney Houston "I will always love you".

CHAPTER TWO

For the next month there are e-mails to and fro, loving, funny...
lots of sexy attachments... They are able to speak on the telephone
a few times... But they have not seen one another for twenty years.
Mike keeps asking Michelle to send a photo of herself by e-mail.
But she is afraid to send one, as she has obviously aged 20 years!!
But she is also cautious that there would then be a photo of her
somewhere on his computer. What if anyone else saw it by
accident?

E-mail from: Mike
To: Michelle
Date: 13 February 2012
Subject: "I WILL ALWAYS LOVE YOU"

Hi Michelle

Whitney... What a sad loss! All of her songs have memories of
you. Long before her biggest hit "I will always love you". Do you
remember giving me the cassette with all her songs? I played this
many times in the car when I was alone and just thinking of you.
"I will always love you", how this still brings back many
memories every time it is played, it can never escape in my mind
from the day you gave this to me and the particular timing when
this song was released.

I am not going to get your picture unless I send mine first. So I
had better take the lead, but I expect to get your picture in return
and no ifs and buts, okay! These were taken on my computer cam
in the summer, yes my hair is this colour!! Not bleached by the

sun either! You can have it shredded, deleted, ripped up in pieces, chewed and thrown in the bin, but I do want you to send me your picture.

Finally, and yes, a little ending note… "I will always love you".

Take care

Love always…
Mike
xxx

Date: 14 February 2012

Both send each other very loving e-Valentines Cards.

E-mail from: Michelle
To: Mike
Date: 15 February 2012
Subject: I WILL ALWAYS LOVE YOU

Hi Mike

WOW!!! Still that handsome, sexy hunk I see!!! And… you still have those 'sexy, brown, come to bed eyes' that seduced me every time I looked into them. You have hardly changed at all ~ the years have been very kind to you. UUuuuummm UUuuuumm VERY NICE!!!… I will treasure these two photo's…

I suppose this means I have to send you a photo of me now!!! As long as you PROMISE ME, nobody else will ever see it!!! … I will sort you out one. As I take most of the photo's, there are less of me than anyone else I know, most pictures of me include other people. But… I will sort through and find you a recent one… and as long as I have this promise from you, I will send you one by the end of the week.

Oh dear… Whitney… You can't help but wonder if drugs or alcohol were involved? Such a waste of life, such a waste of a brilliant talent. All Whitney records remind me of the times we spent together. Yes, I do remember giving you a cassette or two of her songs... And the iconic timing of her release of "I Will Always Love You"... I think she released that song was especially for 'US'!!!... Over all these years Whitney has always reminded me of YOU... On a purely selfish note, I'm glad I have all this internet contact with you now, as the world will be playing her records non-stop for a while. Ironic 'Fate' I would call this... You fill my head all too often again at the moment... and Whitney records will be played all over again, to the world!!! ...

And, yes... "I WILL ALWAYS LOVE YOU"

Love always and forever
Michelle
Xxxx

E-mail from: Michelle
To: Mike
Date: 16 February 2012
Subject: "TOP SECRET FILE... FOR YOUR EYES ONLY"

Hi Mike

Thank you for the lovely Valentine's e-card... And, also for your holiday pictures of scenery in Austria. Absolutely Beautiful... The slide show also very beautiful (did you put that music to it?). Yes, I would love to go there one day (don't think I will be climbing that rock either!).

As requested I have attached a photo of myself... In fact, as you sent me two of you, I have sent you two!! Well here I am almost 20 years on...

Please put your 'rose tinted glasses' on before viewing!!!

They were taken by my daughter before we all went out 'New Years Eve 2011'.

And please make sure they don't end up anywhere else on your computer, enabling anyone else to see them.

With my love
Michelle
xxx

E-mail from: Mike
To: Michelle
Date: 16 February 2012
Subject: "WOW"

Hi Michelle

Thank you very much for sending me your two photographs. I
will treasure them always and I promise for my eyes only. I
certainly would not be sharing these with anyone else.

Wow... Very nice and in a slinky black dress and holding a glass
full of drink. Champagne? Just tell me when your lips first
touched the glass to take that first sip of drink, was my kiss there
waiting for you inside, eh? You know I will always remember
this. You have not changed at all, still lovely like I remembered
you all those years ago. Still that beautiful golden blonde hair.
Still those sexy blue sparkling eyes. Still those luscious inviting
lips. You are as gorgeous now as you have always been. OMG...
I love you just as much now, as I loved you all those years ago...
Where have all the years gone?... Everything seems the same to
me now as it did back then.

Love always...
Mike
xxx

The e-mails continue throughout February.

---

5 March 2012 ~ Live Interactive Text

*Michelle logs onto her e-mail account, and showing online is
Mike... Her heart skips a beat to know he is there looking at their
e-mails at the same time she is... Is he typing her another e-mail,
as she has come here to type him one? She skims the curser over
his name where it is showing he is there online. To her surprise
this gives her the option to 'Live Text' with him? She has never
done this before... But no harm in trying... She clicks onto his
name, and a little box appears for her to type a message to him...
She starts to type:*

Michelle: Hi Mike.

A few seconds later a message pops up on her screen from him…

Mike: Hi Michelle.

Michelle: Wow… are we able to instant text here Mike?

Mike: It looks that way Michelle!!

Michelle: OMG… but how do I know this is actually YOU?

Mike: Who else is it going to be?

Michelle: We cannot be too careful… Give me a code word.

Mike: "DITTO"

Michelle: OMG… it is you… I cannot believe this…

Mike: You are crazy Michelle… Always, always my crazy Michelle… One of the reasons I fell in love with you… Well here is a new game for us to play!!!

Michelle: Oh Mike… I am going to love this with you… But I cannot stop now… Maybe we can catch up like this another time? Maybe even tomorrow? A little earlier than this?

Mike: I will look for you here tomorrow Michelle… And… I LOVE YOU

Michelle: I LOVE YOU MIKE… Hope to find you here tomorrow…

Mike: Bye… MWAH…

Michelle: Bye… MWAH…

---

6 March 2012 ~ Live Interactive Text

Mike: Hi Michelle… here we are again!!

Michelle: Hi Mike… Oh Wow!!!… I love this!!!… I could not get to sleep last night, thinking about you, and hoping we would be able to text chat today.

Mike: I could not get to sleep last night, just thinking about you… BUT, when I did… I dreamed about you!!!!

Michelle: MMMmmmm… I hope it was a nice dream?

Mike: It was a very nice dream… we were making love…

Michelle: OMG… tell me more… Wish I had've been there ☺

Mike: It felt very real to me… I am sure you were there.

Michelle: Oooo… tell me more…

Mike: Well Michelle… In my dream we were kissing… Just like we used to… and then I laid you down gently on a bed, and we were both naked…

Michelle: Wow Mike… Tell me more!!!

Mike: Our kisses were very sexy and passionate… and then my hands were skimming all over your body… Just like they used to… Followed by my lips… My lips skimming all over every inch of your body, planting kisses all over you… Just like I used to…

Michelle: Oh Mike… I remember all of this so vividly too… The way we kissed. The way we made love… So special… So tender.

Mike: My dream was special and tender… I ran my fingertips all over your nipples, and kissed and sucked them… just the way I used to.

Michelle: MMMmmmm Mike… I am getting all hot and bothered here… I remember this so well…

Mike: You were hot in my dream… Your nipples were as hard as 'American hard gums', just like they used to be… And then I ran my fingers down to your clitoris and circled it just how I remembered the way you loved it… and you would groan with delight…

Michelle: MMMmmmm… Mike I have never forgotten your tender touch.

Mike: And in my dream, you could not get enough of me when my tongue replaced my finger, and circled your clitoris, and gently I sucked it, flicked it with my tongue… and you were in heaven.

Michelle: Yes Mike, I used to love it when you did that to me… So sensual… What are you trying to do to me here?

Mike: And then in my dream Michelle, you were as greedy as you always could be when we made love, and you orgasmed before me… So I decided to drive you completely crazy, and just carry on, more and more of my tongue. You tasted so good.

Michelle: MMMmmmm… Mike… I used to love this with you.

Mike: And in my dream when you were working up to your second orgasm, I stopped. Moved up your body, sucked those lovely nipples again… Took my hot rod in my hand, now fully erect, and gently circled your clitoris with the end of my hot rod, just how you used to love it… Then gently slipped it inside of you, just the tip… You were wiggling, trying to get more of me inside you… Then I slipped a little more into you… By now, we were both in heaven… And then I slid it in all the way… Deep inside that delicious love tunnel of yours, where your muscles inside would grip me so tight.

Michelle: Oh Mike...... Soooooo nice!!

Mike: And then I thrust my hot rod in and out of your love tunnel, just the way you loved me to... On and on... Pumping you with my love... Until we both climaxed together. I filled you with gallons of my love juice, because you always drained me of every drop. You were always so greedy for me Michelle. But if I recall, we were always very greedy for each other... We could never get enough of one another...

Michelle: Oh Mike... You make me remember this so well, I can almost feel you doing these things to me right now. No we could never get enough of each other.

Mike: I have never stopped loving you Michelle

Michelle: I have always loved you so much Mike, and this has never stopped either

Mike: Our love will never die

Michelle: Never... tell me more about your dream.

Mike: We just lay cuddled up together after we had made love. My arms around your naked body. Our naked bodies entwined. Your lovely boobs laying on my chest and your hard nipples pressing into me.

Michelle: HEAVEN!!!!!

Mike: Oh yes Michelle, pure heaven.

Michelle: Mike... is this safe sex?... or have we just had cybersex? ☺

Mike: I was just telling you about my dream, that is all... ☺ But, maybe as we are here typing this it could be called cybersex? ☺

Michelle: Woweeee... we should do this more often...

Mike: MMMmmmm... Yes please. You can tell me about your dreams next time.

Michelle: Ok... Will do... I have to go now, and I expect you have to also.

Mike: I should go... But as always I don't want to leave you... ☹ It is always so hard to say good bye to you.

Michelle: We never wanted to leave one another... We would always hang on for just one more kiss... And make ourselves late home... but, I would do it all again with you... All the trouble we both ended up in was worth every minute I spent with you.

Mike: Likewise…

Michelle: I LOVE YOU MIKE…

Mike: I LOVE YOU MICHELLE…

Mike: Bye for now Michelle, maybe see you here this time tomorrow?

Michelle: BFN Mike… I will look for you here tomorrow… and maybe tell you what I would dream of doing with you!!!!

---

7 March 2012 ~ Live Interactive Text

Michelle: Hi Mike… My sexy lover

Mike: Hi my sexy babe

Michelle: I love it when you call me that

Mike: I call you that because you are sexy!!

Michelle: MMMMMmmmm… Always sexy with you

Mike: So, did you have a dream about us last night?

Michelle: Mike, I hardly slept, let alone have a dream. I could not get to sleep because I just lay there thinking about our texting on here yesterday… I laid awake for hours!!

Mike: I could not sleep either, thinking about you… Shame you do not have a dream to tell me about though…

Michelle: I could tell you what I would like to do with you right now if you like?

Mike: MMMmmmm… Michelle… Tell Me…

Michelle: I would love to have a Jacuzzi bubble bath with you… Share a bottle of champagne… And make love with you in the Jacuzzi…

Mike: Wow… Still a sexy little minx… I would love that too… Start from the beginning and tell me in detail…

Michelle: We run a bath full of nice warm water… put in plenty of bubbles… turn the Jacuzzi on… Let it bubble up… I get the chilled champagne and two glasses… You get into the Jacuzzi and wait for me…

Mike: MMMmmmm… Michelle… Take that as done… What next?

Michelle: I come into the bathroom, put the tray on the floor, with our champagne and glasses, hand you the bottle to pop the cork… And then…

Mike: Yes... you could always pop my cork, no problem, you did this so well...

Michelle: And then... I start to peel my clothes off... One piece at a time... sexy little seductive wiggles, just for you... until I am naked...!!!!!

Mike... Michelle... You are always so sexy!!!

Michelle: I climb into the Jacuzzi with you... Settle down beside you... We pour the champagne, and have a little toast... 'To the love that we share'... we sip away at the champagne... Cuddle up together... talk and laugh, like we always used to...

Mike: Michelle, you are the same as you have always been... you have not changed one bit.

Michelle: And when we have nearly finished the bottle, you take both of our glasses and place them on the side... We kiss......

Mike: I could always kiss you for hours!!!!

Michelle: These are very sexy, sensual kisses... eating one another...

Mike: MMMmmmm... I love those kisses with you...

Michelle: I am feeling very sexy now Mike... I move and position myself over the top of you... My knees either side of your hips... My arms gently around your neck, and kiss you with all the love that I feel for you...

Mike: Surely now my hands would move to those lovely boobs of yours... I would caress both of them at the same time... My fingers and thumbs would tantalize those gorgeous nipples...

Michelle: MMMmmm yes... and I would skim my hands all over your chest... Kiss all down your neck, and nibble at your shoulders...

Mike: Move up a little Michelle, I want to taste these nipples......

Michelle: Ok... I've moved up... And one of my nipples just brushes your lips...

Mike: My lips would open, and take that nipple into my mouth, and suck it...

Michelle: MMMmmmm... So nice...

Mike: Then I would do the same to the other nipple...

Michelle: My hands would skim down your torso, down your tummy, down, down, down, until I find that hot rod of yours... MMMmm I have found the complete crown jewels here... A hot rod and two golden nuggets... I will have to caress them... Gently, gently play with them... I know how you love this...

Mike: MMMmmmm... Michelle, I surely do...

Michelle: I can feel that your hot rod is fully erect and ready for more action... I move myself up a little... Now you can see me smiling at you... The sexy look in my eyes, you always said I had... You can see my boobs and tummy... The bubbles are just running down my body... Sliding off the ends of my boobs...

Mike: You are such a sexy minx Michelle... I remember you so well... always teasing and tantalizing me... Michelle you drive me crazy, as you always have... I want to see more of your lovely body... I brush the soapy bubbles off of your skin... and now I can see all of you... Gorgeous... Sexy... Irresistible...

Michelle: I put both of my hands around your hot rod... It is so ready for some action... Hard as a rock, pulsating... I run a fingertip gently over the very tip... You gasp with the sheer pleasure...

Mike: Be careful Michelle... You will send me over the top so easily here...

Michelle: Now your hand comes down and slides between my open legs... one finger circles my clitoris... I think you have found my 'hot spot' here... Wow... so nice... And then the finger moves around and slides gently into my love tunnel... MMMmmmm... Oh wow... And whilst that finger is slipped inside of me, your thumb moves to my hot spot and circles slowly...... OMG... This is heaven...

Mike: MMMmmmm... Heaven for sure!!!

Michelle: I take your hands, and place them back onto my boobs... With my hands I take hold of your hot rod, and work the tip of it around my hot spot...Both of our eyes light up at this... then gently I run it right down the valley of love, to find the entrance to my love tunnel... It is there at the entrance, just touching the open lips of my love tunnel...

Mike: You drive me crazy Michelle... I want you so much right now...

Michelle: Come inside of me then Mike... So gently I ease you inside of my love tunnel... slowly... gently... I let you all the way inside of me... It is so good to feel you right there inside of my very core... So deep... I put my arms around your neck and kiss you so passionately... You put your hands onto my hips... And thrust me so tightly onto your hot rod... now you are in so far, you could not be any further inside of me... So deep inside me I can feel your golden nuggets rattling at the entrance of my love tunnel.

Mike: MMMmmmm... Michelle...

Michelle: And slowly I start to move up and down on you... My boobs are right at your eye level... Your hot rod right inside of my love tunnel... and I am letting you almost back out... But not quite... And then back down on you... all the way inside of me... I can feel you swelling up inside of me Mike... I know it will not be long before you explode... So I move faster... Harder... and kiss you with more passionate kisses...

Mike: Oh Michelle... Now it is me who is hot and bothered!!!

Michelle: Come on Mike... Let's share our love the way we used to... Now, I am thrusting myself up and down on you with a force... vigorous... pumping... Oh Mike... you are on the edge here, I can tell... I grip your head, and plunge you into my boobs... And work you for all I am worth... OMG... I can feel your love juice pumping into me, as you grip me tighter and tighter... This sends me over the edge... And my orgasm is out of this world... my head is spinning... My nipples so hard... your hot rod and love juice just filling me... the pleasure ripples right through me... my orgasm starts from my love tunnel, and radiates throughout my entire body... I am shuddering with the uncontrollable pleasure now... It goes on and on... mind-blowing......

Mike I know you will remember all of this as I do... We were so good together... When we made love, I would get completely lost in you... the pleasure was so good, I would not know where my body ended and yours began. We were as one!!!!

Michelle: I am only brought back to earth, by your teeth gently tugging at one of my nipples. I hug your head so tight, and press my boobs right into you...

Mike: Wow... Michelle... I remember all of this so well with you.

Michelle: I hold you tight inside of me... And just hug you with my arms... kissing all over your face... Kissing your lips...

Michelle: Then I sit right up again, still with your hot rod inside of me... We look at one another... All of the love that we shared once, we still share...

Mike: Our love will never die Michelle... it will go on and on forever!!!!

Michelle: It is a good job I can no longer have babies Mike, I think you would have given me triplets there. ☺

Mike: For sure Michelle

Michelle: I love our love making Mike

Mike: Me too Michelle… And I LOVE YOU

Michelle: "DITTO"

Mike: I have always loved you Michelle… And I will always love you…

Michelle: Our feelings for one another are the same Mike… Our love is eternal…

Mike: You probably need to go now, look at the time.

Michelle: OMG… yes, I must go… I cannot see you on here tomorrow, but I will e-mail you.

Mike: OK… I LOVE YOU MICHELLE

Michelle: I LOVE YOU MIKE…… Bye for now…

Mike: Bye my darling… I hope we share the same dreams tonight.

Michelle: This is just the beginning, as we have now become 'Cyber Lovers'… Our loving making here will get more and more sensual, sexy and full of passion.

Mike: I think you are right… The world is our oyster here… We can do whatever we want… And, I am sure we will.

Michelle: MMMmmmm… What a lovely thought… Bye darling. Mwah.

Mike: Bye Michelle. I love you. Mwah. Until next time……

CHAPTER THREE

Many more e-mails and live interactive text take place throughout March, with funny attachments and videos.

E-mail from: Michelle
To: Mike
Date: 2 April 2012
Subject: Cotswolds Anniversary

Hi Mike

As we have both recently remembered, this, the first week of April in 1992, was the week we went off to the Cotswolds together. Where we spent a wonderful five days, and five wonderful nights living together… a time I have never forgotten…

Where I got to spend my days wandering around with you, holding hands, not having to look over our shoulder all the time, cuddling, kissing, laughing and loving with you. And five wonderful nights tucked up in bed with you. Your arms around me… So much love… I got to wake up in the mornings with you lying next to me… I have never forgotten this… and have always been so glad we did that… Every single year since then I have thought about that time, at this time of year… and wondered if you have thought of it too, when the blossom is on the trees, the daffodils everywhere, the birds singing, and the spring is here. I remember all the love we shared when we lived together there; although really it was only a brief time, it's a time I have treasured in my head and heart for twenty years…

I have never met anyone else in my life I would rather have done that with. When you said the other day, take care you are very precious... I couldn't agree more... you were precious to me then... you are precious to me now...

I love you Mike Turner. Enjoy your day off today.

With my love
Michelle
xxx xxx xxx xxx x

E-mail from: Mike
To: Michelle
Date: 2 April 2012
Subject: We may not be together, but we will never be apart.

Hi Michelle

Yes like you, I remember us spending these five wonderful days in the Cotswolds together. I caught the train in the afternoon from home to the station we had agreed to meet at, on Sunday 5th April. I remember saying to you, it is the end of the tax year. When I met you at the station and put my case in your car you told me your Mum had packed us a big food parcel of goodies. This even included our favourite drink, a bottle of Southern Comfort. If I recall, you said to me: I am pinching myself to make sure this is true. Then we both looked across at each other nervously when we spotted two police officers coming over our way!! This could only happen to us, eh!! We must have looked suspicious?... and we were only looking at a map to plot our journey!!

Anyway with my good navigational skills and your excellent driving skills we made it to the Cotswolds early that evening. We even made telephone calls back home, we would never have got away with this today, eh! How wonderful it was to share and feel our love and warmth together. I remember you saying to me which side of the bed do you want to sleep on and you slept on my left side. This was because we had never actually 'slept' together, and spent the night together until this time. Our time in bed before this had been making love. But, just to hold you in my arms and hug and cuddle you and to think I had you all night to myself made me feel so good. It was like a fairy tale come true and I was even starting to pinch myself.

Can you remember the Monday? I am sure you can because we had torrential rain all day and it was our excuse to stay in bed. You were cold and we got the logs and had a real fire. The poor guy, we used all of his winter stock of logs by the time we left. We walked hand in hand, though still thinking we would be recognised by someone. It was perfect, and I will never forget this time we had together. It was when we went back to your parents' house and the way they greeted me even though I was a stranger. Your Mum said we were a couple and what wonderful parents you had there my darling. I know your Mum was very understanding and you shared everything with her like a sister. It must have been difficult for them under all the circumstances, but they seemed to accept us as a couple! I will never forget these times we shared and had together. I loved you then, like I still love you today and my feelings never changed. In so many ways we are so alike in what we do and what we think. I am even beginning to think there is some sort of telepathy going on between us. Like I say, we may not be together, but we will never be apart.

Love always…

Mike Xxx

---

2 April 2012 ~ Live Interactive Text

Mike: Hi Michelle

Michelle: Hello darling. Thank you for your e-mail this morning, it touched my heart.

Mike: Yes an anniversary date to remember for sure

Michelle: Most definitely… always remembered

Mike: It does not really seem that long ago.

Michelle: I know… I think we both still remember things from them as though it were only yesterday.

Mike: Five wonderful days and nights, to treasure in our hearts forever.

Michelle: It certainly is… If we were there right now, would we stay in for dinner this evening or go out?

Mike: Let's go out for a nice meal and a few drinks.

Michelle: OK where shall we go?

Mike: You choose.

Michelle: Do you like Thai food?… or Italian food?… or what do you like when you go out these days?

Mike: Italian is good, not sure about Thai but if it is like Chinese food that is fine. You know I am a fussy eater, so for me it must smell and look good and I must be able to identify what is sitting on my plate. No fried rat and such like for me, thank you.

Michelle: Trust me with the Thai food, I'll help you choose something really nice, always fresh ingredients, lightly spicy… very, very nice. No rats, mice or cats…

Mike: That's good, you know I do not experiment too much when it comes to food.

Michelle: I see from the picture you have just put up that you are going to wear a white shirt then… Uuuuummmmm, smart, sexy and handsome as ever… yummy I could eat you right now…

Michelle: Do you want to know what I'm going to wear for this dinner date then?

Mike: Do you mean to wear and can be seen. Maybe you still wear no knickers!!! ☺

Michelle: ☺ Only sometimes when I used to meet you, to turn you on. So you will have to wait and see this evening. So I will wear my nice blue dress, figure hugging, to the knee, plunging neckline… hang on and wait

Mike: I would love to hang onto them my darling!! Maybe you have no bra on either? ☺

Michelle: No bra, for your benefit later. Oh and black lacy French knickers because I've remembered you like them… oh… and the beautiful earrings you once bought me, little blue sapphires surrounded with little diamonds… and the perfume you like

Mike: Yes I remember those earrings, and didn't I buy you the necklace to match?

Michelle: My hair brushed up on top, twisted round with a clip to hold it in place, but quick release for you later… sophisticated and elegant… yes, you gave me the necklace at another time. I still have them all… and I love them. A memory of you I have hung on to all this time.

Mike: I remembered they matched those lovely blue eyes.

Michelle: I always remember this whenever I put them on… Thank you for buying them for me, I have always treasured them. So no bra, naughty knickers, but only you know that, not everyone else in the restaurant…

Mike: Well I should hope not!

Michelle: So do you still drink white wine with your meal? Without the bra, I thought you might enjoy the view with your dinner, and save you time later?

Mike: I drink little wine, but still love the occasional Southern Comfort. This is still my favourite drink. You hooked me on this, if you remember?

Michelle: Yes, I remember. Southern Comfort it is then. Filled to the top with lemonade, lots of ice, times two please

Mike: Yes… Doubles even… if we are not driving.

Michelle: Doubles it is then…

Mike Turner: Or, like abroad just tip it in and half fill the glass with alcohol. ☺

Michelle: Not too strong though, it spoils it… just lots of them

Mike: Yes true, double is okay or even just single shots.

Michelle: This restaurant is opulent and luxurious like Thai restaurants usually are, they even have a small band playing…

Mike: Have I told you lately… I love you…

Michelle: No… not for ages ☺

Mike: You are so cheeky! ☺

Michelle: There is an electric piano… drums… saxophone… and they are playing music softly…

Mike: Okay sounds pretty good to me.

Mike: Sorry I have to go… Cheryl has just come home… I love you and see you soon.

Michelle: Bye darling… I love you… I'll e-mail you so you can read it later x

Michelle: I have one last question before you go. The band are playing our song… what is it?

Mike: "I will always love you"…

Michelle: That's the one… bye darling… I will always love you xxx xxx xxx xxx x

Mike: You know this is so true. Every time it reminds me of us. Bye for now darling x

Michelle: Me too. Bye darling mwah x

Mike: Mwaaaaaaaaaaaaaaaaaaaaaaaah! Big hugs and tons of kisses…

Michelle: Thank you xxx xxx xxx xxx x

E-mail from: Michelle
To: Mike
Date: 2 April 2012
Subject: Our out to dinner experience!

Hello darling…

We ran out of time on Skype, but I have to finish this story today…

So we've finished our Thai meal, and we've had a few Southern Comfort and lemonades each… and the band are playing 'our song'… so as a few other people are up and dancing, would you have a little smooch with me? Our bodies pressed firmly against one another as we sway to and fro with the music… Our thighs pressed firmly together, our tummies, my boobs soft and gentle, pressed firmly against your body. Our arms around one another… my head on your shoulder… smooching, swaying gently and nice. I'm singing very quietly to you… "I will always love you"… I'm looking into those sexy brown eyes of yours now, and watching those lips that I love kissing me… when this music has finished I think it's time we walked back to our little cottage in the Cotswolds…

Where… one clip is going to let my hair fall wild and sexy round my face…

One zip is going to let my dress fall to the floor…

And all I will have on will be those sexy black French knickers… and high-heeled shoes…

To be continued…

My love to you always

Michelle

xxx xxx xxx xxx x

E-mail from: Mike
To: Michelle
Date: 2 April 2012
Subject: Re: Our out to dinner experience

Hi Michelle

It is nearly midnight and I thought I would check my e-mails.

Wow… How do you expect me to sleep now, eh? You have just again turned me upside down and inside out. My mind is going crazy… How I would love to have you tonight, us both naked of course in bed and you laying your lovely boobs on my chest and us having nice hugs and cuddles and kisses until daybreak. You know you would get no sleep. You have just made my day complete and I hope I dream about this.

Love always and I cannot wait to read the next e-mail…

Love you always…

Mike xxx

E-mail from: Michelle
To: Mike
Date: 3 April 2012
Subject: I just love you so much

Hello darling

I really do just love you so much… we are closer now than we have been able to be for so long… I don't think there is any doubt, for either of us, of just how much we love one another… I love this world with you… and, I love you making love to me in this world… and, at the moment, I can barely think of anything else other than you. We really did steal each other's hearts… I think maybe I have yours… and you have mine???

This is for you to read later, or in the morning. Really early start for me tomorrow 7.30am start... until 4pm... But I will look for you on Skype about 5pm, don't worry if you are not able to. There will be plenty of other times, I'm sure of that. Mwah...

I LOVE YOU DARLING... AND...
I WILL ALWAYS LOVE YOU...
Michelle
xxx xxx xxx xxx x

---

3 April 2012 ~ Live Interactive Text

Michelle: Hi darling

Mike: Hi gorgeous

Michelle: So where did we get to yesterday then?

Mike: I think we are down to a bra and French knickers. Woweeeeeeeeeeeeeee!!

Michelle: So have you still got your clothes on? No bra if you remember, just the French knickers and high-heeled shoes ☺

Mike: I think I had better slip you into bed before you get cold.

Michelle: I think it's time for me to remove your clothes then...

Mike: Okay... You can start on me.

Michelle: Running my fingers down your chest, unbuttoning your shirt...

Mike: Yes you liked to wear my shirt. You used to put it on sometimes when we were together, with you completely naked underneath. You looked so sexy in my shirts!!

Michelle: MMMmmmm.. I remember this too, so slipping your shirt over your shoulders... and off...

Michelle: Un-buckling your belt on your trousers... and... off......

Mike: Wow... You are quick.

Michelle: Throw them across the room like you do my clothes!!!

Michelle: I can't hang about... I'm getting cold here

Mike: No... I only throw your bra out.

Michelle: Yes, I remember this too...

Mike: I like those boobs natural looking.

Michelle: I'm all yours!!!!

44

Mike: OMG... I LOVE YOU ☺

Michelle: Make love to me then Mike!

Mike: No foreplay do you mean, straight in! hee hee hee

Michelle: Well... maybe a little!!! ☺

Mike: I am sure you need a bit of foreplay to get you going. You used to love it when I started with some kisses down your neck, so that is what I will do now

Michelle: MMMmmmm... so nice...

Mike: Just to make your hairs on the back of your neck stand on end...

Michelle: They are... just at the thought

Mike: Working across to your cheeks, and back to your lips because I love the taste of them.

Michelle: MMMmmmm... yummy...

Mike: Very long lasting passionate kisses.

Michelle: Wow... I love them...

Mike: Then to those gorgeous lips with more wild passionate kisses.

Michelle: MMMmmmm...... I'm loving this...

Mike: Your boobs are pressing into me, so I think I need to give them a kiss and then move my tongue around your nipples to start you going.

Mike: Like the hairs on your back they are now standing up on end too.

Michelle: WOW... they are tingling at the very thought

Mike: American hard gums now, I love them.

Michelle: "American hard gums"... your favourite

Michelle: Snap... we said the same thing, at the same time?

Mike: OMG... Telepathy again is kicking in.

Michelle: I know, we live inside of one another I am telling you...

Mike: These nipples taste nice and hard and sexy.

Michelle: MMMmmmm so nice. Carry on... I'm really enjoying myself here with you.

Mike: I can almost wrap my tongue around them now.

Michelle: WOW... really? Nice, nice, nice, nice soooo so nice

Mike: I am working down to that part when I have finished sucking and caressing your boobs.

Michelle: Really!!

Mike: I am moving down now… You can feel my hand starting to stroke your pussy. You are beginning to get excited. Starting to go mmmm… mmmm… your heart is beating faster like a drum… dom, dom, dom.

Michelle: Very fast indeed… and I am just loving every moment of it…

Mike: You are saying stroke me gently and I like my hot spot kissed.

Michelle: Am I ???……

Mike: You are opening your legs and my lips have replaced my hands and my tongue is stroking and kissing your clit… OMG… YOU ARE SHOUTING.

Michelle: Oh… My… God… Mike…… what are you doing to me?

Mike: You are loving this, just let me get faster.

Michelle: Oh… My… God… I am loving this

Mike: I can tell, you are getting wet here now.

Michelle: I bet…

Mike: Be patient, I want to just kiss you some more and give you more tongue and caress that clit of yours, sorry I obviously mean your hot spot… ☺

Michelle: I'm loving every single moment of it… I'm not rushing you…

Mike: Your heart is racing now.

Michelle: It's nearly exploding…

Mike: Your boobs are shaking with every heartbeat… Now tell me… Is it you on top or me?

Michelle: You on top…

Mike: Okay so I will lay you gently down and you are opening your legs. You are about to receive me slowly at first.

Michelle: I'm ready for you… I'm kissing you… I Love You…

Mike: Just gently… not fully inside yet, just little strokes in and out.

Michelle: Oooohhhhh wow……

Mike: With each thrust you are getting excited and you are saying, "Further in Mike I love it".

Michelle: Mike… I am in heaven with you… right here and now…

Mike: I am putting myself deeper and deeper with each thrust and you want to close your legs on me so you can feel it tight every time I come inside you.

Michelle: I'm gripping you tight with my inner thighs…

Mike: I am just caressing your boobs at the same time. I can feel you getting very wet and slippery down there now.

Michelle: And inside with my pelvic muscles… tight, tight, gripping you oh so tight. I love you inside of me… it's where you belong…

Mike: You have really squeezed me tight, so tight I am right inside you and it will penetrate no deeper. I am sure I am right there deep within you.

Michelle: You are… right there deep inside of me… And I am holding you there oh so tight.

Mike: My hot rod is so hard and tight now, but warm and nice inside you.

Michelle: We fit together so well… we were made for one another.

Mike: Your nipples are so hard and I love them. I am starting to fill up with every movement.

Michelle: I bet they are, with everything you are doing to me… I am just loving it…

Mike: I want to hold on for as long as I can, I want to come at the same time.

Michelle: Come on then… give me your love juices… I want to feel them inside me… and when you do that… it will be together.

Mike: This is really coming now, I am about to explode these warm love juices inside of you.

Michelle: OH… MY… GOD… MIKE I JUST LOVE YOU SOOOO MUCH

Mike: I cannot hold it back any more it is coming. Like a mass explosion I have come and it is shooting everywhere and you are so wet and our love juices are mixing up and so warm with our love for each other.

Michelle: UUUmmmmmm UUUUmmmmmmmm… I am loving this so much.

Mike: You still want to take every last drop and I will give you all my love.

Michelle: Give me all of your love… because you already have mine…

Mike: I can feel your heart beating fast whilst I am still caressing your boobs. You whisper Mike I loved that, and you know we share the same love and the same feelings for each other.

Michelle: I am absolutely in heaven… that's why… my heart is racing, my blood pressure is up… my skin in flushed… and I just love you so much

Mike: You are warm now from our love making and our body heat means we need to cool down.

Michelle: Don't move away from me yet… I like you inside of me…

Mike: But only until the next time, eh!

Michelle: Just cuddle me… and love me… we will cool down together… you still inside of me…

Mike: MMMmmmm… I would love to cuddle you my darling and hug and hold you in my arms, (for real) with those American hard gums pressing into me…

Michelle: Let's stay like this tonight then. You inside of me…… while we sleep…

Mike: Okay we will do that. Have I told you Michelle… I LOVE YOU.

Michelle: I Love You Mike, so very very much

Mike: You know I have never stopped loving you.

Michelle: I have never stopped loving you either

Mike: The times I have thought about you… and yes our song when it plays… My mind just thinks about nothing but you. I so remember that day when you gave me this cassette.

Michelle: I loved what we had all those years ago… and I love what we have right here, right now… Yes, our song has always done the same to me about you……

Mike: It broke my heart, and I still remember this.

Michelle: We don't need to be sad about it anymore… we are closer now than we have been able to be for so long. It broke my heart too…

Mike: Every time I have heard that over the years, it has broken my heart over and over again.

Michelle: We don't need to be sad about it anymore… we know how we both feel…

Mike: I know… but you just cannot forget.

Michelle: Now we both know, we have carried the same feelings for all these years... we have both been made sad by the sounds of things. I have cried a river of tears over you

Mike: My tears filled the river and became an ocean, you know that.

Michelle: I am sorry darling. We have both been very sad then... obviously that is why neither of us could completely let go... We did what we did back then to minimize the distress to other people. But we obviously paid a very high price for this ourselves

Mike: I love you Michelle... See you maybe tomorrow? Just never change and be the same always.

Michelle: OK darling. I will look at 5pm but don't worry if not suitable... I Love You darling. I have loved you for so long, and wished you were mine

Mike: Bye... Take my love to bed with you tonight and I hope our telepathy gives us the same dreams to share.

Michelle: Me too...... Mwaaaaaaaaah mwaaaaaaah mwaaaaaah

Mike: Mwah! Big Hugs and tons of kisses.

Michelle: Bye darling. Hold me tight and cuddle me in your dreams tonight, and I will do the same with you

Mike: Bye... You know I can almost feel you here in this Skype world, like it is real.

Michelle: xxx xxx xxx xxx x

Mike: I LOVE YOU... I LOVE YOU

Michelle: I LOVE YOU... AND... I WILL ALWAYS LOVE YOU

Mike: Bye now.

Michelle: Bye darling

From: Mike
To: Michelle
Date: 4 April 2012
Subject: My Love

Hi Michelle

It has turned midnight, but I am here still thinking about you. I just want to send you my love, with big hugs and cuddles and a heap load of kisses.

Good night…

Mike xxx

Michelle: Hello darling. I'm here looking for you, because I Love You and I have really missed you today…

Mike: Hi my darling… A busy day for you at work today!… I probably cannot stop too long, so if I suddenly disappear I will see you maybe tomorrow around the same time.

Michelle: Very busy day… I'm really tired now… I was tired when I got up at 6am this morning, because I hardly slept, just laid there thinking about you… I've only just got home…

Mike: I hardly slept either, I was wide awake at 00.30 last night. That was when I decided I would tell you about it, and send you that e-mail last night.

Michelle: We still touch each other's hearts!!

Mike: We sure do!!

Michelle: If we were in the Cotswolds today, I would be saying to you right now: Lay on the sofa with me, cuddle me, let me have a little snooze and then I will cook us dinner.

Mike: Maybe you should have a long relaxing soak in a bath my darling. But do not fall asleep in the bath. You could be drowned.

Michelle: Hey… I can swim.

Michelle: So what would you choose for dinner if I were cooking it for you tonight in the Cotswolds… maybe a nice roast dinner? Or something simple like lasagna?

Mike: Either, I do not mind. I always like a nice roast dinner.

Michelle: I'll cook you nice roast dinner then, with a nice dessert, and you can get us both a drink

Mike: Maybe I could have you on the menu and I could help myself to some nibbles.

Michelle: Maybe you can help me cook it… I'll teach you to cook… while we are waiting for it to cook there could be a few nibbles

Mike: Okay… Two Southern Comforts and lemonade to the top and some ice, eh!

Michelle: Yummy…

Michelle: So would you help me cook then? Shared cooking is nice!

Mike: I am best with the drinks, no good with cooking. I even still burn water.

Michelle: I will teach you... stand here and watch to start with... some nice music on... a few drinks... and some nipples... I mean nibbles

Mike: Naughty Michelle ☺

Michelle: Then I would lay the table with candles. Have a nice dinner with you... What would you like for dessert? I love cooking desserts. You name it... I will make it for you.

Mike: Do you know I could go without the dinner and just live on love with you.

Michelle: We would both get very skinny. Let's have our dinner, throw the dishes in the dishwasher... and go lay on the rug in front of the log fire... more drinks? A nice cuddle in front of this fire... listen to the music with me... kiss and hug.

Mike: Yes I am sure we can, you are such a sexy, wild and passionate little thing anything could happen.

Michelle: You see... I'm tired... and you make me want you right here and now...

Mike: I would love to just hold you in my arms and cuddle you Michelle.

Michelle: I would love that too... with all my heart... I would truly love that...

Mike: MMMmmmm... Michelle.

Michelle: MMMmmmm... My Mike...... have I told you today that I Love You?

Mike: I think we are madly in love with one another, eh!

Michelle: Are you hugging me in front of this fire?

Mike: Yes I have my arms wrapped around you holding you gently tight.

Michelle: Are we lying on the floor on a rug? Or on the sofa?

Mike: On the rug.

Michelle: I love your arms around me gently tight... oh I was hoping it was the rug

Mike: Yes more room to move there on the rug.

Michelle: You, my darling are looking quite hot and flushed... I'm going unbutton this shirt of yours...

Michelle: And slowly and gently kiss your chest…

Mike: Okay I could be getting warm here.

Michelle: Kiss it all over…

Mike: Can I do the same to you?

Michelle: Gently running my hands all over you…

Mike: Mind your long nails, please.

Michelle: In fact I'm going to remove this shirt altogether… I am being careful of my nails on you… I don't want to damage you

Michelle: So the shirt is now off…

Mike: Yes I have to watch those tiger claws.

Michelle: And my hands have found that buckle on your belt again…

Michelle: So slowly… because I'm teasing you… I start to undo it…

Mike: You had no trouble with that last time.

Michelle: It's undone now…… and

Mike: You may find a surprise!!!

Michelle: I'm going for the zip on your trousers…

Michelle: Slowly down it goes…

Michelle: My hands are quite firmly rubbing all against you

Mike: Please be careful there!!!

Michelle: I am… don't worry… I won't damage you… you are loving it

Mike: Yes I am loving it.

Michelle: Off with these trousers…

Michelle: Wow… you are down to your underwear, and I am still fully clothed…

Mike: MMMmmmm Michelle, I am getting a big boy now!!

Michelle: I can see that… and feel that… a very big boy!!!

Mike: I know you like it big and hard. ☺

Michelle: Now let me investigate this area thoroughly… I don't want to leave anything untouched here… Wow… I have found a complete set of crown jewels… and you are getting very excited here now…

Mike: Just be careful it does not hit you in the face!!!

Michelle: Domestic violence!!!

Mike: Maybe you would enjoy this kind of domestic violence?

Michelle: Maybe I should play games with my tongue, like you did yesterday?

Mike: You know best

Michelle: Ok I will then…

Mike: Do you want to suck a big lollipop?

Michelle: MMMmmmm yes… I like lollipops!!

Michelle: My kisses are working their way down your body… wow you are loving this…

Mike: I think I surely am loving this now.

Michelle: My hands are caressing you, all over your delicate parts… all over these lovely crown jewels of yours… The hot rod… And the two golden nuggets… and my kisses are getting nearer and nearer to this area

Mike: MMMmmmm… Yes this is good Michelle

Michelle: MMMmmmm, yes now my lips and tongue have found you… gently, gently, licking and kissing you…

Mike: MMMmmmm… Yes I love your lips there.

Michelle: You are tasting so good, I'll stay here for a while then, kissing, licking, sucking… And both of my hands are playing with your crown jewels too…

Mike: MMMmmmm… Do you like a milk shake?

Michelle: Don't make me laugh, I am concentrating… the licking has turned to sucking… oh yes… you are liking this a lot… gently, firmly… just like your hugs.

Mike: Be careful Michelle, my hot rod is so far in your mouth, it is nearly touching the back of your throat!!

Michelle: You are such a big boy!!! I'm really getting the taste for this now…

Mike: You definitely like your lollipop Michelle, you are sucking me so hard…

Michelle: Sucking you harder… but only for pleasure, not pain

Mike: Yes I can feel it tickle the back of your throat. Yes I am loving this very much

Michelle: My hands are caressing each of those golden nuggets, and your hot rod is going in and out of my mouth… MMMmmm… So tasty.

Mike: But, you know when I was deep inside you yesterday I could feel myself filling up with love juices!!!... It's happening again!!!

Michelle: I'm going to have to finish you off like this... sucking, nibbling, quite firmly now... let the juices flow... you know I love your juices...

Mike: Yes I can feel it pumping up now and I cannot hold it.

Michelle: My tongue is flicking the very tip of your hot rod... over and over... And now I am sucking on you quite hard... your hot rod in and out of my mouth... My hands gripping onto your hot rod too...

Mike: OMG... Do not stop the flow of my juices or you will blow my nuts off

Michelle: Don't make me laugh... I'm not going to stop... until you have finished pumping those love juices...

Mike: There are live bullets shooting everywhere now.

Michelle: I know... I can taste them... I am loving it, and so are you...... in heaven Mike

Mike: Yes, yes, yes... I love you.

Michelle: My tongue is still going wild on you... and its driving you wild...... yes, there are still live bullets showering everywhere... and still your hot rod is throbbing...

Mike: Yes I want every last love juice delivered.

Michelle: I want every last drop of you... inside of me...

Mike: You have it Michelle... All my love juice... All my love...

Michelle: MMMmmmm Mike... I love you... And you taste soooo good

Mike: MMMmmmm Michelle, the things you do to me

Michelle: The things we do to each other

Mike: I will always love you Michelle, always!!

Michelle: "DITTO"

Michelle: I have to go darling, look at the time

Mike: See you here tomorrow if we both can

Michelle: Ok darling, I will try... Mwah xxx xxx xxx xxx x

Mike: Bye Darling... Mwaaaaaaaaaaaaaaaaaaaaaaaaaaaah

E-mail from: Mike
To: Michelle
Date: 6 April 2012
Subject: Cotswolds and us!!

Hi Michelle

Do you remember the 6th April when we were down in the Cotswolds? It was a Monday and a very different day in contrast to the sunny warm day that we have today. Well you can probably remember that day because it was bucketing down with rain all day. Until quite late in the day we were in bed together listening to the sheep. I was not sure if they were giving birth or not, but they certainly made a lot of noise.

Now you need to be careful in front of that log fire especially naked. Do you remember the log sparks spitting out of the fire and burning the carpet!! Maybe we should just play safe and go back to bed.

Do you know, I cannot see you, I cannot touch you and I cannot hold you in my arms, yet there is a sense of you being very close to me now. Your love, your warmth, your laughter and smile all seem very real. It is nice to feel this again with you.

I love you and I do miss you.

Mike xxx

E-mail from: Michelle
To: Mike
Date: 7 April 2012
Subject: Still in the Cotswolds with you

Hi Mike

Well here is a taste of next week... you are lying on that rug, in front of the lovely log fire, naked. Yesterday, during our interactive live text, I managed to keep all my clothes on I believe, but I'm going to strip them all off, with you watching, and lay down with you. Cuddled right up close to you, for the next four days… until we meet again… This means we have to extend our stay here in the Cotswolds for another week…

So if you think of me at all this weekend, this is where we will be. Cuddled up together, naked, on the rug, in front of the fire. Cuddled so close our hearts are touching one another. My finger tips, slowly, gently, running up and down your body…

To be continued…

I will try to e-mail you over the weekend. I have enjoyed this week with you. I love you.

Michelle
xxx xxx xxx xxx x

E-mail from: Michelle
To: Mike
Date: 10 April 2012
Subject: Another 24 hours in the Cotswolds for Mike & Michelle

Hi Mike

Here is 24 hours in the Cotswolds for Mike & Michelle…

It's early in the morning, and I am awake, but my eyes are not open yet, and I'm cuddled right up close to you… I can remember when we were there, in the middle of the night, when you thought I was asleep you covered me up with the bed covers so I didn't get cold in my sleep… I have always remembered this… but here in this 24 hours, you have woken now also, and we lay here listening to the birds singing outside our window, and the 'confused' sheep that lives there. As it's your turn to make the coffee, off you go… and bring us back a nice cup of coffee each to drink in bed… then a nice little kiss and cuddle until we decide it's time to get up…

Maybe we should start our day with a shower together… Nice warm water spraying all over the two of us… and as you have now made my hair wet, you are going to need to wash it for me… So I'll just stand still and behave for a while whilst you lather the shampoo all over my hair… Oh but as usual I can't keep my hands off of you, so maybe I'll just stroke my hands up and down your sides whilst you rinse my hair off... Out comes the shower gel... oh there is a whole new one for us to use... MMMmmmm coconut... I'll wash you, and you can wash me... slippery lather everywhere... yes, now you have washed my boobs for five whole minutes, 'American hard gums' have appeared... so you wash them quite firmly... one in each hand... firmly brushing your thumbs over my nipples... UUUUUUuuuummmmm UUUUUuuuummmmmmm... And, of course I have to wash you everywhere, yes, everywhere... with loads of the shower gel, let me clean this 'delicate tackle' of yours... these crown jewels need a whole lot of my attention, nice and gently... let's not miss anything here at all... one, two, three compartments, all being massaged gently, gently, gently... Oh now I have to kiss your lips as well... gently, gently, gently... Gentle hands, gentle lips brushing against yours... so, you decide it's time to wash my 'hot spot'... OOOOOooooooo just the thought, all that warm water, all that shower gel, and you!!!... heaven!!!... Now do we make love here and now? or do we go have breakfast and save it for later? Only you can decide??? So a nice brisk dry off with a towel each, of course I have to dry you, and you have to dry me...

Breakfast, well I know what this has to be... chopped up fresh fruit... what do you drink with this?... tea?.. coffee?... fresh fruit juice?... Whilst we have our breakfast together, we decide we really should go out today, in daylight, and see some of the Cotswolds... So we get dressed, and off we go. In the car, we drive around and admire the beautiful views, yellow fields of rapeseed in flower, dry-stone walls everywhere... sheep all over the place, and little baby lambs... daffodils everywhere... and blossom on the trees... and for us today the sun is shining... We stop in a quaint little village/town with some shops, and hand-in-hand we stroll around them... laughing, joking, and so very in love... It's lunchtime already, so we stop at a lovely little pub by the river, and have a light snack, and one drink each... We sit outside by the river bank, and the sun is shining on us... here comes the photo... I've told you about this earlier this year... engraved in my mind, and deep within my heart, this photo of you has stayed right there for 20 years. You sitting under the shade of a tree, the sun dancing on your face, you laughing, drinking your drink, and the river with a little bridge behind you in the distance… And, I am thinking to myself… just how much I Love You… how sexy you look, how handsome you are, how loving and gentle you are… what fun you are… how I always enjoy everything with you… always… whatever it is… wherever it is… We go for a little walk along the river bank, and just enjoy the sunshine and each other…

Then we decide to buy ingredients for our dinner later, and head off home, to our temporary home in the Cotswolds… I make us a cup of tea, and you load up the logs on the fire, and light us a nice fire because it has got cold outside and is raining again. We snuggle down on the sofa together and watch kids' TV… until we decide it's time to cook dinner… Now here's a thing. You have chosen the dinner… and I am going to teach you how to cook it!!!… stop screaming!!!… hee hee hee… I'm taking a gamble here on spaghetti bolognese (as you said last week you would eat lasagna) and spag bol is quicker for your first lesson… so we chop the onions together, just a little garlic (I don't like too much garlic), we'll cook it in a wok (so you don't make too much mess, more room to move)… on with the cooker, wooden spatula in your hand, I'll pop the ingredients in and you mixy mow (stir)… in with the onion and garlic, mix… in with the mince, mix… keep it all moving so nothing sticks to the wok… in with chopped fresh tomatoes that I have taken the skins off, and chunky-diced, mix… in with chopped tinned tomatoes, mix… I've chopped up some mushrooms (I don't know if you like these?… I do, but you are cooking, so only put them in if you like them)… in with dried herbs and seasoning… keep mixing, don't let any of it stick to the wok… I've poured us a small glass of wine each… Pinot Grigio, or Frascati??? You can choose… with ice in, nice and cold, and makes the wine last for longer… So now you are drinking wine with one hand, and mixing your bolognese with the other… and you told me you couldn't cook??? I'm cuddling you now, just watching, and drinking my wine… wow, this is smelling good. On with a saucepan of hot water, let it come to the boil… in with two handfuls of linguine spaghetti… I'll lay the table… It's got dark now, so we will have candles… I've put music on… CDs of 'love songs'… you know how I like meaningful words in songs… Oh, what's this first one? arrrrhhh… yes… "Nobody loves you like I do"… good choice, tugs at my heart strings… OK, pasta cooked for 12 mins, we are ready to serve... drain the spaghetti, rinse under hot water to get rid of the starch (and so it doesn't stick together)... Into our ready and waiting hot dishes... on with the bolognese mix you have made... a little grate of parmesan cheese on top... and to the table... more wine... dinner 'perfecto'... 'delicioso'... its official, you can now cook... yummy... and to finish I've made us tiramisu... quick and easy, and very tasty...

I'll load the dishwasher, you put more ice into our wine glasses, and we'll take the rest of this bottle and go sit on that rug in front of the fire... drinking our wine, listening to the music... but... now I have drunk half this bottle of wine, I am going to 'tease and tantalize' you... oh yes!!! (This could be Skype when we next meet there, tell me if you want to hear it?)...

And once we are tired, and the fire has died right down, we should go off to bed. Where we will be naked, and cuddled right up close together... cuddled so, so close... our last words of the day are me saying to you... Thank you Mike for such a nice day... I love you with all my heart... cuddle me tight, all night, even when I am asleep... I'll kiss you, and you will feel all the love I have inside of me... for you...

Michelle

xxx xxx xxx xxx x

E-mail from: Mike
To: Michelle
Date: 7 April 2012
Subject: Re: 24 hours in the Cotswolds

Hi Michelle

I really miss you and love you so much.

OMG... You are really going to do this to me... I am going to tease and tantalize you... oh yes!!! ...

Wooooooooooow... I cannot wait now, please continue, you know I am all yours! I just love you!

I am reading this and at the same time trying not to be heard laughing. Have I told you lately "I love you", but you are driving me crazy!!!

You know I have always wanted you in a long slinky black dress. See attached file.

How I would like this to be you and me. Me just unzipping this long black slinky dress and letting it slip off your shoulders and dropping to the floor. Your lovely naked body pressing those long hard nipples into me when I hold you so very close. I will let you finish this off now and quote again… I am going to tease and tantalize you… oh yes!!! … I am looking forward to the next bit!!!

It is difficult to see you this week, but you are forever on my mind and in my heart.

I will always love you…

Mike
Xxx

CHAPTER FOUR

E-mail from: Michelle
To: Mike
Date: 11 April 2012
Subject: I am going to tease and tantalise you

Hi Mike

You should tell me more often the things you like!!! e.g. the long slinky black dress!!!... I have such a dress in my wardrobe. I'm sure you would love it... Well we will save this for tomorrow's 'Another 24 hours in the Cotswolds' instalment. Where maybe we could go out for dinner, me in this dress, and you in a dinner suit with a black bow tie... oooooohhh my very own James Bond... MMMmmmm...

For today, I will fill in the missing instalment of yesterday's e-mail... where we have finished dinner, almost finished this bottle of wine... and back by the lovely log fire... I've finished my wine, and I'm going to take your glass from you, put it down, and kiss you to thank you for cooking me such a nice dinner... I give you a long, lingering, loving, kiss... very long... very lingering... very loving... and gently to the music my thighs are pressing against yours...... just swaying to and fro... maybe I am pushing slightly more firmly against you now... my arms are resting gently around your neck, and we are smiling at one another... Oh, the dinner was so nice, I really should thank you more... I gently undo the cuff buttons of your shirt, and kiss you again... Slowly, gently, I undo the top button of your shirt, and then another... I kiss you some more... I run one fingertip across your lips, down your neck, and down your chest, and undo another button... and another until they are all undone... slowly I pull your shirt out from your trousers, and it's all loose now... your hands have been around my waist, but now you undo the top button of my blouse, and reveal my cleavage... I whisper in your ear... "No Mike... I have to get you undressed first this time"... You squeeze my boobs through my blouse... "No Mike... be patient"... gently, seductively I slide your shirt off your shoulders, and off it comes... across the room it goes, and lands on the sofa... more sensuous kisses... I undo the buckle on the belt of your trousers, and then the button... slowly, slowly, gently, gently I undo the zip of your trousers, and gently slip them down to the floor... you step out of them, and with one foot, flick them across the room, and they land on the sofa with your shirt... OOOOoooooo nice, you don't seem to have much on now... just your underwear... OK Mike, sit down on the rug in front of the fire to keep warm, finish your wine, while I get undressed...

With the music still playing, I'm standing right in front of you... swaying to the music...... I undo the bottom button of my blouse, watching you all the while... I don't take my eyes off of you... and then I undo another, slowly, seductively, more buttons until they are all undone... Now I have revealed my nice black lacy bra, all that cleavage, and all that bare skin... slowly I slip the blouse off one shoulder, and do a little shimmy for you... you are smiling at me... I am smiling at you...... those brown eyes are twinkling at me in anticipation... what's next???... I uncover the other shoulder, and the blouse falls to the floor... A little shimmy to the music, and a little twirl... just for you... I undo the button on my skirt, and slowly unzip the skirt... with a wiggle of my hips... it slides slowly down my legs, and falls to the floor...... OOOOoooooo nice... you make me feel so sexy... I'm still swaying to the music... my hips are rotating...... all I have on now, yes you know... are the sexy, lacy, black French knickers, and bra that matches them... you are holding out your arms for me to come to you... I whisper to you, "No Mike... wait... just be patient... we have all night"... I reach my hands behind my back, and unclasp my bra... I can see you licking your lips now... you must have enjoyed the wine?... I do a little shake of my boobs forward, and the bra straps slide down my arms, to reveal my boobs, I catch the bra in one hand, place one strap around my finger, and swirl the bra around over my head… Aaaarrhhh you are liking this… you are really smiling now… your eyes are sparkling… Oh, and you are licking your lips again… you must have really enjoyed the wine?… I toss the bra, as I have seen you do, but it lands on the light fitting on the ceiling… oh dear, I will have to get this later… You are making me feel really sexy now, keep licking your lips like that… I put my hands up, and around the back of my neck, and under my hair… I am still swaying to the music, and I slide my hands up the back of my head, taking my hair with it, until my hands are on top of my head, holding my hair there… my boobs have moved up too… and because you make me feel so sexy, my nipples are really hard and sticking out a lot… just like the 'American hard gums' I know you love… My eyes are closed, and I'm still swaying to the music… I do a nice little shimmy for you… and a twirl, as I sway my hips to and fro… I let go of my hair, and it falls back down… In fact I will rough it up slightly for you… wild and sexy… You are asking me to come to you now… but I am smiling at you, and whisper "SSSsshhhhh, just be patient Mike… good things come to those who are patient and wait"… All I have on now are those knickers you like, and the perfume you like… I'm trying to decide… do I come closer to you?… or do I remove the knickers???… MMMmmmm… I'm liking the music, so I carry on, with my little shimmy to the music… right in front of you… another sexy little twirl… a wiggle of my bum, a jiggle of my hips… my hands go up to my hair again… and this time when they come down, I run my fingers and hands down my neck… around the front of my neck, slowly, slowly and down… down over my boobs… oh you like this?… over my nipples… and down they go further… over my tummy… and now they are at the knickers… with my two thumbs I slide them into the top of the waist of the knickers, and just move them down one inch… I am looking right at you… smiling… "Teasing and tantalizing you!!"… oh yes!!!… down one more inch they go… you are licking your lips again… down one more inch they go, and still I'm swaying to the music… down they go a little further… slowly… seductively… down a bit further… down… down… down…… and with a last little wiggle of the hips they are on the floor…

You are reaching up to me now… and take both of my hands in yours, and gently pull me down onto the floor with you… We are kneeling, facing each other, right on that rug, right next to that fire… You take one boob in each hand and start to caress me… your thumbs rubbing quite firmly against my nipples… Oh Mike, I love you, so, so much… My hands are caressing your shoulders and back… I love your body… we are kissing, quite passionately… I slide one hand down to your underpants, and gently feel you through them… UUUuummmm UUUUUuuummmmm you have been enjoying watching me get undressed, I can tell…!!! So I gently rub my hands all over these pants of yours… and I can feel you growing inside them… best I stop doing that… you are enjoying it too much… we don't want you exploding just yet!!!… so time to remove the pants… and lay you on the rug… you need to calm down a bit I think… but I am on my hands and knees now, crawling up the front of you… you take my boobs in your hands… but… I gently remove them… still time to 'tease and tantalize'… I kiss the palms of each of your hands, but I need to move them out of the way, so with one hand I put them over your head, and gently lay your hands on the rug above your head… and I whisper to you… "You're not allowed to interfere… just stay still and enjoy yourself"… be careful… you are so excited now, that your 'not so delicate at the moment tackle' has just touched my boobs… SSSsshhh Mike, we will save that for another day… so with my free hand, I take hold of 'your tackle' and barely touching you, gently stroke up and down… oh no… I mustn't do this for long, you will explode… So holding you quite firmly, I start to brush you against me… just with the tip of your hot rod… I find my hot spot with this, and gently rub you against my hot spot… and then a little faster… Oh wow… you are loving this… so I flick you faster and faster there… "No Mike… wait"… still holding onto you, I lean down and kiss you on the lips… we are both feeling very excited and passionate now… I lower myself onto you… just slightly… only letting one inch of you into this love tunnel of mine that is so ready for you… and right back out again… I hear you say, "Michelle, enough teasing and tantalizing, I just want to come right inside of you now"… still holding onto you with my hand, I guide you back in again… just the tip of you… where all the sensitive nerve endings are… how does that feel???… and back out again… with a very gentle

fingernail, I graze the tip of you… Do you like that???…
"SSSSssssshhh, no Mike… keep still"… I lower myself onto you
again… and you are trying to get right inside of me… So gently,
gently, I let you slip right inside of me… warm… wet… and
ready for you… keep still Mike, and feel this sensation… you can
feel the rings of muscles right inside my love tunnel gripping you
tight… so, so tight… keep still… I am gently, gently, little
butterfly kisses, kissing your lips, licking your lips… gently
sucking your lips… so soft and gentle… Our bodies are not
moving, but you are right deep inside of me… and all you can feel
is me gripping you with all these muscles inside. Just tight firm
rippling twitches… Our hearts are pounding against one
another… gently and slowly I move away from you a little, and
allow you to move back out… but… you can stand it no longer,
and your hands move down and grasp my body, pulling me right
tight on top of you, until you are right back inside of me once
more… so far in there is no further to go… and my muscles are
gripping you hard… then releasing you… gripping you hard…
and releasing you… and with the tiniest of movements, I move up
and down on you, because inside of me is where all the work is
being done… I can feel you are going to explode… so I move to
your enjoyment… and it happens… once more you are filling me
with your love juices… well, this is enough for me, because once
you do that, I can contain myself no longer, and I too orgasm right
there with you… I am completely lost in a world of wonderful
sensations… My orgasm ripples throughout my entire body…
And it goes on and on… Wonderful sensual sensations… Oh
wow… oh wow… oh wow… oh sorry, I think I got so carried
away there I have been nibbling at your neck, and left some marks
behind… so I'll kiss them better… my lips all over your neck…
kissing… nibbling… Mike… I love you … We stay cuddled up
like this for a while, just gently stroking each other's bare skin,
until we decide it's time to go off to bed.

Well, I hope you have enjoyed the missing part of the 24 hours…

Feel free to invent the next 24 hours… with the slinky black dress,
and dinner suit… we can do anything we want in this world… we
have no restrictions from other people, or time constraints… it's
just 'us'…

You know what they say darling ~ Home is where the heart is ~ and my heart is right here with you, in our cyber world we call home.

I Love You darling
Michelle
xxx xxx xxx xxx x

E-mail from: Mike
To: Michelle
Date: 13 April 2012
Subject: 'Our Cyber World'

Hi Michelle

I am going to tease and tantalize you… oh yes!!! Well you certainly did this to me Michelle. Wooooooooooow… It is like spending one night in heaven!!!

I am sorry I could not make live text today, but you have still been on my mind. I have just read your very long e-mail again and even now I am trying not to laugh out loud. I just love you so much.

In this cyber world I hope you know we are both barking mad. I know you say it is me that puts you on a high, but believe me you do the same to me. You have not changed a bit, not that I would ever want you to change, so just stay the way you are now and forever. This cyber world really brings us closer together and I can almost feel like I can touch you, even though I cannot see you. My feelings for you are the same and I cannot help the way I still feel inside.

You really want no reminders about Friday 13th and for us it is a lucky day. Every Friday 13th I think of you. I think of us!! I love you now, I will love you tomorrow, I will love you forever.

Love always…
Mike Xxx

E-mail from: Michelle
To: Mike
Date: 13 April 2012
Subject: Dreams come true ~ Friday 13th April 2012

Hi Mike

Another wonderful day for us in the Cotswolds… and we go back to our lovely temporary home there, as we are getting ready for a really nice evening out…

We have decided as we are going out on a date this evening, we will get ready separately, you in one bathroom and bedroom, me in the other… So off I go (we all know girls take longer to get ready than boys)… I wash my hair, wrap it in a towel, and lay in a nice bubble bath for a soak, thinking about you, and the wonderful evening ahead… We are to meet, dressed and ready to go out, in the hallway at 7pm…

I dry myself off, put on a dressing gown, blow-dry my hair, put really nice make-up on, plenty of the perfume you like, ooohh a couple of extra squirts all over my body, you never know what might happen later??? I decide no underwear at all under the dress… so do I put any on, or not??? I put on our little golden clown 'Ditto' for good luck later – he hangs on his long chain, and settles where he always does, right snuggled between my boobs… I've decided… no underwear!!! On goes the beautiful dress… on with high, high-heeled black shoes… sexy!!!… seductive!!! It's 7pm so I go into the hallway, and there you are Mike… looking fantastic… standing there in your dinner suit, white dress shirt, and black bow tie… and my favourite aftershave… WOW!!!… my very own James Bond for the evening!!!… how lucky am I?…

You have ordered us a taxi, because you said I might get cold in my dress otherwise… off we go… we are going to the casino… where first of all we have dinner… then we wander around the casino deciding where we are going to take our chances… as any sensible person does, we have set a budget to gamble with: only gamble with as much money as you are prepared to lose… Our budget is £100 between us… so we change our money into casino chips, split it in half, and wonder around some more. We each play blackjack… we've won some, and lost some… we each play poker… we've won some, we've lost some… my favourite, we go to the roulette wheel and sit down… we each put small amounts on… we win some, we lose some… we count our chips up… just over £50 between us… we put the £50 to one side, and play separately with the remainder… we lose it… OK, we have had a really good evening out… we've had a good run for our money… so we decide to go for it… the whole £50 on one bet… between us we lean across the table and put the whole lot on… there's only one thing it could be… '13 Black'… the wheel starts to spin… I kiss little Ditto for good luck… you briefly kiss me for good luck… The croupier says "No more bets please"… our hearts are in our mouths… the wheel slows down, and the ball jumps in and out of the compartments… it settles in the slot next to our number 13… ooohhhh noooo… but with one more little jump it lands just where we want it to… 'Black 13'… The croupier calls the win… "Black 13"… OMG we have won!!!!… £50 x 32… is £1600, plus our stake money back… £1650 of chips are passed in our direction… OMG…… we kiss one another because we are so happy!!! (This has really happened to me, I thought of you when I placed the bet, and I kissed Ditto for good luck, and I thought of you when I won…) It's time to call it a day… we cash our chips in, do we want a cheque?… No thanks we will take it in cash… You kiss me again and say it must be my lucky dress… I say maybe Ditto helped too… you ask me if I have anything on under my dress… I just smile at you, and my eyebrows go up in the air, and tell you, you will have to find out later…

We order a taxi, and go back home… Once inside, you take me by the hand and lead me to the kitchen, where you take out a chilled bottle of champagne, collect two glasses from the cupboard, expertly held all with one hand… and with the other hand you take hold of mine, and lead me to the bedroom… you take off your jacket… and then pop the cork of the champagne, and pour us a glassful each…… we toast to our successful evening… and to our love… we sip at the lovely chilled champagne… then you take our winnings out of your jacket pocket and throw it all up in the air and it showers down all over us… we are laughing… and very happy… whilst I am standing there drinking my champagne, you remove your bow tie… ooooooohhhhh and then your shirt…

then your shoes and socks... you said you thought you needed a head start, because you didn't think there was much under this dress to remove... you take the glass from my hand and place it on the side... and kiss me... passionately... MMMmmmm... heaven...

Now, your wish comes true... the lovely long slinky black dress that you have loved me wearing ... You slide the tiny straps off of my shoulders... and then... you unzip that long zip right down my back as you are kissing me... slowly, gently... and the dress just slides down my body slowly... and falls to the floor ... this now shows you, there was no underwear this evening... I'm naked... you kiss me hard and very passionately... our bodies pressed firmly together... my boobs pressed hard against your chest... my very hard nipples pressing right into you...

You scoop me up, and lay me gently on the bed... remove my shoes... remove the rest of your clothes... and lay beside me on the bed... and so passionately you kiss me, more and more... all the lovely kisses down my neck that you do... your hands are on my boobs, you are playing with my nipples... your kisses get lower until your tongue is all over my nipples... kissing, gently sucking... ooooohhhhhh wow... I now think there is a direct link here with you doing this to 'my love tunnel'... already I want you inside me... your hand moves down, and you start your magic there with your fingers... OMG... it's only seconds and I'm having an orgasm... You are smiling at me... I can see all the love in your eyes... you tell me how much you love me... OMG I am in heaven with you...... your tongue goes back to my nipples ~ I feel like there is an electric current passing through my body with all of the things you are doing to me... your kisses move lower, you are kissing all over my tummy... OMG... you make me feel so sexy... your kisses move lower still... heaven!!!... we both know what you are doing now... kissing me, gently sucking me right on my hot spot... OMG Mike!!! ... and with your expert techniques you give me yet another orgasm with your tongue... OOOooooo Mike ...Unbelievable tingling throughout my body... unbelievable, wonderful sensations. You climb on top of me, and enter me slowly and gently... and make the most wonderful love to me... taking your time, making sure I enjoy every moment... and when finally you climax, the feel of all your love juice just pumping into me, again it brings me to yet another orgasm... how greedy of me... but it was all your doing!!!... Undeniable sensual pleasures with you Mike... always...

Eventually, we get into the bed, and just cuddle up... close and tight... and I ask you a question...

Mike... can we please stay here for one more week? Maybe you could answer this yourself for me next time you e-mail me?

Wow... lucky for some 'Friday 13th'...

I love you darling, with all my heart
I just love you so much
Michelle
xxx xxx xxx xxx x

---

13 April 2012 ~ Live Interactive Text

Mike: OMG... How can I reply to my lovely Michelle and express all my love feelings for her. I think you have covered everything possible other than a repeat performance...... Yes, another week and how many repeat performances could we get in during a whole week? You know Michelle and I may have told you this a million times already... I LOVE YOU...

Michelle: Did you enjoy all of that as much as I did?

Mike: Oh Michelle... I did... believe me, I did... Just tell me something... I remember very well that you had big nipples, that was even before I started to caress them. I do remember them has American hard gums. Is this correct?

Michelle: You are making me laugh... but yes, this could be a fair description!

Mike: MMMmmmm Michelle... how I would love to have a little taste of them right now. I remember, if I did not get your bra off and I had my hand down your bra and I remember finding it difficult get my hand out again because they would get caught up around your nipples.

Michelle: Do you remember that one day we had off together, we spent the morning in bed in a hotel, got up and dressed, and went out to lunch, and I went out with no bra on, I hope nobody else saw the American hard gums?

Mike: As if I could ever forget... I could not take my eyes off your boobs and nipples whilst we were eating lunch... and I could not wait to get you back to that hotel bed. I think we cut lunch quite short, and rushed back to that bed, where we spent the most wonderful afternoon.

Michelle: So, what did you think of us winning all that money in my last e-mail, and the long sexy black dress?

Mike: MMMmmmm... I think you would look sexy with no bra and your nipples sticking through that black dress my darling. And, if only we had've won all that money. Well yes... It would be black 13 if we were to go for win all or lose all.

Michelle: I did actually do this once for real... £50 on black 13... and that is how much I won!!!! Our little Ditto was with me then...

Mike: Wow... He is a lucky Ditto in more ways than one. How I would like a home like he has living down there between your boobs. That chain is the perfect length for him. Nestled right in between your boobs.

Michelle: He loves it there... and thanks you for buying him for me, and allowing him such a lovely soft warm home.

Mike: He must be blind now!!!!! Still when you are blind you tend to go more on feel. Again lucky Ditto

Michelle: You always told me he would be... he has been with me through thick and thin...... and I think he loves living down there... he has never complained... When I have Ditto with me, really it's a little part of you I have taken with me

Mike: Yes... When I got him for you I did not realise he would be retired to such a lovely lifestyle.

Michelle: He loves it... we have taken care of each other. He has had a million kisses from me over all these years

Mike: His only complaint can be when you squeeze him between your boobs when you laugh...

Michelle: That's when he sticks the boot in.

Mike: Yes but his ears must be ringing!!!

Michelle: You are making me laugh out loud here, the cat thinks I've gone mad. You always could amuse me Mike.

Mike: If ever Ditto started talking you would be in deep trouble.

Michelle: So now you have read all of the messages I've left you everywhere for the past week... have you picked up on the vibes at all that I've been missing you... and... just how much I love you

Mike: Well I have read them, but didn't realise you were missing me. You may have to tell me again. ☺

Michelle: Honestly, and truly… I love you with all my heart……

Mike: "Ditto" = "I love you", but also says my feelings for you are the same

Michelle: The love that we share is priceless darling.

Mike: Completely. And, Michelle you do make me laugh at times too…

Michelle: We amuse one another for sure.

Mike: Yes… I had never heard of love juice and love tunnels… I thought they were some sort of cocktail drink until now… ☺ You seem to like the taste anyway.!!!

Michelle: ☺ We have developed a secret lingo here

Mike: Can you imagine going up to the bar and saying Michelle would like a love juice cocktail please?

Michelle: OOOOhhhh I like cocktails… 'Sex on the beach' is my favourite!!!!!!!

Mike: Love juice on the rocks

Michelle: I have loved our imaginary week in the Cotswolds this week, please can we stay for another week?

Mike: Well in this cyber world there are no restrictions and we can be anywhere in the world

Michelle: What a lovely thought… anywhere in the world together

Mike: I have to go now… see you soon.

Michelle: Ok darling, e-mail me over the weekend when you have time… Maybe another story of us in the Cotswolds?

Mike: OK, will do… Bye for now… I want to give you all my love and nibble you all over.

Michelle: Wow…… that would be nice, very nice…

Mike: Bye now. Mwah

Michelle: Bye darling…… I love you xxx xxx xxx xxx x

Mike: Bye my lovely passionate wild and sexy Michelle… I will always love you

Mike: I just cannot get enough of you…

Michelle: MMMmmmm… I will always love you… and that is a fact…

Mike: Bye… Going now but I just want to say you mean everything to me Michelle

Michelle: I feel so happy to have you back in my life in this way…

Michelle: Bye darling xxx xxx xxx xxx x

Mike: Do you know saying goodbye is so hard and it really means I love you.

Michelle: I love you… Happy Friday 13th…

Mike: "DITTO"

Mike: I

Mike: LOVE

Mike: YOU

Michelle: You are heart-melting……

Mike: Take care… Byeeeee

E-mail from: Michelle To Mike
Date: 13 April 2012
Subject: Re 'Our Cyber World'

Hi Mike

Thank you for your e-mail this morning… I just love it so much when I am reading words you have written telling me you love me, you melt my heart every single time you tell me… and always so nice to talk to you on the phone…

I love this cyber world of ours… all the fun, laughter, and love we share here… I just love it so much… A world where I feel so close to you… a world where I can actually feel you… I feel the love we share which is very real… we may not actually be touching, but I remember what you feel like… and I love you as much now, as I did all those years ago. This is a world where I now realise all my wildest dreams and fantasies come true… because my dreams and fantasies would always include 'you'… We feel so close together now and our two hearts are as one touching places we never knew we had … this is so true of you with me. This world with you is heaven to me… I am in a very happy place in my life right now, and it is because of you.

Here in this world, I share these dreams and fantasies with you… nobody has ever made me feel the way you have, and still do…

maybe you will find time over the weekend to share some of yours with me???

Oh Mike… What I wouldn't give to have just one real kiss with you…

My love to you always and forever
Michelle
xxx xxx xxx xxx x

E-mail from: Mike
To: Michelle
Date: 14 April 2012
Subject: I will meet you in my dreams

Hi Michelle

"I Meet You in My Dreams"

As I close my eyes and drift off to sleep
I want to find you in my dreams waiting for me.
I see you in my dreams almost every night,
And you are so very real to me.
I hear you softly whisper, come with me my love
And then we will dance the night away.
I reach out, as you offer your hand
As a symphony begins to play for just us
It is the most beautiful music I have ever heard.

You take me into your loving arms,
And hold me so close
Our bodies fit together as if we were made for each other
And then we begin to dance the night away.
Romantically, we gaze into one another's eyes
All we can see is the love that we share
Then I feel a kiss you tenderly place upon my forehead
I return this with a gentle kiss upon your cheek
I look into your loving eyes and tell you…
You are my lover, my friend, my darling
These words come so deep from within my heart
And I wonder to myself, will you ever truly know
Just how deep my love is for you?

I love you more each and every passing day
And nobody else makes me feel this way
Our love just grows stronger as time goes by
For I will love you more tomorrow than I love you today!!!
No other can make me feel this way but you.

You kiss me tenderly on my lips
As you whisper I must leave you now my darling
I don't want this night to end…
But the dawn of a new day arrives
I whisper softly to you
I hope we meet in my dreams tomorrow

~ Until we meet again~

Love always…

Mike xxx

E-mail from: Michelle
To: Mike
Date: 15 April 2012
Subject: Cocktails and dreams

Hi Mike

I've logged on here to send you an e-mail, and found messages
from you, from this morning… yes, by the time you sent them I
had signed off, put everything away and gone off to work. So if I
was showing online, I don't know why? Ditto said to ask you a
question: Have you ever seen the film *Indecent Proposal*… with
Demi Moore and Robert Redford?… and if you have you would
know what he means, when he says that, he would not swap the
place he lives… even for a million dollars!!!… but, he also said
thank you for buying him, and giving him to someone, where he
has found such a good home… he says he is well looked after,
and loved. He is warm and content, and I'm not quite sure what he
means when he says he likes the scenery. Mike, I don't know
what you have been teaching him, but he won't keep still at the
moment… he says these nipples are more erect than they usually
are these days, and he is doing gymnastic displays around my
nipples!!!… I know he is happy… but what is that about???

I loved the e-mails you sent me this weekend. The poem 'I will meet you in my dreams'... soooo lovely... you know how I love meaningful words... thank you darling... I really liked that a lot... you melt my heart. I love this world with you, and all the things we do here... the things you send me... being able to communicate with you on almost a daily basis... I love the 'you' I have always known, and together here in this world we share so much. We can now share anything we want to!!!... Mike & Michelle's world just keeps getting better and better. I really can't tell you just how much I do love you. I think about you almost constantly at the moment... all day long; whatever I'm doing (or supposed to be doing), I can still have thoughts of you pop into my head. When I go to bed at night, you are the last thought in my head before I go off to sleep. Sometimes I dream of you. And, you are the first thought that comes into my head when I wake in the morning, before my eyes even open.

And... OMG... I loved our evening out... dressed to kill you say!!! wow!!! I may have to start calling you Mike (James Bond 0013). I am loving the world we are creating here... I can't wait until it's your turn to write the next chapter!!! I love sharing our thoughts, and turning them into one thing... You + Me = 'US'... and the things we are getting up to... WOW, WOW, WOW my wildest dreams coming true...

Meanwhile I've been giving some thought to our 'cocktail inventions' what do you think of the following?

'Love Juice Cocktail'
1 measure Southern Comfort
1 measure Cointreau
Coconut Milk
Ice
into a cocktail shaker ~ shaken, not stirred, as Bond 0013 would say!!!
into a nice shaped long glass (see attached files)
garnished with 2 cherries on a cocktail stick (the cherries represent whatever your imagination wants them to be?)

'The Love Tunnel Cocktail'
1 small strawberry in the bottom of a champagne glass (see attached files)
1 shot of Southern Comfort
fill to the top of the glass with chilled champagne
gently place a swizzle stick inside, and jiggle until the bubbles rise!!

Well, tell me what you think??? Colour, taste, visual?

I think we are onto a winner here Mike… we will patent these, as you suggested… good idea!… and they will sell all over the world. We will be rich!!! And thinking about something you said to me last week ~ you are right ~ we can go anywhere in our world here… so maybe we will have enough money to go on a nice holiday… wow Mike… a holiday abroad with you!!! fantastic!!! YES!!! … You can take me to somewhere nice you have been in the world… or I can take you somewhere nice I have been… Oh Yes… brilliant idea!!! We need to go somewhere we can wear our 'dress to kill' outfits!!!

"I will always love you"
Always & forever…
Michelle
xxx xxx xxx xxx x (13)

E-mail from: Mike
To: Michelle
Date: 15 April 2012
Subject: Love juice cocktails

Hi Michelle

This cyber world that we live in feels so very real. I feel your love and warmth. The feelings and love we share for each other are the same now and like we have always had for many years.

So you have asked me to follow on with another week together in the Cotswolds. It has been so lovely to share your very wild, passionate and sexy love with you, Michelle. You know we often talked about you being in a long slinky black dress, but only now have I ever imagined how sexy you would look when you start to write a book about it. We share so much here, I have learned about 'love tunnels' and 'love juices' and how well they seem to go together!!!

Anyway, I will continue our story. We are both dressed to kill and we have won a lot of money. So tonight I thought we would hit the town and go and spend some of this cash together. I know you like cocktails, so why not go to a nice cocktail bar? Deep in the Cotswolds I have found a lovely cocktail bar. So off we go again......

You and I are dressed to kill and you are still wearing no knickers and no bra under this slinky long black dress, but those lovely nipples really stick out and show like American hard gums and you are looking so very sexy!!! I feel sure all eyes will be on you tonight...

So we go to this cocktail bar and behind the bar is a guy mixing up some cocktails. I say, Michelle what cocktail would you like to order?, and the guy brings out a long list of cocktail drinks. You have a long look down the list of cocktails and you reply, but my favourite cocktail drink is not listed. It is not listed, I say, why???... I then just happen to look down at your boobs and I can just see Ditto popping his head out. Obviously enjoying himself down there, but probably starting to get a little hot now in between those lovely boobs. He needs to come up for some fresh air every now and again in order that he does not suffocate down there and get smothered. Very quickly you shuffle those boobs around him and he sinks back down again.... Lucky him, I say to myself, it must be like living in heaven down there!!! Anyway, back to the order for the cocktail drinks. You say to the guy behind the bar, I want to order a 'love juice' cocktail. The guy looks a little bewildered and then he says does this love juice cocktail have to be shaken up and down for a little while before it is stirred together???... You reply OMG... I always truly shake it up and down and get it really well stirred up before I take this love juice inside me. The guy looks even more bewildered and says, is it shaken slowly at first and then gets faster with every shake? You reply yes of course, it takes a lot of shaking and mixing and takes up a lot of energy to get it to perfection. The taste must be absolutely right for the taste test on the lips, and then slip into my mouth, and then swallow... Ditto can now feel you getting very excited and he is now kicking you down there and shouting it is time to go. Ditto is shouting, the only way you are going to get what you want here to satisfy your sensual, sexy, wild and passionate love needs is to make love to Mike. Your boobs are getting very hot now and your nipples are so long and hard they are sticking out... So much so you could hang posters on them. Mike says I will give you the biggest love juice cocktail ever and it will go down well, giving you a very warm feeling deep inside you!!! You will simply love it inside your love tunnel!!! Your nipples are getting bigger and harder just thinking about it. Anyway Ditto tries to raise his head again but quickly gets shaken back down again amongst those lovely boobs. Mike thinks to himself...Ditto is so lucky living down there in between those lovely pair of assets. I so wish I was Ditto, I would never keep still down there!!!! Anyway taking the advice of Ditto and looking into Michelle's blue eyes, there is only one look, which simply says... Mike take me home to bed and make love to me!!!... Mike can see Michelle is hungry for love and wants a big long stiff cocktail with plenty of shots of love juice inside her...

Hey Michelle... Do you think we should patent this name 'Love Juice Cocktail' because I think the name alone would make it a 'Number One' seller cocktail!!! What do you think, eh?

I think I could be in heaven, so I am leaving you to continue with your next chapter in this book!!!...

Finally just in case I have not told you lately... I LOVE YOU!!!

Mwah!... with big hugs and kisses...

Love always...
Mike xxx

---

16 April 2012 ~ Live Interactive Text

Mike: Hi Michelle... I miss you!
Mike: I love you...
Mike: I
Mike: L

Mike: O

Mike: V

Mike: E

Mike: Y

Mike: O

Mike: U

Mike: I need a cuddle now...

Michelle: Oh Mike... I love you so much, and I need a cuddle too

Mike: Do you remember when we first met and you told me about this kiss in the glass... To this day and whenever there is a celebration toast my mind thinks of you... Do you know why it is??? Because I will always love you...

Michelle: I always think of you too when this happens, and always at midnight on New Year's Eve.

Mike: I cannot help but love you and you make me feel good even though I do not see you or cannot touch you. This is our cyber world that we have created and like you this is the nearest we can get to being real.

Michelle: Oh Mike... What I would not give at this moment, to actually feel your arms around me... and to kiss your soft and tender lips?

Mike: Me too... Oh damn, sorry I have to go now. BFN Mwah

Michelle: Ok darling. BFN Mwaaaah

---

17 April 2012 ~ Live Interactive Text

Michelle: Have I told you lately... that...

Michelle: I LOVE YOU

Mike: Have I told you lately that... I LOVE YOU

Michelle: We need to sell our cocktail menus then... and a holiday for us

Mike: What a wonderful thought... if only!!

Michelle: I would love to make love with you right now......

Mike: Come on then... Just come and don't bother putting your knickers on...

Michelle: I've only got a little nighty on at the moment... as it is first thing in the morning, no bra... no knickers...

Mike: Can I put my cam on and see you?

Michelle: You are so naughty ☺

Mike: Just kidding… we both have to go, and get ready for work.

Michelle: Bye darling. Have a good day.

Mike: Take care and remember I love you Michelle… with all my heart…

Michelle: "DITTO" with all my heart.

Mike: Our little Ditto lives next to your heart and that is his home!

Michelle: He lives next to it… but… you live inside it…

Mike: Wow… I love it.

Michelle: You live inside it… where nobody else ever has…

Mike: I nearly forget to tell you…

Mike: I wanted to shout these words… I LOVE YOU.

Michelle: Schhhhh… somebody might hear you, and it is our secret.

Mike: I LOVE YOU… I LOVE YOU… I LOVE YOU.

Michelle: Gooooooooooooooooooooooo … but I Love You too…

Mike: I need a no bra cuddle first!

Michelle: We are both going to be late for work.

Mike: Bye my darling… Maybe we will see each other here later today.

Michelle: I will look for you here for sure… Bye darling.

Later that day… …

Michelle: Hi… MY SEXY LOVER. I am waiting to give you that 'no bra cuddle'… …

Mike: I wish I lived with little Ditto. With those big mountains on either side and Ditto in between in the deep valley where he must be getting some loud echoes with no bra on and your boobs knocking from side to side around his head.

Michelle: I've got him on at the moment… and I have sent you an e-mail… there is a 'no bra cuddle' waiting there for you.

Mike: I am sure I will enjoy it… thank you.

Michelle: My pleasure.

Mike: I am in love with a mad, sexy, wild and passionate woman.

Michelle: So how about a no bra cuddle now then?

Mike: So you now want to rip my shirt off and rape me, eh!!!

Michelle: WOW… Now there is a thought.

Mike: Yes I need a cuddle.

Michelle: So if this is a no bra cuddle, you need to undress me!!

Mike: No problem. I am thinking you would have a jumper on as it is chilly today, so arms in the air, and I will slip this jumper off over your head… MMMmmmm nice, now I can see a very sexy black lace bra. I'm unclipping the bra… and off it comes!!

Michelle: Very nicely done Mike, but now I am cold… I need to get closer to you.

Mike: I have flicked your bra across the room and it has landed on the door handle.

Michelle: Yes, I remember when you used to throw my bra across the room, so I could not retrieve it easily!!! ☺

Mike: Now come on, press those boobs into me Michelle.

Michelle: So now… I am moving closer to you… and my nipples (which are cold and hard) are touching you, and pressing onto your chest

Mike: Yes I can feel them very hard.

Michelle: And I am looking at your sexy brown eyes, and longingly at those lips of yours.

Mike: Which part of your body do you want my lips on?

Michelle: I'm right up close to you Mike, just touching your lips with mine, so so so gently.

Mike: Okay lips on lips. But… Do you think I should start on those American hard gums soon, they look so tasty.

Michelle: Just some loving gentle little kisses to start with, gentle, and tender. So so so soft and gentle… barely touching…

Mike: I will be gentle with you, like handling a precious gemstone.

Michelle: So, so, so soft and tender MMMmmmmm…

Mike: To go with these tender loving kisses, my hands are now on your boobs, squeezing them gently… Oh wow… I love these boobs so much… Just as I love your tender and loving lips… In fact I love all of you.

Michelle: I love all of you… inside and out… your mischievous brain… your sexy body… your expert fingers and tongue… and more.

Michelle: Hold me close to you Mike

Mike: I am, Michelle… So close our hearts are almost touching.

Michelle: Oh Mike... if only we could really do this... let's sell our cocktail menus and disappear together... with all the money we are going to make... where would you like to go on holiday with me?

Mike: Do you know, with you is all that matters.

Michelle: You are so right, anywhere together would be wonderful

Mike: Paradise Island, Nassau in the Bahamas is nice.

Michelle: I've been there too... Yes beautiful.

Mike: Shall we go there then?

Michelle: Yes... let's.. I think we would have a fantastic holiday together there

Mike: Just to be with you is enough... I love you!!!

Michelle: Ok... I'll book it... we go in two days...

Mike: Is this a one-way ticket to never return?

Michelle: OOOOOoooooooo it could be......

Mike: Well I think if ever we did this there would be no return for either of us!!! We would both be dead meat!!!!

Michelle: Now there is a thought, would they ever find us if we did this?

Michelle: Would you get up at 6.00am and come down to the beach with me, and watch the sunrise...... hear the surf crashing, and just sit on the sand and cuddle me?......

Mike: Definitely, I would love to do this with you... So, no problem.

Michelle: I have to go now darling... I love you... enjoy the e-mails later.

Mike: Bye. I will read them later... Mwaaah... Big hugs and kisses.

Michelle: I want a real cuddle with you right now!!!

Mike: You are so close to me with your boobs. I can feel your heart beating, our hearts are beating together now as one.

Michelle: Bye darling.

Mike: Bye darling.

E-mail from: Michelle
To: Mike
Date: 17 April 2012
Subject: Another cocktail invention

Hi Mike

I have thought of cocktail number 3… what do you think of this one? It is called:

'A Lovers Kiss'
in a champagne flute pour
half a measure of peach liqueur
fill to the top with Champagne (see attached file)

MMMmmmm sweet, tasty and irresistible!!! another best seller Mike.

Today I will do my market research, and we will take it from there…

We are going to make loads of money here… think about our holiday… where would you like to go and when? I have an idea already, but will let you get in first if you want to… bearing in mind, there is more than one holiday for us here, with all this money coming our way.

If I could have given you that 'no bra cuddle' this morning, or yesterday when you wanted it… it would have been something like this… both stripped naked to the waist… I would have walked slowly towards you, taken hold of both of your hands, looked into your 'oh so sexy big brown eyes'… got a little closer… my nipples are touching you now… we are both smiling… I would oh so slowly move my lips closer to yours, but not touch them… nearer, and nearer, but not touching yet… I can feel you gently breathing, we are that close… a tiny bit nearer… our lips barely, barely touch… I close my eyes, because I am in heaven being this close to you… so, so, so gently our lips just brush against each other's… sensual… loving anticipation… and then your arms go around me, and the kiss really happens… long, lingering, smoldering, and oh so loving…

I Love You darling ~I will look to see if you are on Skype at 3pm.

Love always
Michelle
xxx xxx xxx xxx x

E-mail from: Michelle
To: Mike
Date: 17 April 2012
Subject: It's all systems go

Hi Mike

I nearly made myself late this morning sending you that last e-mail. Skidded in by the skin of my teeth, and said the traffic was bad… whoops!!! See what you do to me… I just can't get enough of you at the moment… that's my problem!!!

Well, I'm home again, cuppa made, laptop back out, and things to talk to you about… Anyway, I've been conducting my market research today (have you seen cocktail number 3 yet?)… and well, better than we even could have imagined… from 100 people surveyed, 100% loved them. First of all, the names are (as you said they would be) a big winner. People just couldn't wait to try them… and then they thought they looked great… and they tasted wonderfully yummy!!!… So, off I went, and we now have the patent on all three of them… registered to Mike & Michelle… Their recipes will be dispatched to cocktail bars, clubs, pubs and restaurants all over the world as from today…… So, let's book our first holiday… how about we go in a couple of days' time???

Also… (see attached file of a very sexy little black nighty)… OOOooooo Mike, I like this… you must do too… MMMmmmm… I am going to source this from the internet, and purchase it to take on our holiday… UUUuuummmm UUUUUuummmmmm… I think we will both enjoy this… I know you… you just want to slip those straps off my shoulders, and slowly unpeel it… yes, I know, uncover my boobs and nipples, and have a little taste, before the whole thing just comes right off… I'm going to look for it now…

Maybe see you later darling

Love always

Michelle
xxx xxx xxx xxx x (13, in case you never count them?)

E-mail from: Michelle
To: Mike
Date: 17 April 2012
Subject: Mike & Michelle's Holiday

Hi Mike

Oh how I would like to just sit on the sand next to you Mike, and watch the sunrise, with the waves from the sea crashing towards us, and not another soul around… just you and me!!!!!! God knows how many wood carvings we would buy between us, with nobody else saying, "What do you want that for?"… We both love our wood carvings, and it is only Simon that stops me, and Cheryl that stops you, from buying more.

How wonderful it would be to travel around the world together. We have both individually been to so many places… But, only ever the Cotswolds together. Paradise Island is as good a place as any… for a start… I think we could trek around the world together, you take me to your favourite places, and I will take you to mine!!!…

Love always
Michelle
xxx xxx xxx xxx x

---

18 April 2012 ~ Live Interactive Text

Michelle: Hello darling

Mike: Hi Michelle… How is my sexy cyber lover today?

Michelle: I am fine darling… been looking forward to this part of my day

Mike: There is one place we should be right now!!!!

Michelle: Tell me? Is this in bed darling?

Mike: You are getting too excited now.

Michelle: I've stripped you naked whilst you have been messing about...

Mike: Messing about? I would love to mess about with that body of yours!!!

Michelle: Get the rest of my clothes off then, and into this bed...... and you can...

Mike: I am naked in bed waiting for you.

Michelle: I'm getting in there with you... right now... move over...

Mike: Do you want to come on top?

Michelle: Which do you prefer?

Mike: I prefer you on top and then you have control, and you can show me all the things you like best?

Michelle: Wow... interesting!!! Let's start with some nice kisses, because I have been missing you

Mike: MMMmmmm... Yes please I like that, plenty of long passionate kisses.

Michelle: MMMmmmm Me too!!

Michelle: Then I'm going to slide down this bed a little, and kiss your nipples like you do mine... lick them... kiss them... suck them... just like you do to me.

Mike: My nipples are not so good, your boobs are much better Michelle.

Michelle: I've seen your nipples before, remember?... and I love them... so I'm carrying on... I'm going to slide down this bed a bit more... and...

Mike: This is getting interesting... whatever you say.

Michelle: I've now got hold of your 'delicate piece of tackle', these lovely crown jewels, and I'm touching the end of your hot rod on one of my nipples... rubbing it round and round all over my nipple... what do you think of that?

Mike: OMG... Yes Michelle... It is rising to the occasion!

Michelle: Yes... I thought you might like that... so I will carry on... all over my boob now...

Mike: Wow it is hard and erect now with you doing that

Michelle: In that case, I'm going to place it right in between my boobs and squash it there... snuggled right in between them... how does that feel?

Mike: Yes... I love it there and so glad Ditto is in the drawer and out the way, he would be jealous now.

Michelle: I've put him right out of the way... he couldn't bear to watch this... and I am rubbing my boobs up and down... on you... and you are really pushing yourself hard up and down against my boobs... so far up, that if you do that again... my tongue is going to touch the end of your hot rod......

Mike: Yes nice and warm there too and your boobs around my tackle feels really good. My hot rod and two golden nuggets snuggled so tight in between your lovely boobs... OMG...

Michelle: My nipples are touching your tummy, as I move up and down...

Mike: Yes so nice, but when you do this Michelle, I can feel myself starting to have love juices rushing from my nuts into this tackle... My hot rod is hard as a rock for sure.

Michelle: I love you between my boobs like this... is this what you would call a 'no bra cuddle'... or was it more than you expected???

Mike: I was just waiting to see what would develop. I am just waiting to see your next move. I think you are addicted to love juice cocktails now. You want my love juice, in your love tunnel... you want to drink it... and now cover your boobs in it... OMG Michelle, what are you trying to do to me here... You drive me crazy!!!!!

Michelle: Up and down I slide on you... That hot rod of yours well and truly gripped tight there in between my boobs... My nipples trail up and down your tummy.

Mike: I am filling up and ready to explode... Just let it explode naturally and do not stop it from shooting everywhere, otherwise you could blow my nuts off... ☺

Michelle: ☺

Mike: If you stopped now the backfire would kill me!!!

Michelle: I won't stop you, don't worry... just let them juices flow... all over me... and stop making me laugh here... this is very serious stuff.

Mike: Well I am coming... and my love juices are shooting everywhere... ooppps sorry... all over your boobs. Some has just shot over your lips, you seem to like the taste.

Michelle: I love your 'love juice'... I like it all over my boobs... and I like the taste of it.

Mike: You are now licking your lips for more!!!

Michelle: Stop saying the same things as me, sometimes we type the same things at the same time.

Mike: You stop reading my mind!!! ☺

Michelle: Come on Mike... give me everything you've got... I'm sliding up and down on you now... because you have made me all slippery...

Mike: It is shooting everywhere, it is like a machine gun repeater with live bullets spraying everywhere. Yes your boobs have love juices everywhere.

Michelle: Yes... you are right there... I thought it was only actually meant to be a teaspoonful at a time... I don't know where that fact came from... I think there is at least a cocktail glass full here Mike... and yes it's all over my boobs... I love it...

Mike: Oh dear... I have just had a thought... I have just flooded poor little Ditto's home.

Michelle: You do make me laugh darling... I had better have a shower then, well at least before he finds out. ☺

Mike: I love you... Your heart maybe on fire, but I have just tried to dampen it down a little with my love juices.

Michelle: Nothing... Nobody... will ever dampen my love for you Mike.

Mike: I can hear it beating now from here, you are still hungry for love...

Michelle: I am always hungry for your love, you know that,

Mike: Oh no... guess who has just come home? Sorry my darling, but I have to go now.

Michelle: OK darling

Mike: We will carry on from here another time... I have to satisfy my sexy Michelle.

Michelle: It's a deal... Go darling before you get found out, go go go!... See you soon. Mwah

Mike: I love you Michelle, and I mean I really really love you.

Michelle: DITTO Mwaaaaaaaaaaah

CHAPTER FIVE

---

19 April 2012 ~ Live Interactive Text

Mike: Throughout life, you will meet one person unlike any other, to that person you can tell anything to, you could be with them forever and never get bored, and you could tell them things that they won't judge you for. This person is your soulmate, lover and best friend. This person is you Michelle… and all the time there is the internet, I will have you here and I don't ever want to let you go. I need a cuddle now. Do you think it should be another no bra cuddle?!!! OMG!!!

Michelle: Hi Mike.

Mike: Hi Michelle. Have you read my opening line today?

Michelle: Yes, I have… Thank you… I do love you, you know…

Mike: I want to show you my love today Michelle.

Michelle: OOooo… sounds as though I am going to enjoy this.

Mike: I want to cover your lips and body in kisses

Michelle: MMMmmmm so nice, I am definitely going to enjoy this!!

Mike: And then, I am going to give you some choices

Michelle: Wow… what are the choices?

Mike: Now you want to know… and are curious, eh!… Well be patient…

Michelle: Very curious! Are you teasing me here?

Mike: Be patient… All good things come to them that wait. Your choice is…

Mike: Wait just a minute… I should explain this a bit first…

Michelle: Come on… tell me… ☺

Mike: Your 'hot spot' is your clitoris just in case I need to remind you. You know what I am talking about now.

Michelle: Yes darling… I know what my hot spot is… and I know you know as well, so continue… please…

Mike: Do not get impatient the choice is coming…… ☺

Michelle: OK… I am ready and waiting in anticipation!

Mike: I know you are getting excited about this already!

Michelle: I am getting excited, and you are making me laugh here.

Mike: Okay… anyway moving upward and onward… or should that be only moving downward… ☺

Michelle: I am ready and waiting for your choices.

Mike: Okay… you have a choice of how you want that hot spot caressed.

Michelle: WOW…… carry on……

Mike: 1… Kiss and caressed with my lips.

Mike: 2… Kiss and caressed with my lips and tongue.

Mike: 3… You can get my tackle out and my hot rod which you know very well now and you can have it caressed with this, it may get wet and moist doing this!!!

Mike: 4… You can have may warm hand down there and have a nice gentle massage.

Michelle: OMG… so many choices… hang on I'm thinking about this…

Mike: 5… You can have all of them but obviously there's not enough room there to have them all at the same time!! ☺

Mike: 6… You can have a choice of order, if you are feeling really sexy.

Michelle: ☺ WOW!!!!… My pheromones are highly aroused now!!! Can I have them all please… in that order?

Mike: I thought you would say this… ☺

Michelle: You know me so well… ☺

Mike: I know… You are so sexy…

Michelle: You make me feel so sexy Mike

Mike: I can do the first two, kisses, lips and tongue.

Michelle: WOW!!!… nice… I love it when you do that…

Mike: They can come together, but my tackle and hot rod, you may have to do a bit of work there to get my hot rod extended to the full length.

Michelle: This is no problem at all… I can do that at the same time…

Mike: I take it you want my hot rod fully erect and hard on your hot spot.

Michelle: Wow… that would be very nice… So put my hand where you want me to start…

Mike: Hey… No putting inside your love tunnel just yet, either…

Michelle: I'm not… I want to enjoy your lips and tongue first……

Mike: You sexy thing… You must be patient and wait a bit longer for that bit.

Michelle: You are being naughty to me today… you are teasing me!!

Mike: I am rolling my tongue over your hot spot now, you are loving this.

Michelle: YES… I am loving this… you are quite right there Mike.

Mike: You are saying Mike this feels sooooooo good.

Michelle: This feels reeeeeeaaaaally good Mike… soooooooo gooooooood… I just love it sooooo much when you do this to me. You know this.

Mike: Oh… You are now asking for a little suck too…… You are so greedy Michelle.

Michelle: Ohhhhh Wow… ☺ I am just loving this Mike.

Mike: You are now asking for what???

Michelle: MORE… of the same…

Mike: You want my tongue in your love tunnel?

Michelle: Oh Wow… yes please…

Mike: Be patient Michelle… I have a proper tool for that my darling.

Michelle: You are making me really laugh here.

Mike: I must try and laugh quietly here, you are okay there on your own… I can hear you laughing from here… and shouting, Mike I want more!!

Michelle: You are teasing me… carry on…

Mike: In a minute my hot rod will penetrate to the bottom of your love tunnel, are you saying you want my nuts inside too?!!

Michelle: Wow… YES… I would like that very much…

Mike: Anyway you have me aroused here, my hot rod is hard and long and waiting to stroke your hot spot...

Michelle: Come on then Mike... I am ready and waiting for you......

Mike: Do you want me doing this, or do you want to take control of my hot rod, if so you will need both hands?

Michelle: You can do it Mike... I am in heaven with all of these sensations!!

Mike: I am surprised Michelle... I thought you would want to take it in hand and massage your hot spot... But... I will do it for you, it will be my pleasure!!... and I will give you such pleasure

Michelle: MMMmmmmm... So nice......heaven...

Mike: So you have your legs wide open just waiting for me to press myself against you. You say, Mike put it in my love tunnel and then bring it up to my hot spot slowly...

Michelle: WOW... how nice is that?... My love tunnel is warm and wet, and waiting for you... you are right, I am on fire now......

Mike: Do not worry, I have a repeater gun that will put out the fire and dampen it down a little...

Mike: OH NOoooooooooo!!!... I am going to have to go now!!!... I am sorry!!!

Michelle: Oh Darling!!! What a place to have to leave this on hold.

Mike: OMG... How can I stay like this, I will not get my trousers back on now?

Michelle: You do make me laugh darling... well, don't forget where you are today. Mike...... You have really got me worked up here......

Mike: This will continue... I want to leave you fully satisfied and happy...

Michelle: Good... I like the sound of that...

Mike: Bye... I love you...

Michelle: Bye Darling... I love you... xxx xxx xxx xxx x

E-mail from: Michelle
To: Mike
Date: 20 April 2012
Subject: Our life together

Hi Mike

You are right... we are truly lovers and friends... and I do feel I can talk to you about anything... I would share everything about me, with you... and I would love to share everything about you... 'Soulmates'~ yes!!!... I have loved you for a very long time... and I just get to love you more and more with each passing day.

Tell me Mike... has it ever crossed your mind over the years, what a sort of life we would have shared together if we had made different choices all those years ago?

From time to time, this thought has crossed my mind... And, I did think all those years ago, we would have been very happy together. Now, I know for sure we would have had a very 'caring and sharing' life together. A life full of happiness, laughter and fun... we can always lift each other's mood... we really enjoy one another... and above all else we truly love one another... Our love has stood the test of time, against all odds, I might say!!!... if only we could have seen a clearer future for ourselves 20 years ago... I would have given everything up in my life at that time to be with you... but... I know you could not see a way forward for us...... so we tried to let go!!!... But this has never really happened ~ we have always each clung onto the tiniest thread... In trying to spare everyone else's feelings, we both now know this came at a great cost to each of us!!!

But now we have our cyber world together, where nobody else can see us, or touch us... This will be ours for as long as we both want it... I hope that is for a very long time to come... In this world we freely share our love, our thoughts, our feelings... We have talked recently about the Whitney record "I Will Always Love You"... it would seem this has not only reminded us of one another for all these years, but also torn at each of our hearts. That record can come on anywhere you are in the world ~ and for me, it has felt like a sledgehammer smashing into my heart... it has brought tears to my eyes on many occasions... but now maybe we can each hear this, and our feelings be different?... not different in the love we share... but, I think for me now, I will just think of us together in our cyber world, when you held me in your arms, and we danced to 'our song', telling each other how much we love one another... Our night out in our cyber world... the long slinky black dress, the James Bond outfit, the casino, the cocktail bar...

and then going home, and the most wonderful love we make with each other here… My dreams have come true in this world with you Mike!!!… and I just love you so much… and I will always love you… we both know this now.

I love you darling, with all my heart.
Michelle xxx xxx xxx xxx x

Mike: Hi Michelle

Michelle: Hi Mike

Mike: Have I told you lately, not only do I love you, but that you are also crazy?

Michelle: Noooooooooooooooooooooooooooooo

Mike: Okay I know, not since Friday, eh!

Michelle: That was ages ago… Have I told you lately that I LOVE YOU?

Mike: Our love will never die… But… You were crazy back then and are still crazy now.

Michelle: Yes crazy then… crazy now… hyped up when I am happy, always…

Mike: I read your e-mail and it's so true what you have said there.

Michelle: I think we would have been very happy don't you?… and still now…

Mike: Yes… well I guess we would never know, but so often like you, I did think about this… We have shared so much love… We have shared so much pain.

Michelle: I know……

Mike: Oceans of tears and sleepless nights, so sad and painful.

Michelle: At least we have this now… and I love this world with you too…

Mike: Yes we have our Skype world… and safe from others, here in our cyber world.

Michelle: I've never wanted to lose you completely… never…

Mike: We have never really let go, we never will…

Michelle: I know… and I love it here with you

Mike: Do you know if tomorrow never comes, I am still glad we met and that we shared a part of our lives together.

Michelle: Me too... I have never been sorry it happened... and I am glad we have this together now... I wished we had done this bit a whole lot earlier

Mike: Nothing can take that away from us. Yes we laughed, we cried and we had pain, but here we are still here now. Nobody can separate us!!

Michelle: A whole lot of pain...

Mike: OMG... yes!

Michelle: But... here we are still making each other laugh (most of the time).

Mike: Our love will last forever... and forever has no end

Michelle: I would like a cuddle with you right now...

Mike: I know you would have given up all. But there were so many complications. Our love was so strong, but everything else held so many problems at that time.

Michelle: Things like that don't happen without some reason... Neither of our marriages could have been perfect... or it never would have happened between us!!!!!

Mike: Tell me, how are you and Simon these days? And I mean be truthful here!

Michelle: I know in the past I have said OK... OK is what I mean... but we have never been the same since all that happened all that time ago. Let's say we keep up appearances for our now grown up children, and other people.

Mike: Do you love him?

Michelle: If I am to be honest, and we always say we will be honest with one another, I love him in some way, but I think this is a love out of loyalty nowadays, and has been for the past 20 odd years. A marriage of convenience now.

Mike: But you have a happy life together?

Michelle: Our life is happy through our family. Simon and I are not that close really.

Mike: But I thought you were again now?

Michelle: Probably so does everyone else... But it has never been the same... I can never love him the way that I once did... because I love another man... 'YOU'

Mike: Oh Michelle...

Michelle: What about you and Cheryl?

Mike: Pretty much the same... we keep up appearances for others... No, our situation has never been the same either. Probably most other people think we are OK... and yes, you could have worded that well... my love for her, is also probably now out of loyalty to her, and for the family.

Michelle: Oh darling... what have we done to ourselves? To our lives?

Mike: If only we had of had a crystal ball all those years ago, to see into the future

Michelle: Yes, if only.

Mike: This may surprise you.. I have not slept in the same bed as Cheryl for 10 years!

Michelle: Really?

Mike: Really!!

Michelle: This does surprise me... I suppose I thought you just slipped into your marital bliss again, and that was that

Mike: No.. there has always been a certain distance between us... since you and I fell in love with each other.

Michelle: I caused the distance between Simon and me, because I could not bear to make love with him... could not bear for him to touch me... because... I wanted it to be you.

Mike: I know what you mean... it is me who has created a distance between Cheryl and me... we just tick along.

Michelle: Oh Mike... I need a cuddle with you now... a real cuddle... I just want to feel your arms around me, and hold me close

Mike: I know Michelle... I know... Come on then, I need a cuddle now too.

Michelle: If only that could happen.

Mike: I wish I could actually put my arms around you right now. Hold you close.

Michelle: Me too darling... if only!!!

Michelle: Look at the time, we both need to go.

Mike: I know darling... I love you... I have always loved you... I will always love you.

Michelle: "DITTO"... Bye darling

Mike: Bye darling

Michelle: Hi Mike

Mike: Hi Michelle. How are you today?

Michelle: I'm OK Mike... how are you?

Mike: I am okay I guess... I hope we did not make each other sad yesterday?

Michelle: Maybe we surprised one another with our feelings, and how our marriages have not been the same since you and I... Why have we never mentioned this to one another before?

Mike: I guess I thought you and Simon were OK again... so I have never wanted to rock your boat again

Michelle: And, I thought you and Cheryl were OK...

Mike: On the surface yes... but deep down inside, not really.

Michelle: Again we mirror one another.

Mike: In so many ways Michelle.

Michelle: We like the same things... we dislike the same things... We think the same things... We say the same things... Our marriages are each patched up, but have never been completely repaired.

Mike: We have caused each other so many problems... because we fell in love with each other the way we did.

Michelle: I know... and I have always tried not to think of you putting your arms around Cheryl the way you did me... I tried to never think of you making love to her, the way you did me... telling her you love her, the way you used to tell me.

Mike: Do you not think I have had all the same thoughts about you and Simon?

Michelle: I love you Mike... I want to feel your arms around me now.

Mike: I would if I could, you know this.

Michelle: Let's not be sad today... put your arms around me... and love me.

Mike: Well, I will love you like you have never been loved before!!!

Michelle: You have loved me, like I have never been loved before, or since!!!

Mike: Our love is so special... so true... so meaningful...

Michelle: You are so right there... love me here and now Mike...

Mike: How I would love to for real...

Michelle: This is real... we are both here... we tell each other our true feelings... we tell each other the things we would love to do to one another, if we could... and besides... I am feeling sexy!!!!

Mike: You are always sooooo sexxxxy!!!!

Michelle: I've just realised I didn't put a bra on today... so my warm soft boobs are pressing against you, and my hard nipples are already sticking into you...

Mike: MMMmmmm... nice......

Michelle: Mike... what would you say if I said I was going to make wild, passionate, sexy love to you right here and now? Right where I am standing, in my kitchen!!

Mike: I cannot wait!!!

Michelle: OK... I'm going to just 'rip' your shirt right off you...... without even bothering to undo it...... just rip and throw... whoops... buttons pinging all over the floor now...

Mike: Wowee... sexxxy!!! And you have no bra on... so I can see your nipples really looking sexy pressing through that blouse.

Michelle: I like your style... off with the blouse...

Mike: A very sensual sexy looking Michelle.

Michelle: My warm soft boobs and hard nipples are pressing right up against your bare flesh... MMMmmmm that feels so nice...

Mike: Yes I remember that feeling well. When you would lay your boobs across me and we cuddled and kissed.

Michelle: MMMmmmm I remember that well too... nice... very nice......

Mike: Engraved in my mind for eternity.

Michelle: Here is a smouldering, sexy, long lingering kiss... and...

Michelle: I'm feeling passionate today Mike... I'm going to...

Michelle: just rip your trousers off, like I just have your shirt...

Michelle: off... and thrown across the room...

Mike: Okay, but it is cold today, so I need warming up pretty quick.

Michelle: And off with your pants too... wow... that was quick...

Mike: Wow... I need to whip that skirt off you then...

Michelle: Whoops... I've just realised... I forgot to put my knickers on this morning as well???

Mike: You are so sexy Michelle.

Michelle: You are cold you say... well let me gently get hold of these crown jewels of yours, and gently caress you to warm you up a bit......

Mike: MMMmmmm... I am yours my darling, whatever you want today, just take me.

Michelle: MMMmmmm nice... I am going to take that hot rod of yours, in both of my hands, play with it a little... and then... I'm going to just slide this hot rod of yours gently into my 'love tunnel'...

Mike: OMG... heavenly...

Michelle: How warm and nice is that Mike?

Mike: Yes much warmer in there my darling, warm and wet...... and quite humid inside you. Yes I can feel you are squeezing me hard deep inside of you.

Michelle: I'm also going to gently caress your golden nuggets at the same time... and...

Mike: You know they are filling up already with my love juices.

Michelle: Wooooo!!!!! We are getting hot and sexy here!!!!! I'm going to have to pin you against the wall, and make very 'wild and passionate love' to you

Mike: Yes I can feel, it is a good job you are getting very wet, or there could well be a fire down there below.

Michelle: We are both on fire here Mike.

Mike: Yes hot and steamy!... I love it. You could say my golden nuggets are now like fire balls.

Michelle: I'm pumping you in and out of me, hard and fast... you are going inside me so far... (note to self) remember to do it standing up more often... the penetration is wonderful...

Mike: My hot rod has become a big cannon and about to fire the biggest 13 gun salute ever... ☺

Michelle: I know I can feel it... We are well hot here Mike, and frantic... you are even biting me...... hot steamy kisses as well.

Mike: Just do not stop...... let it fire and pump the shot everywhere.

Michelle: OMG... Mike...... your 'love juices' are pumping inside me already......

Mike: I am just feeling those lovely boobs at the same time. And you have taken me so far inside of you... pumping me in and out... OMG... heaven!!!! I am going to explode any minute.

Mike: Take all my love inside you… let me just give you all my love.

Michelle: Your hands are everywhere… all over my boobs… my hips… my bum… and you are pulling me so hard against you, I think this is the tightest cuddle you have ever given me… I can feel your love juices exploding right inside of me…

Michelle: My body loves the sensations… my mind loves the sensations you give me… and my world explodes into endless pleasure… an orgasm rips right through my entire body and mind… I am completely lost in you…

Mike: Loving it…… this is how I will love you always.

Michelle: Your 'love juices' mixed with 'my love juices'… flowing and mixing already… Sooooooo, soooooooo nice Mike… I love you inside me like this… This is the best 'love juice cocktail' in town…

Mike: Yes and I love to share this love potion with you my darling. There is nothing else quite like it.

Michelle: My boobs are pressed so hard against you… I can feel both of our hearts beating fast and furious against each other… Our hearts touching each other through our skin…

Mike: Yes two hearts now beating together as one…

Michelle: Yes… two hearts as one.

Mike: Gosh, look at the time, I always forget the time with you, just shows how much fun we are having here.

Michelle: You need to go now, don't you?

Mike: I need to… but I don't want to… ☹

Michelle: I think you are developing an 'insatiable' appetite for this loving making with Michelle in our cyber world.

Mike: I love you… Just to have a kiss would make my day now.

Michelle: Have I told you today that I LOVE YOU…

Mike: No you never tell me this!!! ☹

Michelle: Well… I do with all my heart…… and then a little bit more…

Mike: Bye… Must go, take care, see you tomorrow.

Michelle: Bye darling xxx xxx xxx xxx x But, no Skype for me tomorrow, I'm on that course tomorrow, won't be home until about 6pm… sorry… hopefully today made up for that xxxx

Mike: Okay ☹ The best every training course I have attended was with you my darling… I miss you.

Michelle: MMMmmmm… The Cotswolds… I loved living there with you. Go on darling… you have to go now… just remember… I LOVE YOU.

Mike: Our two hearts have separated, but only until the next time.

Michelle: Catch up with you later in the week

Mike: Bye… I love you to bits…

Michelle: I love 'your' bits… ☺

Mike: Love, hugs and tons of kisses.

Michelle: Bye darling……

Mike: Can I just say…

Mike: I LOVE YOU… forever!

Michelle: One last thing…

Mike: You want my body again?

Mike: You are really sexy today..

Michelle: I could keep going here for another hour!!!!! Could you keep up is the question?

Mike: It's been up, what do you mean?

Michelle: Up… yes… well I would give you 15 minute recovery time here and there… I would keep you fit… that is for sure…

Mike: I am just recharging now and ready to fire another round of shot.

Michelle: WOW… I'm ready as soon as you are…… because I am really up for this today!!!

Mike: Bye… I love you Michelle… Enjoy your course like you have just enjoyed this inter-course!!!

Michelle: Hee hee hee… I'm sure it won't be that good. Bye darling…

Mike: Bye

Michelle: MWAH

E-mail from: Michelle
To: Mike
Date: 30 April 2012
Subject: My sexy passionate dream

Morning Darling

Oh Mike… I had the most wonderful dream about you/us last night… one of those dreams that when you wake up, you wonder if it could have been real…!!! I woke up really hot… and had to go get myself a drink of water to cool down… and I thought to myself… WOW… that was so real… I wondered if you could have been having the same dream at the same time??? I'm telling you, I really enjoyed myself in that dream… and so did you… My God… I have never forgotten your sensuous, passionate kisses, that is for sure… they were so real in my dream… let alone everything else!!!

Thank you for the sexy files you sent me yesterday, they also featured in my dream… maybe my dream was because they were sitting here waiting for me, and you must have been having such thoughts yesterday evening.

I love you darling… have a good day, and I hope we meet up on Skype tomorrow, as the past few days have been impossible for one reason or another.

Michelle
xxx xxx xxx xxx x

---

1 May 2012 ~ Live Interactive Text

Michelle: Hello darling
xxxxxxxxxxxxxxxxxxxxxxxxxxxxxxxxxxxxxxxxxxxxxxxxxxxxxxxxxxxx

Mike: Hi Michelle… Wow… When am I going to get this lot of kisses?

Michelle: The next half hour is all about 'you and me'… nobody else… nothing else… just us!!!!! And… you are going to get these kisses right here and right now.

Mike: I just cannot wait!!!

Michelle: I think you need some of my loving?

Mike: I sure do!!! Lots of it!!!

Michelle: You need a cuddle… a special cuddle… a no bra cuddle…

Mike: Yes please… I love those boobs!!!

Michelle: Just put your arms around me and cuddle me… and my boobs… and we will share kisses, lots of sexy passionate kisses… I'm all yours for the next half hour!!!

Mike: Yes your boobs rubbing up against me. Your lips are on mine. Your nipples are starting to get hard pressing against me… now look what you have done… American hard gums already!!!!! I love those American hard gums.

Michelle: Mike… you have just put your hand down my knickers, just like you did the other day…… MMMmmmmm… Sexxxxxxxy!!!

Michelle: Erotic and sexy

Mike: I do not think they will stretch enough to get all my hot rod in there! I may have to slip them off my darling.

Michelle: Come on then… take them off me… and make love to me……

Mike: Okay I have slipped then down and they are over your ankles and you have just kicked them off. What a shot… on the door handle again!! ☺

Michelle: I'm all yours then …

Mike: Now I can get to that hot spot of yours.

Michelle: MMMmmmm… you know how I like that…

Mike: With my hot rod I have put it right there where you like it. Just putting the tip of my hot rod right there.

Michelle: Wow……

Mike: Oh… Some of that love juice is getting excited and a little has popped out the end and making your hot spot moist.

Michelle: Oh…… wow, wow… I'm liking this……

Mike: I am just going to massage the end of my hot rod over your hot spot to try and dampen down the fire. I do not want a bush fire to start here…

Michelle: Oh… my… god…… I love it when you do that…… no we don't want a bush fire! I am getting rather warm here, I can tell you.

Mike: You are loving this Michelle.

Michelle: I am loving it Mike… and I am loving you…… the most sensitive part of a female… her hot spot, and the most sensitive part of a male, the tip of his hot rod… so carry on……

Mike: Yes… there are more sensual nerve ends in this part of the body for sure. I am doing it now up and down all over that hot spot and then I will do some circular massaging for you.

Michelle: The two together are magic…… Oh… nice… very nice…

Mike: Opppps… Sorry a bit more juice has just popped out the end.

Michelle: Mike… I am loving this… carry on… we will let the juices flow…

Mike: No not yet… be patient you sexy thing!

Michelle: I am feeling very sexy at the moment……

Mike: I need to save most for that love tunnel.

Michelle: Oh… nice… I love it…

Mike: Do you want me to lower it and start to open the door of your love tunnel?

Michelle: Come on then…

Mike: Okay… Do not rush, be patient…

Mike: Okay it is at the entrance to your love tunnel and gently I am pushing just the tip inside you. Just little gentle strokes… in and out… with only the tip going inside you.

Michelle: Oh Mike, I just love it when you do that…

Mike: The door is really opening now and inviting me inside you. So are you ready for a little deeper penetration?

Mike: Ohhhhhh nooooooo… I must go… Sorry!

Mike: OMG… what bad timing… Bye.

Michelle: Bye darling… shame about the timing… ☺

Michelle: So if I don't see you before your holiday… have a lovely time… I will miss you…

Mike: I'll try and text with you here before I go… If not, I will e-mail you

Michelle: I LOVE YOU

Mike: "DITTO"

Mike: Leave your Skype turned on if you can, I will try to come back later.

Michelle: OK darling. Mwah.

Half an hour later………………

Mike: Hi again Michelle

Mike: OMG... You have got tired of waiting and gone off to make yourself a coffee, eh?

Michelle: I'm back

Mike: On your back then, it is me on top? ☺

Michelle: Yes... definitely... I'm enjoying this...

Mike: So the tip of my hot rod has just let out some moist love juice and I have just popped the end inside you. You are loving this and shouting Mike, let me have all that hot rod deeper inside me.

Michelle: Come on then Mike... deeper inside of me... I am really wanting you now...

Mike: You must be patient, I will give you a bit more at a time, and I need to be gentle with you.

Michelle: Be gentle with me... I'm loving every minute of it... I'm kissing you... I'm cuddling you... I'm wanting you......

Mike: Okay, a little more pushing and a bit deeper inside you now and then I have eased back. So are you ready for a little bit more penetration down this love tunnel?

Michelle: Oh... Mike... I love this with you...

Mike: Okay, another gentle push and my rod is half way inside you and it is really warm.

Michelle: OOOOooooooo I love you inside of me... It is where you belong...

Mike: I will ease it back a little and then go a little deeper.

Michelle: MMMmmmmm...

Mike: You are so warm and slippery, is this me or you doing this, or both of us?

Michelle: I think it is both... our love juices already mixing together... more... more... more...

Mike: I can feel my end must have a premature leak, it does just feel like pumping. But wait... be patient.

Michelle: I can feel it throbbing inside of me... and I am gripping you tight... so, so, tight...

Mike: I am now going really deep and my golden nuggets are now knocking at the door to come into you.

Michelle: Wow... nice... come on then, see how far in your golden nuggets can go...

Mike: My golden nuggets cannot get in there too, no way my darling, it will not all fit inside, so just stop screaming that you want more. ☺

Michelle: Stop making me laugh ☺

Michelle: Come on Mike... give me everything you have got...

Mike: You want this 13 gun salute shot everywhere inside you? It is hard now and filling up with shot.

Michelle: Come on then... fire away... all 13 shots... pump them inside of me... I am in heaven here with you today...

Mike: Oh Yes... it is pumping... 1, 2, 3, 4... all the way now and all 13 have fired and splattered everywhere.

Michelle: OMG... you see when that happens, I go right through that orgasm chart you were telling me about... Oh yes, oh yes, oh yes... O... M... G... heaven

Mike: It is hot and steamy down there now my darling, I do not think your bush will set fire now, it is like it has been in the rain, really wet.

Michelle: OMG... I am in love with you... there is 'love juice' everywhere... well it's all inside of me... yours... mine... 'our love juice cocktail'...

Mike: Yes I think you may have got more that your share today, I could not hold it back and you copped the lot.

Michelle: You do make me laugh sometimes...

Mike: I will massage some of this around your bush back up to your hot spot, would you like me to do this for you?... Yes I want you to get going now and become fully aroused you sexy passionate adorable Michelle and stop shaking those boobs at me. You know I love them so much and they tease me.

Michelle: I told you... I'm all yours today... do what you want with me......

Mike: I just want to suck the nipples and kiss then for a minute.

Michelle: Come on then... they are just waiting for you...

Mike: They are so lovely and nice to feel... Your lovely 36C's Wow! You certainly have a lovely pair of assets there my Michelle.

Michelle: Oh Mike... I am just loving this with you today...... hey, don't tell everyone what size my boobs are... ☺

Mike: I think we need to take a little rest so come and cuddle in my arms and lay your boobs across me, this is how I like you.

Michelle: This is how I like you too… always have…… cuddled up close, so so close… kissing you, loving you… just cuddled together… you and me……

Mike: I want to wrap my arms around you and just hold those boobs gently in my hands.

Michelle: Hold me as close as you can… and never let me go…

Mike: MMMmmmm… You know I would love this.

Michelle: MMMmmmm… Me too…

Mike: Just to touch you and feel you, it would be great.

Michelle: I agree with that… just one little touch… one little cuddle… one little kiss…

Mike: I would even allow you to keep your clothes on!

Michelle: ☺

Mike: This is how it all started with a Christmas kiss!

Michelle: It was that kiss that did it for me……

Mike: I have a bone to pick with you anyway… Do you now that Christmas all I ever thought about was YOU?!!!!!

Michelle: 'YOU' were all I thought of that Christmas too…

Mike: YOU… Sent me crazy!!! I have never been the same since…

Michelle: I've told you before… for me that was the very moment I started to fall in love with you… and the very moment of that kiss… I knew……

Mike: Did you know it would lead to World War III?

Michelle: NO… I thought that would be it… One meal… One kiss… But, by then I knew I would never forget that kiss… ever… And, I never have…… I didn't expect to fall in love with you the way I did…… But, it just happened…

Mike: I had loved you for a long time by then… But did nothing about it…

Mike: I must go now… Love you forever… I'll be in touch after my holiday

Michelle: I LOVE YOU DARLING… I will miss you… but just to say have a really nice time…

Mike: I will miss you too… and you will always be on my mind.

Michelle: You will be on mine too…… safe journey… keep safe. Mwaaah

Mike: Mwah

Michelle: Mwwaaaaaaaaaaaaahhhhhhhhh...... Hello Darling

Mike: Hi Michelle... How are you today?

Michelle: I have really missed you...

Mike: I have missed you too Michelle

Michelle: How was your holiday?

Mike: Location very nice... Hotel very nice... Weather very nice... BUT...

Mike: You were not there!! ☹

Michelle: I am glad you are back now... I need some of your loving... I have missed you so much

Michelle: I am wearing something I know you are going to love!

Mike: Gosh... Okay tell me?

Michelle: Just one dress... with one zip... and when you undo the zip...... the dress is just going to fall to the floor... and I will be naked!!!

Mike: Wowwwwwwwwwwwwwwwwwwwww

Michelle: So, what are you waiting for?

Mike: You are getting me excited now.

Mike: So I do not need to fight with your bra or your knickers today.

Michelle: No bra... no knickers... just one zip to go...

Mike: Sounds good to me and this is almost like unzipping a lovely banana which is fleshy, ready and ripe to eat. I know you like a bit of nana yourself!! . So I have just taken the zip to the end and about to slip it over your shoulders and let it fall to the ground.

Michelle: And to the floor the dress goes... now I am naked!

Mike: Yes that is a lovely naked body... Love it!!! Plenty of nice ripe flesh here.

Michelle: And so are you... naked

Mike: Gosh... You are a quick worker, I didn't feel a thing.

Michelle: I've taken hold of your hands... and kiss the palms of each of your hands... then place them on my... you choose!!!

Mike: It is going to have to be on those lovely boobs and nipples of yours... Then followed by my lips

Michelle: OOOOoooooooooo sexy...

Mike: I love your boobs my darling… and have I ever told you I love you? I think we both need some hugs and cuddles today.

Michelle: We need lots of TLC… and this is… tender, loving, care at its best……

Mike: At its breast… sure!!!

Mike: Do you know what?… I love you!

Michelle: "DITTO"

Mike: I cannot feel you… I cannot touch you… I cannot see you,… But, I feel you are here right next to me. Lucky for you right now maybe we are apart, because I would be really naughty.

Michelle: I think we are both naughty! And, I think…

Michelle: I am in love with you…

Mike: That is dangerous!! You know the power of love!!

Michelle: Very powerful… but it's too late I'm afraid…

Mike: BIG TROUBLE…

Michelle: I 'AM' in love with you Mike…

Mike: And I 'AM' in love with you Michelle…

Mike: At least in our cyber world we can express our true feelings for one another and not be in trouble with anyone else.

Michelle: We have each been in so much trouble, because we loved one another… if they knew about our e-mails and this Skype texting… OMG we would both be dead meat!!

Mike: Let's hope they never find out then… I never want this to end between us…

Michelle: Me neither… I wonder how many other people share their secret love on the internet?

Mike: Plenty I would think.

Michelle: But, I bet not many have been 'Secret Lovers' for more than 20 years!!

Mike: No… maybe we hold the world record for this?

Michelle: Our love is special…

Mike: And priceless…

Michelle: Timeless…

Mike: Forever… with no end

Michelle: ☺

Mike: We both have to go now, look at the time

Michelle: OMG… Bye darling

Mike: Bye Michelle

Many e-mails take place with funny and amusing video clips for the next couple of weeks.

---

28 May 2012 ~ Live Interactive Text

Michelle: Hi my darling

Mike: Hi my sexy Michelle

Michelle: What a lovely sunny and warm day today

Mike: Yes you know what the sun does to me…

Michelle: Yes, I remember this well… We both love the sunshine.

Mike: I think you must need some sun lotion on today.

Michelle: I think I need to put some on you?

Mike: Oh, yesssssss please……

Michelle: OK… lots of lotion on my hand… nice flat hands, fingers and thumbs firmly but gently massaging into your body…

Mike: Tell me I hope you have no top on doing this… I want the full works today.

Michelle: Round and round the shoulders, and then down your back, my thumbs pressing firmly into your spine… this is to make you tingle from head to toe…… I still have bra and knickers on at the moment…… be patient you……

Mike: Oh no… get them off you.

Michelle: Back up your spine… and firmly down your sides… be patient Mike…

Michelle: Come on then let's turn you over……

Mike: I want to feel you stretching across me putting this lotion on me and your hard nipples dragging across me whilst you do this.

Michelle: Now this part is going to be like your video clip… I am behind you, and going to apply the lotion to your chest… well you know what happened next… boobs in the face…

Mike: Yes… I hope that bra is off now. I may have to see if I can catch a nipple for a little kiss and suck.

Michelle: I'll come and kneel over you… you are lying on your back now… my knees are either side of your hips… and I am taking your hands and placing them on my boobs so you can feel these hard nipples through all the lace and silk… and then…

Mike: Your boobs are like movers and shakers and keep moving around, but I am working hard and will catch one soon… What?… Your bra is still on… come on you, get it off.

Michelle: I am going to slowly undo the bra, and let it slip off… so now your hands are on my bare boobs and nipples!!! UUUuuummmmm nice…

Mike: Yes and about time too, I am really getting excited.

Michelle: I'm going to lean over you and give you some gentle little butterfly kisses, on your lips, my lips barely touching yours… erotic anticipation…

Mike: My hot rod is really hard and long… are you going to try and hurdle over it now? Be careful Michelle…

Michelle: And then… I'm going to move up a bit… and instead of my lips, it's one of my nipples gently brushing against your lips… be patient Mike… this might be a two-part story…

Mike: ☺ This is good and much better than the video clip I sent you… but I am ready to go… So move on quickly…

Michelle: This is going to be much better than the video… be patient Mike ☺

Mike: Just jump on top of this hot rod, it is erect and waiting for you my darling.

Michelle: So now you want to taste the other nipple to make sure they are the same flavour… Mike be patient…

Mike: Yes I have had both nipples… I am like a big baby with them.

Michelle: Now… I am going to apply suntan lotion to your front… warm it in my hands… gently massage into your chest… then down your middle… to your belly button… and then…

Michelle: I am going to rub some in my own boobs… all over my boobs… and nipples… so when I lay them on you they will be nice and slippery……

Mike: MMMmmmm… Yes I like them slippery.

Michelle: OK… time to take your towel off…… I still have my knickers on, but I will explain that in a minute…

Mike: I have just slipped my hand down your knickers to see if you are wet. I know it is a hot day today, but yes I can tell you are getting excited.

Michelle: I'm going to wipe my hands dry, because you will not want suntan lotion on your crown jewels… it might sting?

Michelle: and I am going to give you a gentle, nice little massage here too… oh yes… you are a very excited boy today……

Mike: What, no lotion!!!… what if it catches the sun!!!… it would burn!!!

Michelle: I think the suntan lotion may sting

Mike: The hot rod could turn into a red hot poker!!! ☺

Michelle: Oh dear!!!! Maybe I should move in with my tongue?

Michelle: So, with my tongue… I am gently flicking the end of your hot rod… gently but firmly… and then…

Mike: Can't wait for then?

Michelle: I am taking all of your hot rod into my mouth… MMMmmmmm Yummy!!!!!!! You did say I like a bit of nana!!

Mike: Oh! You want some ice cream with this on a hot day, eh! ☺

Michelle: But I can't do this for too long, because you are too excited… so I will move onto the golden nuggets… licking and kissing… oh so gently… with gentle gentle fingers too…

Mike: Oh… Ice creams now with nuts… I am spoiling you my darling, or should this read you are spoiling me?

Michelle: Humm ice cream with nuts… good one!!!!

Mike: Yes but you know when I come I cannot hold back!!

Michelle: Time for me to sit up… still kneeling across you… it's time to move on… don't want you exploding just yet!!!

Mike: Can you jump on top? This is a big hurdle to jump over now. Certainly raised higher by a few inches now!!

Michelle: I'll place your hands on my hips… because my knickers just have little ties at the sides there, and once you pull the ties, off the knickers will come…

Mike: Okay… Gosh it is taking time to get you stripped off today Michelle.

Michelle: Be patient Mike… you will enjoy the end result more…… we are getting there slowly but surely… pure sexual pleasure for both…

Mike: I am enjoying this, I just want to do what nature tells it to do my Michelle.

Michelle: So now I am naked… and so are you… and I'm kneeling right over you… my love tunnel only a couple of inches from your hot rod…

Mike: At last… ☺

Michelle: I'll move your hands back up to my boobs… and…

Mike: Yes I need to take care of them in case they start shaking everywhere, they can be dangerous. I could so easily be knocked out with them my darling, once they get shaking about and with your nipples so hard and long they could poke my eye out!!

Michelle: They will be shaking in a minute when I start bouncing up and down on you…

Mike: This is what I mean… I think I am already ahead of the game here my darling… Get shaking…

Michelle: I am going to gently take hold of your hot rod… and gently caress my hot-spot with it… Ohhhhhh nice…

Mike: Yes that would be nice for us both. Both tips pressing together, eh!… So sensual and sexy… Love it.

Michelle: So nice… yes… sexy and sensual… and so seductive.

Mike: Opppps… I am a little excited and some love juice has just come out of the tip. It will keep you moist whilst doing this.

Michelle: I have to go now darling… So this will have to be continued…

Mike: WHAT…!!!!! How can you do this to me, this is cruel and like punishment?… You will just have to finish me off somehow now.

Michelle: Be patient Mike… I will later…

Mike: What!!!! You have taken me right up to this hot spot and then tell me to wait until later… You cannot do this to me!!!

Michelle: You will be putting me in for the Olympics rodeo riding, after this session!!! We will carry on from here darling, I promise…

Mike: E-mail me the rest…… Bye.

Michelle: Bye… I love you … you will get it big time, later or tomorrow… I promise… Mwaaaaaahh

Mike: You are definitely going to get something!!!

Mike: I love you… Bye

Michelle: Mwah xxx Bye

Mike: You may be in for a rough ride!!! ☺ Bye

Michelle: I'll hold on tight, don't you worry… you are going to 'get it'……

Mike: MMMmmmm… Nice

E-mail from: Michelle
To: Mike
Date: 29 May 2012
Subject:... To be continued

Hi Mike

So... here is a quick re-cap... You have had a really nice massage, which you enjoyed very much... I like massages, whether it is to give or receive... I have massaged your hot rod and golden nuggets... and there was even 'ice-cream and nuts' involved... yummy... this really got you going... and now we are both naked... I am straddled across the front of you... my knees either side of your hips... I am sitting up, and your hands are caressing suntan lotion into my nipples... and I have your hot rod gently in my fingers, caressing my hot spot with the tip of it... OOooooo sooooo, soooo nice... sexy... sensual... erotic... you are fully loaded and wanting to come inside of my love tunnel... I am looking at you, and you are looking so horny and sexy... that I am wanting you inside of me... so here comes some sexy, wild, passionate loving...

I think we both really enjoy the 'play time'!!!... Well, we are both well and truly fired up for today, that is for sure... OOOOoooooo the end of your hot-rod rubbing against my hot spot... oh soooo nice... sexy... round and round, flicking it up and down... I can feel the sensation right now... and I have to go off to work feeling like this.

Well, I am going to have three Weetabix for my breakfast today, so I do have plenty of stamina for later... you are going to get it!!! ... this will be a sensational finish... as I am kneeling right up in front of you, I'm sure you can see my boobs and tummy glistening with the suntan lotion... sexy and shinny... and all for you...

I love you...

Michelle
xxx xxx xxx xxx x

E-mail from: Mike
To: Michelle
Date: 29 May 2012
Subject: Re:... To be continued

Hi Michelle

Well you are going to have to mount me high and ride me high like a bronco kid rider later. Your boobs will take a lot of slapping up and down riding out this finish. My darling, you are going to have me so deep inside you it will be like riding bareback on a stallion.!!! How can you do this to me when you are rubbing me and pressing me into your hot spot and then leave like this?!!!...

I think later you are going to get both barrels shot inside you and you will take all of me with my nuts exploding and no holding back this time. Naked it will be like you riding bareback in the Grand National with you jumping up and then down on me at every obstacle fence all the way around on this long intercourse race with you on top of me... Into the long running straight you will have to shuffle back and forward and really ride and work me off because it will be a hard stiff finish!!! I want my oats after all this and you will work up a real sweat and be hot until I put out that fire!!! You are really wild and sexy, but I may tame you in the end.

Have you got the stamina for this? We will see later!!!

I love you...
Mike
xxx

---

29 May 2012 ~ Live Interactive Text

Michelle: Hello my darling. Are you ready to carry on from yesterday here???... or do you need any more re-cap??? I am still caressing my hot spot with the tip of your hot rod... and then...

Mike: Hi my darling... I can tell you are feeling sexy, but let me say now you are the bronco kid and you will have to ride me real hard and stiff to the finish. I mean the finish... That is me finishing off what naturally should have happened yesterday when you loaded me up and the decided not to fire it. You will be in for the ride of your life now. I will hold those boobs tight with both hands, because you are a bareback naked rider and your boobs will start slapping around everywhere once you get into the galloping position!!!! You are going to cop it today my darling.

Michelle: Wow... OK...

Mike: Yes I have just made that hot spot moist again, these tadpoles want to get off racing again. They have been waiting so long, they could have changed into frogs by now!!

Michelle: I am now guiding your hot rod nearer to my love tunnel... and gently and slowly I direct you in there... slowly... gently... only halfway in... and back out again...

Mike: You are riding me my darling so you have control. I will lay back and enjoy the ride, but I will hold your boobs with my hands otherwise with all the rocking you or I could be slapped with them.

Michelle: But now I am moving down closer to you... and slowly and gently it moves in again... further this time... OOOOoohhh sooooo nice...... yes you are caressing my nipples, as we go...

Michelle: Out a tiny bit... but... back in again... right in this time...

Mike: Yes, I can feel I am going deep and penetrating well inside you now.

Michelle: Deep, deep inside of my love tunnel, which has been waiting for you for 24 hours... so warm and nice in there...

Mike: Yes these tadpoles have been swimming inside my nuts for too long.

Michelle: And gently to start with... I begin to move up and down on you... gently, gently, slowly, slowly, up and down......

Mike: I want you to ride me hard and stiff so you get full penetration.

Michelle: I can feel you Mike... Deep, deep, deep inside of me... so I'm getting a little faster... up and down, up and down... and pushing you right inside of me... OOOOOoohhhhhh sooooooo nice...

Mike: Yes I am holding onto those boobs tight so we do not get slapped in the face with them. They are bouncing everywhere and I think you should have left the sun lotion off, it is hard to hang on now. But, OMG... I am loving you riding me...

Michelle: Sexy, erotic and sensuous... up and down... hold on to them, because I am picking up more speed now... moving you further into me with each move... you are right there deep, deep inside... just where I like you to be.

Mike: Yes I know this will be a hard stiff finish, but you will see, it will be worth all the hard work you are putting in. You are shouting I am riding hard and low with this deep inside... OMG... That is so hard now.

Mike: Yes I think you need to go all the way this time and ride out the finish.

Michelle: I am going to keep still just for a few seconds... so... you can feel my muscles in there gripping hold of you... tight, tight, grip... and then release... tight, tight, grip and then release... yes, very hard now... especially with the position I am in... you can go no further inside... you are as far in as it will go...... so... in and out we go again... right in... not quite right out... right back in...

Mike: Well I know you cannot fall off my dear with this inside you. You are well and truly held on my hot rod.

Michelle: And now I am getting faster... wild and sexy... I have you so far inside of me... and I love it...

Mike: My nuts are now like they were yesterday, fully loaded and ready to fire. Are you ready for this.

Michelle: Your hands have moved down to my hips now, because you are saying, come on Michelle... more... more... more... harder... faster. So that's just what I am doing... wild and passionate love with you today......

Mike: You are really fast... top of the jockey league table for you my darling.

Michelle: Harder and faster... fast and furious... wild and passionate...

Mike: My nuts cannot hold on any more, so here goes. With that last push you have me deep inside and I am exploding... Pumping everywhere. You must feel my stiff hard rod just not stopping, just pumping my love juices inside you.

Michelle: I can feel your hard stiff hot rod... pumping your love juices into me... OOOOOOoooooohhhhhhh Mike...... how I love that feeling......

Mike: Yes I think I must be inside up to your belly button now, so deep... Hey check my nuts, have they gone inside too? ☺

Michelle: The lips of my love tunnel are kissing your nuts...

Mike: I said you would be in for a rough ride today... ☺

Mike: Kissing them... I think you have swallowed them!! ☺

Michelle: Your love juice is still pumping Mike... and you know what this does to me... My orgasm is ripping right through me...

Mike: OMG... can I ever reverse out now?... I think I may be stuck there for good.

Michelle: Oh yes Mike...!!! OMG...!!! HEAVEN...!!! Hey, I am going through your orgasm chart here, and you are talking about reversing out???

Mike: I think you have more than two days' worth here.

Michelle: My God... there is love juice everywhere... both of ours mixed together...

Mike: I think there is a problem... I think with all that riding so fast you have crossed my nuts and they are stuck inside. Now what?

Michelle: Don't make me laugh... we just stay here for a while...

Mike: Can you untangle me please?

Michelle: And I am going to lay my body against you... my boobs across your chest... whilst everything else is still inside me...

Mike: I think there must have been some crossfire in the finish...

Michelle: We will just lay still, and everything will be fine darling...

Mike: Yes you know it is starting to die down a little but... that was one hell of a ****

Michelle: Wild and passionate love with you today Mike... our hearts are beating fast and furious...

Mike: You sure do know how to ride out a hard finish. I think you deserve a cup and with so much of my love juice there inside I think you could fill it up now. I think there is enough love juice there to put your fire out down there, so hot!

Michelle: So hot... So nice... sensational loving with you... I love these intimate moments with you......

Mike: You are so lovely... I can only say you are the best bronco girl rider of the day. But... You made me wait 24 hours for this, it wanted to come yesterday and I told you it was already leaking when you were rubbing my rod all over your hot spot.

Michelle: I haven't finished with you yet... because there is more to come...

Mike: What, Tell me... I get some oats?...

Michelle: More ice-cream... with nuts... for me... I told you... you are going to get it big time today......!!!

Mike: Look... you have sucked me...!!! f****d me...!!! and now you want to kill me off.

Michelle: It's too late... I've started... so I will finish...... yes, sucking you again... licking rolling my tongue all over your hot rod... hot rod and golden nuggets... and I will keep doing this until... you have a second lot...!!!

Mike: Well okay I will start on the hot spot and get you really going my darling... my tongue will be like a whirlwind around this now, you will say... oh Mike I love it..!!

Michelle: I told you... you were going to get it big time today... good job I had three Weetabix for my breakfast... plenty of stamina...

Mike: I will say Michelle I love you... How can you give me all this pleasure today? I know it was to make up for yesterday and you certainly did this my darling.

Michelle: I wouldn't be stopping until you had a second lot today I can tell you... with my tongue and mouth this time...

Mike: I think I pumped every last juice inside you my darling, there is nothing left in the tanks now.

Mike: Michelle I am awarding you top jockey today and you won a true run ride on top of me. Anyway I enjoyed today my darling, this was a long fast ride today by you my lovely jockey. Maybe your boobs have settled down now with all that bouncing about and rocking, I sure did enjoy hanging on for dear life on them when you were riding so fast.

Michelle: So how about a nice cuddle before you disappear?

Mike: MMMmmmm... Promises, promises!!!

Michelle: MMMmmmmm... ONE DAY!!!

Mike: Well... put it on the slate!!

Mike: I love you this long<--

> forever. Bye now, must go... take care. Mwah!

Michelle: Thank you... sometimes you just melt my heart...

Mike: Take me to bed with you in your dreams tonight and I will surely be naughty again.

Michelle: I will think of that when I go to bed... You take me to bed with you...

Mike: Bye Michelle

E-mail from: Michelle
To: Mike
Date: 29 May 2012
Subject: Even more loving for you

Hello my darling

Well, hot, exotic, loving... but... I haven't finished with you yet...!!!

So now we have had a shower and cooled down... your batteries have re-charged... and I am still feeling sexy, sexy, sexy... So... even although you seem to think you cannot manage two lots in one day... I'm about to show you... you can!!!... I really must not have three Weetabix for breakfast again, it gives me too much energy...

I'm taking you off to bed... we will have a fan on, so we don't get overheated... so a nice cool room... a bed, and you and me!!!... In fact because it is hot, we can have a bottle of champagne, to drink in bed (like we used to). So a nice cold glass of champagne each... cheers!!! and we clink glasses... you know what is waiting on the rim of the glass for you... my kiss... So we will drink the first glass each, and then a lovely, long lingering kiss... sexy, sensual and seductive... more kisses... and lots of cuddles...

More champagne... more kisses... steamy sexy kisses... and maybe this time you want to give me a massage???... I'll lay on my front first, so you can start the massage on my back... shoulders... down my spine... the cheeks of my bum!!! and down my legs... More champagne... I'll turn over, and you can start on my front... arms... shoulders... neck... OOOOOooooo you plant lots of lovely kisses on my neck... MMMmmmm nice...... your hands move lower... over my boobs... your thumbs playing with my nipples... OOOhhhhh so nice with you Mike... Always... down my tummy you go... up my sides... over my boobs and nipples again... and there you stop whilst you kiss me lovingly on my lips... the kisses move down my neck... lots of lovely

kisses… down to my boobs… oh yes they are getting a lot of attention from you now… from your lips and tongue……
OOOOhhhhh sooooooo nice…!!! your hands move down… down my sides… down my hips… down my thighs… right down to my toes… you massage my feet… and then the kisses start on my legs… moving up my legs… right up my legs… until you find my 'hot spot'… Oh… My… God…… so, so, so niceeeeeeeeeeeeeeeeeeeeee!!! You are gently kissing, sucking and licking my hot spot now… Oh Mike… you have now poured champagne over my hot spot and you have started lapping it up with your tongue and it is driving me crazy… Mike if you keep doing this, it is me who will have the orgasm here… and it was about you having another lot!!! OMG Mike… if you don't stop now, it will happen … but you carry on… and… it happens… Oh Mike… I just love you so much… I love the way you make love to me… yes, you are slowing moving down now… but it has happened and my whole body is tingling …

So we change positions… and it is you laying on your back now… and I am planting kisses all over you… your neck… lots of lovely juicy little kisses… I whisper in your ear… Mike… have I ever told you that I love you?… Well I do… with all my heart…… The kisses move down your neck… all over your chest… down your tummy… and there I gently take hold of your hot rod and golden nuggets and massage them so gently… that you are in heaven…!!! and my kisses move lower… until it is my lips and tongue are on that rod and tackle of yours now… so gently… sexy, sensual, juicy kisses… my tongue everywhere… you are loving it… and yes, I have your full attention here now… You are standing to attention yet again today… See… you didn't believe me… but it has happened… with just a little gentle persuasion… well it would be a shame to waste this… so… it's time I got on top of you again… but this time, it won't be as wild, it will be gently and slowly… just gentle movements up and down… in and out… yes, already you are back inside of me… and we are loving one another so much… I am going to lay myself down on you this time, so my boobs are rubbing all over your chest… yes my American hard gums are rubbing all over you… and your hot rod is sliding in and out of me gently and slowly… and again it is as hard as a rock… We are moving together in rhythm… and then the firework display starts… yes… yes… yes… yes… we orgasm together… so gently, so slowly…… such love … sooooooo, sooooooo nice … We just lay still… our hearts beating together as one… you still inside of me… just cuddled up… and you are stroking my hair… Oh Mike I love you so much… So we get ourselves more comfortable, and you cuddle me up in your arms, as we lay side by side… cuddled so tight… this is how we will sleep tonight…

I love you Mike ~ Goodnight
xxx xxx xxx xxx x
Michelle

E-mail from: Mike
To: Michelle
Date: 30 May 2012
Subject: Re: Even more loving for you

Hi Michelle

OMG!!!… I can tell you have not finished with me yet!!!

I have decided to award you a Certificate of Excellence for 'Bronco Riding' and then I thought I had better include 'Endurance'.

You are surely some passionate, exotic and wild sexy lover. Red hot is an understatement. This afternoon made up for yesterday and yes maybe despite you leaving me in such a state yesterday… you are forgiven!!!

Do you know what!!!… I know I have probably told you a million times now already … I love you!

MMMmmmm… How I would love to just give you a hug and cuddle!!! I want to take you into my bed with me and hold you close all night.

Goodnight my darling…
Love always…
Mike
xxx

CHAPTER SIX

E-mail from: Michelle
To: Mike
Date: 2 June 2012
Subject: Our Safe Cyber World

Hi Mike

I love the world of Skype and e-mails with you… I'm so glad we have done this… but Skype time always goes by so quickly… I love the silly things we talk about… I love the fun and laughter we have… I love all the memories we have shared… I love the loving we share… and I love the comfort you have given when I have been down the past couple of weeks… I have always enjoyed you… The saddest time of my life was when we could no longer go on seeing one another… So, I am pleased to be in this safe world with you… and, here we share so much.

I will e-mail you when I can next week, but even that will be limited for me, because as you know Simon will be at home. But know this… even if I can't e-mail you very much next week… thoughts of you will often pop into my head… because that is what happens to me… I can be quite happy with what I am doing, or who I am with…… and then I have a little thought of you just pop into my head, out of the blue… or, I think of something naughty we have been up to…… UUUUUuuuummmmmm what nice thoughts to hold inside of me !!! where nobody else can see them… only you and I know…

I love you Mike…

I have loved you for such a long time… somehow over this past 5 months that love has grown even more… I have never stopped loving you… But, my love for you just continues to grow stronger and stronger.

I will always love you…

You are one of the very special people in this world, and I am glad to have you as part of my life.

Michelle

xxx xxx xxx xxx x

E-mail from: Mike
To: Michelle
Date: 2 June 2012
Subject: Re: Our Safe Cyber World

Hi Michelle

I know it is difficult for you to send me emails or to see me on Skype this week. But, I miss you here in our cyber world.

Our cyber and distant relationship is not always ideal because I want to hold, hug and cuddle you!!! In fact, it can be really tough when I love you so much… Michelle.

I spend countless hours just sometimes thinking about you, with you always inside my mind. I can now talk to you on a telephone or through a computer screen. I know I can't see you when I like or when I need you most… but I can love you!!… I know I can't hug you, I know I can't hold your hand, I know I can't kiss you. How I would just love to hold you in my arms and feel you so nice and close to me again!!… How I loved you when wearing my shirt looking so lovely and sexy!!… How romantic, when we gazed into one another's eyes, only seeing the beauty of the love that we shared together. I lose the intimacy in a physical sense… But our relationship now becomes our cyber world sharing our love with each other and we are able to stay in touch. I love sharing this precious love that we have for each other in our cyber world. Here we learn to share our love in our very own world, where we can communicate openly, because a distant relationship without communication is nothing. I learn to love you without ever being able to feel and touch you and not able to look into those lovely blue eyes… But when we share laughter, it's twice the fun. When we share problems, it's half the pain. When we share sad times and tears we are always here for each other and to help when are feelings are sad. When we share secrets, it is our hearts that we share and reveal. You see, what draws everybody closer and makes us all care is not the material things we have in life, but the love that we share. We share and have a strong love and nobody can take this way… I love you!!

I know we may never see each other, or know everything of where and what we are both doing. I learn to sacrifice, because I know I cannot have Michelle, the person that I love… I learn to appreciate what I share with you, and this our love, in our cyber world. So often, we take for granted the people and relationships in our lives because we think they will always be there, but we all know tomorrow is never promised… But even when I only have a limited amount of time with you, I want you to know I love you!!… I learn to appreciate and cherish every single moment of our time here with you. I have you in our cyber world that we have created and built which has become our home. When I see you, it is only in my dreams, but who knows maybe I will see you for real one day!!!… Oh! Don't panic!!!… I love you!!

After years of not seeing each other it is so nice that we can chat through a computer screen. I have no regrets in loving you and I am so glad that I shared a part of your life. I have the same feelings and love for you now like all those years long ago. I have waited for something to bring us back together and I now feel you close to me. I really can love you in our cyber world and I can cherish our love and friendship that we share together. The key to our relationship is the love we have always shared together. If both of us are not willing to give this up, our love will last forever, and forever has no end… I will always love you!!!

A cyber relationship means we are not together, but we will never be apart. There is no need to be fearful, it's good to know this is our safe home. It's for those who are willing to spend a lot of time just thinking about each other in exchange for the precious time when we can chat and I can say… I love you!!!

It's our way of knowing we can stay in touch and sometimes this makes me feel you are here with me. Even though I cannot get nearly enough of you... I love you!!!

Love has its time, its season, its own reason for coming and going. Love always has been and always will be a mystery... I am so glad fate played a part when you came into my life. Thank you for your love and for sharing a part of your life with me. These memories will always be held close to my heart... Have I told you I love you?

Love always...
Mwaaaaaaaaaah!
Mike
Xxx

E-mail from: Michelle
To: Mike
Date: 7 June 2012
Subject: I love you Mike Turner

Hi Mike

Thank you for the email you sent me yesterday... at times you just absolutely melt my heart!!! How I would love to be with you right now ~ wearing your shirt. We had some really good times together, you and I... and still we do now in our cyber world. I love it here with you... where there is just you and I and nobody else. We share so much here... and mostly is it based upon our love for one another... A true love ~ that will never die.

I am missing you like crazy this week... where I cannot just pick up my laptop and e-mail you... or read something you have sent me... or Skype with you... I am just missing you so much... and thinking about you so much. But, this evening I have time to myself, where I could have Skyped with you if you were about. But...

I love the photos of your garden... how artistic you are... and your beautiful summer house... I will send you some pictures of my garden next week, when I have had time to dig some out... and how are we so alike??? I have in the past had a couple of little topiary animals… a little cat, and a little squirrel, and they were doing really well after five years of my clipping and nurturing… but then I got two real kittens, that 'peed' all over them and killed them!!! The little monkeys!!! I was not amused… But now I only have one of these cats, and he is almost 5 years old now and much better behaved,

As it is nearly your birthday… we had better start thinking about some options for you!!! Ooooohhhh what could these be???

If you by any chance read this email within the next couple of hours of me sending it… I will be on Skype waiting for you.

I LOVE YOU ~ MIKE
Take care

"I will always love you"
Michelle
xxx xxx xxx xxx x

---

7 June 2012 ~ Live Interactive Text

Michelle: I hope you check your e-mails this evening, because I am here looking for you, with a whole evening to myself, as Simon has gone out…

Two hours later…

Michelle: Hello darling…

Mike: Wow… Michelle, how come you are here in the evening? Is Simon down the pub?

Michelle: He has gone to play darts… I am picking him up later… yippy… some time with you…

Mike: Wow… How long have you got?

Michelle: I don't know… at least another half hour I would think?

Michelle: I've had this laptop on my lap for 2 hours hoping you might appear… whilst watching a film.

Mike: Oh sorry… I did not expect this, but I thought I would check my e-mails… What a surprise!!! Glad I did this now! ☺

Michelle: I'm glad you are here now… I'm really missing you…

Mike: MMMmmmm… Miss you too… I was not expecting to hear from you this week.

Michelle: It is difficult… but I have managed to sneak the odd little e-mail in here and there… but I have to be careful…

Mike: No point of putting yourself at risk… Or risking what we have here!!

Mike: I love you…

Michelle: I love you too… You know I do

Mike: Can we ever see each other on cam? I cannot talk of course, so mute the mic and sound? What do you think?

Michelle: Maybe one day… if I do that… I will want to see you for real… so not now…

Mike: Oh! ☹

Michelle: Maybe one day…

Mike: The nearest to real is to see you on cam

Michelle: I would want to touch you……

Mike: Pleaaaaaaaaaaaaaaaaaaaaaaase?

Mike: Just a quick open cam and close?

Mike: Just one minute?

Michelle: One day…

Mike: ☹

Michelle: Don't be sad……

Mike: If I live video call you would you open your cam?

Michelle: Noooooooooooooooooooooooooooooooo…

Mike: Ohhhhhhhhhhhhhhhhhhhhhhhhhhhhhhhhhh…

Michelle: I would just want to touch you, if I did that.

Mike: Don't be mean, I really would like to see you. No harm here!!

Michelle: You can see me… you have a photo… in fact two photos

Mike: Come on YOU!

Michelle: And I would want to kiss you…

Mike: Just a quick open, a wave, and close.

Michelle: What are you trying to do to me here?

Mike: I miss you… It has been a long time.

Michelle: I miss you… BUT…

Mike: Come on!

Michelle: I love you.. and I would like a kiss and cuddle with you right now…

Mike: Michelle… Pleeeeeeeeeeeeeeeease!!!

Michelle: Not today…

Mike: It is my birthday soon… remember you said you would have to think of something special for my birthday. What could be more special? So no better time than now.

Mike presses the button on his computer to video call Michelle. Michelle declines the link.

Michelle: NAUGHTY …

Mike: I know… ☺

Michelle: Don't be naughty!!!

Mike: Your fault… see what you do to me. Okay… No, it is I suppose ☹

Michelle: It's because I will want to see you for real if I did that with you… maybe nearer your birthday… if that's what you want for your birthday…

Mike: You know we can never take that risk for real.

Michelle: Well that's what I mean…

Mike: This is our world.

Michelle: I know…

Mike: We should make the best of what we have here, seeing you here is the nearest to real we will ever get.

Michelle: Maybe one day… I have to go now… taxi service required…

Michelle: Nice to talk to you, even if you are being naughty…

Michelle: Maybe one day, we will do that… not now though

Michelle: So… are you not talking to me now? or have you been interrupted? Well it's a good job my face wasn't on your screen is all I can say……

Mike: I am not naughty!!!

Michelle: Bye darling. take care. I am missing you so much this week… ☹

Mike: I love you and take care

Michelle: I love you darling

Mike: Come on you… I need you now! Just open your cam and close for me.

Michelle: I have to go now honestly xxxxxxxxx Byeeee
Mike: Michelle… please… Just for 13 seconds

Mike presses the button for live video link again. Michelle declines it.

Michelle: NAUGHTY…!!!
Mike: Please…

He tries it again. She declines it again.

Michelle: I have to go …
Mike: Bye then! ☹ I think you are being mean… But, I still love you…
Michelle: Bye darling… "I LOVE YOU"…

Mike tries one more time. Michelle declines, and signs out.

---

11 June 2012 ~ Live Interactive Text

Michelle: Hello naughty one!! ☺
Mike: Meeeeeeeeeeee… I am never naughty… you maybe!!
Michelle: You always… So… are you on your own at the moment?
Mike: Yes darling, I am just here on my own, chatting with you my darling.

Michelle presses the button on her computer for live video link.

Mike: Oh no! You said I cannot do this… it is NAUGHTY!!!

Michelle presses the live video link again. Again he does not accept.

Mike: Can you talk? I have to be careful and switch off the mic when Cheryl is due back, she would hear me talking in the front when she arrives back home. But… We can talk for a while?

Michelle presses the live video link again… And this time Mike answers… For the first time in 20 years they talk to one another face to face, albeit thanks to modern technology and a video link. They talk for 20 minutes, and then revert back to text.

Michelle: Naughty us…

Mike: Michelle, you are looking good… You look the same as I ever remember you

Michelle: You are still the same as I remember… and you are looking pretty damn good yourself

Mike: Wow… I want to be naughty with you now… The more I see you the more I want YOU!!!

Michelle: That has knocked the wind out of both of our sails!!

Mike: You are lovely… and very special…

Michelle: This reminds me of just how much I love you……

Mike: It has been a long time… and a long wait for today, and we can see each other again.

Michelle: I would like a cuddle now…

Mike: It is also easier to chat and see you on cam than for us to type text. I said last time… This is the nearest we will get to being real… I love you!

Michelle: I love this world with you… and, I still love you as much now as I always did. I want a kiss now… and a cuddle… It feels safe here with you

Mike: Come on then!!!!!! I am yours and waiting!!!

Michelle: Come on then!!!… I'm all yours……

Mike: Naughty… It is you that is naughty… Not me!

Michelle: Well we got to see each other today… and that was good…

Mike: Yes really good and so nice to see you after such a long time. A really long time! You know, I want to cuddle you and hug you now, just to hold you close in my arms and whisper… I love you.

Michelle: I would like that now too… cuddled up to you… and I would whisper, Mike I just love you so much …

Mike: I LOVE YOU… I LOVE YOU… Yes I am now shouting it out over the rooftops… I love my Michelle

Michelle: Hee hee hee… you always make me laugh…

Mike: Michelle, you have turned me inside out and upside down today. I may have looked relaxed on that cam… But, my heart is still racing.

Michelle: You looked as cool as a cucumber to me… Like you always did… My heart is racing too… So nice to see you.

Mike: I am sorry darling, I have to go now, Cheryl has just come home

Michelle: OK darling... "See you again soon"

Mike: Maybe we can come back on here later?

Michelle: Don't worry darling, I know it is difficult for you now Cheryl is back. See you soon. Mwah. Bye

Mike: Bye x

Two hours later.........

Mike: Oh!... I am here wanting a cuddle and you are probably doing your dinner. How I would like you for dinner!!! What is on the menu?... Oh yes... Michelle's Delight!! I wonder what that this? I say to myself. Some tasty dish for sure. It surely would be if I had you my darling. I would have to sample you from head to toe with many in between, some nice bits there I know. Those really nice bits I may even come back for second helpings to satisfy my hunger for your love.

Mike: You know I like the sweet menu and I know you are very sweet. What is on this menu?... Oh Yes... Michelle's Surprise!! I wonder what that is? I say to myself. I know you are so full of surprises and I cannot ever predict what you will do next!!!... But this is you, just full of fun and full of surprises.

Mike: I have to say it was great to see you today, you are lovely and you will always be close to my heart and in my mind. It is so nice to chat and share our love and friendship here together and to see you... Wow!!! That is the icing on the cake. I love you...

Mike: I guess you are not coming back here on Skype now and I am just talking to myself again here. Surely a sign of madness, do you recognise these symptoms?. Am I really going mad here, or am I just so madly in love with you? You know you were so close to me, yet so far away, I felt I could almost reach out and touch you.

Mike: I do not know when we can chat next. Have I ever told you... I love you... Today you have made my day complete... So nice to see you again... Take care and take all my love with you for in spirit I will be with you forever. Love always... Mike... xxx

Mike: When you go to bed tonight and if you feel tingles all over your body, don't worry, it is me just caressing you and loving you. I just hunger for your love and wanting second helpings!!!!...

E-mail from: Michelle
To: Mike
Date: 11 June 2012
Subject: Soooooo nice to see you today

Hello Darling

So nice to see you... after what I know is almost 20 years...
OMG... well, you are looking as hot, handsome and sexy as I
always remember you... how little you have changed in that
time... yes, I'm sure we will see each other occasionally on here,
but for me that has to be when we are both 'home alone'... I
could not risk anyone coming into the room and seeing my face
on your computer screen... OMG fireworks!!!... I almost
answered your calls the other evening... because yes, I wanted to
see you... but... when we are alone. I love you so much... and to
see you... you melt my heart... always have... so, because we
live in this safe cyber world, as you remind me... I'm sending you
a loving cuddle, with my body pressed right up tight against
yours... my arms gently wrapped around your neck... and a very
long... loving... lingering... kiss... very long... very lingering...
very sexy...... I love you ~ Mike...

So, tomorrow you have a man coming to check out your
worktops... so no Skype for us... I will email you and dig out
some pictures of my garden, that we talked about, and show you
instead.

Wednesday, I think I am working until 4pm... so probably no
Skype for us then either... but, will let you know. What do you
think of the possibility of ad hoc Skype evenings for us sometimes
then??? I may even be able to Skype with you Tuesday, or
Wednesday evening this week, for an hour max, I think Simon is
going out. So I will e-mail you in the morning, and let you know
which evening, and a time, because I will know by then...... and
you can let me know if this fits in with you. Maybe we will get a
whole hour here and there... OOOOooooohhhhhh... time enough
for some serious 'loving'!!!... and... you don't even have to be
naughty... you just have to say 'Michelle ~ give me some of your
loving'... and it will happen...

I LOVE YOU DARLING… I've loved you for such a long time… and "I WILL ALWAYS LOVE YOU"… Such a long time ago we came into each other's lives, and I think there has been a mutual attraction since that time… of course which developed as the years went on… and here we are now, all these years on… still loving each other, against all odds, I have to say… and wanting just that little bit more of each other… which we both know, will now, be limited to our cyber world… But, I love this world with you. 'Serendipity + Fate'!!!… here we share so much… our thoughts, our feelings, our love.

I love you…
Michelle
Xxx xxx xxx xxx x

---

18 June 2012 ~ Live Interactive Text

Mike: Hi Darling

Michelle: Hi Darling

Mike: Do you want to talk on video today? On the cam?

Michelle: I cam… If you cam!! ☺

Mike presses the button for video link, and they talk together for half an hour. Laugh a lot… And thoroughly enjoy seeing one another again. They each place their hand on the screen of their computers… If only these hands could actually touch one another… Time is up, they revert back to text… Cheryl will be home soon…

Michelle: I wish I could have a kiss down this camera lens…

Mike: So do I Michelle… I love you so much…

Michelle: I love you so much too… always and forever…

Mike: I have even put a tattoo across my heart… I love Michelle

Michelle: hee hee hee… you make me laugh…… that's one of the reasons I love you

Mike: I wish… I wish I could…

Michelle: Wish what darling?

Mike: Just to see you for real… but I know it will never, and must never happen! So I must delete the impossible from my brain. It is nice to see you here... and this is as near to real that we have in our Skype world.

Michelle: MMMmmmm I know... I would like that too... but... we have to stay here (for now anyway)... you can never say never... We both love this world... our own little world...

Mike: The advantage here is that we now have our cyber world. All the time there is Skype we can still at least see each other now and again.

Michelle: A world all of our own... with nobody else...... just 'You & Me'... MMMmmmm... soooooo nice

Mike: I love you so much... And in this world we are so naughty!!

Michelle: Yes, and very nice to see you after such a long time...... I love this world with you... we are both naughty don't you think?... but hey ho... who cares?...

Mike: Time for me to go I am afraid

Michelle: Ok darling... Bye for now... Hopefully see you tomorrow

Mike: Yes... Mwah... Bye

E-mail from: Michelle
To: Mike
Date: 18 June 2012
Subject: A wishing well wish...

Hi Mike

So nice to actually see you for a while... and chat to you... you are still 'so the same' as you have always been. Still that same person I fell in love with all those years ago... the person I have fallen in love with all over again, over the past six months...

Oh Mike Turner ~ I LOVE YOU...

I have been out and put a penny in my wishing well re the wish discussed earlier... you never know... maybe... just maybe one day??? we will see each other again for real...

But... until then... I love this world with you. I enjoy you here very much. Well, as you earned yourself a bonus today, you will have to let me know what the bonus is??? 13 items you say??? Compile a list, I'll see what I can do???

I love you darling.
Michelle
xxx xxx xxx xxx x

E-mail from: Mike
To: Michelle
Date: 18 June 2012
Subject: Re: A wishing well wish…

Hi Michelle

Please throw thirteen thousand pennies in the wishing well for me… I want them all to be for the same wish… "One day we can see each other for real"… so that I can hold you for real in my arms… kiss those lips of yours for real… look once again into those sparkling blue eyes of yours… MMMmmmmmm… Michelle…… if only!!!

I don't need to compile a list of thirteen items as a bonus!!!… This is the only bonus I would really want.

I love you…
Mike
xxx

E-mail from: Michelle
To: Mike
Date: 19 June 2012
Subject: A no bra cuddle

Hi Mike

Soooooooooooo nice to see you, and talk to you again today… the problem this gives me is I want to touch you… and hug you… and give you a little kiss… or two…

So right at this moment I want to put my arms around you… look into those sexy brown eyes of yours… and give you a nice gentle little kiss… and then another… and yes you know what I'm going to say here… and then another… and then a nice tender long and lingering kiss… and then a very passionate one… and then…

As you already had the top couple of buttons undone on your shirt... I would undo another one... look into those sexy brown eyes again, that are sparkling and laughing at me now... so I will undo another one... and then another... and another... OOOooooo they seem to all be undone now... so I will tug that shirt out of your trousers, and slip my arms inside of your shirt and around you... gentle tiger claws up and down your back, and another smouldering sexy sexy kiss... and press my body up close against yours, and hug you oh so close... MMMmmmm... nice...

I know what you are thinking now... If she has undone my shirt... I'm going to do the same with her blouse... come on Ditto where are you? I am coming in there to look for you!!!... So you undo my buttons, find Ditto fast asleep nestled in his home... "Sorry Ditto, out you come," you say to him. And undo his chain, take him off me, and lay him on the side... and back you come and remove my blouse completely... and cuddle me again... and then you say "Michelle, I want a no bra cuddle now"... so quick as a flash you undo the clasp on my bra, off it comes... and yes, you know what you do next... throw it across the room... and cuddle me tight to you... A no bra cuddle... my boobs brushing against your chest... OOOOooooo sooooooo sooooo nice... Off with your shirt then... all this bare flesh... my tiger claws are gentle brushing up your arms, around your shoulders, down your back... and your temperature is rising... a little nibble of your neck... OOooo yummy very tasty, lots of kisses... my arms are around your neck now, and very passionate kisses... and slowly but surely you undo the zip of my skirt, and let it fall to the floor... OOOOhhhhh Mike...... you know what is going to happen now... As I only have my knickers on now, I have to make this even... so... I undo that belt on your trousers... undo the button... undo the zip... in goes my hand to gently caress and massage you... UUUUuuuuummmmmmmm...
UUUUUuuuuummmmmmmmmmmm... nice!!! and off with your trousers... and across the room they fly!!!... Now we each only have one item of clothing each left on us... more kisses... lots of hugging... our bodies pressed firmly against one another... OOOoooo so, so, so nice...

You decide it's time we went off to bed... so you pick me up... yes pick me up... and carry me and put me on the bed... I'm all yours Mike… you can take it from here and finish this e-mail if you like… what would you like to happen next???

I love you darling
Michelle
xxx

PS… I did not have 13,000 pennies… so I just had to throw 13 in for you… I made them all for the same wish, as you asked me to!!!

E-mail from: Mike
To: Michelle
Date: 19 June 2012
Subject: Re: a no bra cuddle

Hi Michelle

MMMmmmm… I would love those boobs pressing into me… MMMmmmm… Those nipples of yours so hard and so long just standing up on end. This is how I remember them!! But what about me picking you up here? Are you not shouting very loudly… Don't pick me up… put me down, put me down!! Well maybe this should continue in our cyber world for another time, eh!

It is nice to see you and Ditto who is still alive and kicking and it must be his birthday again soon. He has not aged at all in all these years and he is obviously living a good life and enjoying every minute cuddled in amongst those lovely boobs. He is a lucky Ditto and in return you say he given you some luck too.

I love you… Mike
Xxx

PS… Thank you for making my thirteen wishes for me… OMG… I hope they come true one day!!!

E-mail from: Michelle
To: Mike
Date: 20 June 2012
Subject: You Cheeky Monkey

Hi Mike

You cheeky monkey!!!… So, you have a way you can take pictures of me whilst we are on Skype?… I wanted to take a picture of 'you'… not you take one of me… so I have been looking to see how I can do this… but it would seem not, on this version… so maybe you could send me another one instead (of you)… Thank you darling… and send me a copy of the one, even two, you took of me today… you cheeky little monkey.

Not long until your birthday… I'm taking you out on the town, in our cyber world… Oh Mike all my wildest dreams come true in this cyber world with you… I love it here with you… seeing you, chatting with you, texting with you, e-mails with you… "I LOVE YOU"…

How I love you…
Always and Forever
Michelle
Xxx xxx xxx xxx x

E-mail from: Mike
To: Michelle
Date: 20 June 2012
Subject: Re: You Cheeky Monkey

Hi Michelle

I am not a monkey!!… I miss you!!… I just wanted a couple of pictures of you!!! Well maybe now you may tell me off… I have attached here the thirteen pictures I took of you today… My lovely Michelle… You look so happy in these pictures, just like I always remember you being…… You are so lovely.

I love you…
Mike xxx

They send one another many emails over the next couple of weeks, sharing photos of their gardens, sunset photos they have each taken. Holiday photos from exotic locations, all around the world, that they have each been to… They send one another love songs… They call it 'Sharing is caring'…

---

26 June 2012 ~ Live Interactive Text

Mike: Hi gorgeous

Michelle: Hi sexy cyber lover

Mike: Gosh… If you were here on Saturday, when I was sawing all that wood up and see the dust cloud outside, you would have to strip naked.

Michelle: Not in your garden, naked, surely???

Mike: Yes the work took place in the garden.

Michelle: I would wait until I was back inside with you… then you could strip me off!!!

Michelle: Dust me off… then shower me off…

Mike: You would have to shake off outside and then go naked to the bathroom for a shower with me… Plenty of liquid soap to get that dust off your lovely naked body. Then rub you down with a nice soft towel… Oh, and by the way, do not write on my bathroom mirror in lipstick 'I love you', like you did once in a hotel room!!

Michelle: Oh yes, I did do that didn't I?… ☺… And then we would really get down and dirty…

Mike: Yes dirty for sure you naughty Michelle.

Michelle: Would you rub the soap all over me?

Mike: I would rub the soap all over you… I would not miss a bit… a single bit… Just like we did in the Cotswolds!!

Michelle: MMMmmmm… yes please…

Michelle: I would let you wash my hair, and I would wash yours…… soap bubbles and lather running everywhere… I would give you lovely, sexy, kisses… Our hands would each wash every single part of each other's body!!

Mike: Do you know I feel like when we first met and when I first fell in love with you… I never thought this would happen again.

Michelle: No neither did I…!!! But here we still are… being naughty…

Mike: I must go now… I love you, big hugs and tons of kisses…

Michelle: Bye darling… Hugs, kisses and cuddles for you too… mwah

---

E-mail from: Michelle
To: Mike
Date: 27 June 2012
Subject: Your birthday treat from Michelle

Hi Mike

So, here we are the day before your birthday… and off we go for your birthday treat with Michelle… We have each packed a small overnight bag, and board the train to London… your treat is for 2 days, and one night…!!!! We arrive in London late morning, and check into our hotel near Covent Garden… I have booked us into somewhere really nice… luxury for us for these two days and one night, because it is your birthday darling. We quickly check out the room and facilities… oh, yes this will be perfect for us… a huge bed… a huge Jacuzzi… and a shower big enough for two!!! Quickly unpack our bags, and hang up our clothes to go out in tonight. But, come on Mike, first of all we are going, to have a little wander around Covent Garden, enjoy the street entertainers, the sun is shining. A little meander in and out of a few shops. And then we decide to have lunch… but this is a light lunch, as we are out for dinner this evening. So we sit outside a little restaurant in the sunshine, have a light bite and a drink… oh we should have a proper drink, it's your birthday… what would you choose here?… I know, a large Southern Comfort and lemonade each, lots of ice ~ yummy… We soak up the atmosphere and the sunshine, how nice ~ to do this with you!!!

By now, it's mid-afternoon… and we decide we should go back to our hotel, order a bottle of champagne and relax in the Jacuzzi together… after all, it is your birthday. So back we go, order a chilled bottle of Veuve Clicquot, and by the time we have filled the Jacuzzi with water and bubbles, our chilled champagne arrives in a bucket full of ice, and two nice champagne flutes… So we slip our clothes off, and into the nice warm bubbles… you uncork our champagne, I hold our glasses, and you pour us one each… we make a toast… "Happy Birthday To You My Darling"… a little sip each… OOOOOoooooo YUMMY!!!… talking of yummy, I settle myself down beside you, give you a nice little kiss, or two. And then lay my head back against your shoulder, as your arm has now gone around me, and your hand has already found its way onto one of my boobs… and there we stay for a while, drinking our drinks, talking, laughing, nice and cuddled up together. Oh wow… how nice… drinking a bottle of bubbles, in a tub full of warm bubbles with you ~ HEAVEN..!!! Nice and relaxing… Intimate moments with you Mike!!!… The more of the champagne we drink, the more giggly we get… OOOoooo these bubbles have gone straight to my head… Now your hand is moving from one of my boobs to the other… and you are saying "Michelle ~ I need to make these nipples stick out like American hard gums"… and the more you play with them the harder they get… Well Mike… I too have a free hand here, so I slip it under the water, down your tummy, and find 'your crown jewels'!!! ~ and I too start to play… nice, nice, nice… you are liking this… I can tell!!!… Gentle massaging and playing… MMMmmmm… wooooo, we have drunk the whole bottle of champagne already!!!… and you are saying, Michelle, put that glass down, and turn around so I can have a taste of those American hard gums… "… It's my birthday ~ and my day of choosing ~ and I want to taste them now…" and I say, "Mike, you won't eat your dinner if you have sweets beforehand???"… but you move me around, and wiggle yourself underneath me until I am straddled over your middle, and you are caressing and nibbling at my boobs and nipples… pre-dinner nibbles you are calling it ~ as you would!!!… Wow, Mike you are right, once you start on the sweet things you cannot stop… but it is your birthday… well, your birthday wish was for a kiss and a cuddle, I hope this is a good start… Woooooo… you have made me feel really sexy now doing that to me… so there is only one answer for this… so I undo the plug and water starts to drain out… and now I am giving you some very passionate kisses (after all, it is your birthday treat)… My arms are around the back of your neck… my fingers are entwined in your hair… MMMmmmm Mike… your brown eyes are sparkling at me… how I love you… my hand moves down,

and gently I again massage your 'hot rod and golden nuggets'...
gently, gently, gently... everything is growing here Mike...
MMMmmmm you are a sexy little devil... now I'm thinking,
what would he like next?... but I've already decided, which is
why the water is going down, I stroke up and down that 'hot rod'
of yours, to get the bubbles all off... and then I move down, and
replace my hand with my tongue... licking you... and then so, so
gently, put my lips around the tip of your hot rod... gentle, gentle
little sucking... OOOooohhhh Mike you are loving this... your
breathing is becoming more rapid...... I take more of you into my
mouth... and work my lips up and down the full length of your
hot rod... and then twirl my tongue, and flicker it all over the end,
right where all those nerve endings are... Mike, you are getting
really worked up here... and say, Michelle. Be careful. Because. I
am. Going to explode... if you keep doing that... Well, there is
only one answer to this Mike... I take all of your hot rod right into
my mouth, and suck on you... how delicious you are... I surprise
myself here, with just how much of you I can get into my mouth,
and one hand is caressing your golden nuggets... Mike, you can
hold back no longer, and explode right there in my mouth... salty,
warm, love juice... I love the taste of you Mike...
MMMmmmm... your hands are on my nipples now, and you are
tweaking them quite hard... because they are sooooo aroused...
MMMmmmm Mike I hope you liked the pre-dinner nibbles... but
now we have to go get ready to go out...

So, after we have washed each other 'all over' (because that is
what you wanted to do... and it is your day of choosing), we get
out of the Jacuzzi, because the water is getting cold... and there is
not much water left now anyway, you grab a huge towel and
decide you are going to dry me off... but you don't get too far,
before you wrap the towel around me, and get inside there
yourself... your wet body is rubbing all over mine... oh how
nice... you are a real randy little devil today!!! but it is your
birthday... I suddenly realize the time... Mike, it is 6pm
already... we have to get ready to go out, our taxi is picking us up
at 7pm... But you are still kissing me, and say "Michelle, I don't
want to go out to dinner... I want dinner here... I will have
American hard gums for starters... Michelle's Delight for my
main course... and Michelle's Delight for my dessert..." You are

looking at me with those sexy brown eyes of yours, OOOoooohhh Mike how tempting... but... I have booked something really special for us... come on, get ready... So off I go to dry my hair you have made all wet, put my make-up on... and something special to wear... Oh yes... it's that lovely long slinky black dress you love... and you are getting ready and put on your dinner suit, white dress shirt, and black bow tie... yes... we are dressed to kill again... you look so sexy and handsome I almost want to stay in too... and you have now put my favourite aftershave on... you walk towards me with that cheeky little smile of yours, and I know you are up to something... you give me a little kiss... MMMmmmm Michelle my favourite perfume and 'that dress'... And then... you start tweaking at my nipples to see if I have a bra on under this dress... ??? No... is the answer, and now I have American hard gums again... your hands move further down... checking to see if I have knickers on??? No... is the answer to that as well... All I have on is... little Ditto around my neck, hanging down into my cleavage, and the dress you love. Michelle, how can I go out and sit and eat dinner knowing you have the dress I love you in so much... and no underwear on???... But the phone rings in our room, and we are told the taxi is waiting for us... Off we go...

You still don't know where we are going? But the taxi driver does, and he takes us off to Ronnie Scott's Jazz Club ~ not far from where we are staying... wow what a treat... In there we go, very, very nice... Large and spacious with lots of people... we go straight to the cocktail bar, look down the menu... and... one of our cocktails is on there... 'Love Juice Cocktail', well obviously we would have a knowing little smile at one another regarding this... and we order one each, go and sit down where the waiter will bring our drinks over when they are ready... In the distance we can hear one of the jazz bands playing, soft music... really nice atmosphere... Our cocktails arrive... and we enjoy them as we listen to the music... By now it is 8pm, and that is the time we are booked into the 'A La Carte restaurant, so off we go. Wow... this is really posh... we sit at our table for two... look down the menu, and order a drink each... Southern Comfort and lemonade this time... then order our dinner, which is wonderful... and you are spoiled for choice when it comes to ordering the desserts... we are really enjoying ourselves here, talking, laughing and just enjoying one another and where we are… A couple of hours later, we leave the restaurant, and go into the main part of the club, where the music is being played… We are seated at a little table for two, and order yet another drink… it is your birthday!!! People are up dancing to the music… I nip off to the loo, but on my way back, I put in a request for the band to play… (don't panic here Mike, I know you would not want me to tell everyone it's your birthday… but we know!!), and it's not long before they play my request… yes Mike, you know what this will be… 'our record'… "I will always love you"… have you ever heard this played on a saxophone… fantastic… no words, just the music… so we get up to have a nice smooching dance… Oh Mike, how wonderful… nice food, nice drinks, and dancing with you somewhere as lovely as this to 'our song'… heaven… and I sing softly in your ear, Mike I will always love you… And you smile at me and say, "Michelle… I love you… thank you this is a wonderful birthday treat"… our arms are around each other, and my head is on your shoulder as we gently sway to the music… Bliss… and when our record's finished, they play another Whitney… so we stay and dance some more… in fact we dance to many, because we are enjoying ourselves so much… Oh Mike… what a wonderful evening this has been!!!… You slide your hands down the sides of my dress, and over my hips… and say, "Michelle press those boobs closer to me… and I want to go soon…… because I want some of your loving"… So as it is nearly midnight we order our taxi to go back to our hotel.

Back at our hotel room, you close the door and stand looking at me, and say, "Michelle, I am so aroused, I have been able to see your nipples through that dress the whole evening… I love you in that dress… but I love you even more out of it"… I smile and walk over to you, and slowly, gently, seductively undo that bow tie of yours, and slip it off of you… you remove your jacket, kick off your shoes and socks… and back you come to me… your arms around me, giving me tender loving kisses… your hands go around the back of me… and slowly, slowly, slowly you are pulling the zip of my dress down… and when it is right down to the bottom, our kisses become very passionate… You step back, and slide the straps of my dress over my shoulders, they slide down my arms… and the dress, slowly, slowly, falls down my naked body, until it lays on the floor around my feet… now I am naked… except for 'Little Ditto', you undo the chain and lay him on the side… and stand looking at me, smiling…

MMMmmmm… you are licking your lips at me… I undo your shirt, slowly but surely… off it comes… tantalizingly, slowly, I undo your trousers, and gently slide them off of you… and then still at a slow pace off with your underwear… now we are both naked!!!… OOOhhhhh the kisses are very passionate now… sexy… steamy… and erotic!!!… Onto the bed we go… rolling around kissing, touching, enjoying… (nothing about a quickie here Mike!!)… You lay on your back and ask me to make love to you, as it is your day of choosing, and there is nothing in this whole wide world you want more than that right now… so Mike, your wish, today, is my command… I crawl up the bed, and place my knees, one either side of you… you caress my boobs… you play with my nipples… MMMmmmm Nice. Nice. Nice… I first of all kiss you on the lips… then I nibble at your earlobes… then nibble all around your neck and round to the other ear… and down your neck some more… Mike I am going to kiss every part of your body… make every nerve ending you have stand on end… nibbling, sucking at your neck, and then your shoulders, and down to your chest… my tongue is everywhere here… my hands are running all over you, these gentle tiger claws working their magic, gently, seductively, and tantalizing on your skin… yes, now your nerve endings are going wild… but still the kisses and nibbling continue… right down your chest, down your tummy, and further down I go… you tell me if my tongue touches your hot rod, you will explode immediately here, so I won't do that this time… But, gently I take hold of your rod and tackle, and gently play with you… our eyes are locked to one another's… I gently place the tip of your rod on my hot spot, and make circular movements with it… Wow. Wow. Wow… how nice is that??? And so gently I slide just a little of you into my love tunnel… MMMmmmm… sooooooooooooooooooo nice… and back out again… again circular movements around my hot spot… and then back into my love tunnel, that is so ready for you… a little further in this time… and just hold it right there, whilst my muscles inside my love tunnel grip you… and back out again… still our eyes are locked together… back in I slide you… even further this time… you take hold of both of my hands, come on Michelle, let me right in there… you gently thrust your hips upwards… and further in me you slide… Mike… we are 'bespoke'… made to fit each other… and with your hands gripping me and guiding me, you move me up and down you on… OOOOOooooohhhhhhhhh soooooooooooooooo, soooooooooooooo nice!!!… Gentle, seductive, sensuous…… the movements are getting, faster, harder… Oh Mike… how I love this with you!!!… every time I move towards you, your hips are coming up to meet me… now it is getting, much faster, harder, OMG… this is wonderful… you are so far inside me… I am thinking to myself, I am going to beat him to the finish line here, because you have me so worked up… but you tell me you are just about to unload everything here and am I ready?… Wow… ready???… Give it to me Mike!!!… And in unison we climax… O… M… G…… your head is buried in the pillows now, as you sooooooo enjoy the moment… Yes Mike… exquisite please!!!… Both of our hearts are racing… we are hot… in fact we are almost on fire!!!… so I slow the pace, but still keep gently moving up and down on you… MMMmmmm… I collapse on top of you… and you pull me to you for more kisses… Mike… "Happy Birthday Darling"… I stay laying on top of you, with you still inside me for a while… but we are both drifting off to sleep, so I had better move, so I don't squash you in the night… I lay beside you, your arms are wrapped around me, our naked bodies are entwined, and my head is on your chest… and as I drift off to sleep, all I can hear is your heart beating… no better place in the world to be Mike, than cuddled up with you like this…

When we awaken it is morning… 7.00am already… no we don't want to get up yet… so we order room service… breakfast in bed together… Oh Yeeeeeeeeeeeeeessssssssssssssssssssss!!! now what was it you wanted?… Melon!!! I'm sure you could eat more than that… we order everything… 'The full monty'… jugs of coffee… and have a leisurely breakfast in bed together… Oh wow… what a birthday this has turned out to be… Then we decide it's shower time… yes, you have guessed it… together!!! So off we go… warm water cascading all over the both of us… shower gel everywhere… yes everywhere… you decide you have to wash every inch of my body… the boobs get it at least 13 times… I wash you everywhere… OOOOoooooo how nice… and then you say you want to thank me for such a wonderful birthday experience... and you make love to me, right there in that shower, with me pinned up against the wall... Oh. Wow. Wow. Wow... can we ever get enough of one another? From today this will be known as position number 13... as per conversation text on Yahoo today...

Mike, where has the time gone? It is time to pack up and check out, it's almost lunchtime... my oh my, we have been busy!!!... Busy making love... we go for another wander around some of the London shops, why not as we are there already... Catch the train back home... home???... back into our cyber home... Well I hope you have enjoyed this birthday treat Mike... I have... oh and did I mention "I love you"?...

Sending you 'All of My Love' for your birthday, darling
Michelle
Xxx xxx xxx xxx x

E-mail from: Mike
To: Michelle
Date: 27 June 2012
Subject: Thank you for my birthday treat

Hi Michelle

Well what can I say because I am simply lost for words?!! Thank you for such a lovely wonderful enjoyable birthday treat.

My birthday treat is to have you in this cyber world that we call home. I cannot ask for more than you have already given to me and I thank you for sharing your love with me. It has been a long time and although we have been well apart, you have always been very close in my heart. Only time moves on, but memories of long ago have never been lost and will never fade away. My love for you is the same now and will be forever... I will always love you.

It was by chance that we met through our work. It was by choice we became friends and by choice we fell in love with each other and then you became a part of my life. You gave me a very special gift... a gift of friendship and love, a love that I have always cherished and memories I will also cherish forever. Thank you for just being you. Thank you for coming into my life and giving me joy, thank you for loving me and receiving my love in return. You are very special to me and I will always love you.

How I would would like to hug and kiss you and make you feel my love and have my birthday treat come true for real... Maybe I could ask?... It is my birthday after all... A small favour!!... Throw £130 in that wishing well to give me 13,000 chances of getting this wish!!... Like they say you have to be in it to win it!! I know we have shared so much love, laughter, joy, fun, even secrets, pain and tears, but there has somehow been a rainbow at the end. In our cyber world we learn to appreciate the rainbow after cursing the rain. It's just like loving again after experiencing the pain. It is love that couldn't separate us apart from our feelings for each other... It's such a wonderful feeling to love and to be loved... I will always love you.

Thank you for a loving and beautiful virtual night out with you. It is a wonderful feeling and thank you for my birthday treat.

Love always...

Mike xxx

Michelle sends Mike a couple of lovely e-cards for his birthday.

---

28 June 2012 ~ Live Interactive Text

Michelle: Happy Birthday darling...... I Love You...... MMmmwwwwaaaaahhhhhh x

Mike: Hi my darling... Thank you for everything you have sent me today and yesterday

Michelle: I love you...

Mike: I love you too... more than you will ever know, even though I tell you thirteen million times...

Michelle: I love you... more than you will ever know......

Mike: Mwah!... I have to go, the family are all just arriving here for dinner

Michelle: Have a nice evening... I wish I could spend it with you......

Mike: MMMmmmm... You make my birthday complete.

Michelle: I LOVE YOU birthday boy... even more messages from me, for you by e-mail for when you have time, tomorrow now maybe

Mike: Thank you darling... I will try to read them before I go to bed. Have to go. Byeeeeeeeeeeeeeee xxx

Michelle: Bye darling xxx xxx xxx xxx x

---

29 June 2012 ~ Live Interactive Text

Michelle: Hello my darling

Mike: Hi gorgeous... So you have decided to get up at last. I have been here since 7.13 am. Where have you been?

Michelle: Wow!! You are up early today.

Mike: Yes... come on you, let us go out for the day! You know what this sun does to us both.

Michelle: That would be wonderful... and I have the day to myself... come on then

Mike: MMMmmmm... I wish... it would be so nice!

Michelle: Would be very very nice... how I wish too...

Michelle: Come on over... We can spend the day in my back garden, nobody will see us there!! We can sunbathe naked... We can put sun lotion all over one another

Mike: OMG... Stop it... You are driving me crazy!!!

Michelle: Make love under the shade of the tree... naked...

Mike: Sounds good... see you in 13 minutes. Make it 13 seconds now... I am feeling sexy already with you talking like this.

Michelle: I'll go and put a rug on the grass... we don't want the grass prickling us... we could stay out there all day......
Southern Comfort and lemonade, with lots of ice for lunch

Mike: Yes please and plenty of extras... I am greedy and hungry for your love.

Michelle: Just us... the sun shining... the birds singing... and us making love...

Mike: What could be better my darling?

Michelle: Nothing could be better!!

Mike: Nothing...... just to have you would be so nice for a day.

Michelle: I agree with that… how I would love to spend the day with you.

Mike… I really, really love you

Mike: Tight hugs… I need those boobs pressing into me…

Michelle: I'm ready and waiting… all I will have on will be suntan lotion… come on then Mike… come over here now…

Mike: Gosh… Hot spot will be in for a good time.

Michelle: WOW… a really good time I think…

Mike: Be careful Michelle… Or one day it could happen!!

Michelle: Promises, promises… Bye darling… I know you need to go to work. Phone me later if you get the chance, I am home all day today.

Mike: OK… Bye for now x

Mike: PS… BE WARNED… THIS MAY ACTUALLY HAPPEN ONE DAY!!!

CHAPTER SEVEN

4 July 2012 ~ Live Interactive Text

Mike and Michelle video call, see each other face to face on their webcams, and talk for half an hour… Then revert to text before they leave one another for the day.

Mike: MMMmmmm… Nice birthday treat, only one complaint.

Michelle: What is that?

Mike: I want it for real.

Michelle: Me too… but…

Mike: When I see you, on the web cam… I look calm, but deep down I am going mad.

Michelle: I love you… and when I see you it makes me want a real kiss with you… like we used to…

Mike: But at least this cyber world brings us closer together than we have been able to be for so long

Michelle: I know… and we enjoy this…

Mike: Yeeeeeeeeeeeeeeeeeeeeeeees! Love it.

Michelle: I am going to stay cuddled up to you all night… with my boobs wrapped around your hot rod… my head on your chest… and just love you…

Mike: Yes please… Heaven! You are always so intimate with me on here, and we have such a close connection. It just reminds me of how we always used to be together.

Michelle: Always heaven with you… Always intimate with you Mike… heavenly, sexy, sensual, romantic, loving and fun…

Mike: We could never get enough of one another, and this is still how we are today... Despite everything else that happened.

Michelle: Do you remember when you used to say to me... "How can something so wrong be so right?"

Mike: That is because we were always so right together... but, we were both married, and knew that it was so wrong...

Michelle: I know... And we still are... Married to other people, but we are so right together!!!

Mike: MMMmmmm... My Michelle...... we will always be right for one another!!

Michelle: Always... and forever!!!

Mike: I must go... Lovely to see you on cam today, and talk to you. Mwah!

Michelle: I LOVE YOU... Mwah... bye

Mike: I LOVE YOU MORE...

Michelle: You say that!!! how do you know?

Mike: Nobody can love you more than I do.

Michelle: Nobody loves you, more than I love you.

Mike: MMMmmmm... I just want you know it`s so hard to say goodbye, everytime.

Mike: I wish I could touch you.

Michelle: I know... but I remember what it was like to touch you... and what I felt like when you touched me... and, I think you truly touched my soul Mike... and not many people in life are able to do that...

Mike: Yes... I feel the same. You engraved your initials on my heart, and told me never to wash it off... Do you remember this?

Michelle: Yes, gently on your skin with my fingernail... when we were in bed together once.

Mike: It is still there engraved in scar tissue...

Michelle: I hope it's not a painful scare?

Mike: I just hope I never die, and my heart goes for a heart transplant... Can you imagine what it would do to them?... and the memories my heart has?

Michelle: I think next time we are on this video you should undo your shirt and let me see it? ☺

Mike: Careful Michelle, because I can remember engraving my initials on your heart too... and as I recall this was all over your left boob... so I may ask to see that on cam?

Michelle: You will never see them on the internet darling...... just you and me for that one... not the WWW!!!

Mike: I am only kidding! ☺

Michelle: I am pleased to hear that ☺

Mike: How I would love to whisk you away, and take you somewhere hot and sunny.

Michelle: How nice would that be?

Mike: Like the Caribbean... or the Seychelles.

Michelle: As you have been to the Caribbean many times with Cheryl, and I have been there many times with Simon, how about we say the Seychelles? We could live in a mud hut

Mike: Come on then... Grab your bikini bottoms, throw them in a bag and we are there. I do not want you carrying too much excess luggage!!!

Michelle: I'm almost packed... and maybe a grass skirt...... other than that, just suntan lotion...

Mike: OMG... Do I need to take some shears for the grass cutting?

Michelle: I know how you like your 'topiary'... be careful when trimming the skirt though... how are you at 'bush trimming'?

Mike: What?... How do I know?... It could be a lawnmower job!! ☺

Michelle: No darling not a lawnmower... ☺

Mike: Can you just give it a short back and sides before we go? ☺

Michelle: Would you be as artistic with this I wonder... No... I'm going to leave you to use your artistic skills darling... maybe you could trim my little bush into a topiary heart shape?

Mike: Yes why not?... I am sure I could do something with it for you...

Michelle: OOOhhhhh... I'm sure you could...

Mike: I like to fiddle and play with your hot spot and bush!!

Michelle: I know you do.

Mike: I had better go now... Mwah!

Michelle: Go pack your flip-flops and shorts

Mike: You know what?... I could so love you now, you are lucky I cannot jump out of your computer monitor.

Michelle: I could love you all the time... you would get no peace with me...

Mike: No peace for us you mean... The wicked!!!

Michelle: We are not wicked... We just love one another

Mike: If we went off to the Seychelles it would have to be a one-way ticket...

Michelle: Two... one-way tickets please!!!

Mike: Well in that area there are pirates! We could say we were just kidnapped and never to be seen again.

Michelle: Good idea Mike... it would not even be our faults then... it just happened, and we could do nothing to stop it...

Mike: My navigation skills go no further than the Cotswold`s, so we can easily explain we drifted into international waters.

Michelle: OOOooooooo... I would love to drift into international waters with you... let's go Mike... we could live happily ever after, with a pure and simple lifestyle.

Mike: It sounds like heaven. Except a friend of mine went there once and went fishing and caught a fish and the next minute a shark took everything.

Michelle: Everything??? Not his tackle surely?... ☺

Mike: Yes, the fishing tackle of course!!! And the fish on the end.

Michelle: We won't go fishing then... I wouldn't want to lose your tackle... I have plenty in mind for this...

Mike: Yes... I think you would be doing plenty of fishing but not in the sea.

Michelle: Daily... `sex-a-exercise`...

Mike: Just pack your bikini bottoms and sun lotion, okay?

Michelle: I'm ready Mike... let's goooooooooooooo...

Mike: I am not sure we can find big enough coconut shells for your 36C's, but we can try when we get out there.

Michelle: OK darling... in the meantime, you will have to protect them so they don't get sun-burnt... do you mind?

Mike: Mind? My pleasure my darling; I just want an excuse to get my hands on them.

Michelle: Mike... there I will be yours 24/7 to do as you please with... and I am sure I could please you!!!

Mike: I think we would be very happy together and just grow old.

Michelle: What a lovely thought... how I would LOVE, LOVE, LOVE that with you my darling. I think we would be so happy, we would live forever... just loving one another.

Mike: I guess the mud hut would have hammocks inside, how are you for screwing in a hammock with me?

Michelle: WOW... what a thought... I would certainly give that a go...

Mike: I think we would earn the title the best swingers in town.

Michelle: Swingers... lovers... friends... always...

Mike: MMMmmmm... Wouldn't it be lovely?

Michelle: It would be wonderful !!!

Mike: We would live on fish and lips!!!

Michelle: YUMMY... and bananas...

Mike: Yes... and melons... Big juicy melons...

Michelle: And I'm sure the island will be a wonderful 'hot-spot'

Michelle: Do they grow nuts there? I like nuts!!!

Michelle: Sorry darling, I have to go, Simon will be home any minute... Or come and get me...... we can leave now...

Mike: One day this may happen... FOR REAL!!! Byeeeeeeeeee

Michelle: I love you Mike... love you soooooooooooo much...

Mike: Gooooooooo... Bye.

Michelle: Love you... love you... love you... forever!! Byeeeeee

---

10 July 2012 ~ Live Interactive Text

They live video call for as long as they dare, then revert to text.

Mike: I need a holiday! And the Seychelles looks good!

Michelle: Ummmm, sounds nice... how lovely that would be... just you and me!!! But it would be forever more... could you put up with me that long?

Mike: A little private island there where you cannot escape from me.

Michelle: I would never want to escape from you Mike... I would just enjoy you... my life with you... and love you...

Mike: I have been thinking about this... Let's go!!

Michelle: I'm ready... let's go!!! ☺

Mike: Except we both have to go to work now… I love you my sexy gorgeous lovely Michelle.

Michelle: Mwaaaaah… "I LOVE YOU TOO" Byeeeeee.

Michelle: PS…

Michelle: Could you stand daily 'sexercise' in the Seychelles with me?

Mike: Yes… 13 times daily!!

Michelle: WOW… we need to do this Mike…

Mike: Bye… Take care and enjoy your day

Michelle: Bye darling… have a good day… mwah

---

12 July 2012 ~ Live Interactive Text

Mike: Good evening Michelle.

Michelle: Hello my sexy secret lover

Mike: I think we have enough text here on Skype to write a book!!

Michelle: Well, here comes another chapter, in our book, `The neverending love story of Mike and Michelle`

Michelle: I am lying on the sofa… with you on my lap, in my laptop, anything could happen!!

Mike: Tell me…

Mike: Are we married, or living together here in sin, in our cyber world?

Michelle: I don't know… have you ever asked me to marry you?

Mike: Well… I was just wondering, that was all. I thought maybe we were, with all the naughty things we get up to

Michelle: Oh… did I miss the wedding?

Mike: We are very naughty!!!… if we are not married!!!

Michelle: Well… let's get this sorted once and for all then…

Michelle: Barefoot on the beach…

Michelle: I take you Mike Turner… to be my 'almost lawful wedded husband'… to love you, cherish you… for as long as we both shall live…

Mike: Really?

Michelle: MMMmmmmm… I do!!!

Mike: Who will be the witnesses?

Michelle: Two random people on the beach...

Mike: ☺

Michelle: Oh... do you have any words to say in this ceremony?

Mike: I have just three little words... "I love you"

Michelle: Not... with my body I will worship you...... to look after you for the rest of our days... For as long as we both shall live?

Mike: Worship!! Are you my sex goddess?

Michelle: To have and to hold...

Mike: I would love to hold you my darling...

Michelle: You are not giving much away here Mike... Am I virtually Mrs Turner your wife now?

Mike: No, you are Ms... You have to prove yourself first ☺

Michelle: Come and give me some experience then... I'll move over so you can lay on the sofa next to me... I've moved right over......

Mike: Okay... I wish I was your lap-top now.

Michelle: I am laid right out here... with you balancing right across my lap... in my laptop

Mike: Oh... Balancing eh! Do you mean I could fall down between your legs?

Michelle: If you were right here with me... I would gently run one finger, softly,over your lips... gently up the side of your face... look into those sexy, seductive, sparkly brown eyes of yours... run that finger down to your chin... and move in nice a slowly for a sexy gentle little kiss...

Mike: Between your legs I would gently run one finger down and around your hot spot.

Michelle: Slow down Mike...

Mike: Well you let me fall down there and now you blame me.

Michelle: No kisses to start... no sexy, sexy, sensual kisses?

Mike: Yes... Just doing this now the other end, here in between your legs Michelle ☺

Michelle: Wow!! Mike... you don't hang about do you?

Michelle: Well... carry on... Don't let me interrupt you.

Mike: You should have had a skirt on when I was on your lap doing this balancing act... Then when I fell, I see you have no knickers on... So here I am enjoying this and you are loving it.

Michelle: You sure know how to relax a girl after a stressful day at work.

Mike: It was a choice of north or south... I went up the valley to the northern point... You like me there!!!

Michelle: Is that the 'hot spot'?

Mike: The south tunnel will come later. ☺

Michelle: Wow... what exactly are you doing to my hot spot?

Mike: Just playing with it for the moment.

Michelle: Is this with your finger(s)?

Mike: Hey... Yes, who's a fast worker now? Be patient. You need to relax, just enjoy!

Michelle: I'm feeling far more relaxed than I was a couple of hours ago... carry on!

Mike: Yes... I can tell... You are looking very sexy now.

Michelle: MMMmmmm... nice...

Mike: I will use the tips of two fingers now. Nice slow strokes up and down and around and around.

Michelle: Oh wow... Heaven... Umm, sounds nice...

Mike: Yes you love this... Just stop shouting, more, more, more... Be patient and stop getting so excited for a minute.

Michelle: Mike... it is your fault... you get me so 'sexcited' here...

Mike: Well it is your time of making some choices... What would you like next? You can have my tackle out and play, then put my hot rod where my two fingers are on your hot spot and you can have the same gentle strokes.

Michelle: Come on then... let's undress you... and get your equipment out...

Mike: Oh... Am I still in your lap top bag?

Michelle: No darling. Just right here with me... skin on skin... nothing else but us!!!

Mike: Good... I do not want the computer to crash at such a vital point!!!

Michelle: Neither do I... I don't want you damaged...

Mike: Okay, so my hot rod is there now and you are holding me and pressing it into that hot spot.

Michelle: Round and round the garden...

Mike: Yes... Ooopss... Something has come out the end of my hot rod... Watering the garden now around the hot spot!!! It keeps

160

slipping down from north to south. It loves to play with your hot spot, but says I should be in that south tunnel and explore.

Michelle: Come and slide inside me… waiting for you… warm… moist… wet even..!!!

Mike: It has just popped its head inside!!! Wow… you like that, eh!!

Michelle: I like that a lot Mike… come on then Mike… I want you now…

Mike: Be patient… It is dark down there. I am just popping the head of my hot rod in and out to get acclimatized to the dark. You seem to like these short thrusts in and out.

Michelle: Yes Mike… I do like that a lot… short… and gentle to start with…

Mike: Don't worry, my hot rod will soon give you full enjoyment and all the way in… be patient. When I go all the way… Is there a rock bottom? I mean like going down a mine, is there a coal face?

Michelle: Come in and see what you can find… it could be a treasure cove

Mike: Wow… Yes… I am going in now.

Michelle: I really want you in there now… come on then… more… more… more…

Mike: Yes, deeper and deeper with each thrust.

Michelle: I'm coming up to meet you a little here, to help you find your way…

Mike: Yes well into the love tunnel now, very warm and hot in here. Hey… Stop squeezing your legs together on me, you could cause a cave-in.

Michelle: I'm squeezing you tight… right inside of me… in so deep…

Mike: It is tight here down the bottom. So hot too, boiling in fact. I think I may need to extinguish the heat and cool it down with some love juices.

Michelle: Ummmmmm… so nice…

Mike: Mmmm… Come with me.

Mike: Oh… Yes… ooppps… I am filling up now and ready to put out your fire down there.

Michelle: Right at this moment Mike… you are the centre of my world here… come on then darling… I am ready… hot… sexy… passionate… and loving your loving.

Mike: Okay this last thrust deep to the bottom inside you will be all guns blazing. Yes... Yes... Yes... Coming now, just pumping away!

Michelle: MMMmmmm... OMG... me toooooo!!!... exploding around you Mike... Ecstasy rippling through my body as the orgasm you give me takes over my entire being.

Mike: You are so goddamn sexy Michelle... Cool and slippery in your love tunnel now and yes you have added to the sexcitement.

Michelle: Give me every last drop of your love here Mike...

Mike: I am just pumping until you have every last drop and not waste it.

Mike: Stop reading my mind again YOU!

Michelle: ☺

Michelle: Wooooooooooooow... every... last... drop... Mike... I am in heaven... my whole body is loving this...you fill my whole body with wonderful sensations.

Mike: Yes I am just taking some respite now after all that 'sexercise'!! Next time you can get on top... ☺

Michelle: Don't move away from me... lay your head on my boobs... and cuddle me... and I will put my arms around you and cuddle you... whilst your hot rod is still inside my love tunnel... my warm velvet tongue sliding seductively across your skin

Mike: Yes please... Ummmmm... Michelle you have an insatiable appetite for our love making... and I love it... Can you feel my heart racing?

Michelle: Yes, our hearts are both racing... And so close together right at this moment. My gentle tiger claws and fingertips are making little circle movements gently over your shoulders and back...

Mike: Yes, I love it when you do that. I need to kiss and suck your nipples now... I am like a big baby now.

Michelle: Come on then Mike... you are still cuddled up to me... inside warm and snug, outside gentle and tender cuddles... Soft loving kisses... You are my baby and I love you...

Mike: I love you... 20 years is such a long time, but I feel close to you now again.

Michelle: I feel closer to you... especially right at this minute.

Mike: I know this is our cyber world, but I feel it is real. I cannot touch, but I can communicate with you and see you… And it feels so real again.

Michelle: I love you darling… really, really love you, how nice to spend an evening with you… making love with you… especially… cuddled up with you… naked bodies!!

Mike: I had better go now and you must soon. Thank you for your time… Thank you for sharing your love with me… Good night. I will always love you…

Michelle: When you go to bed later…

Mike: Yes I hope we have the same naughty dreams together.

Michelle: When you lay your head on your pillow tonight… just remember, really you are still laying cuddled up to me… with your head resting on my boobs… and my fingers will be gently running through your hair…

Michelle: I would love to be cuddled up with you right now…

Mike: I love you Michelle… Sod it… Let us get married!!!

Michelle: I love you darling… yes… let's get married… two hearts always together as one then ☺

Mike: Two hearts beating as one… Yes: part of my heart has always been with you

Michelle: Part of mine always with you darling…

Mike: I think we have now put the two halves back together again, eh! Love it.

Michelle: I think we have.

Mike: I just feel your love and warmth… And I love you like long ago.

Michelle: I do with you too… so much love to share with each other…

Mike: Good night… Mwaaaaaaaaaaaaaaaaaaaah!

Michelle: Good night darling… cuddle me tight all night……

Mike: I will… You cuddle me tight all night too… Never let me go.

---

13 July 2012 ~ Live Interactive Text

Michelle: `HAPPY FRIDAY 13TH` Morning my darling… after your 'romantic' comment last night of… "Sod it, let's get married"!!! this is what I think we should do… You take me by the hand,

and we tele-transport to the Seychelles right here and now… and get married barefoot on the beach, just the two of us… our little guy Ditto can be our witness… we don't need anyone else… Just pure and simple… no fuss… just us… where we can be married in our cyber world on Friday 13th… as the sun rises over the beach and sea… sunrise for new beginnings…

Michelle: To have and to hold, from this day forward in sickness and in health, to love, honour and cherish one another for as long as we both shall live…

Michelle: Mike… do you take Michelle to be your cyber wife? Michelle… do you take Mike to be your cyber husband?

Mike: I Do!

Michelle: I Do!

Mike: And I am going to Do YOU!

Michelle: We now pronounce ourselves husband and wife…

Michelle: You may kiss the bride…

Mike: So we are now Mr & Mrs Turner for real in a virtual world, eh!

Mike: Mwaaaaaaaaaaaaaaaaaaaaaaaaaaaaaaaaah

Michelle: Oh wow Mike… you are my husband in Our Cyber World……
MMMMMMMmmmmmmmmwwwwwwwwwwwwwaaaaaaaaaaaaaaaaaaahhhhhhhhhhhhhhhhhhhhhhhhhhhhhhhhhhhhhhhhhhhhh…

Mike: About time too! ☺

Michelle: The best Friday 13th ever!!!

Michelle: Wow… married and honeymoon in the Seychelles… where we can stay and live for evermore…

Mike: So this will be our anniversary date to remember!

Michelle: Yes… our anniversary date… 13th July 2012…

Mike: You didn't want to wait a month for your birthday?

Michelle: Oh husband… I am going to pamper you… love you… and spoil you for the rest of our days…
MMMMmmmmmwwwwwaaaaaaaaaaaaahhhhhhhhhhhhhhh

Michelle: I am yours… and you are mine…

Mike: Yes… Do you know, that would be nice and we would have some great times together. You would get no peace from me of course; I would just love you 24/7

Michelle: Oh Mike… this would be wonderful… I would live happily for the rest of my days… no peace for you either… 24/7 loving…

Mike: You would be running around the island… not barefoot, but completely naked, with me chasing you.

Michelle: Wow… this is what we will do then…

Mike: It is a good job you can no longer have babies, we would otherwise have a tribe!

Michelle: Yes… I think we would… so thank goodness… we have the little guy though… little Ditto I'm talking about.

Mike: Yes okay… I will adopt him! He will not be getting all the fun though, swinging on his long chain down between your boobs, because you are naked

Michelle: You are his Dad now… he will look after both of us now… he will share with you… You told me he would take care of me… bring me luck… Now he will do this for both of us.

Mike: Well, Mrs Turner… Mr Turner needs to go to work. It is okay for Mrs Turner to have the day off.

Michelle: Bye Mr Turner… Mrs Turner loves you…

Mike: I love you MRS TURNER… A lucky Friday 13th

Michelle: It has been lucky… the best Friday 13th ever… nothing could be better… Or more special… I will always love you… and now I am yours!!!

Mike: And… I am yours!!! You have me… I couldn't be more yours!!!

Michelle: I love you darling…

Mike: I love you more…

Mike: I must go… Busy morning!

Michelle: Bye darling… phone me later if you have time… I am at home all day.

Mike: Bye… Speak to you later… You have made my day complete this Friday 13th

Michelle: You have made all my dreams come true… who ever thought this day would come?

Michelle: happy… happy… happy…
MMMMmaaaaaaaaaaaahhhhhhhhhh

As soon as Mike gets to work he phones Michelle… They laugh and joke that they are now "virtually Married".

Hello there my new husband

Could I be any happier today?...
This morning I married the man of my dreams...
A man I have loved for more than 20 years...
The man I would share everything with... my hopes... my dreams... my love...
The man I will cherish for the rest of my days...
The man I will look after, through thick and thin... The man I will be happy with forever more...

We should start our honeymoon, here in the Seychelles, by making love... slowly and gently, savouring every moment, taking our time... and really enjoying one another... exploring every part of each other's body... MMMmmmm...

And, when the sun-sets we should dance to 'our record' on the beach... still bare-foot... and did we even get dressed today?... "No" you would say... so, naked... I think we dashed off so quickly this morning, we did not even bring anything other than the few things we each packed the other day... but... luckily our little guy Ditto, brought an iPod and solar-powered docking station... so we have music...

I love you so much Mike... "I will always love you"

Your ever-loving wife
Michelle
xxx xxx xxx xxx x

E-mail from: Mike
To: Michelle
Date: 13 July 2012
Subject: Virtually Married

Hi Michelle

Virtually married and making love in the Seychelles! Life is simply beautiful !!!

"I LOVE YOU"

Mike xxx

Sent with lovely romantic attachments of love.

E-mail from: Michelle
To: Mike
Date: 13 July 2012
Subject: Re: Virtually Married

To my sexy, oh so lovable, husband

Mike… This is the best Friday 13th I have ever known… Life is indeed beautiful… it could not be better… Our wedding day, married in the Seychelles… and making love in the sunshine, on the beach with you…

I love you ~ You love me… I am yours ~ and you are mine… Forever and always now…

I LOVE YOU
Your loving wife
Michelle
Xxx xxx xxx xxx x

They send one another romantic and loving wedding day cards.

E-mail from: Michelle
To: Mike
Date: 14 July 2012
Subject: Paradise in the Seychelles

Hello my sexy husband and lover

Our wedding night… Wow Mike… you made love to me all night long… and when I thought we had finished with one episode and drifted off to sleep in your arms… an hour later there you were again, starting with the tiniest movement, so I thought I was dreaming, yes… with one finger and one thumb you start to play with one nipple… gently at first… and then rolling it around with your finger and thumb a little harder, until I realize I am not dreaming… MMMmmmm… and planting little kisses all over my neck… and whispering to me… "Mrs Turner ~ I love you… I am going to make you happier than you have ever been in your life…" I look into your gorgeous brown eyes and I am mesmerized by the fire in your eyes… You capture me with your severe intensity, your grip is possessive and commanding… OMG how can I ever resist you?…

And then… you move to the other nipple, and say it cannot be left out… and you start the whole process again… twiddling, tweaking, gently pulling, gently squeezing… And then… your lips go over my nipple, and you are kissing, sucking, gently biting… and I am loving it… and loving you… And then… your lips work their way down to my tummy, and you cover that with kisses… juicy, succulent kisses… and little nibbles… and you are saying, I love this sinuously sexy body of yours… I love to caress and kiss all of these curves… you are telling me you are hungry and want a midnight snack… and down further you go… OH… MY… GOD… MIKE… now you are doing all of this to my 'hot spot'… you are sending me into orbit here… I am lost in a world of pleasure and sensation with what you are doing… licking… kissing… sucking… blowing… OMG… I am going to explode here any minute, I am trying to hang on… but with you doing all of that Mike… I cannot control myself… and I am lost… lost in a world of delicious, indescribable, exquisite, sensual sensation… and all that eventually brings me back to earth, is you telling me how much you love me… Could I be any happier?… No!!! This is heaven with you Mike… And then… you move up my body and gently slide your hot rod inside of my love tunnel… oh… you are so ready for this… slowly in… slowly out… and then you are thrusting hard and fast in and out of me… and oh so quickly I feel your love juices filling me once more… warm and sensational… and again you send me into orbit… Mike, how do you do this to me?… Every time you touch me… endless pleasure!!!

Eventually you wiggle up my body a little, and lay your head on my boobs, and say they will be your pillow now… and, I cuddle you so close, just stroking your body… and off to sleep we fall again for a while. And as I drift off to sleep with you laying across me, I am thinking to myself... I am the luckiest person in the whole wide world... I am going to love being married to this man... Mrs Turner... Mrs Turner... Mrs Turner...

To be continued...

All of my love... MRS MICHELLE TURNER
Yes... MRS TURNER...
xxx xxx xxx xxx x

E-mail from: Michelle
To: Mike
Date: 15 July 2012
Subject: My New Husband

Hello Darling

This is to say "I LOVE YOU"...

Thank you for my 'very romantic' card on Friday, and over the weekend...

Thinking about you more than ever this weekend...... Wish I was with you now.

With all of my love
Michelle
xxx xxx xxx xxx x

---

16 July 2012 ~ Live Interactive Text

Michelle: Morning my sexy husband

Mike: Good morning my sexy, erotic, passionate, mad, lovely, gorgeous wife.

Michelle: How is the Seychelles?

Mike: It could not be better... But, hey... pop those boobs back in, do you want to drive me crazy?

Michelle: YES!!! ☺

Mike: Seychelles... Hot!!!... Like you!!!

Michelle: How was your wedding night of loving? HOT!!! all night?

Mike: Our wedding night was wonderful… I must go… or I will be late for work. Maybe see you later on Skype.

Michelle: Bye for now… I love you HUSBAND

Mike: My long loving passionate kiss for you… I love you WIFE

Michelle: I want to make love to you now… could you stand me 24/7?

Mike: Yeeeeeeeeeeeeeeeeeees and more!!! I've got everything with you, my lovely wife. Who could ask for anything more?

Michelle: Oh Mike… I am going to love being married to you…

Mike: I am going to love this life time together… Woweeeeeeeee

Michelle: Me Tooooooooooooooooooooooooooooooo!!!

---

17 July 2012 ~ Live Interactive Text

Mike: Hi my gorgeous sexy wife… I love you…

Michelle: Morning lazy-bones… is your honeymoon wearing you out? and you can't wake up… you are late this morning?

Mike: I am glad we got married because now I can love you every day forever!!!

Michelle: I will love you everyday FOREVER

Mike: Get dressed and go to work, otherwise I will have to come over there and DO YOU!

Michelle: That would set us both up for the day… We would certainly have a glow about us, and smiles on our faces when we arrive at work!

Mike: It sure would… I'm on my way over now…

Michelle: Well, I am ready for you… Had my shower, and only have a towel wrapped around me.

Mike: You are so sexy… I know the sun is shining today!!!

Michelle: The sunshine always makes me sexy, sexy, sexy… life in the Seychelles with me would wear you out…

Mike: MMMmmmm… I bet!

Michelle: 28 degrees and sunny most of the time… would I ever leave you alone?

Mike: I may get exhausted due to the 'sexercise' and holding your boobs, but I can manage that.

Michelle: Always 'hot' for you Mike...

Mike: I must go... Bye... Love you forever...

Michelle: Bye darling... Mwaaaaah

Later that day...

Mike: My darling wife Michelle... Normally you would shout to me... Don't pin me down, don't pin me down, so here I am with my hot rod well inside pinning you down hard, but... now you are shouting you love it stuck inside and you feel comfortable being pinned down like this, eh!! I want those lovely boobs out now, swinging in time with the hammock... With your boobs rocking from side to side, whilst I am rocking you up and down on my hot rod... OMG... everything is rocking and shaking here and you are loving this!!!! I am keeping a careful watch on your bouncy boobs just in case I get a slap in the face with those 36C's... What fun!!!... I am now trying to catch a flying nipple in my teeth whilst they are swinging!!! Bouncy, bouncy they are flying now, no chance of catching them at that speed. Those boobs are both rotating in different directions now, one clockwise and one anti-clockwise. Slow up, you!!!... I am not just hanging on in here for my life...

Michelle: Hi darling... hang on here... I think I have some reading to do...

Mike: It is a good job I am deep inside your love tunnel otherwise I could be in trouble here... Bronco riding is an understatement!!

Michelle: OH... WOW .... you need some loving then?

Mike: At least I have some big boobs to grab onto!!! I love your sexy body... So soft... So seductive... And all of its curves... especially these particular bumps... or do I mean mountains?

Michelle: You are sexy... and funny... and soooooo, so, so, lovable

Mike: Look, you have taken me right in, I have filled your love tunnel with love juice and you still want more!!! The tackle is dry now and it needs to replenish its nuts.

Michelle: Well... don't warn me... or wait for me then? ☺

Mike: It had been there a long time, what do you expect? When it comes, there is no stopping it!!! It was you late home from work, leaving me waiting here for you...

Michelle: When I feel your hot rod filling me... And your love juice pumping into me, filling me up... oh Mike... it just sends me into heaven... and off I go... into orbit...

Mike: I love you Michelle. Why didn't you marry me long ago?

Michelle: You didn't ask me ☹ But, I love being married to you now...

Mike: Well there was a leap year in that time too.

Michelle: I thought you would just say "MAYBE"...

Mike: Yes... but you know my "MAYBE" has often turned out to be Yesssssssssssss!

Michelle: I have a question now...

Mike: Okay... fire away!

Michelle: If there is a tropical storm (now we are in the Seychelles) will you hug me tight in your arms... because I'm not too keen on thunder and lightning?

Mike: Yes of course... I have the very picture of us in the Seychelles... You can see how we hug each other, I will send it to you via e-mail.

Michelle: Thank you... do you know what? I could take the world on, wrapped in your arms... I love you Mike... more than you could ever know...

Mike: MMMmmmm..."DITTO"

Mike: Sorry Michelle, time to go

Michelle: All too quickly... Bye darling...... Loving you always.

E-mail from: Mike
To: Michelle
Date: 17 July 2012
Subject: Breaking news... a couple have been found on a deserted island

Hi Michelle

Breaking news!!... A couple has been found after many years on a deserted island in the Seychelles. A news statement says... It is believed they went there long ago when they got married and decided to spend their honeymoon there!!!

Love never dies!

Mike
Xxx

This is sent with a funny attachment of an old couple, suntanned with hand prints all over them of the not tanned parts, where hands have been. They have been there for 25 years.

E-mail from: Michelle
To: Mike
Date: 19 July 2012
Subject: The waterfall

Hello my darling

So we have gone in search of a waterfall... and this is what we found!!!... (see attachment) and naked together we stand under the cascading water... with the sun shining on us... the water pounding over us... wowsa... some power-shower this is... we have brought shower gel with us (coconut of course)...

And I begin by washing your hair... Oh Mike, you like me washing your hair... and then your ears... and then your neck... followed by your shoulders and back... MMMmmmmm... we are kissing passionately and your arms are around me... I step back only enough to wash your chest... and then your arms... back to your chest... and down your sides... around and around your tummy... and then... (my personal favourite here)... down to your crown jewels... I am unabashedly drinking in the sight of your body as you stand naked in front of me. You are so lustrous... healthy, strong and vigorous. MMMmmmm... lots of washing needed here... they need a double dose... and lots of it... no need to rush, we don't need to be dashing off anywhere!!!... And then down your legs... by the time I get to your knees my boobs are caught up on something... Oh it's you... the crown jewels are standing to attention, and that hot rod of yours is between my boobs... oh let's give that a little wash with my boobs... and down further I go, finish washing your legs... and your toe-toes... Oh now I am down this low, I need to make sure all of the shower gel is washed off of your crown jewels... so I lick the crown jewels, and two golden nuggets with my tongue... and slide your hot rod it in and out of my mouth... yes nice and clean... and ready for action!!!... Back up I stand, look into those sexy brown eyes of yours that are smiling at me... your lips are smiling at me... And then, you say, "Michelle Turner, my wife, I love you"... I take hold of this hot rod of yours and gently slip it into my love tunnel... and still we are smiling at one another... "Mike Turner, my husband, I love you"... the water is pounding over us... and you start to pound into me... thrusting hard and fast... and so quickly you find your release... and are pumping me full of your delicious love juices once more... Mike, you make me feel so sexy, so loved, and my world just crumbles around you... as I have the orgasm of a lifetime... OMG... will we never tire of all this love making?... Noooooooo... we will live long happy lives, living from fresh produce to eat... and plenty of daily 'sexercise'...

And then... you say to me... "Michelle... it's time I washed you now"...

To be continued... by you, if you like!!!

I love you my wonderful husband... I love my honeymoon with you...

Michelle xxx xxx xxx xxx

E-mail from: Mike
To: Michelle
Date: 22 July 2012
Subject: Hotting Up

Hi my lovely sexy virtual wife

It is warm today and the forecast is to be getting hotter!! Although it cannot get much hotter than your e-mails... I love them... I read the one you sent me yesterday, and then went to bed... And then what happened... I was thinking about your lovely boobs all night and was it you pressing your nipples into me?

I think I need to get the sun lotion out and protect those white parts and gently with my hands work all over your body!!! That gorgeous sexy body of yours!! I know what you are thinking those bouncy bouncy boobs will be slippery, but I want to just say when I am finished `DOING YOU` somewhere else will be very slippery… I want you… "I love you"… Anytime, anyplace, anywhere with you my darling!!!

I loved your last e-mail of us making love in the waterfall… You are so sexy and provocative… I can never get enough of you. You have well and truly captured my heart and soul…

Enjoy your day, always be safe and take care…

Love always…

Mike
xxx

---

24 July 2012 ~ Live Interactive Text

Michelle: Morning darling, what a lovely sunny day today… What would you like to do today, if we could spend the day together?

Mike: Wherever you want. Your day to make a choice on anything and today it is yours!

Michelle: A walk along the beach… holding your hand

Mike: Granted!

Michelle: Thank you darling… ☺

Mike: You can have two more wishes!

Michelle: Really?

Mike: Yes because I love you…

Michelle: I love you Mike… so my second wish is a kiss……

Mike: Walking on the beach holding hands… and a kiss… Granted!

Michelle: Thank you… ☺ and because I love you so much… my third wish… to spend the whole day with you laughing in the sunshine… cuddling you…

Mike: I am sure that would happen anyway… Yes, granted! I think we will always laugh together over anything! We so easily make each other laugh over absolutely nothing at times.

Michelle: We certainly do that darling.

Mike: Even the most silly of things, eh! ☺

Michelle: What I would not give for just one touch… Just one kiss… just one cuddle with you in the real world…

Mike: I know darling, but we both know this would be such a risk for us to take.

Michelle: I know…

Mike: We both have to go get ready for work now… Love you… bye

Michelle: Bye darling… Mwah… I love you, now and always.

Mike: Mwaaah… Now and always.

E-mail from: Michelle
To: Mike
Date: 24 July 2012
Subject: A virtual day with you

Hello my darling… my virtual husband…… the man of my dreams…

What would be my ideal day with you, you asked… well, as we are currently in the Seychelles: it would be to walk along the beach, hand in hand with you, with the waves gently lapping over our feet as we walked along…

But, I would be just as happy to be anywhere with you… hand in hand, walking through a crowded street somewhere… just being with you would make me the happiest person on the planet.

Yes… you are my friend… my lover… my virtual husband… and my soulmate… and I will love you forever…

Michelle
Xxx xxx xxx xxx x

E-mail from: Mike
To: Michelle
Date: 24 July 2012
Subject: Re: A virtual day with you

Hi my sexy virtual wife

Come to bed with me tonight and I will give you some hot love!!… Your boobs should be tingling… I have been playing

with them all day!!!… Miss you!!… I love you Michelle
Turner!!…

Good night…
Mike
xxx

E-mail from: Michelle
To: Mike
Date: 25 July 2012
Subject: A honeymoon of love and happiness

Hi my darling

Well, as we are still on our beautiful island in the Seychelles,
surrounded by the crystal clear Indian Ocean… it has occurred to
me that my husband still cannot swim… so… yes Mike I hear you
now… "OH NO"… this is a swimming lesson day!!! So down to
the ocean we go… just our toes in the water… lovely and warm…
up to our knees we go… don't panic, I'm holding your hand. You
will be safe with me Mike ~ I will look after you ~ I will never let
anything happen to you ~ You just have to trust me…

You decide it's time for a splashing game… and start splashing
me… OK; two can play that game… so we splash each other until
we are both well and truly soaked. I know what you are up to here
Mike, trying to distract me so I forget about your swimming
lesson… OK… I will sidetrack you here!!!… So I lay down on
my back on the sand where the waves are just gently lapping over
me… Oh yes, that has got your attention… and you come and
kneel over me, and start kissing me… and I pull you down so you
are laying on top of me… the waves just lapping over us…
swooshing up and down the beach… and over us as we roll
around kissing, cuddling, laughing… you say if we make love
first, right here, right now, you will be more relaxed and be able
to concentrate on your swimming lesson… and with that you start
to kiss my nipples… my boobs… and you are saying "Yummy…
salty Michelle"…… and before too much longer we are making
love… yes, in broad daylight, on the beach, right on the water's
edge… Nice…!!! I hope there are no people here… we haven't

seen any yet, in a week and a half... (although little Ditto got our bottle of Southern Comfort from somewhere?)

Half an hour later, after we have just laid there on the beach exhausted, back into the water we go... I am going to lay in the shallow water, and you are going to lay on top of me... me on my back... you on your front, holding onto Michelle's buoyancy aids... you are so busy hanging onto my boobs and kissing me, that you don't notice I am edging us further and further into the sea (don't worry, you could still stand up, with your feet touching the bottom here)... and gently we just float around on top of the water... you on top of me... you are OK... Mike... trust me; we will have you swimming in no time at all. OK... a change of position here... we both stand up... I stand behind you, and hold under your arms whilst you take your feet off the bottom, and lay back against me... you rest the back of your head against my boobs... your arms out beside you... your legs just floating in front of you. Your eyes are closed, and your face up into the sun... and you say... "Michelle, what on earth have I been worried about all these years?... All I needed was the 'right float' to get me going"... Yes, you are relaxed and just floating on top of the water, with me giving you just a little support... and your head resting on my boobs... You look like you are in heaven!!!

Mike, we will have you swimming in no time at all... this has given you the confidence you needed... We will leave it at that today... so just lay back, relax... and enjoy... I have got you... and you are floating!!!

I love you Mike... I love my honeymoon with you...

I will always love you...
Michelle
Xxx xxx xxx xxx

E-mail from: Mike
To: Michelle
Date: 25 July 2012
Subject: Re: A honeymoon of love and happiness

Hi my darling...

Yes I would love to hold your hand…
Yes I would love to go to the Indian Ocean with you…
Yes I would love to have fun and have laughs with you…
Yes I would love to cuddle you…
Yes I would love to hug you…
Yes I would love to kiss you…
Yes I would love to try your buoyancy aids…
Yes I would love to hold your boobs…
Yes I would love to kiss your nipples…
Yes I would love to make love to you…
Yes I love this honeymoon with you…
Yes I would love to share that bottle of Southern Comfort with you..
Yes I do trust you…
Yes "OH NO" definitely no swimming lessons for Mike…
"OH YES" definitely I love you…

Mwaaaaaaaaaaaaaaaaaaaaaaah!!

Mike
xxx

CHAPTER EIGHT

E-mail from: Michelle
To: Mike
Date: 1 August 2012
Subject: Our mud hut... Our new home

Hello My Darling

What do you think of this attachment? It seems like a good place
to start... we can build it from scratch... bespoke, Mike &
Michelle's home... A beautiful little mud hut... we can add to it
later if we feel the need... I think we need somewhere we can
shelter if it rains!!! And... I'm sure we will enjoy building it
together... although as I mentioned... I will smear you with mud
now and again... just so I can drag you off to the waterfall to
wash you off... and what a view we will have from our mud
hut... The Indian Ocean. Wow... wow...

What a wonderful way of life... Pure and simple... Just the two of
us!!!... Heaven!!!...

But... this is what we spent our day together doing today... we
started with our walk along the beach watching the sunrise...
went to our waterfall for our shared shower... MMMmmmm...
we found some fresh fruit for our breakfast... we went fishing in
the sea... and caught some fish for our dinner... and at sunset we
built a little fire on the beach and BBQ`d our fish... Our little
Ditto, has, from somewhere, got us two glasses, some lemonade
and a bucket of ice for our Southern Comfort: where does he get
all this stuff from? There must be life on this island somewhere?

We have been here for two weeks now, and seen nobody!!!... but Ditto obviously has!!!... We must find the time to walk further around the island, and see who else lives here... but there is nobody where we are... just you and I... BLISS...!!! After sitting by our fire on the beach and eating our fish supper... we play music (love songs) on our iPod... drink plenty of our Southern Comfort... and decide to dance in the moonlight, under the stars, on the beach... How romantic!!!... sexy salsa dancing... smooching cuddled up together dancing... oh... how wonderful... and you say, "Come on Michelle... it's time for bed"... "Bed Mike!!... we haven't slept in a bed for two weeks, we have been married for two weeks now, and not even had sex in a proper bed," I reply... but off to our hammock we go... Ditto has got us some candles now, and lit them all around our hammock... he loves us being together, and says he he has never been happier, now he has a Mum and Dad... he wants us to stay here forever, and all three be happy... we don't need anybody else or anything else... Ditto, your one wish is granted...

Now here is a thing... you jump into the hammock first... and sprawl yourself out, so there is no room for me to lay beside you... and with that cheeky little laugh of yours you say, "Michelle... you will just have to get on top of me!!!"... So carefully up I climb onto the hammock... one knee balanced each side of you, and kneel over you... and of course you get hold of my nipples!!! and start twiddling and tweaking, smiling at me... and then you say... "Michelle... make love to me!!!"... Well, who could resist that? Not me, with you, that is for sure!!!... Well... I am going to have to be careful here so that I don't rock this hammock about too much, so that we do not fall out, and land on the beach for the night... I start to slide my warm velvet tongue seductively across your skin. My finger tips gently start to play with 'your crown jewels'... Oh yes... I now know exactly what you like here... the two golden nuggets are getting the treatment... gentle, slow, sensual, seductive massaging... MMMmmmmmm... and lots of it... now the hot rod... yes standing to attention, and ready for action... Well... this is how I am going to stay, sitting on top of you... because I have discovered, you like playing with my boobs through the duration sometimes... and I can watch you... our eyes are locked, and you have that smouldering sexy look in your eyes... I am mesmerized by the fire in your eyes. We are smiling at one another... Oh Mike... you have that look of love all over your face... capturing me with your severe intensity... and gently I slide your hot rod into my love tunnel... OOOOOhhhhhh... soooo nice... Yes Mike... I have discovered you like to watch my boobs bounce up and down, as I move up and down on you... We are in heaven... And, all too quickly here we reach a climax together... at exactly the same time... MMMmmmmmm... Sooooo Sooooooo nice with you Mike... So much pleasure together!!!... Ecstasy rippling through my body as the orgasm you give me takes my entire being. Sexy, sensual and satisfying!!! ... then I move down, and lay on top of you... and give you the best kisses you have ever had... they are slow, sensual and oh so loving.

We shuffle around, and lay next to each other, and cuddle up... the stars are twinkling... and candles are still glowing... and then you move around a little, until your head is resting on my boobs... yes, this will be your pillow tonight... I stroke your hair, and massage your head... You will sleep well tonight darling... and so quickly I think you have drifted off to sleep... I don't know if you can hear me, when I whisper to you... "Mike, I love you so much, and I am so glad we have got married, you make me so happy"... but you do hear me because in your sleep you squeeze me tight, and mumble, "Ditto"...

I love you darling
Michelle
Xxx xxx xxx xxx x

E-mail from: Mike
To: Michelle
Date: 1 August 2012
Subject: Love in our natural shower

Hi My Michelle

How on earth do you expect me to go to sleep at night, when I check my e-mails and find sexy, passionate, erotic activities of us in the Seychelles?... But, oh, how I love to read them.

Well... It looks as though we are going to start to get dirty building our mud hut, so I have looked out some beautiful pictures from the internet. And, this is our natural shower in the Seychelles!

I cannot wait to start reading about the build... How dirty we will get... and how I am going to shower you off in this waterfall... And I am sure, without a double, make love to you in our waterfall.

Lots of love, big hugs and tons of kisses...
Mike
xxx

E-mail from: Mike
To: Michelle
Date: 2 August 2012
Subject: Topiary Heart Shape

Hi my sexy Michelle

Well, as I suspected, it is now 2am in the morning, and I cannot sleep, because I am thinking about you... About us... Sometimes you are just so outrageously flirtatious... I cannot sleep for thinking about us making love in the beautiful waterfall that we will use as our natural shower together... You have asked me to put my topiary skills to good use, and create you a topiary heart... so here goes...

We have just left the shower and you think your precious little heart down there in between your legs needs a little topiary trim, eh! No probs!!! So just lay back on the hammock and drop that towel and open your legs wide for me. I promise I will be gentle with you and this will not only look great, but you will feel great when I have finished with you my darling!!

Out come my little topiary scissors and yes, I can see it does need a little trim!!... I could find it hard to find that hot spot otherwise in amongst the bush without some little trimming up!!

Legs nice and wide apart and yes a snip, snip here and a snip, snip there. I will need to push my fingers around there a bit to make sure I do not clip anything else and make sure I just clip and shape your little topiary heart. Nice little gentle fingers around and around. You know to get a nice true cut, it should be a bit wet!! So yes you guessed it, my tongue will just moisten it up a little for you. Nice lots of licks… MMMmmmm… Yummy, yummy, looks nice and tastes delicious!! MMMmmmm… I need to just part your vagina (sorry I mean love tunnel) a little just to get to the edges and give that a little snip, snip!! Oh!!… Your hot spot looks nice now with some neat trimming and much less bush there having given your heart some shape. I just need to get the shape of the heart right and I will be finished, well not quite yet!!… snip, snip and yes that is coming good.

OMG… Michelle where I have been moving my fingers around your hot spot, you are also coming good!! This has got you so sexcited!! It is masturbation time and you love this!!…… But you are playing with me and my pop up has just done that… popped up!!! You are screaming, "Hang On", so I grab your lovely big melons and do just that… Those nipples are so long and hard and really not only look good, but feel good!!

Well, I think it is time to give you a treat; after all, your topiary heart is looking so good now and the final bit is making you feel good too. So with your legs still wide apart let me ruffle your topiary heart and see if it is still looking in good shape. Yes, just perfect if I say so myself and what a good job I have done on it for you!! I think I need to get it wetter, inside now, yes all the way in and you are shouting, Mike that feels so lovely when you do this to me…

To be continued…

Love always…
Mike
Xxx

---

1 August 2012 ~ Live Interactive Text

Mike: Hi my gorgeous sexy Michelle.

Mike: Well a little bit of scissoring and a little bit of shaping and you have the perfect designer heart there now in between your legs… I think I made a good job myself. ☺

Michelle: WOW… good morning my darling… I think you made a good job too ☺

Mike: I hope you enjoyed the e-mail I sent you in the night, when I could not sleep?

Michelle: Mike… I have just read that e-mail, and I loved it… I like the new design… A perfect heart shape… love it, thank you.

Mike: Yes… It was throbbing too!!!

Michelle: Ummmm, sounds nice… yes throbbing for 'you'…

Mike: Yes, it pulsates whenever I touch it…

Michelle: I've got your breakfast ready… Melon?

Mike: Nice… big melons… I love them.

Michelle: Ready and waiting… just for you!!!

Mike: Nice! My mouth is watering already!!!

Michelle: You should check them out for softness… before taking a nipple… I mean nibble.

Mike: Nothing better than a nice melon for breakfast and a nice little cherry on the top.

Michelle: Come on then…

Mike: I would love to come on them, for sure and I would like a little bouncy on them.

Michelle: MMMmmmm nice… come on then…

Mike: Early morning sexercise!

Michelle: OOOoooooohhhhhh… I like early morning sexercise…

Mike: Come here I want you NOW!

Michelle: I'll call in to see you on my way to work… you sound hungry.

Mike: Hungry for your love.

Michelle: MMMmmmm… I love you, and I love being MRS TURNER.

Mike: I LOVE YOU MORE… MRS TURNER.

Michelle: More than chocolate?

Mike: More than sliced bread.

Michelle: Oh… ☹ who likes sliced bread?

Mike: I would love you in a sandwich… between the sheets…

Mike: Come to bed with me, I am fresh out of the shower and ready now for you my darling.

Michelle: Come on then… not much to take off… just out of the shower myself, only a towel on… coconut flavoured Michelle again… MMMmmmm…

Mike: Good… straight down to business then, what are we waiting for, eh?

Michelle: I'm all yours…!!!

Mike: WOOOOOOOOOOOOOOOOwwwwww! Michelle: We can check out this topiary you have created.

Mike: I will stroke it smooth… and then gently ruffle it up again.

Michelle: My topiary heart shape is throbbing again now… just like when you were fiddling with it trimming it into a heart shape… and somehow my nipples are standing to attention!!!

Mike: You have all my attention now… you were good, I must say… You just stretched you legs wide apart and said to me… Get on with it!! ☺

Michelle: OOOooooo Mike…… did I? ☺

Mike: I was not sure what you meant… the scissor job or a hand job!

Michelle: Well starting with the scissors… would have lead to much more I'm sure…

Mike: I decided to give you one anyway!!! ☺

Michelle: I am sure you did ☺ I do love you…… you always know how to push all my buttons…

Mike: I love playing with your buttons… Bye… we will both be late for work

Michelle: Can I play with your crown jewels?

Mike: They belong to my virtual wife so help yourself.

Michelle: MMMmm nice… bye darling… a kiss for your lips… and two kisses for your crown jewels.

Mike: Michelle, I have to go to work now, thinking of your lips on my crown jewels.

Michelle: I hope this does not distract you too much?

Mike: How will I get any work done today now? Byeeeeeeee

Michelle: Bye darling… Mwah… for your hot rod too… hee hee hee… Byeeeee

E-mail from: Michelle
To: Mike
Date: 1 August 2012
Subject: Starting our mud hut

Hi there my sexy husband

Wow… I am loving this topiary heart you have given me… A topiary heart surrounding my hot spot… you are so romantic.

So, time to start building our 'mud hut' then… We leave the beach and climb up the hill, so we are safe from the sea, and elements of the weather if it ever gets bad… we don't want our little home getting water-logged… so we find a nice spot, with a lovely view overlooking the Indian Ocean… under the palm trees… a flat surface… and mark out our spot… you mark out a big circle (13 feet diameter) and say, that will do for a start. And off we go… gathering materials to start building our mud walls… and off to work we get… we start with just 13 inches high, marking out where the door will go… after only 10 minutes you say, "Michelle, we need a drink, this is thirsty work"… but we only have Southern Comfort and lemonade, so this is what we have… more building of the mud wall… then you say you want another drink… more Southern Comfort and lemonade…

After a couple of hours, we have the first thirteen inches high done… just the opening left for the door… and you say, this needs to dry before we go any higher… we are pretty pleased with ourselves, and you say I need a reward… "Come and give me a nice kiss Michelle," you say… and when I do… you… plant your muddy hands right on my boobs… so now I have two muddy hand prints, one on each boob… and you are laughing at me!!!… "Mike… I think you are a little drunk"… you grab me by the hand, and take me off to wash me off… we find the beautiful lagoon, where our waterfall runs into… and we get into the lagoon… Oh bliss… cool and refreshing… and you wash your hands off, and then wash me… you wash my hands free of the mud ~ and kiss them… you wash the mud off my boobs ~ and kiss them… and then you start on the rest of me… washing every little part of me ~ and kissing every little part of me… As you do this, I unabashedly cast my eyes over your naked body, visually drinking you in, as you stand naked in front of me.

And then… you say you need to check on your topiary heart you have created… Oh yes, you exclaim, a very good job… looks very nice with water dripping off of it, and the sun shining on it… good enough to eat… You decide you should dry it, to decide if it looks better wet, or dry… how do you dry it?… by blowing on it… OOOOOHHHHhhhhhh MIKE!!! You drive me wild… My sexy, sexy, erotic, sensual husband… tingling wonderful sensations… MMMmmmmm…… and then you slip a finger inside of me… back out, and start circling my hot-spot with that same finger… OOHHhhhh Mike!!!… and then tell me off, because you say, it is all wet again… only one thing for this you decide, and then you slip your hot rod right into my love tunnel… OMG Mike… how I love you… love being in the Seychelles with you… love being married to you… My whole world is perfect with you… and we make love, standing right where we are, in the lagoon…

I love you Mike Turner…
I will always love you…
from your virtual wife…
your sexy babe…
Michelle
Xxx xxx xxx xxx x
PS… I hope this one doesn't keep you awake tonight ☺

E-mail from: Mike
To: Michelle
Date: 1 August 2012
Subject: Re: Starting our mud hut

Hi my gorgeous wife

You are so goddamn sexy… Here comes another sleepless night for me… You are driving me crazy, then I get into bed and my mind is going all over the place. I have looked out even more phot's of waterfalls in the Seychelles, and have attached them for you… I know how you love waterfalls.

Loving You Always
Mike xxx

Michelle: Good morning my oh so sexy husband… Thank you for the e-mail last night, I love the natural shower you have found for us..!!! Ohhhhh… Wow… wow… I just love it…!!!

Mike: I love you x 13…

Mike: Yes I found a lovely natural shower and how I would love to have you there… Even in the water!!!

Michelle: Oh yes how I would love that too, in that water… Making love with that entire waterfall cascading over us.

Mike: MMMmmmm Michelle… I want you there now.

Michelle: I love you darling, really, really love you.

Mike: I don't want to go to work now, but we both have to, so we have to say bye for now ☹

Michelle: I would rather spend my day with you… but, yes… we both need to go. Bye for now darling.

Mike: Mwaaaaaaaaaaaaaaaaaaaaaaaaaaaah

Michelle: Mwaaaaaaaaaaaaaaaaaaaaaaaaaah

E-mail from: Michelle
To: Mike
Date: 2 August 2012
Subject: Day 2 ~ of our 'Grand Design'

Hi there my darling

OK… second day of our building plan… yesterday's first course has dried well, and ready for the next level… so we gather up more mud, and off we go, building another layer upwards on top of yesterday's… Another 13 inches high… bless him, little Ditto has gone and filled an empty bottle of Southern Comfort with fresh water from a stream for us… he does look after us!!! And slowly but surely we lay another layer… Well I am feeling a little naughty today, and can't resist drawing with mud on your back when you are bending over… hummm… 'I love you' I write

189

across your back... and some hearts and kisses... Oh how lovely and sun-tanned you are becoming, after living here for almost three weeks... you are laughing at me, and tell me the sooner we finish this course, the sooner we can have play time...!!! I'm on it... so we work well together, we have got into the swing of this now... and even quicker than yesterday we have completed this 13 inches... so already our mud hut is 26 inches high... we stand back and admire our work... yes, Mike... we are a team...!!! We high-five with our muddy hands... and then you grab hold of me, and smear your muddy hands all over my back and shoulders whilst giving me a kiss... Mike!!! I draw a muddy heart around the outside of your heart... and write `Michelle` through the middle of it... We are hot, and covered in mud now... so off we go to the natural waterfall that you have found for us...!!!

You are almost running, and have hold of my hand... and shouting, "Come on Michelle ~ I told you this morning I wanted to have you in this waterfall... and that is exactly what I meant..." When we arrive there, it is absolutely beautiful... in we go, and stand under the cool refreshing cascading water... we wash all of the mud off of one another... and then you look into my eyes... Mike, you look so sexy, sun tanned and wet... You kiss me on the lips, soooooooo sensual, our arms around one another... and then you are saying... "Yes, Michelle, I meant every word, when I told you three weeks ago... To have, and to hold... I want to have you, right here, right now... and I want to hold you forever in my arms"... You kiss me all over my face... and as you are still kissing me, between each kiss your say more words... "To love and to cherish... Oh yes Michelle, I will love you forever more... and I will cherish you for the rest of my days"... Your kisses move down to my neck... all over my neck... and you say more words... "For richer, for poorer... yes, our life here is pure and simple, and rich or poor makes no difference to us... we have everything we want... each other"... And as you are saying all of this you are planting kisses all over my neck and shoulders... nibbling at me gently... "In sickness and in health... yes Michelle we are happy and healthy, we will live long and happy lives here"... "For as long as we both shall live... Oh yes, Michelle Turner... I love you... I will always love you..."

You take hold of my hands, and move them up into the air, put my hands together, high above my head, and tell me to keep them there... your hands slide down my arms... down my sides... over my hips and you hold me there... you move your head down and kiss my nipples... nibble my boobs... OOOooohhhhhh Mike..!!! you can be so romantic sometimes... You decide you need to check on your topiary heart you have created... with one finger you trace the outline of the heart... OMG Mike... you set my senses on fire...!!! you trace your finger around my hot spot... OOOOOhhhhhh Mike...!!! the things you do to me...!!! Then you slip the same finger into my love tunnel and start smiling at me... saying... "Michelle ~ you are so ready for me..." You remove your finger, and replace it with your hot rod... our arms are around each other, with wild passionate kisses, just like in the picture you sent me... we make love, passionately... OMG... MIKE... I am just lost in a world of pure pleasure with you... absolute sexual, sensual sensations... You fill my mind and body with absolute pleasurable sensations...!!! I no longer know where my sensations end, and yours begin... where my body ends, and yours begins... we are gelled together as one... What is mine is yours ~ What is yours is mine... OMG MIKE... I just love you so much... my head is exploding with the sensations you are giving me... my climax is heavenly... my whole world is just exploding in sheer pleasure...!!!! And then I feel you filling me with your love juices... and telling me how much you love me... I don't think life gets any better than this Mike...!!!

I love you
I will always love you
Michelle
Xxx xxx xxx xxx x

E-mail from: Mike
To: Michelle
Date: 2 August 2012
Subject: I love you... especially in our natural shower

Hi Michelle

I am glad I have found this natural waterfall in the Seychelles. We can now shower together and get all that mud off our naked bodies!! MMMmmmm… I am looking forward to washing you down all over!! Then we can have some nice love, hugs and cuddles!!… You press your hard nipples into me with our hearts beating together like thunder!!!

Guess What!!!! Ditto has found some `Love You Chocolate` for us!!… Yummy, yummy!!! You and chocolate at the same time, how wonderful is this!! (See attachment photo of chocolate with `Love You` on it.)

MMMmmmm… I love you…
Mike
Xxx

---

3 August 2012 ~ Live Interactive Text.

Mike: Hi my sexy babe.

Michelle: Hi my handsome hunk of a husband.

Mike: Thank you for your email regarding the chocolate.

Michelle: I hope you liked it.

Mike: I love chocolate and I love you… So two good things for the price of one! Have I got to lick the chocolate off your boobs and your love tunnel?

Michelle: Oh Mike… you know me so well…

Mike: Yes… I bet you have smeared a lot around your hot spot so I have to wiggle my tongue around to get it… Yummy, yummy and you will love it and probably go wild.

Michelle: And… golden nuggets… covered in chocolate… YUMMY…

Mike: Oh… Mine too, eh! Chocolate and cream cocktails… sounds like another new drink to me.

Michelle: Hee hee hee…… yeeeeeeessssssssssssssssssss!!!

Mike: Just tell me… Is the chocolate inside your love tunnel too?

Michelle: Would you like it to be?

Mike: Do I have to put my tongue inside?… Would you like tongue, fingers, or hot rod? Which would you like of the three?

Michelle: Mike, it is you who makes me so greedy... You know what I am going to say now don't you?... All three please... in that order.

Mike: I just knew you would say that... ☺ You are really greedy!!

Michelle: You set me on fire Mike... even the very thought of you...

Mike: That is because my tongue is twirling around down there, right inside of your love tunnel

Michelle: OMG...

Michelle: HEAVEN...

Mike: Yes you are getting sexcited! I had better lick that hot spot, you have given that a double helping of chocolate.

Michelle: OMG... MIKE... I love it... I love you...

Mike: I think I need to lick from top to bottom down here... all that chocolate is sticky around your hot spot, I am just going to suck it off.

Michelle: OMG... please carry on from here next time... because I hate to say it... but I have to go... Simon will be here any minute

Mike: Just tell him you are busy!! You could tell him you are about to climax.

Michelle: You drive me crazy... sexy, sexy husband

Mike: Byeeeeeeeeeeeeeeeeeee

Michelle: Byeeeeeeeeeeeeeeeeee

E-mail from: Michelle
To: Mike
Date: 3 August 2012
Subject: Day 3 ~ of our Grand Design

Hi My Darling

We are up bright and early, as always... had our fruit for breakfast... and... little Ditto has found us a jug of coffee from somewhere, white, no sugar, he knows us so well... and refilled our bottle of water... he is good to us!!! Oh, hang on before we go off for our bespoke building experience, I need to do some housework... a quick shake of our hammock... all done!!!

At the mud hut, we find that yesterday's work has dried well... we are doing well my darling... and off we go again, finding our mud, and up we go a further 13 inches... packing the mud wall, yes it is quite straight... (not so 'cock'-eyed after all... hee hee hee)... Oh Mike... I cannot resist smearing mud on you again... and you on me... my nipples have got it... but quickly even with all the messing around we are now up to 39 inches... Wow... it is looking good... and you say to me, "Michelle, how could I have ever doubted you as my jobber's mate... you do work hard... and yes, you are fun to work with..." We have a little kiss, and off we go to our waterfall for a shower...

Oh, it is so beautiful here... into the cool water we go... you wash me off... every little bit of me... MMMmmmm... I wash you off... every little bit of you... all the mud has gone... I start to sing you a song... and dancing for you under the waterfall... what am I singing?... "I've got the hots for you... boom boom de boom boom"... and my arms are in air as I shimmy just for you... a wiggle of the hips... twirling around slowly... arms down by my sides... and a lean forward, with a shimmy of my boobs at you... Oh Mike... your eyes are popping out as you say "My boob-a-licious Michelle"...

Then you say it's time for lunch... Chocolate lunch... oh yes I know you like chocolate for your lunch... so back we go to our stash of chocolate Ditto has got for us... When we get there, I am not surprised to learn that you are in charge of the chocolate... so you undo it... but to my surprise you pop the first chocolate into my mouth... WOW...!!! maybe you do love me more than chocolate? (still to be decided)... and then you eat two yourself... Hmmmmm... ??? maybe you don't???... then you hold some chocolate in your hands, and of course it melts in the heat... now you are laughing... I can guess what is coming next... you rub the chocolate all around my nipples, all over my nipples... and again you are saying, "My, oh, my... yes, you are my Boob-a-licious Michelle"... and then you set about licking the chocolate off of my nipples... 'Chocolate covered nipples'. MMMmmmm... I don't know who is enjoying this the most... licking and sucking... MMMmmmm Mike!!! and you tell me you have found your favourite sweet of all time... chocolate covered Michelle's nipples...!!! Well, as I have told you recently my favourite sweets are 'chocolate covered nuts'… so you know what is going to happen next, don't you…!!! I melt a couple of the chocolates in my hands, and gently massage it into your crown jewels… the golden nuggets get it big time… oh, now I need more chocolate, everything is growing here, and I have run out of chocolate… more chocolate on the hot rod… MMMmmmm Mike… yes, you look good enough to eat…!!! And I set about licking the chocolate off… WOW..!!! These are the best 'nuts in chocolate' I have ever tried… YUMMY… licking and sucking… MMMmmmm... Mike… and then you tell me… you love me as much as chocolate…!!! Yeeeeeeeeeessssssssssssssssssss!!! Result…!!!

Down to the ground I push you… and get on top of you… and then I notice you have more chocolates in your hands… and with me straddled across you on my knees, you smear more chocolate all over my nipples and boobs… and with that cheeky sexy little smile of yours you say, "Michelle… make love to me…" And as I slip your hot rod into my love tunnel, you start to lick the chocolate off of my boobs and nipples… WOW… Mike… more heavenly sensations… I cuddle your head, and hold you against my boobs… OMG… so nice… I am gripping your hot rod tight, so, so tight inside of my love tunnel… feel all those muscles inside of me just gripping at you… so tight… and gently I am moving up and down on you… all the while you are licking and sucking the chocolate off of my boobs… OMG Mike… this is heaven… and all too quickly you are telling me you can hold on no longer, the love juice is about to explode… I hold you tighter, and move even faster, my heart beating like thunder… and yes, your love juice is filling me… you are biting me now, in your own sheer pleasure… and with your panting breath you are saying… "Michelle… I can never get enough of you"… All of this just sends me over the top, and I climax in pure pleasure… "Oh Mike… I love you… I love you… I love you…"

Yes Mike… I love you
I will always love you
Michelle
Xxx xxx xxx xxx x

E-mail from: Mike
To: Michelle
Date: 4 August 2012
Subject: Love in the Seychelles

Hi Michelle

I thought we were alone on this island in the Seychelles… So who took these pictures? I hope Ditto was not watching us… He will get jealous!

Anyway he has had years of fun playing with your lovely boobs… So I need to make up for lost time!

Check out these very sexy files I have attached.

Love always…
Mike
xxx

---

6 August 2012 ~ Live Interactive Text

Michelle: Good morning my darling… I did not want to leave here Friday evening, when my eta happened early… and have spent half my weekend thinking about your tongue, chocolate and my hot spot…!!!

Mike: Hi my sexy virtual wife… And they say the weather is going to get hotter towards the weekend!!… Wow I say to myself, how much hotter can my wife get?

Michelle: We are 'HOT' together

Mike: I am glad you spent your weekend thinking of all the things I would do to that hot spot of yours, and that beautiful little topiary heart I have created for you,

Michelle: Yes… You drive me completely crazy!!

Mike: Not only was my tongue enjoying your hot spot… but my lips were enjoying your nipples too…

Michelle: Stop it Mike… you are driving me slowly insane here!!

Mike: I want to do all of this to you in the real world, not just our cyber world.

Michelle: How I would love that too…

Mike: But, we know that cannot happen!!

Michelle: No... if we got caught again, it would blow both of our worlds apart.

Mike: For sure!!

Michelle: But, what I would not give... for just one touch... just one kiss... with you in the real world... Now I am being really greedy!!

Mike: We are both greedy Michelle, this is what has got us into so much trouble.

Michelle: I know...

Mike: Bye darling, we both need to get ready for work.

Michelle: Bye darling... I love you.

Mike: "DITTO"

E-mail from: Michelle
To: Mike
Date: 6 August 2012
Subject: Day 6 ~ of our Grand Design

Hi there my sexy, oh so lovable husband

Nice sexy files you sent me over the weekend... little Ditto must have a camera from somewhere now, if you say this is us in these pictures, although obviously nobody can see our faces, so who knows?

So over the weekend more building of the walls of our mud hut... day 6 (today) another 13 inches of the mud walls... so now 78 inches high (six and a half feet high)... so Mike, is this high enough now?... can we start thinking about the roof, once this has dried?... In looking back at the original picture found (see file attached again here) what type of roof do we need to think about???? a palm leaf one?... or a thatched one?... Now can we manage the thatching? I hear you thinking... of course we can... there is nothing we cannot do between us!!!... it must only be like a 'latch-loop rug'???... so I think we could do either!!!... What do you think?

And after our shower together, naked in our natural waterfall... we celebrate our hard work for today (see other file attachment)...

Mmmmmm... my hard nipples pressed hard against 'you'... and a kiss... in fact 130 kisses... and a cuddle... infact an endless cuddle, for all of those kisses... I hope you don't drop me!!! Do we make love today?... or am I wearing you out?... I need you to be on form Friday evening, when we have a whole evening to video cam with one another... "Sod it..." (as my cyber husband would say) there's plenty of time to recuperate before Friday!!!... Yes Mike... we make love... slow... gentle... sexy... seductive... and oh so sensual... endless pleasure for us both... Our daily 'sexercise' to keep us fit and healthy... Our hearts beating together as one..!!! Savouring every kiss... every touch... every moment... and feeling all the love that we share...

My lover... My sexy husband... My forever friend... I love you so much...

Michelle
Xxx xxx xxx xxx x

E-mail from: Mike
To: Michelle
Date: 7 August 2012
Subject: Attachments of topiary heart shapes.

Hi Michelle

Wow... I love your emails and the very intimate love that we share together... Just to prove a `maybe` is not always a No!!... I have attached a picture taken on cam of me only recently, as you have asked me to. Just for you and this is to show you that I have kept my side of the bargain, just like you have kept your side of the bargain in the continuation of your heart topiary. Your pictures will follow in an email another day. Have I told you you're lovely and I love you?

I have also attached some pictures of topiary hearts... I hope this was not our little Ditto with the camera again!!

Love always...
Mike
xxx

Mike: Hi my gorgeous babe

Michelle: Morning my darling… Mwah

Mike: I need a cuddle

Michelle: I want a cuddle… with my nice warm boobs pressed into you… my hard nipples pressed even harder into you… Your arms around me…

Mike: A BIG YES!!

Michelle: Nice start to the day… MMMmmmmmm… cuddle me tight then…

Mike: I want to kiss your nipples and suck them to get them hard so they are like American hard gums.

Michelle: Yes, I would like that too…

Mike: Delicious… so tasty and OMG… so long now I have had a play with them.

Mike: Bye… I must go.

Michelle: Mike… Wind me up… Sex me up… set me on fire… and then you say Bye ☹

Mike: Cheryl has just come out of the shower… Byeeeeeeeeee

Michelle: Bye darling

Michelle: A whole evening alone for us to Skype… My heart skips.. skips.. a beat…

Mike: YOU ARE BONKERS!!!

Michelle: You say I am bonkers… I say you are sexy..!!!

Mike: So, we have two hours!!!… Cam we cam?

Michelle: I cam, if you cam… ☺

For the next two hours, they video link, talk and laugh, and just thoroughly enjoy one another, as they always do… then finish off with some text.

Michelle: I love you Mike Turner… I love you as much now as I always have… and that is… with all my heart…

Mike: You know I feel like a child when I see you... So tempting and I am saying to myself I want you... But no, I cannot touch and cannot feel you. You know this is driving me crazy!!!

Michelle: You drive me crazy... and I want you...

Mike: I would love to have that heart of yours!!!

Michelle: I know it is too late now... but I wish we had done things differently all those years ago... I wish we had ended up together... I love you as much now, as I did then... you have my heart Mike Turner

Mike: I love you so much and I cannot ever get enough of you now. How I would love to feel your heart beat next to mine and I would love to cuddle into those boobs like Ditto has done for all these years... The lucky little SOD!!!

Mike: Just to say, thank you for tonight and so nice to see you and have this precious time with you. You know I wish I could have you and take you to bed with me now.

Michelle: I would love to come to bed with you right now... naked... and cuddle you all night......

Mike: Mwah! BIG HUGS... and take all my love to bed with you... Good night my darling...

Michelle: Goodnight darling... I will take your love to bed with me... and you take mine...

E-mail from: Michelle
To: Mike
Date: 10 August 2012
Subject: Day 10 ~ of our Grand Design

Hi there my darling

So, what have we been doing over the past few days on our idyllic island in the sun?... day 6 we completed the mud wall... day 7 we had a chill out day, where we just caught fish for our dinner, and drew plans on the sand of our roof design... Now, obviously I am just the jobber's mate here, so I am relying on the excellent carpentry skills of my cyber husband here... and you design the frame you want to put up for the roof (see attached files)...

Day 8, off we go exploring the island, in search of more materials... and to see if there is actually anyone else living here.

Now, we obviously suspect someone else lives here, some sort of civilization?... Mike, we have lived here for four weeks, and seen nobody... just the two of us!!!!! Oh wow, wow..!!! We have needed to put clothes on today, you just in your shorts and flip-flops ~ me in a short skirt, vest top and flip-flops... and off we go... we walk for miles, but around the beach edge, because we said if we got lost, eventually we would end up back on 'our beach'... hours later we find signs of life... yes, there are other people here... we find a little village, on what we think is completely the other side of the island to where we have set up home. Little mud huts... a few basic shops... the natives are surprised to see us, but very friendly towards us... There is a little store here that sells everything we need to finish our mud hut... we order our doors... we buy wood for the frame of the door, and frame of the roof... we buy the thatch for the roof... you buy a few tools... and they say they will deliver the goods for us, and give us a lift back to our side of the island... but we still want a few more things... we buy a couple of bottles of Southern Comfort, lemonade... and find some food... Mike, I don't think you would want to live off of fresh fish forever more, so we buy chicken, bacon, coffee, milk... and coconut shower creme... MMMmmmm... and 'chocolate'!!! Now, we are ready for our lift back, in a tatty little pickup truck, and we are driven back to our beach... the guy who gave us the lift says we should set up home on their side of the island... but we say we are just fine... don't call us... we will call you...!!!

By now it is late afternoon, and soon to be sunset... so we have a shower in our natural waterfall because we are so hot... you build a little fire to BBQ our dinner on, and I prepare the food... chicken wrapped in bacon tonight, and fresh vegetables... yummy... we settle down on the beach to watch the sunset with a large Southern Comfort and lemonade each... me wrapped in your arms (no better place to be in the whole wide world)... and watch the most beautiful sunset... what could be better than this Mike? Nothing..!!! We put our chicken on to cook... it takes a while... more Southern Comfort and lemonade... then put some water in a little dish, put it on the BBQ to heat up, place our chopped vegetables in it, wrap the bacon around the chicken, and put that back on to finish cooking... more Southern Comfort and lemonade… and when our dinner is ready it is wonderful… now it is dark, and we are just sitting by the little fire, and under the stars… Mike. this is my idea of heaven..!!! we have our iPod on, playing romantic music… and life is sheer bliss… and then you tell me you want dessert… Hummmm what will this be… you want a Bounty bar you tell me, but we only have chocolate… I say, I will make you some… you say, can you do that really? so you tell me to make mine first, because you are sure yours will be better?... I find a coconut, break into it, shred the coconut, melt some chocolate and pour it over the spread-out coconut… and when it has set a little we break pieces off and try it… YUMMY..!!! Ingenious!!!… now you say it is your turn… you take off my top, and say Michelle's boobs are already coconut flavoured, because you washed them twice for me earlier in our shower… you get some chocolate and rub it all over my boobs and nipples… MMMmmmm… and then you set about licking it all off… Oh yes you say, this is much better… My bouncy Bounty boobs bars… win hands down every time… Boob-a-licious Michelle's bouncy Bounty bars… yummy, yummy, yummy… More Southern Comfort and lemonade to wash it all down… I think we are a little tipsy now… we make love, under the stars… wild and passionate love… MMMmmmmm… Life is just wonderful here with you Mike…

The next morning, we are up bright and early to start the frame for our roof… we have a little practice by making a tiny section, then put mesh over it, and have our first try of thatching… Oh yes Mike… we can do it… of course we can… with our joint skills there is nothing we can't do between us… we are a team… 'Team Turner'… so the next few days will see us making our wooden roof frame… I know I will be impressed with your carpentry skills here Mike… My clever, clever, skilful husband…

Life could be no better than this Mike… Pure and simple… no hassles… just us… and it is heaven on earth…

I love you darling… love you so much…
Mrs Michelle Turner
Xxx xxx xxx xxx x

E-mail from: Mike
To: Michelle
Date: 12 August 2012
Subject: Thirteen reasons why I love you

Hi Michelle

There are so many reasons why "I love you"… I have attached just thirteen of them!! 13 lovely pictures of you, taken on my webcam. I have also attached a slide show of photo`s I thought you would enjoy. Something as special as I can give you in 'our cyber world'.

Have a wonderful day and very `Best wishes` to someone very special and very close to my heart.

I will always love you… today, tomorrow and forever…

Mike xxx

Mike also sends a couple of romantic e-cards to Michelle for her birthday.

---

13 August 2012 ~ Live Interactive Text

Mike: Hi Michelle… `HAPPY BIRTHDAY`. How I would love to spend your birthday with you, but I know you will have a wonderful day and that you will be pampered and spoilt and you deserve it… why not?… Enjoy!!

Michelle: Hello darling… thank you for all of my birthday messages… Thank you for the video slide show you have sent me… All the attachments we have sent each other of the Seychelles… our honeymoon… and all the pictures you have taken of me on your webcam… how I would like a real kiss with you right now…

Mike: You know, you take a lovely picture and do you know in every one you were either laughing or smiling.

Michelle: You monkey… I knew you were taking loads of pictures the other evening, when we were on video cam for a couple of hours… it is you that makes me laugh and smile…

Michelle: As it is my birthday, and my day of choosing… I would love a real kiss with you… Put it on the slate…

Mike: Okay… OMG… History repeating itself, eh!!

Michelle: I could not get you off my mind Friday night… your smiling happy laughing face… a face that I love… I love you so much Mike… two hours just talking to you, and seeing you… I loved it so much

Mike: I know you are just going off for your pamper day… When you relax on that massage table, let your mind drift off to the Seychelles and us on the beach and me massaging your body with lots of lotion all over. I will make certain it is the full works and concentrate on those bits which may not get the full massage today!!

Michelle: OMG… my nipples will be standing to attention if I do that… what will the woman think of me?… but now you have said it… it will happen……

Mike: Did you like the music I put to our slide show today? I had to put on our song… You know the one… "I will always love you"

Michelle: You just melt my heart… I loved it

Mike: Enjoy your day.

Michelle: Thank you for being here this morning, I know that is not easy for you… you have made my day…

Mike: You're lovely and have a lovely special day… Bye.

Michelle: I will be home at about 5pm… I will turn this on for half hour, in case you get a chance… but I know that is difficult…… how I would love a cuddle and just one kiss with you right now…

Mike: Next best… A virtual cuddle and some big hugs… and of course lots of kisses…

Michelle: I would love to feel your arms around me today… but I almost can…

Mike: Go and get ready… you will be late.

Michelle: I'm not going for an hour

Mike: OMG… what I could do with you in an hour!!

Michelle: I will think about you… whilst having all my pampering… OMG… one whole hour with you in the flesh… I would be straight in that shirt with you…

Mike: Come on then you gorgeous, sexy and loving passionate wife… I am here waiting for you now… I remember when we spent afternoons in bed together; when you got out of the bed, you would put my shirt on to go to the bathroom... So sexy, nothing else on underneath...

Michelle: I remember that too... I would love to do that now... slowly unbutton it... one button at a time... one kiss at a time... slowly... seductively... my gentle tiger claws skimming across your chest... and come right in that shirt for a sexy sexy kiss and cuddle...

Mike: How I would love to share your love today!

Michelle: Me too... as I told you Friday evening... I would never be able to leave you alone...

Mike: Good!

Michelle: I need to slowly take this top off... and... slowly undo the bra... and let it slip off... and look into those sexy brown eyes of yours... and then cuddle you with my arms... my boobs... my body... and wrap my arms around you.

Mike: Sounds good to me... I will tell you what... put it on the slate.

Michelle: And just kiss you a million times... On the slate it is...

Mike: Bye now... Enjoy your birthday!

Michelle: Bye darling... "I will always love you"...

Mike: I will love you forever and always... sends lots of little symbols

Michelle: Wow... a birthday cake... drinks... a hug... and flowers... you spoil me...

Mike: I would more than spoil you!

Michelle: Oh Mike... you melt my heart... how I want you right now...

Mike: See you soon... Take care... Go enjoy your day.

Just after 5pm that day...

Mike: Hi my darling... I hope you are having a wonderful day!

Michelle: Hello darling... thank you so much for the photos of 'our honeymoon'... all the attachments we have sent one another, of beautiful natural scenes in the Seychelles, so, so nice... you melt my heart darling... you have sent me e-mails throughout the day... loads of them... thank you

Mike: We cannot stay long now, but I have been thinking of you all day... I just love you to bits!!! Have you enjoyed your pamper day?

Michelle: I have been pampered beyond belief today, and really enjoyed my day... I'm ready for you to finish off the bits they didn't do... all my rude bits... ☺

Mike: MMMmmmm... No problem!... Can't wait... ☺

Michelle: ONE DAY MIKE...! ONE DAY...!!!

Mike: I hope they didn't see my artwork and the heart topiary!

Michelle: Not a chance... I kept it hidden.

Michelle: Maybe we should have a day of pampering one day... where nobody can find us... just locked away together for the day... I'll pamper you... and you can pamper me...

Mike: That would be very difficult for both of us, you know that.

Michelle: ☹

Mike: Go get ready for your evening, enjoy your meal and evening out.

Michelle: I LOVE YOU and you have made my day so much more special...... my sexy cyber husband...

Mike: I LOVE YOU MICHELLE TURNER... more than you will ever know.

E-mail from: Michelle
To: Mike
Date: 17 August 2012
Subject: Day 17 ~ of our Grand Design

Hi there darling

Mike, we are doing so well with our 'bespoke' build here... my clever husband has put up the wooden frame for our thatched roof... and as jobber's mate, I have held all the wood whilst you cut it... and you didn't even saw any of my fingers off..!!! and then... I held onto everything whilst you banged things into place!!!... We have put the wooden frame up, ready to hang our doors on... wow, wow it is looking good, and taking shape... We have started our thatching on the roof... well this is quite a task, as neither of us have done this before, but as I have said to you before Mike, nothing is impossible for us, together we make a team, and between us there is nothing we could not conquer..!!! We are doing well... but it is going to take us some time... Especially as...

You keep looking at me, covered in sawdust, and saying, "Come on Michelle, you are all dirty again, I need to take you off to the shower, and wash you off..." Well Mike, I am not going to argue with this... with those sexy brown eyes of yours I feel you would get far too much of your own way with me... Those skilful hands of yours, wash me off... every little bit of me... MMMmmmm... and then, I wash you off... Oh Mike, I would never leave you alone in this world... my hands washing all over your body, gently caressing every part of you... with lots of tender loving care... In the waterfall, we kiss, just like our picture you found... congratulate ourselves on our home we are building so well between us... and you say to me, "Michelle ~ you are the best jobber's mate I have ever had..." Oh Mike, this earns you a reward...

Out of the water we get, and lay on the grass beside the waterfall and lagoon... kissing and cuddling... the sunshine dancing on our bodies through the palm tree above... a lovely warm breeze... MMMmmmm Mike... I cannot resist those luscious lips of yours... but then my kisses move down your neck, my gentle tiger claws skimming over your chest... MMMmmmm... I love you all wet... I lick the water off of your chest, with very juicy kisses... nibbling and biting you gently... Yes... you love this!!!... and just lay back and enjoy it... down to your tummy my kisses go... MMMmmmm... my delicious sexy husband... my hands are creeping towards those crown jewels of yours... and gently with my finger-tips, I caress them... OOOOoooo nice... further down my kisses travel... until my lips are on those crown jewels... Yummy!!! I pay lots of attention here... licking and sucking... MMMmmmm Mike, you taste so good...

But then you say, "Michelle... hold fire here... or this will be over and done with all too quickly, you have me so worked up..." And, you roll me over, and get on top of me... your turn now, you claim, and start the whole process on me... you start on my neck, gentle little kisses... down across my shoulders... down the insides of my arms... and then to my boobs... and my nipples... MMMmmmm... and when my nipples have become American hard gums, you move down to my tummy... and then... you decide it's time to inspect your artwork, of the topiary heart... you trace your finger gently around the heart you have made... and say you think it may need a little trim up within the next couple of days... and then... your fingers find my hot spot... Ohhhh wow... I love it when you do that... until you replace your finger with your tongue... Ohhhh Mike... I love it even more when you do that...!!! It drives me absolutely crazy... but you know that... and then... you are smiling at me... "Yes, Michelle... we are both on the brink now... it's time I put this hot rod inside of you"... And with the tip of your hot rod, you caress my hot spot... OMG... Mike... I love it, love it, and love it when you do that... I am in heaven... and then you slide inside of me... but pull right back out... smiling at me... "Mike... I want you... come and give me all of your love..." You slide back inside me again, this time with more force... your body so lustrous, healthy, strong and vigorous. Woooo that makes my eyes light up...!!! And with each thrust, I am lost... lost in a world of sensations, of your body and mine... and when I feel your love juices filling me, my world explodes around you... of wonderful pleasure... the sheer and utter pleasure of your body and mine joined together... Lost in a world where I am yours, and you are mine...

When our hearts slow down a little, you roll over, and gently pull me on top of you... we are holding each other tight... my boobs are cuddled onto your chest... you kiss my hair, and tell me how much you love me... Your grip on me possessive and commanding. Mike... I could never love anyone as much as I love you...... and I will always love you this way...

Always and forever
Your ever-loving wife
Michelle
Xxx xxx xxx xxx x

---

20 August 2012 ~ Live Interactive Text

Michelle: Thank you for sending me all the pictures you have taken on your web cam... Do you know, I didn't know you had taken that many.

Mike: ☺ I think I did a good job here. You are really looking cheeky in most of them.

Michelle: I am cheeky... and naughty with you...

Mike: Fun, sexy and lovely.

Michelle: As my cyber husband would say… "Sod it… let's bunk the day off together"…

Mike: Let us go for it then!!!

Michelle: Let's have a nice day together… I will phone in sick…

Mike: Yes come on then. I will say I have to see my virtual wife she is not feeling too well… She has love sickness… She is starving for love… I need to spend the day with her.

Michelle: Oh yes… she is… hungry for you Mike-Turner.

Mike: I cannot get enough of you.

Michelle: And I can never get enough of you… I would love you to myself 24/7… for the rest of my life…

Mike: You would certainly not have love sickness then my darling.

Michelle: I would be happy and healthy for the rest of time… and so would you… I would keep you fit…

Mike: Look at the time… We are both late… Bye now and see you soon.

Michelle: Bye darling… I do love you……

Michelle: And…

Michelle: I am so glad to be married to you… in our world…

Michelle: A very special world…

Mike: Very special…… Bye

Michelle: Bye

Michelle: Hi Darling

Mike: Hi My Darling

Michelle: Do you know, it is 10 years today that my Mum died?

Mike: You still miss her…

Michelle: Yes… She was more than just a Mum to me

Mike: I know she was.

Michelle Do you know my Mum said to me many times, that one day, somehow, she didn't know how or when, but you and I would find each other again…

Mike: Oh! Why would she have said this? But, she was right, because in our cyber world we have!

Michelle: She always told me she hoped she would still be around to see it... so she would be happy we have found each other again in this way... I know she would...

Michelle: She cried a million tears with me all that time ago... she really liked you...

Mike: Yes, I know I only met your parents for a short while but I could feel their same love and warmth that I have always found in you. I do not believe in life hereafter and life hereafter is our children and their children, like nature and how the world has evolved for billions of years... But yes, if only our parents knew what happened after death.

Michelle: I wonder if people do still know things after death?

Mike: I personally think like nature, regeneration is life and nobody comes back. I know some believe and if they help retain memories it is good for them. I am sure many people say I will communicate after death, but I cannot believe it, but maybe I am wrong and I will be singing "I Will Always Love You" from above, eh!!!

Michelle: I don't believe they can communicate... but I believe there is some sort of awareness...

Mike: A spiritual awareness? Maybe sometimes the mind?

Michelle: Sometimes I can feel my Mum... I know that sounds strange...

Mike: I still cannot believe that you told your parents about 'US'

Michelle: I know... it took an awful lot of courage for me to do that... but, our situation had been blown wide open by then, and everything was everywhere. I cannot believe they accepted the situation as they did... they thought I was happily married up until that point...

Mike: I know

Michelle: But, when I took you to meet them that day, they really liked you... My Mum said to me afterwards, we looked like we belonged together... we made a really good couple.

Mike: Yes, I remember you telling me this.

Michelle: Anyway, we should get off of this topic.

Mike: Don't be sad about your Mum today darling... She would not want you to be...

Michelle: I know… and I also know she would be so happy we share our love once more…

Mike: I think you are right…

Michelle: Anyway, moving on…

Michelle: Have you thought of a name for our 'mud hut' yet?

Mike: No… Have you?

Michelle: Yes…

Mike: Are you going to share it with me?

Michelle: If you want me to.

Mike: Come on then… tell me…

Michelle: OK… ready…

Michelle: `M & M's LOVE SHACK`… what do you think of that then?

Mike: Yes it has the chocolate theme about it too, sweet and delicious M & M's home… Yes, that will save me putting this in my think tank.

Michelle: Mike & Michelle's home.

Mike: I am glad you said "SHACK"

Michelle: M & M… with a double meaning…

Mike: Yes, that is good… I like it… I was thinking you were going to say "M & M's LOVE SHAG"

Michelle: Love Shack… for shagging… OMG MIKE… now look what you have made me say…!!!

Mike: I LOVE YOU MICHELLE TURNER…

Michelle: I LOVE YOU MIKE TURNER…

Mike: Have a nice day and a nice weekend, enjoy! I will always love you… Maybe your Mum really did know something!

Michelle: I think she knew… I would always love you… and she was right…

Mike: Mwaaaaaaaaaaaaaaaaaaaaaaaaaaaaaaah!

Michelle: A long very sexy passionate kiss for you my darling.

Mike: Bye and be safe and take care.

Michelle: I LOVE YOU my sexy cyber husband… Bye

Mike: "DITTO"

Michelle: Hi darling

Mike: Have I told you that I have fallen in love with you? And, I am missing you my sexy virtual wife.

Michelle: and I with you Mr Turner

Mike: I need an appointment...

Michelle: What kind of appointment?

Mike: A real one.

Michelle: Really?

Mike: Michelle, I would love too... but, it would be too risky

Michelle: Now, you are teasing me?

Mike: Not teasing... just telling you...

Michelle: I would love that too... maybe one day we will?

Mike: We will have to come up with something good.

Michelle: Put your thinking cap on then.

Mike: You too... Very risky, whatever the situation.

Michelle: I know, but what I would not give for just one touch... just one kiss...

Mike: You're naughty and I would love too... BUT...

Michelle: Let us both have a think about this.

Mike: I think this is how it started a long time ago, history repeating itself?

Michelle: MMMmmmm... We must think about this carefully!!!

Michelle: I love you... I miss you... just one touch... one kiss......

Mike: Stop it, you are driving me crazy now.

Michelle: Have a good day darling...... Mwahhhhhhh

Mike: Bye... mwaaaah... I just love you...

Michelle: "DITTO" Bye...

E-mail from: Michelle
To: Mike
Date: 28 August 2012
Subject: Just one touch… Just one kiss…

Hi Darling

Could you disappear off the radar for an hour one day???… It would be so nice to see you… just one drink… just one touch… just one kiss…

We could meet up at a little pub in the countryside somewhere, way away from where we both live?

I love you Mike ~ and what I wouldn't give to just see you for an hour… just one touch… just one kiss… to just be able to feel your arms around me once more… for our lips to touch… and our hearts beat next to one another, just for a short time.

Michelle
Xxx xxx xxx xxx x

---

28 August 2012 ~ Live Interactive Text

Mike: Do you know you are so `tempting`. In answer to your email… Maybe!!! But… We need to discuss this in detail.

Michelle: OK…

Mike: Anyway… This is your heart talking and not your brain, eh!!!

Michelle: They are connected…!!! ☺

Mike: I love you…

Michelle: I love you… more…

Mike: That is impossible because I love you more than anything in the whole world…

Michelle: Sometimes you just melt my heart Mike Turner…

Mike: We both need to give this serious thought. I must go… See you soon and enjoy your weekend.

Michelle: Bye darling… enjoy yours too…

Mike: Mwah! and be good…

Michelle: I love you… don't ever forget that… mwah

E-mail from: Michelle
To: Mike
Date: 30 August 2012
Subject: Day 30 ~ of our Grand Design

Hi my darling

Well, in less than a month we have completed our project… We have finished our thatched roof, and are so pleased with it… We have been across to see the 'village people' again, and have bought paint, some wooden flooring for the inside, a couple of coconut mats, and some lanterns with candles for when we want them… Our doors were delivered and we have hung those… and soooo pleased with them… painted the mud walls (like the attachment picture), bought a hammock for inside, so we will be OK if it rains now, and all in all, other than that we need to tidy up outside, the hut is finished… It looks just like our picture… Mike… it is the best mud hut I have ever seen… I simply love it..!!!

Have you thought of a better name for our hut???… Do we both like the `M & M's LOVE SHACK` suggestion? Because now we need to make our wood carving of the name to go over the door…

So we have watched the sunset from outside our hut… beautiful… paradise… cuddled up close together… me sitting between your legs, leaning my back against you, my head on your shoulder, and your arms around me… I can feel your heart beating against my back… I can hear you breathing against my ear… Oh Mike, just being this close to you touches the depths of my soul… I just love you so much… nothing could be better than being right here with you… And once the sunset turns to the darkness of night, you say it must be time to 'christen our hut'… Mmmm I like the sound of this… but you jump up and say I have to go hide behind a palm tree a little way away, and count to 1300… out loud so you can hear me… and I must not peep… you make me put my hands over my eyes… Mike what are you up to now???… Into the hut you go… and I am counting… and waiting… I can hear you laughing…

But, to my surprise before I reach 1300 back you come, with two drinks… Two large glass full of Southern Comfort and lemonade, with lots of ice… Oh yummy… you sit down next to me and we drink them… then you hand me your glass and tell me to carry it with my own… and scoop me up into your arms to carry me…!!! Do you know what? ~ I don't even complain… I must have mellowed in my old age… Carry me across the threshold, you claim… and that is exactly what you do… Oh Mike, when we get inside you have lit all the candles (13 of course) which are all in little lanterns, so we never burn our roof down… and it looks absolutely beautiful… Oh Mike… Soooooooooooo Romantic … You put me down, take the glasses from me and refill them, and put them next to our hammock… Back you come to me, with a very smouldering look in your eyes… kiss me gently, so gently on the lips… and very slowly and seductively you remove the few clothes I have on… then wiggle out of your shorts (the only thing you have on), and with one foot toss them out of the open doors… they land in a palm tree!!!… Oh no… I can tell you have the devil in you… you pick me up and put me in the hammock… give me another very sexy kiss… but then you start to laugh and get naughty… you tell me to close my eyes… with one hand you take hold of both my wrists and put my arms and hands above my head, and hold them there… and then… you get the ice from the glasses, and start to run an ice cube around one of my nipples… Oh Mike… I am screaming with laughter… please no… it is too cold… Sssshhhhh, you say… and with the same ice cube all around that boob… you get another ice cube, and do the same thing to the other nipple and boob… OMG… I am really laughing, but begging you to stop, because it is so cold… when I say, you have frozen my nipples and I won't be able to feel a thing now… on one nipple your hot mouth goes… flicking your hot tongue across it, sucking with your lips… I am squealing… you are delighted, because you say these are the biggest American hard gums ever… and so tasty…… you have never had hard gums this flavour… Southern Comfort, ice and Michelle flavour… yummy!!! you are shouting!!!… more ice, and more hot tongue and lips on the other boob… you are driving me crazy Mike… and just when I think I have got used to the pleasure and torture of it all… you get more ice… and run it right down my tummy, and straight to my hot-spot… OMG MIKE!!! that really is torture… too cold!!!… and then your hot tongue is on me… Mike, what are you doing to me?… I am sensations everywhere… more ice…

more tongue... and you bring me to a wonderful climax with that expert tongue of yours...

I am only brought back to my senses, by hearing you say, "Michelle you greedy girl, you didn't wait for me"... and then you are in the hammock with me... you are in me... you have slipped your hot rod gently inside of my love tunnel... and your lips are on mine... and you make the most wonderful gentle love to me... gentle... sensual... sexy... romantic... and this time we climax together ~ in a wonderful world of love and sensations of one another... completely lost in one another... the doors of our hut are open, and a cool breeze blows gently in from the sea... You hold me close, so close and tight in your arms; you are still kissing me, and say... "Mrs Turner ~ I hope you like your new home... and... I hope you liked the christening of it"...

Oh Mike yes...
I love our new home...
I loved the christening of it...
and most of all...
I LOVE YOU

Michelle
Xxx xxx xxx xxx x

PS... I love you... more than anything else in the whole world..!!! And the loveliest feeling I have ever had inside of me is... in my heart and in my head being married to you...

CHAPTER NINE

3 September 2012 ~ Live Interactive Text

Michelle: Hi Mr Turner... I am just sending some e-mails, I have my Skype turned on... and you `POP UP`

Mike: Well hello Michelle Turner... You will surely need some sun lotion on today!

Michelle: I sure do... are you offering?

Mike: Yes please, I want to smother your body all over, especially the bits that do not get much daylight... I like the way you say, "And up you pop" ☺

Michelle: Well start on me with the lotion... and I'm sure you will 'pop up' again. ☺

Mike: Naughty us!!! You must stop playing down there!!!

Michelle: My cyber husband 'IS' feeling sexy today...

Mike: Mmmm... Well I need to keep you satisfied.

Michelle: WOW... I like that... I am quite hungry at the moment...

Mike: Yes I can tell... You are like a lion waiting for its prey! Wanting and hungry... for love?

Michelle: Oh... I would never pounce unless you wanted me too...

Mike: OMG... Do not pounce on me, you may not hit the right target first time.

Michelle: I always hit the target Mike...

Mike: Painful... If you miss. ☺

Michelle: I won't miss... And, I am always gentle to start with. ☺

Mike: Yes I am sure you are gentle at first and then pick up speed and bonk away. You like being on top with your prey underneath you, eh!!! ☺

Michelle: Look I will show you… I will just stand in front of you… not touch you… but then so, so gently run my fingertips down the sides of your face… and then so, so gently touch your lips with mine…

Mike: Oh my Michelle… you are outrageously flirtatious… and I love this in you… for sure my lips would touch yours… and my hands would wander all over your sinuously curvy body.

Michelle: Wow… your hands all over my curves!! MMMmmmm nice… and you my darling are such an aphrodisiac… and like no other!

Mike: MMMmmmm… Sounds good to me. So one touch and one kiss… is that on the slate then?

Michelle: Do you want it on the slate?

Mike: Well I have never tried 'it' on a slate before, it could be a bit hard on the back. A bed or even the ground would be far better and more comfortable than on slate. ☺ What about we have a bonk bed for bonking?

Michelle: ☺ A bonk bed… good one!! Well… I am one for variety… but I have never tried on the slate either… or in a hammock until recently in this cyber world with you…

Mike: Well you are hungry… so why not try the lot?

Michelle: Then you will say I am being greedy ☺

Mike: Have I told you… I love you?

Michelle: Have I told you… I love you more?

Mike: You know that is impossible!!!

Michelle: No… it is not…

Mike: I will love you like you have never been loved before… Well, maybe not quite true… We both loved one another like there was no tomorrow when we were in the Cotswold`s together!

Michelle: I love you darling… REALLY love you…

Mike: "DITTO"

Mike: I must go… Bye and see you soon. Love always…

Michelle: Bye darling… see you soon

Mike: Bye now.

Michelle: Bye

Mike: Byeeee

Michelle: Byeeee

Mike: You know I like to look at your pictures, so I have taken some more pictures on my webcam of you and I have a favourite one!

Michelle: Oh dear... which one?

Mike: I cannot describe it here...

Michelle: Please send me one of you... and the one you are talking about, of me... please... come on you have lots of me now... I only have two of you... PLEASE...

Mike: Hummm!!... I will see?

Michelle: Please... Mwah

Mike: You always could get around me with a kiss... I will take one of me on my webcam later, and send it to you.

Michelle: Thank you...... mwah...

Mike: Byeeeeeeeeeeeeeeeeeeeeeeeee

Michelle: Bye darling......... mwah... nice to find you here this evening......

Mike: Byeeeeeeee

Michelle: Bye... and "DITTO"

Mike: "DITTO" = I love you... little Ditto is your lucky charm... he is a very cute little clown, with a smiley face... he probably smiles all the time, because he hangs off that long chain, and sits so snugly between your boobs... He is a lucky little sod ☺

Michelle: He is happy... and he is as lucky as ever... I love him...... he is my little part of you... that's why I love him...

Mike: You know I am very jealous!!!

Michelle: What can I say to that?... You bought him for me... come and meet up with him one day!!!

Mike: This is so tempting Michelle... But... We need to talk about this...

Michelle: OK... talk.

Mike: It is probably easier to discuss this on the phone...

Michelle: OK darling, we will talk about it soon. We both really need to go now.

Mike: For sure... Bye for now darling.

Michelle: Byeeeee... Mwaaaaaaaaaaaaaaaaaaaaaaaaah

E-mail from: Mike
To: Michelle
Date: 3 September 2012
Subject: Thank You

Hi Michelle

Thank you for the e-card... It was lovely to just let your mind wander and think I was there with you. How wonderful that would be if we were truly there together, eh!! Like someone would say to me, "This is truly like heaven on earth." No prizes for who this was of course! I love you and I still remember so much about `us`. Thank you for just being `you`.

Yes, our cyber world which we have made our home and it feels so good. Good, because after a long time I now feel close to you again and here we can say and express our feelings openly. No, it is not the same has being real, but it is second best, plus I can see you for real when we are on cam together. I miss you and I love you.

One touch... one kiss... I think that would be like lighting a short fuse because I know for certain that would set my heart racing and I know we both have the same feelings. Since we have had this cyber world you are always on my mind. Yes, this was a long time ago, and yes so often I have thought of you since then. I am glad this brings us together and maybe your Mum knew something that we would never foresee.

I do wonder about the pictures we have of one another? Should we keep pictures of each other? We need to maintain our anonymity. But, there again, if anyone managed to access either of our e-mail addresses that we use purely for one another we would be in serious trouble anyway... Oh sod it... Let's keep the pictures!

Love always...

Mike xxx

Michelle: Morning... mwah... mwah... mwah... MMMmmmm my delicious husband...

Mike: Good morning Michelle... Have you not had breakfast yet, or do you want to eat me? This must be that lion instinct in you!!

Michelle: I've had my fruit... so I guess I could start on the main course now... ☺ yes... that would be 'YOU'...

Mike: Oh... Well only toast for me this morning, no fruit I am told? I will have to make up for this somehow! Maybe I can share your fruit?

Michelle: See what you think of this for breakfast... my hands gently placed each side of your face... and a nice gentle kiss... then a very sexy kiss... and my body pressed close up against you... come and share my melon then ☺

Mike: Wooooooooooooooooooooow... I love your melons... Yes Please!!!

Michelle: Yes plenty here... ☺

Mike: It was melons and not melon... You know I want to have both melons to play with and build up energy ☺

Michelle: Both melons pressed hard against your chest......

Mike: Nice and juicy those melons. Nice and squeezy and I love it.

Michelle: Oh... and a bonus... nice hard nipples pressed right into your chest... cuddle me tight.

Mike: MMMmmmm... I am coming over there now, so look out.

Michelle: Soft, tender and very juicy melons...

Mike: I want to feel them now!!

Michelle: I would like a nice cuddle with you right now... with your arms around me... MMMmmmm... my arms around you... MMMmmmmm...

Michelle: And nice sensual kisses... MMMmmmmm...

Mike: Do you know, I remember having my hands down your bra once and I was caressing those melons, but when I tried to get my hand out I can remember it was a bit difficult... why you may think?? Well I was trying to get my hand out over those long hard nipples which were sticking out so proud!!!!

Michelle: That's because you get them so aroused!!! They love your touch...

Mike: MMMmmmm Michelle... the sensations you give me are phenomenal... But, for now I must go... Bye... I love you...

Michelle: Thank you for the lovely e-mail...

Mikes: Thank you for being YOU!!!

Michelle: Bye darling... I love you

Later that day...

Mike: You know I do not like quickies... But just to say "I LOVE YOU"... but I cannot stay long. Cheryl is due home any minute.

Michelle: Oh wow... it's my instant pop-up husband...

Mike: Well, if you will insist on playing with my crown jewels it can only be your fault...

Michelle: When I got home from work at 4pm... I decided to have a shower and get changed... and in the shower I realised something and thought of you!!!

Mike: Really? It was me that was missing?

Michelle: My topiary heart needs a trim please. ☺

Mike: Yes no probs... short trim all over!!!

Michelle: Whatever you think it needs...

Mike: It needs a good...

Michelle: But I will keep the heart shape, please... oooohh a good what?

Mike: You know what!!!

Michelle: What???

Mike: My pop-up belongs there!!!

Michelle: You are right... it does... ☺

Mike: Must go... Bye.

Michelle: Bye darling...

Mike signs out... Michelle types him a message for next time they are both online to read...

Michelle Yes... a little trim please... I promise to keep very still whilst you do it... I am going to keep this little topiary heart, because I like it so much... Now be careful not to touch my hot spot because you know you will drive me crazy... well not unless you are going to make love to me after you have finished the trim... MMMmmmmm what a thought!!! I love you ~ Mike Turner

Michelle: I love this cyber world with you… I love being virtually married to you… I love being on honeymoon in the Seychelles with you…

E-mail from: Mike
To: Michelle
Date: 4 September 2012
Subject: Topiary heart shape

Hi Michelle

So you have just come out of the shower and you think your precious little heart down there in between your legs needs a little topiary trim, eh! No probs!!! So just lay back on the bed and drop that towel and open your legs wide for me. I promise I will be gentle with you and this will not only look great, but you will feel great by the time I have finished with you my darling!!

Out comes my little topiary scissors and yes, I can see it does need a little trim!!… I could find it hard to find that hot spot otherwise in amongst the bush without some little trimming up!!

Legs nice and wide apart and yes a snip, snip here and a snip, snip there. I will need to push my fingers around there a bit to make sure I do not clip anything else and make sure I just clip and shape your little topiary heart. Nice little gentle fingers around and around. You know to get a nice true cut; it should be a bit wet!! So yes you guessed it, my tongue will just moisten it up a little for you. Licking and parting the sensitive tissue… Nice lots of licks… MMMmmmm… Yummy, yummy, looks nice and tastes so nice!! MMMmmmm… I need to just part your vagina (sorry I mean the lips to that love tunnel of yours… Oh this must be the bit they call the valley of love). I just need to get to the edges and give that a little snip, snip!! Oh!!… Your hot spot looks nice now with some neat trimming and much less bush there having given your heart some shape.. I just need to get the shape of the heart right and I will be finished soon, well not quite yet!!… snip, snip and yes that is coming good.

OMG… Michelle where I have been moving my fingers around your hot spot, you are also coming good!! This has got you so sexcited!! It is masturbation time and you love this!!... But you are playing with me and my pop up has just done that... popped up!!! You are screaming "Hang On," so I grab your lovely melons and do just that... Those nipples are so long and hard and not only do they look good but they feel good!!

Well I think it is time to give you a treat, after all your topiary heart is looking so good now and the final bit is making you feel good too. So with legs still wide apart let me ruffle your topiary heart and see if it is still looking in good shape. Yes, just perfect if I say so myself and what a good job I have done on it for you!! I think I need to get it wetter, inside now, yes all the way in and you are shouting Mike that feels so lovely when you do this to me...

To be continued... (BY YOU)...

Love always...
Mike xxx

---

5 September 2012 ~ Live Interactive Text

Michelle: WOW..!!! NICE e-mail Mike... My topiary heart, and hot spot are throbbing just reading it... and my nipples are standing to attention..!!! I look forward to the 'to be continued'... are you sure you want me to continue, you were making such a good job there?

Mike: Hi Michelle... OMG... hang on I have some reading to do here.

Michelle: NICE e-mail... thank you...... what a lovely topiary heart shape you have given me.

Mike: I did a go job, eh. Yes my fingers moved a lot around there whilst trimming and this got you 'sexcited' for sure. I did of course do a bit more than necessary with my finger work whilst I had the opportunity, and you just laid back and loved it.

Michelle: Oh WOW... I enjoyed it for sure... MMMmmmm So nice...

Mike: Bye now and enjoy your day and take care.

Michelle: Yes, I have to go now... see you soon... Mwah

Mike: Make sure you have put your knickers on too.

Mike: Bye

Michelle: I have them on... Byeeeeeeeee

Later that day...

Mike: Hi Michelle... How's your day been? It is hot today, and maybe you need a cool shower? Well here I am? I will share a shower with you and then I can give you a nice rub down afterwards or something!!

Michelle: Hi there. Wow... come on then...

Mike: How do you know my name is `there`?! ☺

Michelle: You are a cheeky monkey... ☺

Mike: Can you use the video cam now?

Michelle: I cam... if you cam ☺

They video link, and talk for half an hour... then revert back to text.

Mike: Wow... I have just scanned through the pictures that I have just taken of you... and do you know what? You are lovely and not changed a bit!!!

Michelle: I wish I could take pictures of you on my computer, but it will not ☹

Mike: I'm glad I can take them of you... Well maybe one change that is all???

Michelle: Maybe just 20 years older!!!

Mike: No.. that is not it... You now have a topiary heart... ☺

Michelle: Well, I am pleased you cannot see it in your photo`s... for one I am fully clothed, and for another thing, you can only see me from the waist upwards

Mike: Well... I have a very good imagination.

Michelle: I know you do...

Mike: I love you!!!

Michelle: And, you know that I love you... I know we were just talking about the possibility of meeting up, but I am not sure about coming to where you work... I know you said to me, come on a day that your secretary is off, and nobody will even know I am there... But...

Mike: Well, I am just thinking once you are in my office, that is it... Nobody will see us together... we will think about it...

Michelle: So tempting darling... I loved talking to you today; you make me laugh so much.

Mike: I tell you what; we would both die laughing if we were together all the time.

Michelle: Yes you could be right... but it is better than being old miseries...

Mike: Sure... It is better than any medicine!!!

Michelle: It certainly is... you make me happy, and you make me smile.

Mike: Good, and you do the same for me. Really we are so much alike in many ways and we have the same thoughts and feelings.

Michelle: We have always enjoyed one another that is for sure...

Mike: Yes... you are right... and we are alike in many ways...

Michelle: And although we are now limited to a virtual cyber world... we still enjoy one another.

Mike: That is for sure my darling. I have to go now. But, I may be able to get back on here in an hour, if you can? If not, I will e-mail you and send you some of these pictures... You know the best pictures are always when someone is not expecting them to be taken. Yes, for once I have my own way now and can take your picture whenever I want too. Is that fair you say... ☺

Michelle: You cheeky little monkey... I will pay you back... ☺

Mike: Mmmmm... Another entry on the slate, eh!

Michelle: I will leave this Skype on for a while, as I have some e-mails to send anyway... and one to you...... OK on the slate we have...

Michelle: A sexxxxy sensual kiss for you...

Mike: What happened to the one touch bit?

Michelle: Was that 'one touch, one kiss'?

Mike: Yes.

Michelle: OK... add that as well...

Mike: Maybe I should have my hands behind my back otherwise!!!

Michelle: OOOOhhhhhh I could do anything to you then!!!

Mike: Yes you could... and would for sure.

Michelle: Your crown jewels would get it for sure... ☺

Mike: I am yours anyway, so go ahead and do what you like to me... ☺

Michelle: Wow... OK... I will continue in an e-mail later... "You will get it then"

Mike: Okay my lovely passionate gorgeous wife.

Michelle: I love you husband... catch this very long lingering and smouldering kiss... MMMmmwwwaaaaaaaaaaahhhhhhhhhhh

Mike: I am looking forward to what... "You will get it then", really means.

Michelle: You know what "it" means... ☺

Mike: Stop it you... I want "it" for real...

Michelle: You will get it from me later...

Mike: Yes Please... I am sure I will love it from you ☺

Michelle: Did you like the e-mail with ice cubes in??

Mike: Yesssss... OMG... I can just imagine your nipples looking like long icicles.

Michelle: Do you know what?

Mike: What?

Michelle: I would love a really sexy kiss with you right now...

Mike: Well that sounds good and can you describe to me a "sexy kiss"?

Michelle: Well... it may start with a little gentle butterfly kiss, barely touching... and then when I have got the taste for you... long, deep, meaningful, loving and passionate, my lips firmly pressed against yours, my body pressed firmly against yours...

Mike: Yes, I like this.

Michelle: I remember these kisses with you Mike...

Mike: MMMmmmm... Me too Michelle... I remember your kisses

Michelle: You still make me feel now, like I felt about you then... you melt me from the inside out...

Mike: Sorry Michelle...I must go now... Bye.

Michelle: Bye darling... I will leave this on for a while.

An hour later...

Michelle: Hey are you back?... Yippy!!

Mike: Yes... and I am downloading your pictures! Watch the screen and you will appear.

Michelle: OK... I'm ready

Michelle: MIKE..!!! Just you wait... I am going to pay you back for this, you monkey......

Mike: ☺ ANOTHER SLATE ENTRY!!!

Michelle: This is not fair that you can take pictures of me... and I cannot do the same of you, please send me some of you today...

Mike: I must finish downloading them... Go and have a coffee for a minute.

Michelle: Ok... coffee... do you want one? white, no sugar... milk not cream, I still remember how you like your coffee.

Mike: We still remember so many details about one another...

5 minutes later...

Mike: OK... all pictures downloaded now, on my computer, I will e-mail them to you later, and delete them from my computer, as we have said before, safer to keep as e-mails... where nobody else should ever see them.

Michelle: OK darling

Mike: Can we go over to video link?

Michelle: Not with your family there...

Mike: Gone out.

Michelle: I don't believe you

Mike: Honest... But I can't be long, only for a few minutes.

Michelle: Promise me you are there on your own.

Mike: I promise

Michelle: Hummm...???

Mike: Come on, you

Michelle: OK

They video link, and talk for 15 minutes... then say goodbye by text

Mike: Don't forget to finish the email about your topiary heart... Byeeeee

Michelle: OK... will do... Byeeeee

E-mail from: Michelle
To: Mike
Date: 5 September 2012
Subject: Topiary heart shape cont/…

Hi Mike

OH WOW!!… what a fantastic topiary job you have done with this heart shape… How patient you were with a little snip snip here, and a little snip snip there to achieve perfectly the right shape… How gentle your fingers were when you rubbed them gently around and around… yes, you truly have me 'sexcited' now… And, I surely would indeed have been playing with your crown jewels whilst all this was going on… and indeed you have popped up… So you gently slide your hot rod into my love tunnel…

To be continued… you say…

But back out you take it… and holding onto your hot rod with one hand… you say, point to where you want this to go Michelle… so I point with one finger to my hot spot… and with your hand you guide your hot rod up to my hot spot, trailing my skin all the way and not losing contact, you circle my hot spot with the tip of your rod… Oh wow… nice… you lean down and kiss me, just gentle little butterfly kisses on my lips… Oh Mike… so nice… and then you breathe the words onto my lips with your kisses, and say, where next Michelle? My topiary heart, I whisper… and with your hand you guide the tip of your hot rod all around the edge of the lovely little heart you have made… Oh my God… I am in heaven here Mike… and then you say, "Again Michelle?… do you want me to do all of that again?"… This time I only manage "MMMmmmm," as you are kissing me once more… and you guide your hot rod around my topiary heart once more… rub it quite firmly against my hot spot… and then down to my love tunnel... slide it in further this time than you did last, and leave it there longer, but then slowly take it back out… and slide it up to my hot spot again, circle my hot spot again, I can feel little beads of love juice coming from the tip of your hot rod… OMG… and then you circle the topiary heart again… Oh my God Mike… this 'is' heaven on earth… then you lean down and suck one of my nipples really quite hard, because you say, it is standing up so proud of itself... and then the other... What next? you ask me...

Come right inside of my love tunnel Mike... and give me all of your loving... So this is exactly what you do... slowly and gently slide your hot rod inside of me... right inside of me... deep, deep inside... I squeeze you from inside of me... tightly squeeze... I close my legs tight, so I can feel you even better... you are so hard and thick... and you are so deep inside me now, I can feel your hot rod throbbing... Oh Mike... I love you here inside of me... you kiss me, deep, hard and passionately... I am lost here with you right now Mike... lost in your kisses... lost in your love making... right now you are the centre of my world... and I am the centre of yours, where nothing else matters, nobody else matters... `Just us`... and slowly you move in and out of me... our movements matching one another, my hands all over your back, my hands on your bum... MMMmmmm nice... one of your hands caressing my boobs... and you pick up the pace, and are thrusting quite hard now... Oh Mike... Oh Mike... deep and hard you are penetrating me... so deep inside... hard and fast... fast and furious... your breathing is rapid... and then you are yelling, "Come on Michelle"... Oh My God... I love you so much when you are this sexy and hot... An orgasm is brewing like a storm inside of me, everything tightened and clenched, squeezing... I feel your love juices start to pump inside of me... and yes, you know what this will always do... I climax with you... My head is floating... my body is exploding with sensational feelings of you... my heart is pumping fast... I am hot... Oh wow... Exquisite pleasure!!!... You collapse on top of me... your heart is racing... you are hot... I run my fingers through your hair, which is now damp... and kiss you... I look into your eyes... and in there I can see the love we share... we say nothing... we just look at one another... So much love... we stay like this for a while, while our bodies begin to slow down and cool down.

You roll off of me... lay beside me... and pull me close to you... cuddle me right up to you... you kiss my hair, and stroke my shoulders gently with the tips of your fingers... my boobs are laying on your chest... our hearts are so close together, and still they are both beating fast... and you whisper to me, "Michelle

Turner ~ I love you"… I hug you even tighter and say to you, "Mike Turner ~ Ditto"…

I hope you read this at bedtime… hold me in your arms like this tonight… I will think of you when I go to bed, and maybe we will share the same dream…

I Love You ~ Mike
Nice to see you today
Michelle
Xxx xxx xxx xxx x

---

6 September 2012 ~ Live Interactive Text

Michelle: Hi Mr Pop-Up… I was not expecting you here today!!! What are you doing here?

Mike: I am chatting with my favourite person.

Michelle: WOW… your favourite?

Mike: My favourite!!!… and you call me a pop-up little monkey, eh!

Michelle: Indeed you are… I am just typing you an e-mail…

Mike: Did you think my captions on your pictures fitted the photo of you. ☺

Michelle: OH YES… very funny…

Mike: Especially the "I am ignoring you, look"… ☺

Michelle: No wonder you were laughing so much… you were laughing 'at me' not 'with me'…

Mike: Never at you… Always with you… I love those photos of you… and… I love you.

Michelle: Do you know something?... I Love You, too

Mike: You're lovely… you are lucky I cannot get my hands on you!!!!

Michelle: MMMmmmm… if only you could is what I am thinking now!!!

Mike: Touch technology is improving all the time.

Michelle: I only like the real thing!!!

Mike: Greedy like me, eh!

Michelle: We are the same

Michelle: I want to feel your hands… your body… 'YOU'

Mike: MMMmmmm... I wish.

Michelle: MMMmmmm... Me too...

Mike: That wishing well is not working too well?

Michelle: Did you make a wish then?

Mike: I thought you had £13 pounds worth of wishes for me?

Michelle: Oh well... you will have to tell me when to throw another penny in for you... and make you a wish... Have you got one now?

Mike: We are the same, so your wish will be mine.

Michelle: You have to tell me to be sure...

Mike: I am sure we wish for the same things.

Michelle: If you made a wish right now, what would it be?

Mike: I would wish for a real kiss...

Michelle: Me too ☹

Mike: Will it only ever be on our webcam?

Michelle: Nooooo... I want a real kiss with you,

Mike: I thought you would say this...... I think the same...

Michelle: We are naughty then...

Michelle: So describe me a sexy kiss...

Mike: A sexy kiss... it has to be all over body kisses. Starting and ending everywhere!!!

Michelle: WOW... where are you starting?

Mike: Well starting down the neck with lots of little kisses to put some shivers down your spine.

Michelle: Oh wow... nice...

Mike: All round the sides of your neck... the front of your neck... the back of your neck... and you can feel nice tingles.

Michelle: MMMmmmmm... nice tingles... SENSUAL AND SEXXXXY

Mike: Slowly moving around and to the cheeks on your face.

Michelle: Oh nice Mike...

Mike: Then across to those lovely lips that I want to taste again so much.

Michelle: OH Mike!!!... so, so nice...

Mike: But then... sexy kisses means I need to remove all your clothing to get to those places where you need kissing.

Michelle: OK... well remove them nice and slowly... with kisses everywhere you uncover!!!

Mike: Okay... Do I have a head start?... Did you remember to put your knickers on this morning?

Michelle: Yes... sorry, I did...

Mike: Oh... Okay! And are you wearing a bra now?

Michelle: Yes... and a top...

Mike: OMG... You could have made it easy for me.

Michelle: Sorry!! ☺

Mike: You will be!!!

Michelle: I'll help and seductively remove my top for you... so now I only have a black lacy bra on the top half...

Mike: So first arms up and let me take this top off.

Mike: Who is doing this, me or you? ☺

Michelle: I'm doing you a sexy little dance here, there is a record on the radio I like...

Mike: Okay... Do I have to unzip a skirt?

Michelle: Yes... whoops!!!!... it's fallen to the floor now...

Mike: Okay... Unzipped and you wiggle out of it and it drops to the floor and you step out of it.

Mike: Will you wait for me!!!

Michelle: You are really making me laugh here...

Mike: You are getting too 'sexcited' now.

Michelle: Ok... I'm standing still now... just looking at you...

Mike: Okay so are we down to panties and bra now.

Michelle: Yes... both black and lacy...

Mike: MMMmmmm... My Michelle, you are always sexy and provocative... Okay... just a one-hand flick and your bra is open and you have just bounced out!!! Wow... Nice melons here.

Michelle: Carry on... all yours!!!

Mike: Yes they are gorgeous and I have not even kissed them yet, but I will.

Michelle: MMMmmmm I can't wait...

Mike: Okay... Panties next... hands down your bum and I am just wiggling them down.

Michelle: NICE..!!! I like your hands on my bum...

Mike: Yes, down they fall to the floor and you flick them off and where do they go? Yes, on the door handle.

Michelle: ☺ Good shot... I'll pick them up later...

Mike: I am now just looking and admiring my topiary work... nice and neat. I made a good job there!!!

Michelle: Now look what has happened... my nipples are sticking right out... OOOhhhhhh yes... very nice topiary work... you did do a good job there...

Mike: Okay... I think I had better continue now.

Michelle: OK...

Mike: Yes those nipples are tempting, so I will give them nice kisses.

Michelle: MMMmmmmm... nice... I love it when you do that...

Mike: Yes sticking out so far they are half way down my throat now.

Michelle: Oh... Don't choke on them darling...

Mike: OMG... It is heaven having your tonsils touched with nipples.

Michelle: Oh darling, you are so funny sometimes... ☺

Mike: I love them and I can never enough of those nipples and boobs.

Michelle: I love you touching my boobs and nipples... and kissing them... and sucking them..

Mike: I will not be able to eat my dinner later... I will just say, I am full up thanks... I have been feasting on my Michelle's boobs and nipples...

Michelle: I am really laughing now... I hope you are being quiet there, and not going to get yourself into trouble? And, talking of dinner, I have to go now, and get dinner going; Simon will be home in about 15-20 minutes.

Mike: You cannot go anywhere Michelle... my teeth are around your nipples!!

Michelle: I hope you are being gentle with them... although I did always like it when you gave them gentle little tugs with your teeth... OMG... I am getting myself all 'SEXCITED' here remembering the way you used to do this to me.

Mike: Well Michelle... Maybe one day I will do this again... For Real? Byeeeeeeeeeeeeee

Michelle: ☺ I might keep you to that... Byeeeeeeeeeee

Mike: Good morning sleepy head. Where are you? You are not online yet?

Mike: Having breakfast, having coffee or in the shower??

Mike: I am here early, and you are not around and know where to be seen. I know… you are now saying, how would I know? I am just missing you and I need your loving…

Mike: I have left a message on Yahoo… But you are not there, but showing to be online… What are you doing my darling?… I need you! If you are still in that shower, I want to be there with you.

Mike: Come on you, I need some loving from my sexy lovely Mrs Turner.

Michelle: Morning darling… wow… you are up early!!

Mike: Hello!!!!!!…… At last you are here!! So have you read my messages on Yahoo and Skype this morning? Or, was I just talking to myself again, eh!

Michelle: Why are you up so early this morning?

Mike: I could not sleep because of 'YOU'

Michelle: Are you OK?

Mike: Sure!

Michelle: I wish I could give you a hug… Right now… I want you…

Mike: I want you… and I need you… and one of your cuddles…

Michelle: Are you OK darling?

Mike: I am just missing you, that is all…

Michelle: I just want to hug you…

Mike: I have just one problem at the moment…

Michelle: What is that?

Mike: I want this hug you keep promising me!!

Michelle: I wish I could give you this hug…

Mike: MMMmmmmm… would be nice.

Michelle: I love you Mike… and I mean I really, really love you.

Mike: "DITTO"

Mike: Just in case you have forgotten…"DITTO" = I LOVE YOU… You know it always means this.

Michelle: Do you know, I never, ever, use that word to anyone else… not even in the sense of 'the same as'… because that

word only has one meaning for me...... and it is I LOVE YOU...
Mike Turner

Mike: I have missed not being able to live text you so much recently.

Michelle: Yes, I have missed you too... but we know we can only do this when our lives each allow this... nice to chat with you, I didn't expect to you to be here today.

Mike: I shouldn't be here really, Cheryl is downstairs...

Michelle: OK darling, maybe we should say goodbye for today...

Mike: I should really, but I just wanted to talk to you... well, text with you...

Michelle: I love you darling... Bye for now... speak soon.

Mike: I love you Michelle... Bye for now.

13 September 2012 ~ Live Interactive Text

Michelle: Hi darling.

Mike: Hi Michelle... I am going to DO YOU!

Michelle: WOW...!!! Really? Any particular reason?

Michelle: My God... this is a long reason!!! ☺

Mike: After this morning`s conversation on the telephone... with you saying you were cold and having to change your top because your nipples were hard and showing through your top. Yes... I bet they were sticking up like soldiers to attention. Then this afternoon I tested the new polish on my car you suggested... Yes brilliant and thank you... But then I read the instructions; it said shake it well... I was thinking of your boobs and shaking them well... Then it said use light circular movements and work it in well... OMG!! my mind was doing overtime... Then it says buff it up and get a perfect shine... Well, can I say any more?

Michelle: Oh Mike...... come and do me then!!! I will shake the bottle for you ~ you can watch... bouncy, bouncy, bouncy... and when it is all shook up enough... you can apply some nice massage oil to me... soft and gentle circular movements... and I will be in the buff whilst all of this is going on... ☺

Mike: It also said the surface must be clean and I am thinking Michelle needs a shower and good rubbing down first... and I want to do this for her

Michelle: OH WOW...... put this on the slate Mike...

Mike: Plenty of bubbles to get that body clean first... OMG!!

Michelle: Ohhhhh... I love it... YES PLEASE!!! Put this on the slate for sure...

Mike: Gosh... My mind was on your body, boobs and nipples... not my car

Michelle: Well... if I were helping you do this... by the time you get a really good finish on that car, you will see yourself as a reflection... so if I were there you would have boobs and nipples from all angles... ☺

Mike: But after plenty of rubbing and working in... It comes up perfect. So this is why I am going to DO YOU! My mind was just doing overtime thinking about you and your bodywork, boobs and nipples.

Michelle: OH WOW... I'm pleased you had something nice to think about for the afternoon. That kept you entertained whilst polishing that car of yours.

Mike: Did you feel my fingers doing circular movements on the end of your nipples?

Michelle: Well strangely enough I wondered what was happening to them.

Mike: I am sure they would not lay down after all that caressing.

Michelle: No they wouldn't... not with you giving them all that attention...

Mike: See... I cannot concentrate, even on the simplest task!!

Michelle: Put that one on the slate... I will look forward to this for real one day!!

Mike: You drive me crazy!!!

Mike: I need an official appointment... with you... OMG!!!

Michelle: As today is the 13th... I threw 2 x 1p in my wishing well this afternoon when I got home... a wish for you... and a wish for me... it was the same wish...

Mike: Okay... let me know if and when they come true.

Michelle: Do you want to know what they were?

Mike: No... If you tell they will not come true.

Michelle: But you would want to know, because you may be able to help make these wishes happen.

Mike: It should happen if that is the wish? If not, the fairy has not been listening...

Michelle: The wishes were... that I hope we will 'always' love each other as much as we do right now...

Mike: That is a certainty…

Michelle: I think so too…

Mike: When the little fairy came to me after you tossed the 2 pennies into the wishing well. She said to me: "What is your wish for today?" I replied… "Please take care of the person who's reading this message because I love her and she is very special and precious to me."

Michelle: You melt my heart Mike Turner… and I love you so very much…

Mike: Have I told you lately… I LOVE YOU!

Michelle: Ummmmm… I'm thinking…

Mike: What!!!

Michelle: ☺

Mike: You must be suffering from memory loss.

Michelle: ☺

Mike: I LOVE YOU and… I WILL ALWAYS LOVE YOU… Look at the time; we both need to go…… Bye

Michelle: I LOVE YOU… LOVE YOU… LOVE YOU

Michelle: Bye darling, nice to find you here…

Mike… My day is complete now…

Michelle: Mine too… mwah

Mike: Byeeeeeeeee… big hugs, kisses and cuddles

Michelle: A sexy smouldering kiss for your lips… Bye darling

Mike: I am going to collect that for real before much longer… Byeeeeee

Michelle: ☺

E-mail from: Michelle
To: Mike
Date: 15 September 2012
Subject: Polishing skills

Hi my darling

I could have come and helped you do your polishing today… had the most of the day to myself, as Simon has gone off to play golf for the day.

I hope you have managed to keep focused on the job in hand today!!! and your mind has not been wondering?

Love you loads
Michelle
Xxx xxx xxx xxx x

E-mail from: Mike
To: Michelle
Date: 16 September 2012
Subject: Re: Polishing skills

Hi Michelle

My hands focused on the job in hand for sure, but maybe my mind wondered just a little when I was gently doing those circular rubbing movements. I know it was talking about a car on the instructions, but… when it says the body should be clean before you start… OMG!!… I am thinking of a shower with you!!! Giving you a nice rub down and getting your body work squeaky clean all over. When it then says start with gentle circular movements around and around working with your fingers into the area!!… I am thinking of your lovely nipples!!… OMG!!… Then my mind really wandered and I am thinking??… Yes your `hot spot`. I know you like me running my fingers gently over that area!! Your lovely nipples are hard enough!!… So yes my mind was focused on the job in hand, but just one thing was different, it was on YOU!!

I love you… I love you today, I will love you tomorrow, I will love you forever!!

Have a nice Sunday…
Mike xxx

---

17 September 2012 ~ Live Interactive Text

Michelle: Morningmy sexy cyber husband… Very nice e-mail from you over the weekend… If I had known you were going to take such good care of all my body parts the way you do… all the polishing, rubbing, massaging, caressing… and the topiary!!! I would have married you long ago… Oh you do amuse me Mike… I love your sense of humour… Wake up sleepy head… I will have to plant lots of little kisses all over you to wake you… mwah… mwah… mwah… mwah… mwah… mwah… mwah… mwah…

Mike: Hi Michelle

Michelle: Hi Mike

Mike: Can I see you on cam? I will say if I am taking any pictures okay!!!

Michelle: Only if you are on your own, and only if you pre-warn me of clicking that button and taking my picture.

Mike: I will say if I am taking any pictures of you… promise.

Michelle: Before you take them… not after…

They video call one another, and chat for half an hour; Mike takes endless amounts of pictures of Michelle. Then they revert to text again.

Michelle: I AM GOING TO DOOOOOOOOOOOOOOO YOU!!!!!!!!!

Mike: Yes please!!!… Just tell me HOW… WHEN… and WHERE

Michelle: When I see you on this screen Mike Turner… my heart skip skips a beat…

Mike: When I see you on this screen I just want to jump out and hug you and kiss you.

Michelle: Yes… I would love that

Mike: When did you want to come and visit me at my office?

Michelle: WHAT?

Mike: I think he had something to do with early steam engines! ☺

Michelle: "Oh sod it," as my cyber husband would say… just make me an appointment, and let me know when it is!!!

Mike: Don't panic… You would say to me it will not happen???

Michelle: Never say never……

Mike: Okay… Just a maybe, eh!!

Michelle: Just a maybe…

Mike: Okay… But I want to see those blue eyes again for real…

Michelle: MMMmmmm…… Look into my blue eyes, and tell me what you see?

Mike: You saying… Now look into my blue eyes!!!

Mike: Hey… Stop it… you are reading my mind again.

Michelle: How do we always do that?

Mike: You are inside my head Michelle!!

Michelle: You can tell a lot about people from their eyes… let alone body language!!!

Mike: I am going to have to be careful with you; mind over matter is working here somewhere???

Michelle: Do you know the saying 'Jinx'?

Mike: Yes I do

Michelle: When two people saying the same thing at the same time, you both make a wish…

Mike: I think we have some telepathic communication… and I think our wish would be the same too

Michelle: Time for us to go… bye darling… nice to see you, talk to you, and text with you.

Mike: Byeeeeeeeee

Mike: Hang on!!!

Michelle: What to? not your 'crown jewels'……!!! ☺

Michelle: OH… YES… very nice crown jewels…

Mike: I have put a picture of you up now, can you see it… I love this Michelle Turner!

Michelle: Mike… you are naughty… but I do love you… Mmwah… Catch this… great big kiss…
Mwaaaaaaaaaaaaaaaaaaaaaaaaaaaaaaaaaaaaaaaaaaaaaaaaah

Mike: Got it… But I want it for real…

Michelle: So do I… One day this is going to happen!! One day soon!!! Byeeeeeeeee

Mike: You always like to tease me… Byeeeeeeeee

Michelle: You are always naughty… this is another thing we have in common!!!

Mike: You say catch this… Then you say "pop-up," so where was this kiss destined for, eh?

Michelle: Where would you like me to start?

Mike: I always like top to bottom.

Michelle: Always… I'll remember that… well the kiss starts on your lips then… I love those lips…

Michelle: Sexxxxy… yummy… scrummy…

Michelle: Then down to your neck... slow and gentle... Sensual.

Michelle: All around your neck... gentle little nibbles and sucking.

Michelle: MMMmmmm nice... you are so tasty!!

Michelle: Fingers undoing the buttons on your shirt... and with each button, one kiss on your chest...

Michelle: Are you still there? Have you fallen asleep?

Mike: I am here... Mesmerized by your kisses...

Michelle: I want a real hug with you...

Mike: Come on then... See you at 7pm.

Michelle: OK...... 7.00pm at yours... ☺ make sure you let me in... don't just panic and not open the door!!!

Michelle: Bye darling... see you at 7.00pm... and don't send me an e-mail saying I was only joking, when I am standing on your doorstep.

Mike: Not at my front door... but Michelle... we are going to meet up soon for sure. Bye darling... You drive me crazy!!

Michelle: Book me an appointment when your secretary is off... and let me know when it is...

Mike: Really?

Michelle: Really!!

Mike: Really... Really... Really???

Michelle: Really... Really... Really!!!

Mike: MMMmmmm... Okay?

Michelle: Ok... you just let me know when...

Mike: MMMmmmm... I suppose a Friday is best for you and me.

Michelle: A Friday then......

Mike: MMMmmm... Okay?

Michelle: I'll look forward to it......

Mike: So will I...

Mike: I love you...

Michelle: I love you Mike Turner... you touch my heart always...

Mike: I would love to feel that heartbeat next to mine...

Michelle: Bye darling

Mike: Bye darling... Mwah... I want to give you a kiss on the heart

Mike: "DITTO"

Michelle: "DITTO"

Mike: I just want to ask you a question.

Michelle: Yes...

Mike: If we do meet up... Will this set our hearts pumping and are emotions running high again? What will this really do to each of us?

Michelle: Don't they already at times? Will it be any different to everything we have each said to one another in text and e-mails?

Mike: Will this put our minds into over-drive?

Michelle: Or do we deserve this after such a long time?

Mike: I know, but look what happened after one Christmas kiss all those years ago?

Michelle: We fell in love... and the love is still there...

Mike: I am missing you!

Michelle: I am missing you... missing you because...... I love you

Mike: You know... I love you too, this long <------------------------------
----

--->

Michelle: WOW... that is a lot !!!

Mike: Yes more than 20 years` worth...

Michelle: You melt my heart Mike Turner... I love you.

Mike: I loved you for longer than this really... we had the slate going for a least a year before I stole that Christmas kiss!

Michelle: Yes, the slate was probably about a year long, if I recall... Maybe I just fancied you before this Christmas kiss... but... with that kiss you stole my heart.

Mike: Well I didn't mean too, it just happened.

Michelle: I didn't mean too... it just happened...

Michelle: But, it is done now... over the best, over the worst... and still we love one another. If we were to meet up... would we really feel any different than we do right now?

Mike: I don't know, that is why I asked you the question. Do you remember that Christmas... Our minds were not on Christmas for sure thereafter? I could not get you off my mind, every day I was thinking about YOU!!!

Michelle: I don't think we would feel any different than we do today darling… that is when we fell in love… a million words in e-mails this year have told us both that love has never died…

Mike: I know!

Michelle: So why would we feel any different? The love is there… After all those years, after all that happened, after all the problems it caused each of us… The love is still there.

Mike: When we chat on the phone, I felt something. When we decided to Skype I felt something more… and if we met I would feel something even more!

Michelle: I don't want to hurt you darling… that would never be my intention… if you don't really feel you want to, I understand… Truly…

Mike: What then? We are both greedy and want more?

Michelle: Let's just see what happens… just once…

Mike: Okay.

Michelle: I just want to feel your arms around me… and feel your love…

Mike: My heart is already pounding… can you hear it?

Michelle: I want to feel it… ☹

Mike: MMMmmmm… Let us put them both together and they can beat as one!

Michelle: I love you Mike Turner… Really, really love you.

Mike: "DITTO"… Speaking of which 'our little guy Ditto' will be jealous!!!

Michelle: He will have to come… I couldn't possibly do that without him!!!

Mike: So, I will get to see our little lucky charm again too.

Michelle: He is my little part of you, that is why I have carried with me so many times for all these years

Mike: Well, I suppose in a way I have adopted him. Only seems right that I should see him again after all these years!

Michelle: Yes, You are his DAD now

Mike: I gave him life… and what a life he has had down there, on that long chain, the lucky little sod!!!

Michelle: He is soooooooo pleased you bought him… and sooooo grateful for where he lives… thank you so much for buying him and giving him to me. He is my most treasured possession of all time.

Mike: I gave him the best home ever!!!

Michelle: Well maybe you would like to see him after such a long time?

Mike: What, down there in amongst your boobs?

Michelle: Well... that is where he lives!!

Mike: Would I ever find him down there? ☺

Michelle: I'm sure you could find him if you tried hard! ☺

Mike: MMMmmmm... Well I will not stir him too much.

Michelle: Maybe I could wear him on the outside... that way you won't be telling him off.

Mike: He will be fine down there, besides I would feel I am evicting him from his home. That is where he belongs and that is where he should stay. Wear him, if you come... we may need the luck!!!

Michelle: Exactly!!! He always looks after me... he will look after you too now...... since the day you became his DAD... Our virtual wedding day... 13th July 2012

Mike: I must go now... and you will get your eta See you soon... Love always... Here is your virtual kiss... Mwaaah... but maybe soon a real one?

Michelle: A real one would be so so nice... but for now Mwaaah... Bye

---

E-mail from: Michelle
To: Mike
Date: 19 September 2012
Subject: Two Hearts = One Love

Hello my darling

A love that we have shared for so long... yes, for more than 20 years... and is a very long time... and against all odds this love has stood the test of time. Other people have tried to destroy this love... Our life's circumstances should have destroyed this love... But our love has been so strong nothing has ever managed to destroy it...

This is a 'True Love' Mike, which will last in each of us forever more... Whatever the future holds, this love will always be there.

We both know that for sure now... I heard somewhere once, that if you love somebody enough, you will let go of them, and if they come back to you, the love will last forever... well this is 'us' my darling... We tried to let go, it broke both of our hearts... But, now we share this love as strong as we ever have.

When I have said you stole my heart, I can tell you, you have a bigger part of my heart than anyone else ever has... I don't give my love easily... but to give it to you was too easy... and still is... you are my special one!!!

I don't know if you will read this today?... or tomorrow?... But if I could go to bed with you tonight... I would lay my naked body next to yours... snuggle up so close to you... with your arms around me, I would gently kiss your lips... place a gentle loving kiss on your heart, place my hand on your heart, and let you feel all of my love... A love so strong... A love so deep... My body would be entwined with yours... my heart right next to yours... And we would sleep peacefully, engulfed in 'our love'...

Our two hearts = Our one love

Mike Turner ~ I love you, I will always love you...

Michelle
Xxx xxx xxx xxx x

---

19 September 2012 ~ Live Interactive Text

Mike: Hi my gorgeous Michelle... I love you... I need that hug now.

Michelle: Hello darling... I love you too.

Mike: I need that kiss now.

Mike: I need that touch now.

Mike: Come on you.. I want YOU!

Michelle: I wish I could give you that kiss and hug right now, come close to this screen and I will give you the kiss.

Mike: MMMmmmm... I need a real one now.

Michelle: My hands gently placed either side of your face, just gently touching you... a look into those very sexy brown eyes of yours... and then... my lips so gently placed on yours for a very gentle little kiss... full of all my love

Mike: Yes Please!!!

Michelle: Feel it right now... it's what I am doing to you... and then my arms around the back of your neck... and a really long loving kiss, so sensual on your lips.

Mike: You know real is always better.

Michelle: Feel my love Mike...

Mike: I know, but real is always better... but this is all we can do this morning...

Michelle: This is real darling, we are both here texting our love, feel my love for you now... it is so real.

Mike: I do all the time... when we text... when we see each other on video link... and one day when we touch for real again!

Michelle: Yes darling... that will be so nice... a real touch, a real kiss, a real hug...

Mike: Do you actually want to do this Michelle?

Michelle: I am really tempted, I can tell you.

Mike: MMMmmmm... Me too.

Michelle: Let's just think about it for now then darling... If it happens we both need to be 100% sure.

Mike: OK darling.

Michelle: I have to go now... see you here tomorrow... Mwah

Mike: Bye darling... take care.

---

20 September 2012 ~ Live Interactive Text

Mike: Hi Michelle

Michelle: Hi Mike

Mike: I have an important question for you

Michelle: What is that darling?

Mike: Have you thought about coming over to my office at work?

Michelle: Yes... I have thought quite a lot about it over the past couple of days.

Mike: Is this full proof or are we both mad here?

Michelle: What do you think?

Mike: I was asking you?

Michelle: We have planned what we would each say... to your work colleagues, the reason I am there as a potential client... If our other halves find out, I did not know it was you that worked there... You did not know it was me who had the appointment... until we saw one another.

Mike: What are you doing tomorrow (Friday), say in the afternoon around 2pm?

Michelle: Well, you know I have the day off.

Mike: My secretary is off tomorrow, and it could be a good day to go for it... If you decide, I have to advise security at reception... Give me a ring in the morning and we can decide yes or no then.

Michelle: OK darling...

Mike: I hope you have not collapsed on the floor now.

Michelle: My heart is pumping rather quickly at the moment...

Mike: Look... You do not have to, if you prefer not, and should we take this chance?

Michelle: I want to see you... I'll re-phrase that... I desperately want to see you.

Mike: Visitors report to the main reception and they then ring me to say. Then I would come down to collect you, as my secretary is off tomorrow. This is as safe as it will get there, and once in my office, we are alone.

Michelle: So do you want me to come?

Mike: You know this answer already; I would like to see you.

Michelle: I have the same reservations that you do... but... I would love to see you, if only briefly... and we have a pretty good plan here?

Mike: Well it would need to be like my normal appointments so it looks the same.

Michelle: Obviously we would both be innocent...

Mike: So just a greet and shake hands when we meet... no hugs or kisses okay!!!

Michelle: OK... ☺

Mike: But that will come later maybe!!! ☺

Michelle: But just wait until you shut your office door!!! ☺ OMG is there CCTV in your office?

Mike: No

Mike: Let us chat in the morning on the phone; I will phone you when I get into work… I must go now. Maybe I should order in a defibrillator… I think we both may need it.

Michelle: OK… have a good think overnight about this… we both have to be sure… I would love to see you… and I LOVE YOU…

Mike: Quite a few key members of staff are on holiday this week… work-wise the timing could not be better.

Michelle: So how long do clients usually stay with you for?

Mike: You can stay all night!!! ☺ But normally maybe 30–60 minutes, depending on their business… Maybe we should just have half an hour, not to be too greedy?

Michelle: OK…

Mike: I will phone you in the morning, say 9:15am if that is okay?

Michelle: That will be good…

Mike: Speak to you then… Two hearts doing overtime!!!

Michelle: Yes… and a sleepless night ahead for both of us

Mike: For sure!!! But we do not have to do this

Michelle: I know… see how we both feel in the morning?

Michelle: I have to go now… bye darling.

Mike: Bye darling, speak to you in the morning to decide.

E-mail from: Michelle
To: Mike
Date: 21 September 2012
Subject: Mr & Mrs Turner… together

Hi Mike

I cannot believe we have done this today!!!… Oh Mike, it was just so nice to actually see you, feel you, and touch you for real… To feel your arms around me after all these years. To feel your warm and loving kisses… OMG… I am just in heaven…

Well attached is a photo I will cherish FOREVER!!! A half hour of time I will cherish forever… I am so pleased I brought my camera along, and for the first time EVER we have a picture of just the two of us!! (even if we did take it ourselves.) I have attached the picture here as promised, deleted it from my camera, deleted it from my computer, it is now just in this e-mail for the two of us to see. Look at us Mike, we look so happy. We are both laughing, our eyes are sparkling... OMG we certainly bring out the best in one another.

Well, in and out of your office without a hitch... Let's hope neither of us has any repercussions from this... And if we do... Off to our mud hut we go...

You and I happy to see one another... One touch... One hug... 13 kisses... If we never do this again, I am so glad we plucked up the courage and did it today. The tenaciousness will always be there between us, I cannot see that we will ever really let go of one another now. We both know it is very dangerous for us to meet up, but our cyber world allows us so much expression to one another. We amuse one another for sure... We love one another for sure.

I LOVE YOU MIKE TURNER ~

I WILL ALWAYS LOVE YOU...... ALWAYS...
Michelle
Xxx xxx xxx xxx x

E-mail from: Mike
To: Michelle
Date: 21 September 2012
Subject: Re: Mr & Mrs Turner... Together

Hi Michelle

This is a nice picture of us together... What does it tell us in this picture? We are in love, we love each other and we are both very happy. I can remember your Mum saying to you once "They make a very nice couple," and I think if your Mum could see this picture today these words would be repeated.

Thank you for today and it was really nice to see you. Yes, a touch, a hug and a kiss and all the three wishes came true without any problems. I still have you on my mind. I thought this may happen after seeing you today, but it was a day where I felt your warm love again. A love that we have always shared for so many years.

I will always love you...
Mike xxx

E-mail from: Michelle
To: Mike
Date: 22 September 2012
Subject: Re: Mr & Mrs Turner... Together

Hi Mike

I am still thinking about you this morning... I kept waking up in the night, and thinking about seeing you yesterday... I'm glad we did it... so nice to see you... I just have one problem with it... It wasn't long enough...

Yes, a very nice picture of us!!! You are right my Mum did think we made a lovely couple, and we looked like we belonged together... she thought we had something very special... and she was right... I think we make a lovely couple... two peas in a pod.

I love you darling... I will always love you... My feelings towards you have not changed one single bit...

My love to you always and forever.
Michelle
Xxx xxx xxx xxx x

E-mail from: Mike
To: Michelle
Date: 23 September 2012
Subject: A wonderful 30 minute appointment with my Michelle

Hi Michelle

Thank you so much for letting me see you on Friday. It was so nice to have all three wishes, a touch, hugs and those kisses.

I have to be at work early tomorrow morning so I will not see you on Skype prior to you going to work, but I hope to see you later in the afternoon.

OMG... But there is a problem!!... I just could not get you out of my thoughts and mind, just like that Christmas many years ago!!... I was up during the night on Friday, just wide awake and I went downstairs and watched some TV for a while and then again Saturday, but this time even earlier and just thinking about you... Maybe tonight I will sleep without waking up!! Anyway, I am glad we did it and I am sure my mind will settle down when I am back to work and other things take over my mind.

I hope you are okay?... Love always...

Mike xxx

E-mail from: Michelle
To: Mike
Date: 24 September 2012
Subject: A wonderful 30 minutes with you darling

Hi Mike

Yes, so nice to see you darling... touch you... hugs with you... kisses with you... "I LOVE YOU"...

Friday night I kept waking up all night, just thinking about seeing you... Saturday I kept myself busy all day, but still you were on my mind... Went to a party Saturday evening, my Auntie's 80th birthday, at a social club, where there were plenty of cousins to catch up with, had a nice evening, and was OK there, until the band played 'our record'... quick exit to the loo for me... home about 1.00am Sunday... thought about you all the journey home, and again the record came on the car radio, this time Whitney singing it... OMG... my mind filled with you again... Oh how "I LOVE YOU"...

I slept better Saturday night... by the time I got up Sunday morning, I thought, did Friday afternoon really happen? Or was it just a dream?... I looked at the e-mail with the picture we took on Friday... Yes, it really happened... I'm glad we took the photo... I will treasure this photo, always... yes Mike Turner... "I LOVE YOU"...

Today work will be a good distraction for both of us... I am settling down a bit now... I hope you are too... You looked so good on Friday... You smelled so nice... You felt so good... I loved touching you... those kisses with you... I have no regrets that we did that... I'm glad we did it...

I WILL ALWAYS LOVE YOU
Michelle
Xxx xxx xxx xxx x

---

24 September 2012 ~ Live Interactive Text

Mike: Good afternoon my darling.

Michelle: Hi darling.

Mike: It was so good to see you on Friday... It certainly made the old adrenaline rush...

Michelle: It certainly was nice to see you darling, and for sure the old adrenaline was pumping. I am glad we took that photo, because I keep thinking now, did that really happen? Or was it just a dream? Then I have to open that e-mail and look at the photo... OMG it was real...

Mike: When you had left my office on Friday, I could smell you and taste you on my lips for hours!!

Michelle: Mike... You are soooo 'HOT'

Michelle: But, I know what you mean, because I could smell you on my skin and taste you on my lips afterwards too...

Mike: I am beginning to think I may need another appointment!

Michelle: Me too... BUT... we said we would not be greedy with this!!

Mike: Can I be fasttracked for an appointment with you if I say Michelle Turner is making me crazy? I am having sleepless nights now!!!!

Michelle: Mike... and you always say it is me who is greedy!!

Mike: I am having disallusions about someone called Ditto

Michelle: Our little Ditto said he loved seeing his daddy again.

Mike: How I would love to spend a night with you.

Michelle: For sure you would get nooooooooo sleep that night... But, you would get lots of loving...

Mike: I bet… Sexercise!

Michelle: The best form of medication you can get… nothing better…

Mike: For sure… It cures everything!!

Michelle: Mike…

Mike: Michelle…

Michelle: I want a cuddle now…

Mike: Come on then.

Michelle: I mean, I really want a cuddle now… and a little kiss…

Mike: That is two cuddles now?

Michelle: Make it 13… and 13 kisses… I want to feel your arms around me… my lips touching yours…

Mike: It was really nice to see you on Friday.

Michelle: Really nice, darling… it just wasn't long enough.

Mike: My heart was probably beating faster than normal and we are both greedy… But those 30 minutes was the best appointment I have had EVER!!!

Michelle: Me too…

Michelle: I LOVE YOU MIKE TURNER… WITH ALL MY HEART.

Mike: I have just cancelled my message; because I typed the same… Just stop doing this!!! This is scary!!!

Michelle: The same… `Jinx`… we both make a wish then…… one, two, three, make your wish… don't tell me…

Mike: I think we will make the same wish ☺

Michelle: Let's do it then… 1,2,3… Go

Mike: Done

Michelle: Done

Mike: We both need to go… see you soon

Michelle: Bye darling

---

25 September 2012 ~ Live Interactive Text

Michelle: Morning darling

Mike: Hi my gorgeous Michelle!!

Michelle: Did you sleep better last night?

Mike: No... not much.. I 'still' have you on my mind... Probably because I was downloading your pictures before I went to bed. You are right, I should not keep them on my computer, so I will do as you suggested... send them all to you by e-mail... that way they are only in our e-mail accounts, where nobody else can ever see them.

Mike: Only another 100 or so to do ☺

Michelle: Oh darling... I'm sorry...... you must be tired... so I have a solution...

Mike: WHAT? You are going to DO ME NOW?

Michelle: Well I am thinking you must be tired... and... it is chilly, windy, raining... and there is only one answer for this...

Mike: Solution = We both need to sleep together!!

Michelle: Yessssssssssssssssssssssssssss!!! snuggly cuddles...

Mike: MMMmmmmm... Michelle...

Michelle: Cuddled up warm and cosy with you...

Mike: I love you...

Michelle: Mike...

Michelle: I LOVE YOU.

Mike: Michelle...

Mike: I love you more

Mike: More and more each day.

Michelle: Impossible... for you to love me more... I love you more than...... ANYTHING...

Mike: I still love you more... ☺

Michelle: Bye darling... time for work... Mwahhhhhh

Mike: Bye My Michelle

Later that day.

Michelle: Hello Darling... we are both home early today...

Mike: This is a message for our little Ditto... I have spoken to Mummy about your headaches... Yes I can understand all the head banging that you must go through living down there in the valley between those twin peaks. I know it is sometimes like the peaks are going to squash you and I know you retaliate with the occasional kick-backs. Her heart does beat quickly like a drum when she gets sexcited and therefore I will have a word with her about this. Against this you are rent free and she does keep you warm nestled down there. I also understand you cannot breathe when she gets sexcited and then those twin peaks really start to bounce and shake... I will again have a word with her about this!!!

Michelle: Hee hee hee... you are as nutty as a fruit cake

Mike: You see... I told you... you have driven me completely CRAZY!!

Michelle: Is this cam?

Mike: Sure it is!

They video link for half an hour, then revert back to text.

Mike: I will send you these pictures later and I will delete the rest. Some I have sent you before so I have them in the email.

Michelle: OK darling... yes, that is what you should do... because if anyone else ever saw them?... you don't want to be packing your bags to move to the Seychelles with me just yet... DO YOU?

Mike: ☺

Michelle: Hummm... is that your cheeky little grin?

Mike: ☺ Sure is!!

Michelle: Do you know?...... I love you Mike Turner...

Mike: You are so lovely Michelle... and a woman who has loved me for so long now... and I just love you so much.

Michelle: I know you need to go now really, as you need to phone your secretary.

Mike: Yes, that is it!... You can be my `sexretary`

Michelle: WOW... I LOVE IT... when can I start? I will look forward to that...

Mike: You are so multi-skilled in so many ways. I think you could make love to me and do a thousand other jobs at the same time.

Michelle: OMG... I wouldn't want to... I would just be focused on you Mike Turner... My lover... My cyber husband...... My friend... My soul mate...

Mike: That's good... You will get plenty of job satisfaction and pleasure from your work that way. I love somebody who enjoys her work.

Michelle: Some jobs just need to be focused on... one at a time... and you are one of those... JUST YOU AND ME: no multi-tasking... just us...

Mike: I hope I can sleep tonight... Michelle, do not keep me awake all night tonight.

Michelle: Just lay your head on your pillow... and think that I am folded in your arms... we are completely naked, my boobs laying across your chest... hold me tight all night... and sleep.

Mike: Yes... That is how I like it... your boobs laying on my chest and me holding you nice and tight in my arms.

Michelle: So do I... I always remember this about us... laying like that with you...

Mike: MMMmmmm... I am so in love with you.

Michelle: I remember once in the night, when we were in the Cotswolds... you covering me up when you thought I was cold...

Mike: I remember watching you whilst you slept... it was like being in a dream. You by my side for five whole nights... and five whole days

Michelle: You would need to lock your office door if I ever came there again... I would do more than a little kiss and cuddle, and take a picture of us both... I love that picture of us last Friday...

Mike: For sure... Yes. We do make a wonderful couple Michelle... that picture is proof...

Michelle: I know...

Mike: `YOU`... I just cannot forget US!

Michelle: `YOU`... I cannot forget US either...!!!

Mike: I know... so many times have I thought this through!

Michelle: Thought what through?

Mike: Us

Michelle: We both think about us...... there is still 'US'... there always will be us darling... I am so glad we have had the opportunity to say everything to one another that we have this year...

Mike: Yes... but the best of all was seeing you, and my three wishes coming true... It was so lovely to see you again after all this time. I could not even imagine this would ever happen.

Michelle: I never thought it would happen either... but it did... and so lovely to just have a little hug with you... and all those kisses...

Mike: Sure... Glad it happened. Just love you more and more, that's all.

Michelle: Maybe we will want to do it again one day?... we will have to see how we feel... ?

Mike: History repeating itself?

Michelle: Yes.

Mike: Sorry darling, Cheryl has just come home... I must go now... see you tomorrow... same time, same place... shame it is only on Skype ☹

Michelle: OK darling... one last thing.

Mike: Bye... one last thing? Go ahead...

Michelle: I see that... our love has always been so strong... we are lucky in this respect, because most people never find a love like this...... so just hold onto that thought...

Mike: You could not be more right.

Michelle: Bye darling

Mike: Bye my Michelle

E-mail from: Michelle
To: Mike
Date: 25 September 2012
Subject: An interactive e-mail

Hi my sexy cyber husband

Thank you for sending me not one, but two e-mails yesterday... and three today... WOW!!!! With all of the webcam photos you have taken of me... I'm glad you have now deleted them all from your computer.

I know you are having trouble sleeping at the moment... so I need to help you... On 'our slate' you have an outstanding massage... here is a taste of what it will be like...

I will lay you down... naked... on your front... my massage outfit will be... just my black lace French knickers... nothing else... so I will apply some jasmine oil to my hands, rub it in to warm it up... and gently start to massage your shoulders and neck with soft gentle hands... and then a little firmer, so it really works into all your muscles and relaxes you... and then I will work my hands firmly right down your spine... soft gentle hands, but firm enough that you absolutely love it... all over your back, my fingers and hands will work wonders… a little more of the oil rubbed into my hands… I move them down to the lovely cheeks of your bum… MMMmmmm… nice… a really good firm massage all over this area… I love your bum… down to the backs of your legs I go… firmly massaging all those thigh muscles, strong firm movements… so again you will love it… down to your calf muscles, massaging up and down, firmly… sensual movements… your body and mind are loving this… dare I touch your feet?… No… I don't want you screaming!!!… So… time to turn you over…

Now you are laying naked on your back… I will start on this side with a gentle little kiss or two to your luscious lips… the luscious lips I saw only the other day… I could never resist these lips… I always, always want to kiss them… a long lingering sexy sensual kiss… MMMmmmmm… time to move on… more of the oil on my hands, gently rub it in to warm it up… then myhands on your chest… nice soft hands, gentle movements all over your chest… back up to your neck… I am standing behind you now… I lean down and gently place another little kiss on those lips… then continue with your massage… down to your chest again… down to your tummy… but now I have had to lean right over your face… and (I) all you can see are my boobs… you take advantage of this and kiss one of my boobs… and then gently take hold of one of my nipples in your teeth… MMMmmmmmm… NICE!!!… but I must continue with your massage… I move round to the side of you, massage right down your tummy, over that little belly button, and move onto your hips… strong but gentle movements… seductive… down your hips I move my hands, down to your legs… Oh I have missed out the 'crown jewels'… this was on purpose Mike… down your legs my hands move all over… even to your calfs… really strong massaging here… dare I touch your feet?… no, no, no… back up my hands move… up your calves… up your thighs… insides of your thighs…

Now I need to get myself more comfortable… I kneel over you… one knee each side of your legs… and my hands return to the insides of your thighs… heading towards your crown jewels… gentle little thumbs finely brush the golden nuggets… so very gently… the tiniest of touches… barely touching you… just brushing over your skin… you are loving this… so gently I apply a little more pressure… thumbs working their magic all over and around these golden nuggets… now I use the palms of my hands… just gently, gently, gently… little circular movements… Oh Mike… you are really loving this… we seem to have a 'pop-up' here now… that hot rod of yours is very interested in what is going on here… Mike be patient…

Your hands move onto me… well, onto the black lacy French knickers… you are rubbing your hands all over my hips and bum… MMMMmmmm… nice… nice… nice… until you slip your hands down inside of the back of them, and now your hands are inside of my knickers, and touching my bare skin…… Oh Mike… So, so nice… I am looking at you… the blue eyes are locked onto the brown eyes… I whisper to you… Mike Turner "I love you"…… what would you like to do next???…

To be continued by you darling… an interactive e-mail…

My sexy, adorable cyber husband

I love you so much…

Michelle
Xxx xxx xxx xxx x

E-mail from: Mike
To: Michelle
Date: 25 September 2012
Subject: Re: An interactive e-mail

Hi My sexy, erotic, passionate wife

Interactive e-mail eh!!!… Are you kidding me, what do I want to do next? You have massaged me all over… You are only wearing a sexy pair of knickers, which by the way are lacy, and I can see right through them. Your boobs are flashing at me… and dangling right in my face!!.. AND YOU ASK ME WHAT I WANT TO DO NEXT!!!

Michelle… What I would like to do, 'IS YOU'… I would pull you on top of me… smother my hands in your jasmine oil, massage it all over your boobs and nipples, and then guide you right onto my hot rod, which is as stiff as a poker for sure…

Straight into your love tunnel… and give you some action yourself… and I would pump away inside of you until we are both lost in a world of sheer pleasure!! You would get it big time after all this massaging… Lock stock, and two smoking barrels.

Then I would hold you in my arms… and we would both sleep.

Love always
Mike xxx

---

26 September 2012 ~ Live Interactive Text

Michelle: Hi my darling

Mike: Good morning you sexy woman! Last night… Did I sleep? No… The storm kept me awake and YOU!

Michelle: SNAP…!!!!

Mike: I was thinking about your email and just imagined this was real… How do you expect me to sleep?

Michelle: Oh dear… there is only one solution then… we will have to rent a room for the night… and we will sleep together…

Mike: In a single bed, eh! Taking it in turns who sleeps on top of who!!!

Michelle: Mmmm… make love… then nice snugly cuddles in each others arms… and sleep…

Mike: I would be very happy to squash up with you in a single bed. But… You would wake everyone up screaming… Mike, that feels so nice, do it more and more!!!

Michelle: I will try to keep quiet… and just say it to you… I am also thinking, if we can sleep in a hammock, a single bed should not be a problem.

Mike: I love you… Michelle Turner… we both need to go to work…

Michelle: I LOVE YOU MIKE TURNER… OMG I am going to be late!!

Later that day… They video link for half an hour, and then revert to text.

Mike: Do you know… Whenever I see you on this screen I want you more!

Michelle: I feel the same about you…

Mike: This is like a baby having its favourite treat in front of it and saying... You can look only, but not touch and certainly you cannot have it!!!!

Michelle: I would love to spend a night with you... I would hold you in my arms... and cuddle you tight all night... Am I your favourite treat then?

Mike: Mmmm... Yes please, just you and me and you running those lovely boobs all over me. If you lean over me I may just have to kiss your nipples and make them into American hard gums!!!

Michelle: I want to go to bed with you... Oh don't panic... I know that cannot happen.

Mike: I never panic. With you I always feel at ease.

Michelle: Yes you do... I've seen you.

Mike: Noooooooooooo... Cool as a cucumber that's me!

Michelle: Simon is not due home for an hour... come on over.

Mike: WHAT!!! To your house??? You have gone completely mad!!!

Michelle: ☺

Mike: `YOU`!!! Stop it...!!!

Michelle: I want you...

Mike: You would be in panic if I did?

Michelle: Cool as a cucumber... that's ME TOO!!! Come and try me!!!

Mike: Try you... I would have just one taste and then look out you!!!

Michelle: MMMmmmmmm...... NICE...

Mike: I must go... Bye... Mwah!

Michelle: Bye darling

---

27 September 2012 ~ Live Interactive Text

Michelle: Morning darling

Mike: Hi Michelle... I am just off to work... Yes running late today. Do you know what!!!... I would rather spend the day with my lovely wife Michelle Turner. Just to hold her hand and we go for a walk, find a nice restaurant and a drink and then... Back to bed!!!

Michelle: How nice that would be darling.

Mike: I wish tomorrow was another appointment with you. Mmmmm… See you maybe later; I will be late home today… Directors' board meeting to attend and then lunch out. I wish it was with you instead… Enjoy your day and take all my love and keep it with you.

Michelle: I wish I could spend the day with you too… or even lunch with you… anywhere, anything… All of my love to you… Always and forever… wherever you go.

Mike: Byeeeeeeeeeeeeeeeeeeeee… I love you…

Later that day…

Michelle: Hi my darling

Mike: Hi Michelle… You know I wish I could turn the clock back one week.

Michelle: Me too darling… it was so nice to see you, touch you, kiss you, feel your arms around me… A week has passed and no repercussions from anywhere!! Looks as though we got away with it.

Mike: MMMmmmm… I just love you!

Michelle: I just love you too…… really really love you… I see your face… and think… I love him so much… I wish it was this time a week ago too…

Mike: I think we are going to meet up again somehow???

Michelle: I think you could be right…!!!

Mike: Sorry, I have to go now… Bye

Michelle: Byeeeeeeeee

---

28 September 2012 ~ Live Interactive Text

Mike: Hi… Sorry!!!

Michelle: Hi sexy brown eyes…

Mike: Is it too late to chat for a while now?

Michelle: No I am still OK… how about you?

Mike: Yes okay for the moment… Don't worry if I quickly go. How long do you have before your pick-up?

Michelle: If it is difficult darling, don't worry, we can do it another day. Pick up will be telephone request… at least another hour I would think.

Mike: I am okay for a while.

Michelle: Good… I'll have a nice big kiss then please… because I have been sitting with this on my lap for an hour waiting for you… watching some rubbish on TV.

Mike: Sorry!!! I could not get here until now. Am I in the dog-house… Or will you just say… I am going to DO YOU!!

Michelle: If you give me a kiss I will forgive you… like this: Mwwwaaahhhhh

Mike: Thank you my darling.

Mike: I will love you forever…
Mwaaaaaaaaaaaaaaaaaaaaaaaaaaaaaaaaah!

Mike: I would rather have had the same kisses last Friday.

Michelle: I love you… yes I would rather have those kisses too… your delicious tasty lips… touching mine… MMMmmmmm

Mike: Sorry I was late getting here this evening. You are hardly able to text during the evening, and when you get an evening to yourself, we arrange a time and I am late getting here.

Michelle: It's OK darling…… I understand…… honest I do… We both know, this has to fit in with our everyday lives… it is not a problem this evening, we are both here now for a while.

Mike: "DITTO"

Michelle: "DITTO"

Mike: Hey!!!

Michelle: Stop saying the same as ME!!! Check the time on that darling, we sent that at exactly the same second?

Mike: MMMmmmm… Tell me??… what am I thinking now?

Michelle: What colour bra and knickers has she got on today?

Mike: You have got it in ONE!!! ☺

Michelle: Really?

Mike: I thought you were going to say, I have none on!!

Michelle: It's all I have on…

Mike: Wow… Let's go over to cam and see

Michelle: Come over here and remove them… I have the house all to myself.

Mike: 13 minutes… I will be knocking on the door and shouting… Let me in!!!

Michelle: OK… come on then…

Mike: MMMmmmm… You would panic if I did.

Michelle: There is really nothing I would like, more than to spend time with you…

Mike: Heart racing!!!

Michelle: Heart racing, yes…

Mike: Boobs bouncing with the beats…

Michelle: Would you put your arms around me… to calm me down?

Mike: No… I would probably put my arms around you and flick open the clips on the back of your bra… Wow!!! Free and lose… Nice and natural.

Michelle: Would I get some of those lovely little kisses all around my neck?

Mike: For sure!!… and everywhere else ☺

Michelle: Or would it be straight for the boobs… never mind the lips and neck???

Mike: Be careful Michelle… when I kiss your boobs they are not going to knock me out.

Michelle: I cannot type for laughing at that one!!!…

Mike: So besides… bra off and that only leaves the knickers, eh!

Michelle: The black lacy French knickers… I put them on especially for you!!!

Mike: I am… Sexcited now!!! French… Le removal de knickers!

Michelle: So would you complain if I undid a few buttons on that shirt… and planted lots of sexy succulent kisses all over your neck?… very funny French!!

Mike: No… Gladly take my shirt off me; I much prefer to see it on you.

Michelle: Slowly undo these buttons… gentle fingertips all over that sexy chest of yours…

Mike: Yes… How I remember you… My shirt on you and just a few buttons done up, not many mind, your nipples penetrating out and showing through my shirt. Sexy, sexy Michelle… You make me hot!!!

Michelle: Pull the shirt free of the trousers… run these hands all over your back… and lots of sexy kisses… I used to love wearing your shirt… You are hot!!!!!… my sexy cyber husband…

Mike: You would make me hot if you did this now.

Michelle: MMMmmmmm… my sexy sensual husband… I would love to get you hot……

Mike: MMMmmmmm… Just carry on my darling… I am yours!!

Michelle: And a cuddle for you husband… a no bra cuddle… my boobs pressed firmly against your chest… my nipples sticking right into you… my arms around you… my lips kissing yours… how is that?

Mike: Just lovely… I can feel those hard American hard gums making indentations in my skin… So hard my darling… Love it.

Michelle: And slip my hands down to the belt on your trousers, and undo that…

Mike: That is before I am starting to kiss them and suck them gently… OMG… how much more can they grow?

Michelle: You always make them grow…

Mike: I think there is another pop-up!!!

Michelle: Undo the zip of these trousers… slowly…

Mike: That went together well… ☺

Michelle: Oh Mike… I wish you could hear this…

Mike: Hear this?

Michelle: I have moved into the kitchen to plug in my laptop as the battery is running low… put a CD on… Celine… and the track playing is 'Seduces Me'

Mike: Love too!

Michelle: On this album is also "I love you"…

Mike: Yes… Nice!!!

Michelle: Hang on I have to answer a text on my mobile.

Michelle: Sorry darling, my taxi service is required, I have to go now

Mike: Ok

Michelle: I would love to cuddle you right now.

Mike: Sure… I would love nothing better… Just to have you in my arms and feel you close… so nice!

Michelle: SOOOOOOOOOOO NICE!!

Mike: Mind how you go this time of night. I love you Michelle.

Michelle: I love you Mike… I will always love you… Bye.

Mike: Bye… Drive safely.

Michelle: I never like to say goodbye to you.

Mike: We will never say goodbye Michelle… this is just until the next time.

Michelle: I think we need another appointment soon Mike… I need to kiss those lips of yours and put my arms around you again.

Mike: MMMmmmm… Heaven… Goodnight My Michelle… Mwaaaaaah

Michelle: Mwah ☺

CHAPTER TEN

1 October 2012 ~ Live Interactive Text

Mike: Hi... Where is my sexy wife Michelle? It is 13 minutes past!! Well okay... I can chat with myself!! Thank you for your e-card... and yes I would love to seduce you Michelle Turner... Oh ~ Michelle has just popped up!!!

Michelle: Hi my darling

Mike: Hi and how is my sexy wife today?

Michelle: Friday night was an untimely exit... both stripped of our clothes... sexy kisses and cuddles... I would rather have stayed with you for another half hour!!! Yes, Mike Turner... you 'do' seduce me...

Mike: Yes I forgot on Friday you were naked!! Good job it was only on here or you could have been arrested.

Michelle: Absolutely NAKED!!!! I wanted to stay with you for a while longer...

Mike: MMMmmmm... My sexy, passionate, seductive cyber wife!!

Michelle: Do you know what I would like right now?

Mike: Let me guess... A touch, a kiss and a hug?

Michelle: A nice snugly cuddle... and a long lingering kisssssssssssssss... Shame it is only on this screen. I loved the nice cuddles, and kisses with you in your office.

Mike: So did I Michelle. And I love the picture we took, that picture says everything about us, yes, I think it is written on our faces... happy and in love.

Michelle: Yes... I think it is too...

Mike: I think we could get away with being husband and wife... in the real world...

Michelle: I think people would believe it... We go together well...

Mike: But do you remember all those years ago... we seemed to be like magnets with people?

Michelle: People were drawn to us because... they could see we were in love. Do you think we would ever get away with seeing each other again?

Mike: Maybe?? But... then???

Michelle: Think of a master plan then... I laid awake last night and couldn't get to sleep for ages... then I was thinking of 'YOU'... and I was thinking of a way to see you again.

Mike: It needs to be 113% fullproof... Have you done the risk assessment?

Michelle: Think of a master plan... have a good think, and come up with some brain-storming ideas... Am I just being greedy? wanting just that little bit more of you...

Mike: I feel the same... but weigh up the risk?

Michelle: I would just love to spend some time with you...

Mike: I know, I would with you... but so risky and we both know this.

Michelle: Can I come in your shirt for a cuddle... I am cold...

Mike: Come in my shirt... I need a no bra cuddle with you.

Michelle: Let me in there then... bare skin... that will warm us both up...

Mike: Body heat... is the best way to warm up

Michelle: MMMMmmmm... yessssss!

Mike: Hey... You!!... Stop it... you will have my eye out if you are not careful swinging your boobs like this!!! A & E... Casualty report... Damage to eye caused by swinging boobs with hard nipples.

Michelle: You always make me laugh... you are funny...

Mike: Your twin peaks are warming up!

Michelle: I think skin on skin is working... I'm getting warmer... and your hands on my bare flesh...

Mike: Mmmm... nice... I think we will enjoy this warm-up sexercise.

Michelle: Always sooooo witty!!! ☺

Mike: I will just throw you on the bed then and… Just. 'DO YOU`

Michelle: OOOOOoooooo Mike…… You sexy devil……

Mike: Hard and fast, eh! So hot!!!

Michelle: I've landed on the bed… now what are you going to do to me?

Mike: Okay… Well you have just thrown your legs wide apart, and that topiary heart of yours is just starring me in the face.

Michelle: It's working… I AM warming up now… yes the topiary heart… run your fingers around the outline of it…

Mike: Oppps… My fingers just popped inside… Burnt fingers now!!

Michelle: Do it some more… I like it… come on then Mike… I am ready for you… I'm quite hot now…

Mike: My hosepipe is ready to cool you down now.

Michelle: OOoooo… come on then… slip that hosepipe inside of me…

Mike: Straight in and out… Stop shouting, reel more inside me! How long a hosepipe do you want here?

Michelle: I want all of it…

Mike: What is the end nozzle… Straight jet or spray? I think it is a pressure hose now and getting sexcited.

Michelle: I don't know… start pumping it… and you tell me… WOW… I am very sexcited now… and loving it…

Mike: Build up to climax point so wait for the jet stream!!

Michelle: I love you right inside of me…

Mike: Just one thing okay… Don't try rolling this hosepipe up afterwards… That will hurt.

Michelle: I won't…… just love me… give me your love here Mike…

Mike: I am working fast… I cannot go quicker, just lay back and take my love deep inside you.

Michelle: MMMmmmmm… so so nice… you fill my body and mind with pleasure Mike.

Mike: The trigger is ready to fire and it has rapid automatic pump action.

Michelle: Deep… deep inside of me Mike… this really is a long hosepipe today… come on then… let it go… fill me with your love…

Mike: It has no control when it comes… It just has to automatically release otherwise my nuts would explode. Rapid response is on the scene!!

Michelle: You are so funny… if you do not hurry, I will climax here before you?

Mike: Let us do it together then… After three, or should we make that 13?

Mike: OMG… No too late… it has come!!!

Michelle: My body filled with sensations of you, my husband… Oh how I love you… together…your love juice and mine mingled together… just like our love for one another… devoured and absorbed by the powerful feeling of our joint love…

Mike: I love you.

Michelle: I love everything with you Mike… just cuddle me in your arms…

Mike: Okay… I want to feel you close now and let our pulse rate get back to normality.

Michelle: Hug me really close to you… with your arms around me…

Mike: Your boobs are still shaking in tune with your heart racing…

Michelle: Hug them as well then…

Mike: I love those nipples just bouncing on me.

Michelle: That is just what they are doing… bouncing… touching you… all yours…

Mike: Yes I can feel them… So nice and sensual.

Michelle: I love just being cuddled up to you like this…

Mike: Mmmm… And me… I loved you like this when we cuddled up long ago.

Michelle: So did I…… hug me tighter…

Mike: YOU!… You drive me crazy at times!!

Michelle: I love you Mike Turner… Really… Really… Love you…

Mike: "DITTO"

Michelle: Hug me tighter… cuddle me closer…

Mike: MMMmmmm … YOU!!!… You will not sleep again tonight.

Michelle: No probably not… will you?

Mike: I was up at 2.30am this morning, the rain woke me… but you kept me awake…

Michelle: I love you… I love you making love to me here… my wishing well must be working… all my wildest dreams come true…

Mike: Mmmm… Very wild exotic sexy love!… No wonder you cannot sleep.

Michelle: I would sleep after all of that… snuggled up close and warm with you…

Mike: Yes… Love to with you.

Michelle: You would sleep too… I would just cuddle up to you… my arms around you… you could have one arm around me… and the other hand on my boobs… then you would sleep.

Mike: Always nice to see you my darling, or just text. It brings us closer together whatever way it is.

Michelle: Yes it does always bring us closer together… and I LOVE IT…

Mike: We both need to go now ☹

Michelle: I know ☹

Mike: Bye my darling

Michelle: Bye my darling… I will always love you.

Mike: "DITTO"

Michelle: You brighten every one of my days, when I have contact with you… You are the best tonic in the world… and I cannot get enough of you…

Mike: I feel the same about you ~ we are just one and the same.

Michelle: We are inside of each other`s heads and hearts

Mike: Can we both volunteer to go to another planet?

Michelle: OOooooo good idea… we will say it was for research purposes and… sorry we can't seem to get back…

Mike: MMMmmmm… Research, I would love to do an anatomy research on you.

Michelle: Oh Mike… you would be stuck with me forever then!!! Could you cope?

Mike: I may just cope with you… because I love you.

Michelle: We are in love with each other for sure!!

Mike: For sure 113%… I need to go now… Bye.

Michelle: Bye.

E-mail from: Mike
To: Michelle
Date: 5 October 2012
Subject: Pictures of my Michelle

Hi Michelle

I know you are probably shouting again… "You little monkey", but I just cannot resist you!! I see you on my computer screen when we are on Skype, and I just have to take pictures of you… There are some lovely ones here… You are so sexy, my Michelle!!!

Mwah! Love always…
Mike xxx

---

5 October 2012 ~ Live Interactive Text

Michelle: Hi… it's my darling… MMMmmmm my sexy husband… if I had woken up next to you this morning I would be saying… the weather is windy and rainy this morning… we should stay in bed… and I would snuggle right into you…

Mike: Morning Michelle. Who turned the lights out this morning? Raining and wet, best place isbed on days like this!!!

Michelle: ☺

Mike: I have not read this until now… What are we both thinking? This is weird!!! Stop reading my mind, YOU!

Michelle: Yes darling… I agree… I tell you what… I will make us a coffee… take it back to bed where you are waiting for me… drink the coffee, and snuggle up close for nice kisses and cuddles… We are soooooooooooooooooooo alike Mike Turner, we think and say the same things!!

Mike: So… I am naked in bed, you come in with hot coffee (just be careful you do not spill it) and then you slip your clothes off and lay beside me. I put my arms across you and you come and lay you boobs across my chest and we cuddle and hug each other all day long… Yeeeeeeeeeeeeeeeessssss!!!

Michelle: Yeeeeesssssssssssssssssss!!!!!!! How nice that would be? I was awake for 3 HOURS during the night… thinking about you!!

Mike: I was up at 4.00am this morning, because I could not sleep… thinking about you… Like the song goes I was tossing and turning all night!!

Michelle: We should toss and turn together… ☺

Mike: Yes please…I would Love to!!! ☺

Michelle: Have a good day darling… Late for work… Bye.

Mike: Byeeeeeeeeeeeeeeeee

E-mail from: Michelle
To: Mike
Date: 5 October 2012
Subject: A day in bed

Hi my darling

On a day like today, windy and rainy, we both have the same thought… A day in bed together… Just snuggled up close… away from anybody else… no CCTV… no eyes watching us… Just you and me… locked away on our own…

Our naked bodies entwined… some nice kisses… our naked bodies touching one another… your arms around me, holding me tight… my head on your shoulder… my boobs on your chest… kissing your lips… kissing your neck… you caressing my boobs and nipples… my hands skimming your skin… skimming your chest… skimming your tummy… skimming all the way down to those crown jewels, and just gently caressing them… just to lay peacefully snuggled up to you like this… Oh how lovely…

Then I would get up… put your shirt on… just do up one or two buttons… make us coffee, and bring it back to bed… undo the buttons of your shirt… let it slip to the floor… and slide back in that bed with you… and just love you…

And… you know how I love to draw on you with one finger… Often I have put my initials across your heart… Or written `I love you`, across your heart… Well… How would you like this? With my nipples, I will write "I LOVE YOU" all over your chest; this will obviously be twice… Once with each nipple!! ☺ ☺ You will get this in stereo. You will just have to lay back and enjoy it… And I will hover over you, and do this… MMMMmmmm… Both nipples at once, engraving onto your chest. One day Mike, this will happen for real... One day!!!

Mike Turner ~ I love you ~ I will always love you
Xxx xxx xxx xxx x
Michelle

Mike: Hi gorgeous.

Michelle: Hi sexy.

Mike: It is cold today.

Michelle: Cuddle me... we will warm each other up.

Mike: I like your idea of the engraving on my chest with your hard nipples!!

Michelle: Then... One day my darling... this will happen... put it on our slate!!

Mike: My hands are cold.

Michelle: Where are you going to put them to warm them up?

Mike: Down your knickers!!

Michelle: Wowsa!! Perrrrrfect...

Mike: Tell me,is that why they call this a pussy! ☺

Michelle: I believe so...... ☺

Mike: I should therefore stroke it, eh!

Michelle: Nice pussy...

Mike: I hope it does not bite.

Michelle: No this pussy purrs... it does not bite... but does like a lot of attention...

Mike: It has all my attention... MMMmmmm... I love this pussy!!

Michelle: This pussy loves lots of nice gentle stroking.

Mike: OMG... this pussy is asking for some nice warm milk!!

Michelle: Sexy little kitten then?... hee hee hee... warm milk ☺

Mike: Sexy kitten for sure... and laps it up!!! ☺

Michelle: I was just typing that... lapping it up...

Mike: MMmmm... I told you about this!!!

Michelle: MMMmmmmm... inside of one another Mike Turner...

275

Mike: We are one and the same Michelle... inside one another's heads... and I want to be inside of your pussy!!

Michelle: Come right inside this pussy of mine...

Mike: Well I think you are getting hot now, eh... Time to put out the fire...

Michelle: Come on then Mike... my hot spot is indeed on fire... my cyber husband makes me feel so sexy...

Mike: Oh... Wait, I will slip it out and run it up northward to that hot spot!

Michelle: No... don't take it out right now... I am loving it just where it is...

Mike: Oooops... Back inside again and now you see what has happened... my climax just cannot be held back any longer!!!

Michelle: Come on then Mike... give me your love juices... Fill me with your love... my kisses, would have turned to really passionate ones now... REALLY PASSIONATE... as I am intoxicated by your love, and touch...

Mike: You have them... Just stop squeezing your legs together so tight... it is like trying to extract the last of the toothpaste out of the tube. OK don't stop I love it.

Michelle: Toothpaste... the pussy would prefer milk!

Mike: Whoops!! I forgot where we were... I am filling that little pussy of yours with gallons of warm milk... and she cannot get enough of it. You know when the toothpaste has almost finished, but you think there is enough for one more little squeeze!!! This is you now with your legs squeezing me!!

Michelle: Yes... I would give you one more little squeeze... A really tight squeeze inside of me... My inner thighs gripping you... the muscles inside my love tunnel gripping you... sucking every last drop of your warm milk

Mike: I know this! Just love you to bits. And OMG... I LOVE YOU.

Michelle: I love you...... and...... your bits...

Mike: I must go... bye.

Michelle: OK... Bye Mwah... little pussy says, that was just purrrrrrrr-fect.

Mike: MMmmmm... I love that tight little pussy of yours!!! Bye

Michelle: I would love you to bits if you were all mine.

Mike: Two one-way tickets to faraway lands, please.

Michelle: Yes please, where you will be loving me, and I will be loving you. You will be mine, and I will be yours…

Mike: Lost in cyber space!!!

Michelle: Two ~ one-way to anywhere please.

Mike: The more I played with it that pussy, the more she loved me… she just did not stop purrrrrrrring.

Michelle: This pussy would love you day and night…

Mike: A nice cuddle with you would be lovely.

Michelle: MMMmmmm soooooooooo lovely… just snuggled up tight and close with you…

Mike: MMMmmmm… Darling, how I would love that.

Michelle: Just warm and cosy with you… loving you…

Mike: Come on then!

Michelle: If only…

Mike: I could so love you… you know this!

Michelle: I could so love you too Mike Turner… and you know this…

Mike: I am hanging on the door now, stretching my arms and getting ready to stretch out and hug you. Every day my arms are growing longer and soon I will be able to just reach out and touch you.

Michelle: Wow… I look forward to that day… and I will just snuggle in them, and be content for the rest of my days.

Mike: I just love you.

Michelle: I have to let you go now darling… Mwah

Mike: Mwah… Bye… It is always hard to say bye when you love someone.

Michelle: I know…

Mike: It really means… I love you..

Michelle: Does it? I love you darling

Mike: Now we are both going to be late for work

Michelle: Who cares!!… Byeeeeeeeeeeeeeeeeeeeeeeee

E-mail from: Michelle
To: Mike
Date: 9 October 2012
Subject: Sunrise

Hello my sleepy head

As you cannot get up in the mornings at the moment, I have attached two photo's I took of the sunrise yesterday.

If you lived with me I would sort your body clock out... no waking up for you in the night, well not to watch TV anyway... I would just love you... make love with you... and cuddle you into my boobs all night... you would sleep like a baby...

And, as soon as the dawn was breaking... I would say, come and watch the sunrise with me... Why were you not with me when I took these photo's?

I would love to come to your office today... and make love to you on your desk... wild and passionate love... I hope your security guard does not hear us, or the person in the office below you... I will not be held responsible for all the screaming and shouting... You just get me sooo 'SEXCITED'... And my clothes will be strewn all around your office afterwards!!

Bye darling, enjoy your day at work!!

I love you
Michelle
Xxx xxx xxx xxx x

E-mail from: Mike
To: Michelle
Date: 9 October 2012
Subject: I love you

Hi Michelle

I keep thinking of how much I love talking to you. How good you look when you smile. How much I love your laugh. Always dreaming about you, replaying pieces of our conversation, laughing at funny things that we have shared. I've memorized your face and the way that you look at me. I catch myself smiling again at what I imagined. I know one thing for sure, for once... I don't care, I cherish every moment that we are here together.

I love you...
Mike
xxx

---

11 October 2012 ~ Live Interactive Text

Michelle: Hello my sexy lover

Mike: I am just gobsmacked!!!

Michelle: Really!! Why???

Mike: Why?... Why am I gobsmacked??? Why are you worrying about the noise below or the security guard?

Michelle: I don't know... it's you that has to carry on working with them not me!!

Mike: You are really a sexy sexy cyber wife Michelle Turner... I LOVE YOU...

Michelle: You are a sexy, adorable cyber husband Mike Turner... I love you... and I cannot get enough of you...

Mike: I have taken your bra off the light fitting and I will try and return this to you at some point. I would not want those boobs getting cold or frostbite!

Michelle: You will not believe this... but... my next sentence was going to be... can you return my underwear please, because I have been cold today, with none on...

Mike: You know when you bronco ride you wave your hand around and around in the air, well in your hand was your bra swirling around the office.

Michelle: I am getting good at this bronco riding. Mike... we are soooooooo lik-minded...

Mike: Well, one thing for sure... My rod deep inside means there is little chance of you coming off, I think the phrase maybe you could be coming on!! Just make sure we climax together, okay!

Michelle: Well... I certainly would not have fallen off the table... that is for sure... I would be speared to it... on your hot rod.

Mike: I can guarantee it.

Michelle: You are one sexy husband to have Mike Turner... I love it...

Mike: I could get my lips around those nipples and give them a good old suck!!!

Michelle: They love lots of attention from you...

Mike: No problem... I can give them all my love and attention... Even little ditto could not match me.

Michelle: Will I get lots of warm cuddles this winter?... Oh I cannot wait for all this love and attention... maybe this winter will not be so bad after all...

Mike: Well the weather may be bad, but your boobs they are just lovely!

Michelle: They would love a cuddle from you right now...

Mike: Come on then you!

Michelle: I would love to feel your warm arms around me right now.

Mike: Yes... It would be nice.

Michelle: Very...

Mike: We are only what 7 miles apart, but it is like being 7000 miles apart. I know what I want, but I know I cannot have what I love.

Michelle: I would love to have you too...

Mike: Thank you for sharing your love with me.

Michelle: You complete me Mike Turner... I love you so much.

Mike: I can never get you out of my mind.

Michelle: I cannot get you out of my mind either...

Mike: I am beginning to think you and me just think the same... Almost weird sometimes!

Michelle: Maybe we just share the same love and thoughts about it?

Mike: Have to go now. Bye.

Michelle: Bye sexy husband... mwah

E-mail from: Michelle
To: Mike
Date: 12 October 2012
Subject: Thirteen weeks married today

My Darling Mike

Still on our island of paradise in the Seychelles... I open my eyes, it is still dark outside... and I am wrapped in the arms of my darling husband... my lover... my friend... my everything!!! snuggled together in our hammock... There is no place I would rather be than wrapped in these arms... I close my eyes and drift back to sleep... I feel as though I am in heaven, cuddled up with you... married to you for 13 weeks... every day with you, heaven on earth.

But then I am woken by gentle little kisses on my forehead... I smile, and snuggle even further into you... You are whispering, come on Michelle, wakey wakey, a special day for us today... You are planting kisses all over my face... MMMmmmm shall I just keep my eyes closed?... your kisses move down to my neck, all around my neck to plant the most delicious little kisses... MMMmmmm sooooooo nice... your lips move down to my nipples... Oh Mike... what a lovely way to be woken up... you are kissing and sucking at my nipples, your tongue rolling around and around them... I open my eyes to look at you... you are looking at me... You smile at me, and kiss me on the lips... Mike you are a delight to have as my husband... so sexy... so romantic... so loving... your body flawlessly proportioned is as sexy as hell; it makes my mouth water...

Come on Michelle, up we get... Sunrise... we need to go down to the beach and watch the sunrise... just like the day we married, barefoot on the beach... so off we go... and we walk hand in hand along the beautiful beach, and watch the sky wake up, changing colours, pink, orange, and blue, so beautiful... the sun begins to come up... you stop, look at me, kiss me, and say... Michelle Turner... I love you... I will always love you... Mike you melt my heart... I am so lucky to have you... We walk for miles... This 'is' heaven on earth... Eventually back we go to our mud hut for some breakfast, or should I say brunch as it is now late morning. Then you tell me you have a special surprise for me today… but, as you would, you will not tell me what it is!!!! and tell me I have to wait and see, but I will like it. But before the surprise, we need to go and have a shower, in our natural shower you found for us… Off we go… strip off our clothes, and both naked we get under the waterfall… OOOhhh I love my life here with you… coconut shower gel, we wash every part of each other's body. It takes us forever… you run your hands over every curve of my body, sinuously curvy you say… and then right there under the waterfall we make love… So sensual… So sexy… You fill every part of my body and mind with pleasure…

We then head off back to our mud hut… you say we need to get dressed, as we are going somewhere… somewhere I have never been, but I will love it… You also say, our little guy Ditto needs to come with us, you always say he is a lucky little sod, and today he may bring us luck… OOOoohhhhh now I am really intrigued… so off we go, late afternoon down to our beach… What on earth is he up to? I am thinking to myself… When we get there, a little speedboat is waiting for us… you take my hand, and we climb aboard, and off we go… out into the sea, and around to the other side of the island, where we then see a cruise ship… our speedboat heads off towards it… OMG… I am really excited now, my heart is thumping with joy… we pull up alongside the cruise ship, and are helped aboard… and I am thinking, OMG we are not dressed for this! But you say don't worry Michelle, everything will be taken care of… We look around the ship… well I cannot describe this, because I have never done it… but, I know it would be fabulous… Then we are taken off to where we hire, for one evening only, a tuxedo for you, and a slinky long black dress for me… OMG, my very own James Bond for the evening, my sexy, sexy husband dressed as James Bond… My dress is sexy, long, seductive and requires no underwear… A beautiful dress, just waiting for you to unzip later… Both dressed to kill, off we go… a couple of cocktails each…… then we get another and you take us out onto the deck of the ship to watch the sunset… OMG, the most perfect day with you darling… after watching the most beautiful sunset, we go to dinner, drink champagne and enjoy everything about it… Then onto a show… And then you say, this is where little Ditto comes into it... We go into the on-board casino, and have a little flutter... with the luck of little Ditto, we win on 'Black 13'... you said you knew we would... Your handsome smiling face, a face I love so much... I look into those sexy brown eyes of yours, and you say, do you want to stay here tonight, or go home? My answer is, this has been wonderful, and I have enjoyed every minute of it... but I am ready to go home... home to our little mud hut, on our island of paradise...

They tell us the clothes can be returned tomorrow, so we board our little speedboat again, and are whisked back to our island... I am cuddled up tight to you on the little boat, as it is a little chilly now it is dark... they land us on our beach, and a little giggly and a little drunk, we make our way back to our little mud hut... once inside we light the candles... I watch you... you look so good in what you are wearing... you walk towards me, smiling... take my face in your hands and kiss me... then you are laughing and saying... I think it is time to get you out of this dress, and unleash Pussy Galore!!! Wow... Mike... you are so hot and sexy... slowly you unzip the black dress... and just let it drop to the floor... OMG I am naked... and wanting you so much... Slowly I undo your bow tie, and remove it sooooo slowly... slowly slip your jacket off... slowly undo your shirt... our eyes are locked together... eventually all of your clothes are removed, and we kiss... you pick me up, put me into the hammock, get in there on top of me... and... we make the most wonderful, gentle, sensual love...

My world here it perfect with you Mike Turner... I love you so much... and I am so glad I married you... I am the luckiest person in the whole wide world.

I love you... I will always love you...
Xxx xxx xxx xxx x
Michelle

E-mail from: Mike
To: Michelle
Date: 12 October 2012
Subject: Just thinking of you

Hi Michelle

Well my darling this little monkey has you on his mind again tonight. When you send me e-mails like the last one, I want to be there with you for real… I am here just thinking about you!! This little monkey wants you! I want to hug and cuddle you now and give you tons of kisses.

Well you asked me what colour underwear I like?… This heart shape job looks good to me… I want to seduce you Michelle Turner… Just unleash Pussy Galore! This would surely not want much removing!! I want to feel your naked body next to mine, nice and warm and sensual… MMMmmmm… Let us just make love together… I love you!

Mike
xxx

Hi my darling

I cannot sleep… I am just wide awake thinking about you… So I am going to tell you what is keeping me awake!!!

Hey Michelle… Stop squeezing me so tight with your legs wrapped around me like this!! Well Mike will you stop pinning me down!! What do we both mean? We both love it!!!… He, he, he… see sexy attachments.

Mwah! Good night… I think I am going to sleep now and just dream about you!!!

Love always...
Mike
xxx

E-mail from: Michelle
To: Mike
Date: 13 October 2012
Subject: I would love to seduce you

Hi Mike

OOOoooo lovely e-mails from you... WOW!!! I want you right now... to love you... to kiss you... to cuddle you... to seduce you...

I cannot stop thinking about you at all at the moment...

Addicted to my cyber husband...

I would love to seduce you right now...

I LOVE YOU
Xxx xxx xxx xxx x
Michelle

Hi my darling

I loved your e-mails this weekend... I love the attachment you found of sexy underwear, Yes..!!! I need to locate such an item... the purrrrrrfect shape heart, to wear over my topiary heart... if this does not keep me warm this winter, I am sure you will...

And, the other attachment here... Seduce my mind and you can have my body... Seduce my soul and I am yours forever... Well Mike Turner... I am yours forever... You seduce my mind, body and soul... I love it!!! AND...

I LOVE YOU
Michelle
Xxx xxx xxx xxx x

---

16 October 2012 ~ Live Interactive Text

Michelle: Hello sexy lover and husband...
Mwaaaaaaaaaaaaaaaaaaaaaaaaaaah

Mike: Hi my gorgeous Michelle... Wow, are you going to seduce me?

Michelle: I am always prepared to seduce you, Mr Turner

Mike: Wowee... 50 shades of Michelle Turner!!

Michelle: Fifty shades for sure... heading towards you... for some sexy, sensual kisses...

Mike: I have just slipped off that bra and your nipples are trailing up me so slowly.

Michelle: Mike... I knew you would not leave it on for long... ok... my nipples are trailing right up your body... and pressing firmly into you, whilst I give you such loving sexy kisses...

Mike: Yes... Those nipples make my hairs stand up on end and that is not all!!!

Michelle: Good, I will continue... we both know sexy kisses should be everywhere... so... my kisses are moving down your chest now... and my nipples are sliding down your body also... trailing all over your skin... all over that lustrous sexy body of yours, so healthy, strong and vigorous.

Mike: That is your chat-up line... You want some lollipop eh?

Michelle: Be patient... I am moving slowly...

Mike: Yes I can feel those nipples trailing on my skin!

Michelle: Down, down, down, my nipples go... the nipples will get there before my lips and tongue Mike... the nipples are trailing all over your crown jewels now Mike... and my kisses are skimming down your chest and tummy...

Mike: Well this lollipop has just sprung up into life ☺

Michelle: Well... the lollipop has my nipples trailing all over it too...... MMMmmmm...

Mike: You know those sky rocket lollipops that you can buy, well just look at what you have here.

Michelle: WOW!!!! Well this is a big sky rocket for sure.

Mike: Houston would have nothing like this!!!

Michelle: I think the lollipop likes my nipples trailing all over it... What do you think?

Mike: It sure does darling... This space rocket is ready to gooooooooooo!

Michelle: Where exactly would you like it to go?

Mike: I think there is only one place... Inner space!

Michelle: I might have to have a little taste of if first...

Mike: OMG... You are taking a chance... it is about to ignite. All systems are go!!!

Michelle: NO WAIT... I am going to have to back off, and let you cool down...

Mike: The motors are going already for take off!

Michelle: You are so funny at times... I do love you!!!!

Mike: Are you ready for lift off! ☺

Michelle: I think if I got on that rocket at the moment, it would be almost instant lift off.

Mike: I am sure it would, jump on quick! ☺

Mike: I have to go, I cannot stop laughing. Cheryl is downstairs; she will hear me laughing...

Michelle: SSSHHHHhhhhhh...

Mike: I am trying!

Michelle: Slip that rocket of yours into my launch pad.

Mike: Michelle stop this... I need to stop laughing here.

Michelle: OK ☺ Count to 10 and calm down a little... I won't make you laugh...

Michelle: Have you calmed down?... do you still need to go?

Mike: I cannot stop laughing here...

Michelle: Well, I should let you go then... Or... Do you just want to talk about the weather?

Mike: See you still make me laugh; I am on a roll now... I am going to have to go.

Michelle: OK darling... I hope I can sleep with this on my mind tonight... Your rocket inside of my love tunnel all night...

Mike: Yes... We will imagine it from the time `All Systems Are Ready to Go`!!! Never a dull moment for us Michelle.

Michelle: OMG... how am I going to sleep now?

Mike: You know they say every time you laugh you will live longer... Today I have just put on another 13 years on my life... Bye.

Michelle: Bye darling ☺

Mike: Mwaaaaah for your lips.

Mike: Mwah. Mwah. These two are for those nipples.

Michelle: OMG... Mike... what are you trying to do to me here?

Mike: Send you crazy so you can join me... Bye

Michelle: I am with you all the way... Byeeeeee... Sleep well with your sky rocket heading towards the Venus docking station. ☺

---

17 October 2012 ~ Live Interactive Text

Mike: Morning my sexy gorgeous Michelle

Michelle: Morning darling

Mike: Have I told you recently that I love you?

Michelle: No... ☺

Mike: YOU!!!

Michelle: You will say... I am going to do you one day!!!!

Mike: I AM REALLY GOING TO DO YOU!!

Mike: OMG..!!!!

Michelle: Here we go again!!! come and just love me Mike Turner... let me feel your hands all over my body... let me feel your warm naked body next to mine... come and just let me love you...

Mike: I would love to Michelle... but you will be late for work, and so will I.

Mike: We both need to go, but not before I send you... all my love...

Michelle: Oh Mike... I do love you... you melt my heart sometimes I LOVE YOU... JUST THINK OF THAT... NOBODY COULD EVER LOVE YOU MORE.

Mike: MMMmmmm... Michelle...

Michelle: Bye darling

Mike: Bye... Sexy

E-mail from: Michelle
To: Mike
Date: 19 October 2012
Subject: Sexcited

Hi my sexy lover

I am looking forward to Skype with you later, so hope this is able to happen... If you read this before we meet up then, here is a little pre-warning!!! I am feeling, naughty, sexy, and very loving...

I like the little number you found for me... (see attachment)... So, I am wearing this for you today... it just about covers my topiary heart... so 'maybe' I will need you to warm me up a little later!!!

And for sure I will kiss that arm better for you... little tender kisses all over it... and you need lots of my TLC after your experience yesterday... so I am looking forward to meeting up with you...

I love you...... My sexy lover, my adorable husband...
Xxx xxx xxx xxx x
Michelle

---

19 October 2012 ~ Live Interactive Text

Michelle: Hello my sexy lover... I'm glad you are here because... I am lying on a nice big sofa, watching a Celine DVD, with the fire on (gas flamed)... and all that was missing was you! All that I have on is the article of clothing you found for me last week, the one I sent you an attachment of earlier... and all that it covers is my topiary heart... So I need warming up!!!

Mike: You need warming up, eh!... a whole evening to yourself... well here I am... So you only have that little black see-through heart, just about covering that vital part, eh! No bra, so your nipples must the cold and hard, eh!

Michelle: Jump out of that window, shimmy down the drain-pipe, and get on over here... by the time you get here I will have two Southern Comfort and lemonades lined up, with lots of ice... only the vital part covered, nipples cold and hard!!!

Mike: Wow… That is tempting… Both things, I mean!

Michelle: I am here just waiting for you…

Mike: Well, like I said… I am yours for the taking! You have set the scene so the rest of the evening is up to you!! I can see this is not going to be a quickie!!!

Michelle: And when you get here, I will have to remove that shirt, and that is just for starters.

Mike: Yes my pleasure… nothing I like better is to see my gorgeous Michelle inside my shirt. Most of the buttons undone and her nipples sticking through. Oh how I have never been able to get this out of my mind… All these years!!!

Michelle: Ok… You know how I loved to wear your shirt whenever I could… So I will wear the shirt for a little while, because I am cold with what I have on…

Mike: Well from what I can see… Just a black little heart just covering the topiary heart underneath.

Michelle: The shirt is off… so… up your arm the kisses will go now… and all over your neck… and whilst I am doing this… I will take your hands and you can run them all over my curves…

Mike: MMMmmmm… yes those kisses feel nice. I am just laying back and enjoying this.

Michelle: Lots of tender, loving kisses just for you… because I love you… and my tiger claws just gently skimming over your chest…

Mike: I love you too. Every bit of you!… You have some nice yummy bits. I want your nipples to do this too, skim them all over my chest…

Michelle: Yes… you have some very nice yummy bits too… my nipples are now trailing over your chest…

Mike: Yesssss please… they feel good when they are hard and long… Just gently skimming all over me.

Michelle: Yes… I can do this… no problems at all… my nipples love all the attention you give them… in fact I will trail them right up your chest… nice and slowly… and right up to your lips… because they would like a kiss from you…

Mike: Just keep going up… I want to take them in my lips and give then a gentle suck… Yummy, yummy…

Michelle: Yes… they like this… kiss and suck them gently…

Mike: I am going to suck and roll my tongue over them… Like sucking nice American hard gums, and you know I love Bounty bars and do you know what… I think these taste better!!!

Michelle: WOW... now there is a thing... whoever would have thought you could have liked anything more than chocolate?

Mike: I like something you can get your teeth into and there is plenty of that here.

Michelle: PLENTY!!! And whilst all of this is going on, I am going to slowly remove the rest of your clothes

Mike: I am yours!!!

Michelle: I am all yours too... whatever we want then!!!

Mike: Well I do not have much to remove from the looks of it. Just the little heart knickers and then... completely naked... Mmmm... I am enjoying this... Oh what a feeling! Sensual and loving!!

Michelle: MMMmmmm... I am enjoying this with you... I love these tender and loving moments with you. BOTH ABSOLUELY NAKED... on the sofa, in front of the fire... with Celine singing her heart out...

Mike: Your topiary heart is singing down there too... The song is "I need somebody to love me"

Michelle: I do need somebody to love me...... and that somebody is you!!!

Mike: I think I need to ruffle your topiary and see if it is still in shape! Yes... You like me giving this a little ruffle up!

Michelle: Oh yesssssssss

Mike: Stop getting so sexcited my darling.

Michelle: You make me very sexcited... I am so glad I married you!

Mike: Yes... At least we can say it is virtually legal now.

Michelle: I need to place my body right up close to yours... my boobs touching your chest... my tummy pressed firmly against yours... my legs pressed firmly against yours...

Mike: Okay... But I have something down there that your topiary heart wants from me. So, I have just parted the topiary and yes... I have just popped in a little way to check it out.

Michelle: MMMmmmm... NICE!!

Mike: Yes... It is warm and wet down there; you have obviously got a bit sexcited.

Michelle: That is what my cyber husband does to me... I just get near him... and it happens... I cannot control this... I just want your touch... I want your love.

Mike: I think I need to check your hot spot. Yes... I want to check this out for a while.. You can have my!!! or my fingers to roll around your hot spot... Your choice.

Michelle: What is... my?

Mike: Okay... Penis if you like! There is other terminology like cock, dick, etc.

Michelle: Oh your hot rod!!! why didn't you just say ☺ I'll start with your tongue first if that is OK?

Mike: Hey... who said about tongue?... ☺ Greedy!

Michelle: I'm always greedy with you... Because I love everything that you do to me...

Mike: Before long you will get all three!

Michelle: Wowsa!!

Mike: Okay..Tongue because it is your day for choosing. Let me just make a parting and find my way down here with my tongue.

Michelle: Ohhhh wow... I love it...

Mike: Oh... Yes, right here at the top... It did not want much finding, this hot spot. Let me give it some kisses and roll my tongue over and around... Yes, you love this. I think it needs some wiggle tongue... What do you think?

Michelle: OMG... YES!!!

Mike: I knew you would say this... you are so sexy tonight.

Michelle: Sexy and loving you darling... Always...

Mike: With the tip of my tongue lots of nice wiggles all over that hot spot.

Michelle: OMG... I am getting out of control here!!! This drives me absolutely crazy!!! But you already know this...

Mike: No... Houston Texas will have something to say about this if the rocket is out of control. They will monitor it remotely and put this back on course to land in the love tunnel.

Michelle: I think the rocket needs to head toward Venus... what do you think?

Mike: Rocket back on course and found its target... So get ready for lift off...

Michelle: So what position are we currently in... you on top?

Mike... Yes... You underneath... legs wide apart and ready to take this rocket inside you. It will start its motors and then up, up, and away it will go... Full thrusts...

Michelle: Come on then Mike... come inside of me... full thrust to start with? Wowsa!!! Gently...

Mike: Yes... It is all systems goooooooooo.

Michelle: Come on then darling... take me to the stars...

Mike: You will be taken into deep penetration.

Michelle: Wow... Out of this world... come on then... penetrate that rocket right inside of my love tunnel... I want you right inside of me now...

Michelle: Oh darling!... Where have you gone? You have gone off line!!!

Michelle: Oh Mike... I do not think you will come back now... I hope you did not get into trouble...... I LOVE YOU SOOOOO MUCH... and I love your loving, and these tender loving times we share together.

Michelle: WOW... You are back, how did you manage that?

Mike: Sorry I had to go quick... See you soon and I cannot stop now.

Michelle: Bye darling

Mike: Bye... I LOVE YOU... I WILL ALWAYS LOVE YOU

Michelle: "DITTO" always... Shame you have the internet police on your tail... that rocket was just about to take me to heaven.

Mike: Sorry darling ☹... Came twice asking what I was doing. Problem is she can hear me typing a lot here, not just browsing the net.

Michelle: ☹ Bye darling... fit her with ear muffs!!!

Mike: You were just about to get a big full thrust!!!

Mike: Bye... But, from the time I say "Bye"... I am missing you!

Michelle: I miss you too... a lot..!!!

E-mail from: Michelle
To: Mike
Date: 22 October 2012
Subject: These are the special times

Hi Mike

On Friday evening I was actually lying on the sofa...

I did actually have the fire on...

I did actually have a Celine DVD on…

One of the songs she was singing was one of my favourites… I have downloaded it to my computer this afternoon and tried to send it to you… but failed… so maybe you want to look on 'YouTube' and listen to it… I am sure you will already know it… it is "These Are The Special Times"… listen to the words Mike, because 'these are' the special times, times I share with you…

I love you…
Michelle
Xxx xxx xxx xxx x

E-mail from: Michelle
To: Mike
Date: 26 October 2012
Subject: Kissimmee

Hi my darling

Oh Mike… Kissimmee, what a lovely name… When we were talking about this on Skype, I loved the sound of it.

Florida ~ The Sunshine State… yes, this would suit us perfectly… we both need sunshine to function… Let's go there to hibernate for six months… and then when we both love it, buy somewhere to live together for the rest of our lives. After six months of hibernating with me, you would never want to leave me… I would love you and cuddle you more than my cat (hee hee hee) and he just loves it… YOU WOULD TOO!!!…

Do you know, I have just had a quick look on the internet, and you are right, for £100k you can buy an amazing property… WOW!!! I just knew you would come up with something!!!

Oh yeah… Oh yeah… You have cheered me up on this miserable day!!!

BRING IT ON…
I LOVE YOU…
I LOVE YOU… more than…
I LOVE YOU… more than chocolate…
I LOVE YOU… more than Southern Comfort and lemonade…

I LOVE YOU... more than steak and chips
I LOVE YOU... more than pistachio ice-cream
I LOVE YOU... more than the sunrise
I LOVE YOU... more than the sunset
I LOVE YOU... more than sunshine
I LOVE YOU... more than my cat
I LOVE YOU... more than all my favourite music
I LOVE YOU... more than anything
I LOVE YOU... more than anyone else!!!

In fact I love you more now, than I ever have... I know what you are thinking now, she is crazy... keep taking the pills Michelle... No Mike, it is not pills I need...... it is you!!!!!

All my love
Michelle
Xxx xxx xxx xxx x

E-mail from: Mike
To: Michelle
Date: 27 October 2012
Subject: Re: Kissimmee

Hi my Michelle

You are absolutely crazzzzy!!! But this is one of the reasons I love you so much. Hibernating with you for six months would be wonderful... But then we both know this would be forever!!! We also know we cannot afford financially to do this, not without kicking Simon and Cheryl out of their homes, and as we have recently discussed we could not do that to them now... ☹

So until we manage to win a jackpot on the lottery, our hibernation will just have to be in our dreams... But, you never know... maybe one day this will happen?

I love you Michelle... Always and forever
Mike xxx

E-mail from: Mike
To: Michelle
Date: 4 November 2012
Subject: Time to reflect

Hi Michelle

Time to reflect...

I know this is a difficult time for you darling, with your family situation as it is as present... But, you know I am always here for you. We share everything here darling, and any comfort I can give you... I will...

Time to reflect...

I bet when you opened those lovely blue eyes this morning and you looked out the window and all you could see outside was that it was dark, cold, windy and raining, you said, I am going back to bed and then you dived back under the quilt! Well, it is winter and it is cold outside and like me you hate this time of year. The only good thing about winter is that your boobs get cold and your nipples go hard like American hard gums!!! OMG... Now I am back on sweets I would love a nice juicy suck on your nipples! Yummy, yummy, yummy!!! You said you want to hibernate, eh! Do you mean for us both to hibernate under a quilt in bed for a day and we just cuddle and hug each other and keep warm? MMMmmmm... I would love this my darling. Just to hold you in my arms and feel your warmth and love on me. Yes, your lovely boobs, laying across my chest, and I hug and cuddle you tight and love you... Then my mind thought of something else you said to me recently...

Time to reflect...

You said, "Your pussy does not like to get wet". So I was thinking maybe your pussy wants plenty of stroking. Mmmmm... soft gentle strokes and pussy is in need of some tender loving care!!! With some nice gentle stroking with my warm hands and plenty of loving I am sure your pussy would feel it likes to get wet. With me giving you so much love your `hot spot` would surely get aroused and have you puuuuuuuuuurring again! MMMmmmm... Those sexy blue eyes looking at me and you are just loving this!!

Then your sharp claws slip in between my legs and this pussy now wants to play with some balls!! Wow... You are getting sexy and playful now and really enjoying this, eh!... Oh! Now you have helped yourself from the treasure trove and taken my hot rod in your paws and placed it at the entrance to your love tunnel. I just knew this pussy likes to get wet!! Ooopps... now you have taken it up to your hot spot and you have started to push the tip of my hot rod up there where you have started rubbing it around and around your sensual hot spot. MMMmmmm... I am thinking to myself, nice pussy, but mind the claws!! Then like a cat on a hot tin roof so quickly you whip my rod just inside your love tunnel. Just gently, a little way in at first, but then you also start pushing down and I can feel it going in deeper and deeper with full penetration and only my balls rattling outside knocking at the door of your love tunnel. No darling, they cannot go inside too!!! Mummy should feed you and give you more milk! Yes I know you want my warm milky love juices, but they will come when I am ready to climax with you and we do this together... Sharing is caring!

Time to reflect...

Well my darling I am soon off to bed and you can dream the rest, but please, please do not talk in your sleep or wake Simon shouting out in the night... He, he, he, he,!!! I do not want him in the morning saying that you were shouting in your sleep, "Mike Turner I am going to DO YOU"!

Time to reflect...

Finally just to say three last words... I LOVE YOU
Mike xxx

E-mail from: Michelle
To: Mike
Date: 5 November 2012
Subject: Re: Time to reflect

Hi Mike

MMMmmmm... very nice e-mail from you!! Sexy and sensual... and yes, this little pussy is 'purrrrfectly' happy and contented with you giving her all of this attention. But Mike... you have to tell me, when my boobs are cold and my nipples have turned to American hard gums, or when you have got them so excited this happens to them... what does it feel like for you?... when your hands are caressing my nice warm boobs... when your fingers and thumbs are playing with these American hard gums... when you kiss them... lick them... suck them... tell me Mike, how does that make you feel? What goes through your mind when I trail my nipples over your body... when my hard nipples are sticking into you, and my soft warm boobs are cuddling you... and my arms are around you... how does it make your body feel?

When your hand moves down to stroke this little pussy... how does it make you feel when you are doing this? What goes though your mind, when you hear this little pussy purring at you. And when you touch my hot spot, and you set me on fire, and know that I want you... how does that make you feel?

And no, these tiger claws are nothing but gentle... they are not sharp at all... just gentle, loving, and sensual... so how do you feel when my nice warm hands skim down to those golden nuggets?... what goes through your mind when I cup them in my hands and gently massage them... stroke them... gently play with them? When I gently run my fingers all around them... Tell me how your body feels when I gently but firmly take your hot rod in my hand, and hold it gently tight... and when I move my hand up and down with nice gentle but quite firm strokes... What goes through your mind when I gently, gently rub one thumb over the tip of your hot rod, and a tiny bead of love juice escapes from the end, and my thumb so slowly and gently rubs this all over the tip of your hot rod... how do you feel then?... And what are you thinking?

Tell me how you feel, when I take hold of your hot rod, and guide it to my love tunnel??? Just let it slip inside a little, then back out... and up to the hot spot... and holding it gently but firmly in my hand, guide you round and round my hot spot... what goes through your mind then??? Then back down to the love tunnel, just waiting for you, and wanting you... to be guided by my hand into my love tunnel... to penetrate deep, deep inside of me... What goes through your mind then Mike? Tell me... Tell me how it feels to be inside of me in this way... tell me how you would feel to give me all of your love in this way... all of your love juices... when two people become one...

What are you thinking, when we have been together, looked into one another's eyes, but say nothing? Tell me how you feel when our lips touch... soft and tender... share these thoughts and feelings with me... I would love to know what goes on inside of you at these times. Caring is sharing, you said... I will share my side of this with you if you want me to. How each of these things make me feel... and what I am thinking about each of them... So Mike... if you want to know what makes me tick... just share...

One thing you do already know is "I LOVE YOU"... but I will tell you again anyway, just in case you have forgotten... Mike Turner, I love you... truly, madly, deeply...

Loving you always
Xxx xxx xxx xxx x
Michelle

---

5 November 2012 ~ Live Interactive Text

Mike: Hi Michelle... and how is my lovely pussy cat today? My sexy kitten!!

Michelle: Just purrrrrrrfect...

Mike: Nice pussy!!!

Michelle: She said, do you want to come and play?

Mike: Yes I know she likes to play... Ball games being the favourite game!!!

Michelle: She does like to play with a ball... or two..

Mike: That's good.

Michelle: And... she likes to be stroked...... she likes to be loved...

Mike: Yes I know... Yes she was purring more with every gentle handstroke over her fur coat!!

Michelle: She loved it... Just purrrrrrrrrrfect, she said... and yes, she would perform well to get some warm milk......

Mike: Yes... Likes being stroked all over!

Michelle: MMMmmmm... she loves that

299

Mike: Mummy should give her more milk.

Michelle: Daddy should give her some warm milk…

Mike: She likes sucking it from something!

Michelle: Licking…!! Sucking!!… Enjoying!!

Mike: Just mind the claws!!!

Michelle: The claws are not sharp… gentle claws… very gentle and loving…

Mike: Both paws gripping tight are enough with those long hard sucks…

Michelle: This is a loving pussy… not a spiteful one… don't worry, she is always gentle… treat her nicely and see…

Mike: I do not want to go to the doctors and explain this one!!! Hi doc… what do you think all these scratches are?

Michelle: ☺

Michelle: No, no, no she would not do that… she is a tame pussy… likes to be pampered… and likes to make a fuss of you…

Mike: Well, I did notice it had a winter coat… Maybe time for a bit more topiary.

Michelle: OK… but not too much now it is cold… ☺

Mike: Yes she could get a cold…

Michelle: You would have to look after it then…

Michelle: Sure I would, this would be no problem.

Michelle: Damn… I have to go… and just as my pussy was about to get some pampering from you.

Mike: Don't worry Michelle… it will keep… Bye

Michelle: Bye darling

E-mail from: Michelle
To: Mike
Date: 9 November 2012
Subject: Mr & Mrs Turner together

Oh Mike

Well, your impromptu phone call to me this morning, telling me your secretary was off sick… and then inviting me over…

Resulted in us seeing each other for a whole hour in your office. OMG... HEAVEN!!!

I just love you soooooooooooooooooo much, so very, very much... I have loved seeing you today... You bring so much joy to my life... I love everything I ever do with you... I loved the last time I came over to see you, but today was even better... when we walked around before, I felt as though I was being watched all the time, and we had little time in your office... but today, an hour to kiss and cuddle with you... Oh Wow!!.. soooooooooooooooooooo nice. When I wrote on Skype this morning I was waiting for a loving cuddle, I didn't expect that to happen today...

Don't think that because I am going out this evening I won't be thinking of you... BECAUSE I WILL BE... you are absolutely gorgeous... you are so sexy... my sexy sexy cyber husband... I look at you, and I just want to hug you, cuddle you, and kiss you... what lovely cuddles today!!! what lovely kisses!!!! your sexy sensual kisses... I can never get enough of you... Even though we had to keep our clothes on... My hands all over your body, and inside that shirt of yours... Your hands all over my body... MMMmmmm...... Sheer heaven!!!

And, to get my own back on you for all the photo's you take of me on Skype... well, here are a few really lovely photos of us together today... OMG we both look so happy... The best pictures I have ever seen of you... And the best ones of me... Are when we are together... We never look happier, than when we are together. Don't worry darling, they are deleted from my camera now, and my computer, and just in this e-mail as agreed.

Loving you always ~ with all of my heart
Xxx xxx xxx xxx x
Michelle

---

9 November 2012 ~ Live Interactive Text

Michelle: Hi darling... so nice to see you today. Is everything OK now you are back home?

Mike: Everything is normal... but I just want to say thank you for today and such a bonus to share our love together... You are lovely and I feel so close to you each time we see each other. I LOVE YOU

Michelle: I feel so close to you too darling... and I just love you so much... I will think of you for sure this whole weekend... AND... OMG I LOVE YOU.

Mike: Sending you my love and to Ditto for looking after your bits!!...

Michelle: So feel my love Mike Turner... it will be winging its way to you the whole weekend. Little Ditto says he loved seeing his Daddy today, and even got a kiss from him... I have e-mailed you the couple of photos we took today.

Mike: I have not seen the photos yet but I will look later... I think they tell a story of a married couple in love.

Michelle: He loved his Mum and Dad being together in the same place... he says he cannot wait until all three of us go to live in our mud hut. I cannot get enough of you Mike Turner...

Mike: Yes... He can come with us; we need the Southern Comfort and lemonade with ice. Bye... Love always... I am already missing you... Have a nice weekend.

Michelle: I will be thinking of you all weekend... and I love you... see you Monday on Skype. Bye darling... have a good weekend.

E-mail from: Mike
To: Michelle
Date: 10 November 2012
Subject: Re: Mr & Mrs Turner together

Hi darling

So nice to see you again yesterday. You are right, the photos are lovely. Yes, you are right, we never look happier than when we are together.

I thought about you all evening yesterday... I couldn't sleep just thinking about you... And, again today I cannot get you off of my mind. You are outrageously flirtatious with me... You are so sexy... And so loving... with a forcefulness that drives me wild... you are an extremely provocative young lady. And, I love it.

I love you Michelle... I will always love you.

Mike xxx

Michelle: Morning my darling... I love you so much... I have thought about you the whole weekend... I have re-lived every minute I spent with you Friday over and over in my head. I love your arms around me, it is the nicest feeling in the world, and I love your kisses. I guess I just like being with you... sharing our love!!! A love that is so special, so meaningful, so deep, and unbreakable...

Michelle: Thank you for lovely e-mails over the weekend... thank you for the so very lovely music, I have never heard that before, I just love it, and I love it especially because... you sent it to me!!! You melt my heart Mike Turner... I love you so very much.

Mike: I love you... Mwaaaaaaaaaaaaaaah! I loved Friday... Why?... Because I love being with you!.. Time with you is always so precious...

Michelle: Mind things don't slide off the corner of your desk today, where I sat and polished it with my skirt...

Mike: Mmmm Michelle... I wish I could see you again today.

Michelle: Me too darling... but we have to be very careful.

Mike: I will have to give my secretary more days off...

Michelle: As you said on Friday, we cannot meet in your office too often... So we will just savour that moment of Friday, and wait a while before we do it again.

Mike: I just love you so much Michelle... Always and forever... I have to go now.

Michelle: Bye darling... see you later

Later that day...

Michelle: Thank you for the song you sent me on Friday, I love it... I have never heard it before...

Mike: It was the words!

Michelle: I love the words... the words relate so well to us!!

Mike: I know, this is why I sent it to you.

Michelle: How I would like a hug and cuddle with you right now...

Mike: Yes please!

Michelle: And some of your nice kisses... MMMmmmmm... so nice to see you darling... so, so nice.

Mike: I loved it Friday.

Michelle: What a treat...

Mike: Yes a bonus treat!

Michelle: BIG BONUS...... and a real kiss and real cuddle with my cyber husband...

Mike: To feel you in my arms again, is so nice Michelle.

Michelle: Hey... I have to tell you something little Ditto said to me... he said... his Daddy gave him a kiss on Friday, and he is holding onto it tight, so that, next time his Mummy needs it, she can have it...

Mike: Yes... I know where that kiss will be too!! Right on one of your boobs, where he lives... He is just one lucky LITTLE SOD!

Michelle: He loves his home... especially when I laugh... or start dancing about... you know... shimmy those boobs...

Mike: Yes... I am sure when he gets shaken out of that valley ~ that kiss will be on the end of your nipples. Lucky LITTLE SOD!

Mike: I will download and send you your pictures later, which I have just taken. Wide open blue eyes... OMG... They do things to me!!! I love your blue eyes... I just melt into them...

Michelle: ☺ MMMmmmm......

Mike: And, I love that neck my darling... planting kisses all over it Friday... wow!! Yes... starting on your left side to start you off and to turn you on and raise the temperature and then across to your right and the same that side.

Michelle: Yes... we both know it does raise my temperature too... put to the test on Friday... I arrived cold... and left quite hot... you make me feel so sexy Mike Turner... I could have made love with you, right there and then in your office.

Mike: Yes I felt you, I thought my hands were warm, but placed on you really felt cold. Warm-bodied Michelle... Love it. You can keep me warm any day. Put the making love in my office on our slate!! ☺

Michelle: My hands were cold, as you know... Cold hands... they say... a warm heart... that is me!!!

Mike: I know where to come to warm my hands now... I bet Ditto was sweating down there all the way home! Whew, it's hot Mummy!! And, my darling you certainly have a warm heart, there is no doubt about that.

Michelle: It's the only thing he knows... he said he may share with you one day???

Mike: Really... I would love to live there rent free and enjoy the rides with him... I may just have to do this one day.

Michelle: Come on then ...

Mike: As my cyber wife would say... never say never!!!

Michelle: Just think of how nice and warm we could be cuddled up together when the weather gets really cold outside...

Mike: I do often!

Michelle: Put it on the slate......

Mike: MMMmmmm... That slate could get us in trouble!

Michelle: We won't stick around to take the consequences this time...

Mike: Be careful what you wish for Michelle!!

Michelle: It is just so nice to be this close to you again...

Mike: I know ~ I feel the same... It all suddenly felt the same like all those years ago to me.

Michelle: And to me...

Mike: Only the time has changed.

Michelle: Our feelings haven't though...

Mike: No... Never!

Michelle: They are still exactly the same...

Mike: Will always be the same for me.

Michelle: And for me darling... always remember that... what we have is very special...

Mike: I have never really forgotten. We said a long time ago, we would never forget one another, and we never have.

Michelle: I have never forgotten you either... I never will...

Mike: Maybe you are right Michelle... maybe we should have done things differently all those years ago?

Michelle: We would have been very happy together, for sure... once all the dust had settled... Is it ever too late?

Mike: I don't know darling? Is it?

Michelle: ?

Mike: We both need to go... love you...

Michelle: Love you too darling... so very much.

Mike: MMMmmmm… Lock me up with you… and then throw away the key!

Michelle: How nice would that be… Bye for now.

Mike: Hi my darling

Michelle: Hi darling… I am missing you… I need some of your love.

Mike: Pop over to my office then… I will give you some. ☺

Michelle: Will the chair in your office take the weight of both of us?

Mike: We can try and put it to the test!

Michelle: MMMmmmm… onto your lap I am sliding… with no knickers on… let your hot rod slide right inside of me Mike… deep inside of my love tunnel… how does that feel?

Mike: Nice and wet and warm.

Michelle: MMMmmmm… kisses for that answer… lots of loving kisses… let's put this chair to the test… I am gently going to slide up and down on you…

Mike: Is it the bounce test?

Michelle: Is it bouncy?

Mike: It has a certain amount of bounce!! Your boobs will be bouncing everywhere

Michelle: The boobs are all yours…

Mike: Maybe I should hang on to them. Yes… Both hands full now… OMG… Yes they feel great.

Michelle: Up and down I slide… getting warmer and warmer… wetter and wetter down there…

Mike: Yes… I can feel the heat generating off you. I can feel my hot rod, right inside of you… getting wetter and wetter… warmer and warmer… hotter and hotter…

Michelle: You make me `HOT`

Mike: You are HOT… and yes you are SEXY!!!

Michelle: I love you Mike…

Mike: I love you… MMMmmmm… and I mean really love you.

Michelle: Up and down I slide… getting a bit faster now… oh, now you want to kiss my nipples as well…

Mike: Sure do. Tasty, so very tasty... OMG... at my desk, on my office chair, and my hot rod is deep inside that love tunnel of yours, that I love so much... and one of your nipples in my mouth... I am in sheer heaven here!!

Michelle: Well Mike... I am loving this... and so are you... so faster and faster I move... how is the chair?

Mike: Standing up, like my hot rod. ☺

Michelle: That's good... ☺

Michelle: So faster, and harder I move... sliding right down onto you... so you are deep deep inside of my love tunnel... my arms around you... hugging you tight...

Mike: Yes, full penetration now... My nuts rattling at the door of your love tunnel.

Michelle: Your face is buried in my boobs... you are `HOT`now... your temperature has risen 13 degrees...

Mike: Yes... They are lovely and how I wish I could have them more often like Ditto does all the time... Ride me hard Michelle!!!

Michelle: Mike... you make me feel so sexy, I am going to climax here soon... and give you all of my love...

Mike: Well, this next push be prepared to take my love too.

Michelle: Pull me harder onto you...

Mike: Yes... I am exploding now... pumping my love juices deep inside that love tunnel.

Michelle: Oh wow... wow... wow... Mike I just love you so much... you fill me with so my pleasure!!

Mike: Take every last drop of love my darling.

Michelle: OMG... I love loving you... You get me soooooooooooo sexcited...

Mike: My love is for you...

Michelle: Thank you... My love is for you

Michelle: I have all of your love juice inside of me now... mixed with mine... love juice cocktail... now that I am here on your lap like this I have a question... do you think this topiary heart needs a little trim? ☺

Mike: I have had my hot rod in there, not my head... I need to check that out later. ☺

Michelle: Can you not see from where you are sitting on your chair?

Mike: I can see your pussy is wet now though!!

Michelle: Oh... this pussy doesn't mind getting wet... she loves your love juice... she loves having a shower with you... she loves having a bath with you...

Mike: Yes... I know she likes a lot of loving. She is purrrrring... I am yours... you sexy little kitten.

Michelle: Oh WOW!!! All mine?

Mike: Yes... Body, mind and crown jewels.

Michelle: I wish you were darling... Oh how I could love you...

Mike: Come on then... do it.

Michelle: Come on then... but be careful... we say things like this... and then...... we get virtually married...... or I end up in your office... One day Mike Turner... one day...

Mike: Promises, promises!!!

Mike: It was so nice to be with you last Friday, only in my office I know... not in bed, but I feel such love for you Michelle.

Michelle: I felt it last Friday I told you, we have something so special; our love for one another just grows and grows... The way you look at me Mike, when you just look and say nothing, your eyes say it all... And let's not forget I have actually been to bed with you...

Mike: Oh..How can I ever forget!!! Even although it was a long time ago.

Michelle: We have a combo of the real world, and a cyber world...

Mike: True... Good that we have seen both worlds.

Michelle: I love this world with you... I love the real world with you.

Mike: It makes what we say here so truer...

Michelle: I know... because we do know each other... we have touched each other... we know what the other really feels like... the kisses... the hugs and cuddles... our skin......

Mike: As I said, only time has changed. It feels the same now, as all that time ago... Just the same feelings for me, maybe even stronger now than before.

Michelle: It feels exactly the same for me too... even although we are each twenty years older... you are still exactly the same... my feelings for you have never changed... maybe I love you even more now than I did then... my love for you just grows and grows...

Mike: MMMmmmm... I love you... We have something very special... very very special... I think we had itthen and now... It never really died... it never will...

Michelle: A love that against all odds has stood the test of time...

Mike: Then and now most definitely...

Michelle: Thank you for loving me...

Mike: Thank you for being YOU.

Michelle: OMG, look at the time, we need to go...

Mike: Bye for now Michelle... I love you

Michelle: "DITTO"

E-mail from: Mike
To: Michelle
Date: 15 November 2012
Subject: Our little Ditto's confessions

Hi Michelle

Our little guy `Ditto` wanted to speak to his Daddy in confidence and we have had a heart-to-heart talk. What you would call a Daddy and Son conversation, a man-to-man talk!

I said, So, what is the matter? Come on Son, you can talk to Daddy and get this off your chest!

He replied, well Daddy this is what I wanted to talk to you about just this very subject matter! You know my home is right in the middle of my Mummy's boobs. Yes I do know this, Son... and you are a very lucky little sod to be having all this fun down there living rent free and being kept nestled and warm down in that cleavage between those lovely big boobs.

But, but, but, Daddy!! What, Son? Since meeting you again Mummy has now become very sexcited and her heart starts beating loud and banging like a loud drum... Bang, bang, banging in my ears!! So much so I think I am going deaf!! No, Son... you are just imagining all of this!!

But, but, but, Daddy! What, Son? Since meeting you again Mummy does not always wear her bra!! So apart from all the banging and noise, her lovely big boobs are cut loose and are in free fall. Then when Mummy gets sexcited or moves about with no bra on I get battered and shaken about all over the place. I am in the middle of all this bouncing about down there. No, Son... you are just imagining all of this!

But, but, but, Daddy! What, Son? Mummy is so sexy and hot and it makes me feel sexy and hot down there sitting in the middle of those lovely big boobs. Seeing my Mummy's big boobs turns me on and when they shake and rub all over me like that I feel hot and sexy too. My eyes get big and large with sexcitement watching those big boobs shaking and rubbing all over me. Daddy I then have an orgasm right in the middle of my of Mummy's boobs!!... I now think I am going blind!!... No, Son... you are just imagining all of this!!

But, but, but, Daddy!! What, Son? You know those big hard long nipples which you call American hard gums? Yes, Son! Well, when Mummy gets sexcited they grow so big and hard and stick out.

Daddy, my Mummy's nipples are so nice and tasty... Yummmy, yummmmy and scrummmy. Daddy, there is plenty there for us both to share and we both like sweet tasty American hard gums. Mummy says sharing is caring. Yes, Son!! Well I play with them and give them a little kick around with my feet. When they really start bouncing around I just hang on them and have a good swing around. It is like being on a fair ground and the rides are sexciting and free... Swings, two-a-side football, roller-coaster, bouncy castle, merry-go-rounds, helter-skelter rides and even the tunnel of love! My body and legs are now getting worn out with going on so many different rides!... No, Son... you are just imaging all of this!

But, but, but, Daddy!! What, Son? Mummy says she likes you going through the tunnel of love with her and then getting wet at the end. So Daddy, why does Mummy keep screaming and shouting, push it all the way down inside the love tunnel and then out and back in again. Mummy knows pussy will get soaking wet again!... No, Son... you are just imagining all of this!

But, but, but, Daddy!! What. Son? Mummy says she likes sucking your big lollipop and she likes playing with your gold nuggets.

Mummy likes you stroking her pussy and her hot spot!! No, Son... you are just imagining all of this!!

But, but, but, Daddy! What, Son? What about the bare bronco riding that Mummy has on you? When Mummy jumps on top of you naked she can ride really fast and then she really shakes those boobs everywhere. I noticed, Daddy, that you grab hold of those lovely big boobs tight with both hands. I am glad by then I am in my box out the way because that would make me sea-sick!!... No, Son, you are just imaging all of this!

But, but, but, Daddy! What, Son? All those years ago you named me `DITTO`, How come you gave me this name? Well, Son, this was a special meaningful word for just Mummy and Daddy at the time... It means "I LOVE YOU." Oh!... I love you too Daddy and my Mummy!! I was thinking it meant something very different:

D... Down
I... In
T... Two
T... Tits
O... Orgasms

Oh!! Daddy please do not tell Mummy I was thinking this all these years that I have lived down in the middle of Mummy's lovely big boobs!... No, Son... you are just imagining all of this!

But, but, but, Daddy! What, Son? I am so glad you are back now with my Mummy because she is so happy and sexcited now and I need a Daddy. Yes Son, you have a lovely sexy Mummy and I really love her, but you are still a lucky little sod, but we are now a family again so you are no longer a little bastard, He, he, he...

Good night... I love you...
Mike xxx

E-mail from: Michelle
To: Mike
Date: 16 November 2012
Subject: Re: Our little Ditto's confessions

Hi Mike

I just love your last e-mail... it is hilarious!!! I have read it three times today, and it just makes me laugh out loud each time... I love you when you are crazy!!! I love your sense of humour!!! You always brighten my day... you are my winter sunshine... The crazier you get... the more I love you.

I look forward to that cruise together one day!!! Oh Mike, just imagine... we would have the time of our lives!!! Let's go on that cruise for real... Let's go live in a mud hut...

I will always love you...
Michelle
~x~

---

26 November 2012 ~ Live Interactive Text

Mike: Hi my sexy gorgeous babe.

Michelle: Hi my sexy handsome hunk.

Mike: Do you know I think if I publish this saucy text I could make a fortune... But don't worry, I would never do that unless we spent the money I made on a one-way ticket to wherever we could hide!

Michelle: Where shall we hide?

Mike: I think somewhere warm for sure! Can you imagine us living somewhere cold, we would be SAD! (Seasonal Affective Disorder)

Michelle: We both need blue sky and sunshine.

Mike: Yes, love it.

Michelle: And we both need something else... each other...

Mike: You are not wrong there Michelle

Michelle: Maybe one day we should do this?

Mike: Maybe we should? ☺

Michelle: MMMmmmm what a lovely thought.

Mike: Sorry, have to go darling. Bye for now and nice to chat with you again, my sexy wife.

Michelle: Bye darling… I don't want you to get into trouble… but, I actually really could do with a cuddle right now…

Mike: Okay… Strip off, jump in bed and I will be round, we have 31 minutes. Not exactly a quickie!!

Michelle: Publish that book… and let's go somewhere warm and sunny…… and hide forever.

Mike: MMMmmmm… bye.

Michelle: I am being serious!!… Byeeeeeeeeeeeeeeeeeeeee

Mike: You tease me!!!
Byeeeeeeeeeeeeeeeeeeeeeeeeeeeeeeeeeeeeee

Michelle: Never!! ☺

Mike: Always!! ☺

---

3 December 2012 ~ Live Interactive Text

Michelle: Hello sexy husband… It's cold… and I would like one of those cuddles you sent me yesterday right now please… you tug at my heart strings 24/7.

Mike: You know I love to tug on your nipples!! ☺ I just keep hanging on!!

Michelle: It is cold… and I want to hibernate with you.

Mike: Well Michelle… I think we should both go to bed together for the next six months…

Michelle: So do I darling… we need to hibernate together to keep warm… "Sod everyone else"…

Mike: Well until April, eh! We want to wake up and see the bulbs spring into life.

Michelle: That would be nice… just us snuggled up together for the winter… and then the spring…
yesssssssssssssssssssssssssssssssssssssss!!!

Mike: I like spring!

Michelle: I like the spring too…

Mike: I love bouncy things too

Michelle: Bouncy, bouncy, boob-a-licious Michelle... come and bounce in bed with me for six months...

Mike: Mmmm... I would love to give them a bounce around the bed. ☺

Michelle: So would I... let's do it... maybe nobody will even notice we've gone?

Mike: I may just love you more and more.

Michelle: I would love a cuddle in that jumper with you right now...

Mike: There is room for you, but you would have to face me otherwise the jumper would get out of shape.

Michelle: Ok... I will take my top off and come in there and face you...

Mike: I would love those lovely boobs and hard nipples sticking into me.

Michelle: Do you know what? I would love that too!!!

Mike: I would love it too... If they really pressed hard into me I could bring them up and then I could have a nibble on a bit of nipple!!

Michelle: They would press really hard into you right now...

Mike: Nice and tasty!!

Michelle: Oh how I would love to do that with you right now... I really mean this... cuddled up so, so close, and so, so tight... skin to skin right there inside your jumper.

Mike: Yes... Love it and you would be so tight in here with me, almost like super glued together.

Michelle: You would be saying... "Michelle... those nipples are extra hard today"...

Mike: I love to see them with no bra and you looking so sexy!

Michelle: MMMmmmm... One day Mike!!!

Mike: MMMmmmm... One day Michelle!!!

Michelle: I have to go now darling... Love you... so very much

Mike: Bye for now darling... Love you so very much too. Mwah

E-mail from: Michelle
To: Mike
Date: 13 December 2012
Subject: A wonderful year with you darling

Hi Mike

One whole year has passed since we started to e-mail with each other... How I have loved, and enjoyed this past year with you!!! I have loved reading all the e-mails you have sent me, and some of them, I have read a few times over... I never in my wildest dreams thought I would end up on Skype with you... but it has been fantastic to text chat with you... talk to you, and most of all see you on there... And to top it all off, we have even actually seen each other this year... for just one touch, just one hug, just one kiss... in fact more than one kiss, more than one hug... So, so, lovely to have done that with you darling... Although sometimes I wonder if I dreamed that part? I am glad we took the photos we did, because I sometimes have to look at them to think, yes, it did happen, and it was very real. How, I have loved to feel your arms around me, and feel your lips touching mine... just like they did all those years ago.

You make me laugh... you make me smile... you absolutely thrill me at times... we have made love in our cyber world, you have introduced me to the world of cyber sex ~ and I never imagined it could be so much fun... OMG this has been the best!!! You have given me comfort and joy... I feel your love... I hope you feel my love for you... Here in this cyber world, we have married one another, what a lovely feeling... you as my husband... Our love is timeless, endless, true and meaningful... We share sensual moments here, that I could only ever dream of with you... We have shared so much in the past year... and I love being just a little part of your life... and I love you being in my life...

I just love so much feeling this close to you again... I hope the next year continues as well as this past year...... Who knows what the year 2013 will bring for us? And I mean here `US`!!! I hope it is as good as the past year has been... 2012 has been quite a difficult year for us within each of our own lives, but we have always been there for one another, and this has brought me much comfort at times… We share so much here!!!

I never thought I could love you more than I did all those years ago… but my love for you just grows and grows… Feel my love Mike… feel it with this kiss… my body so close to you we are touching… my soft lips touching yours, with a gentle, tender and oh so loving kiss for you… feel my love with this kiss… if you could hear me right now I would whisper to you, "Mike, I am so in love with you"..

I love you Mike Turner… so very very much…

"I will always love you"…

Always and forever…
Michelle
xxx xxx xxx xxx x

E-mail from: Mike
To: Michelle
Date: 16 December 2012
Subject: The Year 2013

Hi Michelle

How time just flies and goes so quickly and yes, another year has nearly gone. A year when there have been some very sad times, a year when there are still some worries and a year when there has also been some joy, fun and laughter. A year when you became my cyber wife. A year when I have felt your love for real again and yes, that touch and that kiss that I really never thought possible. Let us hope 2013 is a good lucky year for us both. The year 2013 has to be in our favour and 13 has always been our lucky number. Therefore let us both have more tears of laughter and joy rather than any tears of sadness. Life is like a book; some chapters sad, some happy and some exciting. We both know life can change in an instant and tomorrow is never promised. Just live every day to the full and be happy and enjoy. Nobody knows our future, fate or destiny, but if we never turn the page we will never know what the next chapter holds.

I am glad you took those pictures of us in my office. Like you, I now think to myself, did that really happen? Nobody else can see them, but I know when you mentioned your Mum to me the other day, I know she would say, "They make a lovely couple". I will always remember her words to us when I met your parents. Yes, a long time ago now, but like my love for you it never fades.

Always be safe and take care. I miss you and I will always love you...

Mike
xxx

PS... We need to stay healthy, so we need to eat good healthy food and take plenty of sexercise!

E-mail from: Michelle
To: Mike
Date: 19 December 2012
Subject: Merry Christmas

To my darling sexy husband

Just to wish you a very Happy Christmas, and thank you for all the joy you have brought to my life this past year.

Actually, now I come to think about this... I wouldn't mind spending Christmas with you in a mud hut... our mud hut... eating turkey sandwiches and drinking Southern Comfort and lemonade, well it may be difficult for me to cook you roast dinner on our BBQ! Maybe we should install a cooker in our mud hut? Just, loving one another... Making love in as many different positions as we could ever imagine! Who needs anything else?

Never rule out the possibility of this happening one day!!!!

I love you Mike Turner... and I love you being my husband......

ALL MY LOVE ~ MICHELLE
xxx xxx xxx xxx x

Michelle: Hi Darling...
Mwaaaaaaaaaaaaaaaaaaaaaaaaaaaaaaaaaah

Mike: Wowwwwwwwwwwwwwwwwwwwweeeeeeeeee... that is a big kiss!! I love your long passionate sexy kisses.

Michelle: MMMmmmm I would love one of them with you right now... long... sexy... passionate... sensual... MMMmmmm...

Mike: You are feeling sexy tonight, eh!

Michelle: You always make me feel sexy!!

Mike: My cyber wife just drives me craaaaaaaaazzzzzzy!

Michelle: If I were with you right now... I would say... sexy husband... love me!!! I would put my arms around you... and kiss you so softly... so tenderly...

Mike: I know your TLC must be working overtime this week, with your family problems, but you can still find time to share it with me. Have I told you that I love you and you are lovely?

Michelle: These kisses would be so soft they would make your head spin... You have the lion`s share of my love Mike Turner... you have a very large portion of my heart...

Mike: Thank you Leo!

Michelle: You always make me smile... chuckle... laugh... you are so good for me... this has been one hell of a couple of weeks... you are my saving grace in all of this...

Mike: We are both good for each other!

Michelle: Yes darling, I think we are...

Mike: We just have a very naughty streak whenever we meet, or talk, or text each other. Why?

Michelle: I think I am this way with you because... I fancy the pants off of you...

Mike: I have no pants on... I am here naked with only a keyboard to cover my modesty!!

Michelle: OMG... I am going to phone on video link and see for myself.

Mike: Dare you!

Michelle: Will anyone hear?

Mike: No of course not.

Michelle: Never dare me anything!!!

Mike: Dare x 13 ☺

Michelle: I'm going to do it... will anyone hear it?

Mike: No, I will mute the sound.

Michelle phones the video link... they do not talk, as Mike is not home alone, his speakers are on mute, and they sign language to one another for 10 minutes...

Michelle: So... you have pants on after all...

Mike: You are disappointed, eh! I am dressed after all ☺ but, nice to see you for 10 minutes... good sign language we made up... only we could understand it...

Michelle: I want to undo those buttons on your shirt...

Mike: Cheryl just shouted up the stairs... what are you doing up there?... I have just shouted down, I am about to do Michelle Turner!! ☺

Michelle: Did she? Whoops!!!... let's not disappoint her... I want to kiss that hairy chest of yours.

Mike: You are getting very sexcited now!!!

Michelle: I am... what are you going to do about it?

Mike: Come on... Inside my shirt you and give me a cuddle.

Michelle: Yes please... I would really love that.

Mike: Turn that cam back on... I will undo my shirt and let you in.

They video link again, in silence...... Mike undoes his shirt, and shows her just what a naked cuddle with his bare chest would be like.

Michelle: OMG... yes please... Mike you are so sexy!!!

Mike: My sexy Michelle... Take your top off...

Michelle: MIKE!!! Naughty!!!

Mike: ☺

Michelle: I want to come in that shirt with you... and love you...

Mike: I want you here with me right now...

Michelle: I love you so much darling... you always thrill me.

Mike: I am sure you need some cheering up yourself.

Michelle: Well you have certainly done that...... thank you.

Mike: Some Mike magical laughter tonic will do you good.

Michelle: You are sexy, and you are funny darling... you always make me laugh... you have cheered me up a treat today.

Mike: If you were mine... I would just love you to bits.

Michelle: I would you too darling... I really would...

Mike: Nice to see you and text with you this evening, I know you have had a lot on your mind.

Michelle: You have also been on my mind... I always have room for you... in my mind... in my heart... I love you so much.

Mike: You be careful... or we could end up in a mud hut.

Michelle: Maybe one day we will...

Mike: MMMmmmm...

Michelle: You had better go darling, the internet police will be there checking on you again in a minute... good job you have your shirt back on!! ☺

Mike: I cannot leave without saying...

Mike: I LOVE YOU...... so very much

Michelle: Do you know what this if for? Mwaaaaaaaaaaaaaaaaaaaaaaaaaaah

Mike: No, tell me... and tell me where it is heading?

Michelle: It is because... I LOVE YOU SO VERY MUCH... it is heading straight for your heart...

Mike: Wow... Got it... and my heart is pumping now.

Michelle: Goodnight darling.

Mike: Goodnight my darling.

Michelle: I never want to leave you... but you have to go, before you get into trouble...

Mike: You never have left me... You will always have a part of me, and I will always have a part of you.

Michelle: You honestly melt my heart at times...... Goodnight darling.

Mike: Goodnight Michelle... Sleep tight... and cuddle me tight in your dreams.

Hi Mike

Christmas time is a time I have always thought of you...
Christmas Eve especially, the day we shared that first kiss... the
day you turned my world upside down!! We share something very
special Mike... we are two peas in a pod... we have so much in
common, that is for sure... and we still love one another all these
years on, against all odds of everything else... I do question
sometimes, what this really says about each of our marriages???
Are our marriages to other people quite as perfect as everyone
else would assume they are, when you can love another person as
we each do?

Enjoy your Christmas, darling, with your family, as I know I will
enjoy mine too... But I will think of you from time to time over
the festive period, I know I will... Sometimes I just wonder what
you are doing, and where you are... I may find it difficult to look
on here for the next five days, so do not worry if you do not hear
from me... I have sent you an e-card today, that I hope you
receive on Christmas Eve, but never done that before, so hope you
get it then... I love you so very much, I really do... you are one
very special person to me. You have a place in my heart nobody
else has ever touched...

My love to you always and forever
Michelle
xxx xxx xxx xxx x

E-mail from: Mike
To: Michelle
Date: 24 December 2012
Subject: Merry Christmas ~ Happy 2013

Hi Michelle

My biggest reward is to have seen you and your smile, know you are happy and feel our love together. I know life is sometimes cruel and this year has not been easy, but this is what friends are for and show that we love and care. You are more than just my friend. How nice it has been to really hold you in my arms and have that touch and kiss.

Merry Christmas and a Happy New Year. Sending you best wishes for 2013. I wish you good luck, good health, love & happiness. Have a joyous Christmas.

The New Year 2013 will be a good lucky year.

I will always love you…
Mike
xxx

CHAPTER ELEVEN

Much of the communication for the next three months took place on the telephone, or video link... But, still some e-mails and text took place...

E-mail from: Michelle
To: Mike
Date: 4 January 2013
Subject: Happy 2013... Mr & Mrs Turner

Oh darling

Just so lovely to see you... to feel you... to touch you... kiss your lips... to feel your arms around me... to feel your heartbeat... to feel your hands on my body... your soft, gentle, tender kisses just melt me... to cuddle you and listen to Celine on your office computer with you. Listen to that again darling, I love the words, as I told you earlier. And, now when I hear that song, I will remember being right by your side today, and listening to it with you.

Today was an unexpected treat for us!! And when an opportunity arises we are never ones 'not' to grab it with both hands... And, when your office door closed and we were both safely inside (without prying eyes upon us) this is just what you did, 'grabbed me with both hands'. It was just so nice to cuddle you and feel the warmth of our bodies together, for all the times we talk about this in our cyber world, nothing is as good as the real thing.

I'm sorry for all the hassle we had all those years ago, and I am surprised by things you did not know... I know you went to visit my parents when I was on holiday in1992, you will have to tell me sometime what you said to them, and they to you... they did tell me, but I don't think we ever discussed it... they both liked you a lot, and would have been happy to see us end up together, as they told me then, you are both already in the war zone, the dust will eventually settle and everybody will move on... if only we had done it darling...

I loved you then... I love you now... I will always love you...

Michelle xxx xxx xxx xxx

---

4 January 2013 ~ Live Interactive Text

Michelle: So nice to have seen you today my darling... when I said on the phone two days ago, I could do with some of your loving... I didn't expect to get it for real two days later... I love you Mike Turner... I am so glad I married you... I will love you for the rest of my days... and with what has happened in the past, and how my feelings for you have never changed, you know I mean this when I tell you I will love you forever...

Michelle: Hello darling, you are here online, I didn't know if you would be able to. Is everything OK in your world, after us seeing one another today?

Mike: Everything is normal darling... So nice to see you today

Michelle: Phew!!! Good...

Mike: This will be a good 2013.

Michelle: I think you are right darling... just so lovely to see you and touch you...

Mike: I held you in my arms today. We talked a lot. I am sorry for all the problems I caused you.

Michelle: We caused them for each other darling... not one of us... or the other of us... it was a joint effort...

Mike: They say love hurts... and that sure did hurt.

Michelle: It certainly did... hurt me like nothing had ever done before... or since... but we have always hung onto a little bit of each other... and now, I think we have quite a lot of each other again...

Mike: Sure... I am glad we have this little bit to hang onto... and it was so nice to hang onto you today, and just hold you in my arms, so close to me.

Michelle: I love you Mike Turner

Mike: I love you Michelle Turner ~ I even love our little Ditto for looking after you all this time. Thank you for today

Michelle: Thank you darling... you should go, we don't want to have any problems today... Bye darling

Mike: Bye Michelle... I will always love you... Always and forever...

Michelle: "DITTO"

E-mail from: Mike
To: Michelle
Date: 4 January 2013
Subject: "I Love You"

Hi my darling

Thank you so much for today, you really are lovely.

I cannot tell you how much it means to me, just to hold you in my arms for that hour today. Yes, today, somehow we talked about things that happened long ago, and each found our things that we never knew. We went through such a lot at that time darling, and things were so painful and unsettled for both of us. Maybe you are right, maybe we should just have gone for it, and by now have spent these past twenty years together... But... We didn't... ☹

My mind will be on nothing but you this weekend, I already know this. But, my Michelle... It was worth it to see you today.

I love you... Mike xxx

---

7 January 2013 ~ Live Interactive Text

Mike: Hi darling... You tease me now with body chocolate... chocolate coated nipples... I want a taste test please

Michelle: Hi darling... I would love you to have this taste test

Mike: Cover your boobs and nipples with chocolate... Climb on top of me, and let me feast on you coated with chocolate... I will just lay back and enjoy and you can treat me, woweeeeee! Those gorgeous hard nipples of yours dipping in and out of my mouth... MMMmmmm... I know how hard your nipples get, remember!!!

Michelle: They are hard and erect right now... because you make me feel sexy!!! I would lavish you with sexy-ness... I would give you a real pop-up!!!

Mike: I hope you have not had a sneaky look.

Michelle: How I could love you right now Mike Turner. OMG... I love being naughty with you. I cannot wait to get this chocolate... and try it with you...

Mike: Mmmmm... I would be in heaven. Where do you want your chocolate on me?

Michelle: I am going to start with a little message on your chest that says "I LOVE YOU"... then my initials on your heart... and then... down your body I will go with the paint brush... or my fingers... trailing the chocolate... right down to the crown jewels... chocolate covered nuts, they are my favourite sweets!!

Mike: OMG... I may need to give you second helpings.

Michelle: Then... a chocolate coated lollipop!!!!!!

Mike: This is what I meant... Have the full works.

Michelle: Oh... what fun this would be...... licking all of this chocolate off of each other... we wouldn't need lunch... or dinner

Mike: You may find the chocolate lollipop has a creamy warm filling so be careful when you suck it hard.

Michelle: Sucking... licking... more sucking and licking... MMMmmmm YUMMY!!!

Mike: We are naughty... I have probably just made another fortune on this chapter alone when I publish my book.

Michelle: Hurry up and publish it... then we can run away with the money

Mike: I would love you to bits.

Michelle: I would love you to bits too darling...

Mike: You would be placing your life in my hands... What more can I ask for than this?

Michelle: I would place my life in your hands...... and I would love you forever... you know that... I wish I could have one of your kisses right now

Mike: One day Michelle... One day!!!

Michelle: MMMMmmmm... One day!!!!

Mike: Sorry darling, I have to go... Bye... Love you...

Michelle: Bye darling... love you too... so very much... even more than chocolate!!!

Mike: ☺ I love the chocolate, I love the nipples, I love you.

Michelle: I will put one finger in the chocolate tub... then try a little on your lips... finger back in the pot... then rub that finger all over one of my nipples... now see if you want to try it?

Mike: Yes, a little lick with my tongue, and then you know I am greedy... so then a big mouthful.

Michelle: So more chocolate from my finger... this time I will run my finger all over both nipples for you to try some more...... how is that?

Mike: My nipples are not nice like yours!

Michelle: No, that was my fingers over my nipples...

Mike: Oh... Got it. You are getting me too sexcited now.

Michelle: So now, I am rubbing two fingers, one over each of my nipples, little chocolate circles around and around each of my nipples...... how do you like that?

Mike: Yes nice and I will have second helpings now. MMMMmmm... My sexy boob-a-licious Michelle...

Michelle: OK... more chocolate... more on my nipples... and then my fingers are getting wider with the circles, and it is going all over both of my boobs!!!!: try that!!!!

Mike: Michelle... My mouth will not take your full boobs you know this, not all at once darling...

Michelle: You will have to just lick, lick, lick... suck, suck, suck...

Mike: I think your nipples would tickle the back of my throat. OMG, now what am I saying... Chocolate coated nipples tickling my tonsils!!!!

Michelle: MMMmmmm... nice... I like my nipples in your mouth... I like your tongue round and round them... I especially like you sucking them... and even gently nibbling them...

Mike: Oh... Michelle you have put too much chocolate on your boobs and it has dripped down in between your legs... What do you think should happen now?

Michelle: Oh... have I ?... maybe you should lick that off too... ?

Mike: MMMmmmm... Yummy, yummy, I am going for it.

Michelle: MMMMmmmm... OK... do it!!!!

Mike: Well, your pussy may get wet with a bit of licking off.

Michelle: Oh wow... woweeeee!!!! OMG Mike... you get me sooooo sexcited!!!

Mike: MMMmmmm... Yes I think I can get if all licked off okay... Oh!!!... I may have to part your legs just to get the inner bit of chocolate. Your clit that sensual part has got some on.

Michelle: Not the hot spot!!! OMG you should definitely get the chocolate off of there

Mike: I think I had better give that a lick and a little gentle suck and remove the chocolate... Are you reading my mind again here?

Michelle: OMG Mike... you do actually drive me crazy!!! My hot spot is throbbing at the very thought of this...

Mike: I need to just rub over it with my finger to make sure all the chocolate is exposed.

Michelle: Oh Mike... and you say I am teasing you with the chocolate!!

Mike: A nice long lick there now and my tongue twirling around to make sure no chocolate is left there... Michelle, why are you moaning with delight, in the way that you do!!

Michelle: OMG Mike... you send me to heaven, that's why...

Mike: I think it is a moan and saying, more Mike, give me more... I need to make sure, so a nice finger all over and to check there is no chocolate left hidden. Your love tunnel looks tempting now.

Michelle: Oh... what could you possibly fill it with?

Mike: Well, has any chocolate found its way inside there?

Michelle: I don't know... maybe you have a dipstick to test it?

Mike: I sure have my darling!

Michelle: Maybe you could check for me then...

Mike: Long enough to go to the bottom

Michelle: Slip it gently inside of me then...... and see how it feels...

Mike: I will just dip the end in a little way and test. Just gently… in and out… OMG… I have slipped it out and it is covered in chocolate… Now what?

Michelle: I don't know…

Mike: I have a chocolate covered dipstick.

Michelle: I hope you are not chuckling out aloud there

Mike: Maybe it is your turn to do the licking?

Michelle: OK… I will… I am sure I would like a chocolate covered lollipop… so here goes…

Mike: Be gentle with me

Michelle: Gentle little licking with my tongue first… then gentle little sucking with my lips… oh yes… this is very nice… I will try more… gentle sucking with my lips… and take more of you into my mouth… this is so nice, I am going to suck this quite firmly now… hard and fast and firm sucking…

Mike: After cleaning the dipstick, you know it should be plunged in your love tunnel again to check.

Michelle: Mike… you are getting a very big boy here… this chocolate lollipop has grown even bigger… and chocolate coated nuts too!!

Mike: Look you know my chocolate nuts are not for consumption.

Michelle: Well, I will have to see about that… I will only lick the chocolate off of them…

Mike: I think it is ready to check inside that love tunnel again.

Michelle: Maybe it is time for this delicious lollipop to go back into my love tunnel…

Mike: Stop reading my mind, you!!! ☺

Michelle: We are on the same wavelength you and I… ☺

Mike: What wave-length… You have my full length of my dipstick here now. Back to the entrance of your love tunnel and a little push and you are taking me all the way in this time, my sexy baby.

Michelle: My hot spot is actually throbbing here… I can almost actually feel you in there

Mike: I think me licking your hot spot has got you sexcited. You are nice and wet so just let me pump away with nice long strokes in and out.

Michelle: You have got me hot here…… pump me with your love stick!!!!

Mike: Touch bottom and then out... Nice to have you like this and sharing my love.

Michelle: OMG Mike... I love you so much... no more out... I am too sexcited now...

Mike: Just be quiet Michelle, your neighbours will hear you...

Michelle: Come on Mike... fill me with your love juices...

Mike: Let us do it together... Okay.

Michelle: Come on then my baby... together... all of my love for you... coming your way...

Mike: One more deep penetration into your love tunnel and I am leaving it in to explode.

Michelle: OMG... WOW... I am exploding all around you... feel my love for you Mike... feel the sensations you give me... look at my sheer pleasure!!

Mike: Yes I am filling you up now, so nice to give you my love and for you to in return give the same.

Mike: Stop reading my mind again YOU!

Michelle: We think the same things... give me your love juices...... fill me with pleasure......

Mike: I will give you all my love... and forever.

Michelle: And I give you all of my love in return... and this is forever too. For us there is no end...

Michelle: We are bonded together forever with our love for each other... I love your loving... I love you making love to me...

Mike: I love you darling... Look at the time darling... we both need to go

Michelle: OMG... I didn't realise the time.. Bye darling

Michelle: I love the feelings you give me Mike, you fill my heart with love... and put butterflies in the pit of my stomach...

Mike: So in love with you Michelle... Bye

---

9 January 2013 ~ Live Interactive Text

Michelle: Morning my sexy cyber lover

Mike: Morning my always sexy Michelle... I think after all that chocolate yesterday, I need to shower you off this morning...

Michelle: Come on then darling, I have just had my shower, and only have a towel around me at the moment, but more than happy to jump back in that shower with you...

Mike: Come on then darling, lets use up all the shower gel... smother my body in shower gel with your bare hands... How hard can you make my crown jewels this morning?

Michelle: Round to your chest... all over that hairy chest of yours... sexy sensual kisses on your lips... how does that feel?

Mike: I am enjoying this.

Michelle: So down... down... down... I go with my hands... down to the crown jewels... first of all the golden nuggets...

Mike: MMMmmmm... Just waiting for the hands to come down here.

Michelle: They are there... both hands now on your hot rod... MMMmmmm

Mike: It has just grown another two inches.

Michelle: Oh wow... so I see... my slippery hands all over it... checking for any chocolate... down to my knees I drop... so I can study this up close...

Mike: Mind it does not poke you in the eye

Michelle: I think I have just found some more chocolate on the golden nuggets... so... I am going to have to lick this off with my tongue... I really do love chocolate covered nuts... my favourite sweet...

Mike: I think these chocolate nuts already have a good filling inside.

Michelle: OMG Mike... I have just seen more chocolate on the rocket... so...... my hands will take care of the nuggets, caressing them nice and gently... and I am going to lick the chocolate off of the rocket... is that OKwith you?

Mike: Is this on the head of the rocket or down its main shaft?

Michelle: I am starting at the bottom... licking my way right up its main shaft...... right to the top... now I am right at the head of the rocket... flicking my tongue around it...

Mike: My nuggets are full so be careful there in no leakage at the top. It can easily get out of control in this state of mind...

Michelle: My lips are gently all over the very tip of this rocket now... gently sucking it

Mike: I think there is a leak at the top now... I did warn you!... I think you need to jump on now and let me give you a ride!!!

Michelle: I will have a ride in a minute... I like the flavour of this rocket... sliding in gently in and out of my mouth...... sucking gently......

Mike: The pressure is building up all the time and the thrusters are ready to go.

Michelle: So where do you want it to go off?... where it is, in my mouth, with all this licking and sucking... or in my love tunnel... you can choose

Mike: It`s natural place... Your love tunnel is where it belongs. Jump on and I will give you a ride of your life.

Michelle: Come on then Mike... hug me... love me... and make love with me... I am jumping onto that rocket of yours...

Mike: It will be to heaven and back.

Michelle: It surely will be... so I am about to jump aboard the rocket...

Mike: Just slip the nose in and the shaft will just follow all the way in. This booster does wonders!

Michelle: My boobs are sliding all over your chest, because they are so slippery...

Mike: I can feel them... I love those boobs!! I want to hold onto them... but you have taken both feet off the floor now, and have them around my middle, so my hands are both on your bum... pulling you right onto me... So go for it...

Michelle: I am enjoying my ride on your rocket... it seems to be getting faster and faster... pumping hard right into me... OMG... I am in heaven... I think your rocket is about to blow...... and I think I am too...

Mike: This is it Michelle... You are just about to get my full load... Here it comes!!

Michelle: OMG... Mike... Heaven... I can see stars... Shooting stars!!!... Maybe I should make a wish? Your load has landed right inside of me, and docked in Venus!!

Mike: And this is right where it belongs... I can see the shooting stars too Michelle... maybe we should both make a wish?

Michelle: I have made my wish... I hope one day it comes true!!

Mike: I have made my wish too... if it is the same wish as yours, it must come true one day!!!

Michelle: Oh darling... I so hope it does...

Michelle: We are both late for work now!!

Mike: I don't care... I will say... I've been on an important mission this morning before coming into work... It has set me up for the day

Michelle: It sure has darling... Nobody is going to believe me when I say I am late because I have been for a ride on a space rocket... Bye for now... Mwah ☺

Mike: Mwaaaaaaaaaaaaaaaaaaaaaaah ☺

---

11 January 2013 ~ Live Interactive Text

Michelle: Good evening my darling... Oh how nice, I have the whole evening to myself. I know you are not at home alone, but nice to be able to text with you for a while

Mike: Hi, my gorgeous babe... It is so cold outside tonight

Michelle: Really cold... only two degrees... we need to share our body heat

Mike: Body heat is best!

Michelle: I know... come on then...

Mike: MMMmmmm... Michelle

Michelle: MMMmmmm...... Mike......

Mike: I want you right now!

Michelle: I want you too...... really really want you...

Mike: `YOU` !!!

Michelle: The more I see you... the more I talk to you... the more I text with you... the more I love you...

Mike: MMMmmmm my Michelle... you fill my heart with your warm love

Michelle: Do you know how to repair a broken heart?

Mike: Don't say that

Michelle: It is a proper question? I will tell you the answer...

Mike: Okay...

Michelle: I have discovered over the past year... there is only one thing that can repair it...

Mike: I know...

Michelle: Do you know what I am talking about here?

Mike: You take the half back that we both shared and gave to each other a long time ago. They cannot be apart and it is now a happy heart and both together and been repaired.

Michelle: The only thing that could have ever repaired either of them then... Mine feels so much better now...

Mike: What was your answer?

Michelle: The only thing that could repair it... was the thing that broke it...

Mike: Yes I know... I am sorry!

Michelle: Don't be sorry... it wasn't all your fault...... 50/50 We were both in it together darling... We both knew what we were doing...

Mike: Maybe we just never knew how much it would really hurt?

Michelle: No, I don't think we knew that until it happened... But, both much better now???... Yes?

Mike: Yes

Michelle: When I told you I would always love you... this was so true...... and here I am 20 years on telling you...... I loved you then... I love you now... I will always love you

Mike: Let me see you on cam for a quickie... Okay?

Michelle: A QUICKIE??

Mike: Yes a quickie. ☺

Michelle: We don't like quickies ☺

Mike: But I have to turn the sound off... and cannot be long, just in case anyone comes up here

Michelle: OK

They video link in silence for a couple of minutes... hold their arms out to one another... touch their hands on the screens... the love is written all over each of the faces. They revert back to text.

Mike: It is like the silent movies! ☺ Can I see a teardrop in those eyes Michelle?

Michelle: Can I come in that shirt please... please?... I really want to... I really do want to cuddle up with you for the night now

Mike: "DITTO"

Michelle: One day this is going to happen for real...

Mike: I wonder when this will be and where?

Michelle: Who knows?

Mike: I am yours!!!

Michelle: I wish you were mine!!!

Mike: I am yours and always have been. You have never left my heart or mind.

Michelle: I love you darling… You stole my heart a long time ago… hurry up and get our book published…

Mike: Okay.

Michelle: I could drive you crazy for the rest of our lives ☺

Mike: Michelle, you have already done that

Michelle: I would be saying Mike cuddle me…… Mike kiss me… Mike love me… never let go of me… I've got 20 years to catch up on…

Mike: I would say Michelle… okay, you jump on top and enjoy the ride. 20 years` bareback riding to catch up on… OMG! You are going to kill me!!

Michelle: I would love you like you have never been loved before!!!!

Mike: Are you going to love me? Or kill me off with 24/7 'Sexcercise'? I would die with a smile on my face for sure.

Michelle: We will have to share the sexcercise programme… enjoy each other… OMG… I just know we would…… we would either be laughing… or kissing… or cuddling…… or having sex!!

Mike: Yes we would, you know we would make a good couple together…

Michelle: We would make a fantastic couple… we would have the time of our lives…

Mike: You bet we would. We have a lot of time to catch up on

Michelle: Do you think this will ever happen one day?

Mike: I don't know Michelle… I think we would both like it to

Michelle: If only life were that simple???

Mike: Indeed ☹

Michelle: Well, you know what they say… where there is a will, there is a way

Mike: ☺ We will have to see then… what destiny has in store for `US`

Michelle: It is the year 2013… 13 is our lucky number… this could be our lucky year?

Mike: Find a way then…

Michelle: We will have to start doing the lottery, so we can get enough money to go for it?

Mike: Or publish our book?

Michelle: I thought it was going to be your book?

Mike: Everything is 50/50 with us, you know this!!

Michelle: Maybe putting our book together then, could be our answer?

Mike: Maybe we should try this!... and see what happens?

Michelle: Maybe we should ☺

Michelle: OMG... I have company at the door, I have to go darling... Really sorry ☹

Mike: Okay darling... Goooooo!!!... Mwaaaaaaah

---

16 January 2013 ~ Live Interactive Text

Mike: Hi my sexy baby

Michelle: Hello sexy 'YOU'

Mike: How's your American hard gums?

Michelle: Cold... frozen!!

Mike: Come here and I will defrost them for you!!!

Michelle: I'm on my way ☺

Mike: Okay, see you in 13 mins. ☺

Michelle: If only!!!

Mike: Mind how you come, I want you in once piece here. I do not want any broken nipples either

Michelle: You would have to lick and stick them

Mike: No problem... I would stick them back on and like putting ice back together, mould then on again!!

Michelle: MMMMMmmmmm... I will look forward to this... One day!!

Mike: One day!!

Mike: You have all my love now and forever!

Michelle: You have all of my love now... and forever too

Mike: My love for you was there all the time...

Michelle: Thank you darling... you melt my heart at times

Mike: This will warm your nipples back up, and melt them too...

Michelle: I am waiting until you can melt them for me… slowly slowly melt them… long and lingering love with you

Mike: My kisses will warm your nipples, but I think they may grow longer and harder.

Michelle: MMMmmmm Mike…… I would love this with you…… we should go and live in the sunshine together somewhere in the world…… and laugh until the day we die…… oh and I want to die first, don't ever leave me on my own…

Mike: I just love you…

Mike: Sorry, have to go darling… byeeeeeeeeeeeeeeeeee

Michelle: Bye Mwaaaaaaaaaaaaaaah

---

23 January 2013 ~ Live Interactive Text

Michelle: Hi my sexy lover… I would love a piece of you right now

Mike: Hi my sexy babe… Which piece?

Michelle: Those sexy lips… I love those sexy lips… and those sexy sparkly eyes

Mike: Do you know you flash those sexy eyes when you say something sexy?

Michelle: Do I?

Mike: Yes… I have noticed this several times. Body language does not lie.

Mike: This is like being secret silent lovers!!!

Michelle: Nobody I would rather have as my secret lover

Mike: Do you remember that song… `Secret Lovers`?

Michelle: Yes… you bought it for me… do you remember?

Mike: Secret lovers, that's what we are…

Michelle:… And we love each other so…

Michelle: We are not 'only' secret lovers now… we are secret husband and wife ☺

Mike: Yes… Officially in our cyber world… and in our book!! ☺

Michelle: I love the thought of being married to you…

Mike: Legally can only do this here in our cyber world

Michelle: We like illegal moves…

Mike: I like your sexy moves…

Mike: I have got the message in your eyes and they are saying…
  Take me to bed and make love to me.

Michelle: MMMmmmm…… they would be for sure

*They connect by video link for the next half hour, and say goodbye
for the day.*

E-mail from: Michelle
To: Mike
Date: 24 January 2013
Subject: All because of you

Hi my darling

I hope your long day at work went quickly for you today, and was
more enjoyable than when you do not have much to do at work
some days. I hope it gave you something to focus on…… because
for me…… my mind has just wandered off in your direction at
every opportunity for the past 24 hours. Yes, I have had a full-on
day at work, but when not concentrating on the patient in front of
me, I just cannot stop thinking of you today, and when I do it
makes me smile.

I spent half my evening thinking about you yesterday, trying not
to chuckle out aloud when I thought of the funny and entertaining
afternoon we had on Skype. When I went to bed, it took me ages
to get to sleep, because when I closed my eyes, I could just see
your smiling face, chuckling away as you were typing things on
your computer yesterday. It was hilarious asking one another
questions face to face, and then typing the answer to see if we had
the same answers… OMG and how many times did we? It really
is uncanny, just how alike we really are!!

You fill me with joy Mike Turner… I enjoy the things we do
together so much… You are priceless!!… and I honestly love you
so much… You are very very special to me… Even when I tried
to stop loving you all those years ago, I could not… and now I
just love you more than ever… I am so glad that we have found a
way to be together again… this is not just our cyber world, we
have a mix here of a cyber world and the real world. So I just

thought I would tell you... I am positively glowing today... All because of YOU!!

I love you... I will always love you...
Michelle
xxx xxx xxx xxx x

---

28 January 2013 ~ Live Interactive Text

Mike: How's my baby ?

Michelle: Hello my yummyilicous delicious husband

Mike: Are we going over to cam?

They video link for half an hour, have to leave, but come back an hour later

Mike: Be good!!!... If you are going to be naughty, only be naughty with me.

Michelle: Come and play with me

Mike: Just hang on then and then I will play with those double C's

Michelle: I would love to feel your arms around me

Mike: Did you feel my arms wrap around you and undo your bra?... Yes they are natural and free!!

Michelle: Oh wow... come and have a no bra cuddle with me now then...

Mike: Yes please Michelle Turner. Do you like the picture I have just put up there of you?... I love it... sorry I took some earlier, and didn't even tell you

Michelle: I am telling you that woman in that picture is in love with you...

Mike: Here is my gorgeous baby looking so sexy!!

Michelle: She LOOOOOOOOOOOOOOOOOOOOOOOves you!!!!

Mike: I love this baby too... Really love her

Michelle: You should marry her...

Michelle: Oh yes... that's right, you already have ☺ well, virtually!!

Mike: I have already

Michelle: ☺ Again!!!

Mike: Yes stop it you!!! ☺ same time again!!

Michelle: We amuse each other… love each other……

Mike: Do you know we can laugh over nothing… We must both be crazy!!

Michelle: I think we have sent one another crazy!!

Mike: Bye, must go.

Michelle: Bye darling. Mwaaaaaaaaaaaaaaaaaaaaaaah

Mike: I may be able to come back later?

Michelle: OK… I will leave this on for as long as I can

An hour later, Michelle has to sign out…

Mike: Where is my baby? Maybe you cannot makeSkype now, eh? I am just here talking to myself again. I will download your pictures whilst I wait to see if my baby is coming back here. I am just here waiting, waiting and waiting for my Michelle to pop up! You will never believe this 13 pictures!!! Welcome to my world… I am going crazy!! I will send these 13 pictures by email. Just talking away to myself… Byeee

---

4 February 2013 ~ Live Interactive Text

Michelle: Hi My sexy horny husband

Mike: About my tattoo?

Michelle: Tattoo?… What tattoo?

Mike: I have had a tattoo… where? you may ask. On my hot rod…!!

Michelle: Wowsa!!… I did not expect that one!! ☺ I would like to see this tattoo…

Mike: The guy said, how big do you want it?

Michelle: And… you said?

Mike: I said, how big do they come? He says, do you want initials MT or Michelle Turner. I said, I want all the way in full, she likes it that way.

Michelle: Oh darling, you always make me laugh ☺

Mike: He said, what font size… I said, she likes the full works… So start with 13.

Michelle: I should have a look at the tattoo… and see how long it takes me to make it read Michelle Turner…

Mike: He said, OMG... That is talking big if you start at 13.

Michelle: MIKE... I CANNOT WAIT TO SEE IT...

Mike: I said, that is how she likes it, fully blown up and ready to explode.

Michelle: I would like the challenge of seeing just the M T to start with... then I will time myself to see how skilful I can be...

Mike: I said, whilst you are at it can you do anything with the golden nuggets?... I said, I will ask her for any suggestions

Michelle: OMG... I am doing to have to think about that one... Darling... I would say... Don't do it... it would be tooooo painful... I will tattoo those golden nuggets for you in CHOCOLATE!!! melted chocolate... and then... lick it off...

Mike: Okay, that would be less painful.

Michelle: It wouldn't be at all painful... It would be bliss...... you would not get bored with me Mike Turner!!!

Mike: Okay... I will settle for the chocolate bliss... I think you can make the milky creams to go with it.

Michelle: MMMmmmm... I am sure I can do this. It would be the best chocolate treat you have ever had!!!

Mike: He did say to me, does that keep her happy and contented and give her plenty of pleasure?... I said, I think so!!! She shouts out, give it to me Mike.

Michelle: You think you are a choc-o-holic now... wait until you have tried body chocolate!!... yes Mike... "Give it to me... more, more, more"

Mike: MMMmmmm... She does get sexcited!

Michelle: Chocolate hot rod... chocolate golden nuggets... for me

Michelle: And for you... chocolate nipples... chocolate boobs...

Mike: And later plenty of milk creams

Michelle: Chocolate everywhere we want to put it...

Mike: Now I am hungry... I need some chocolate!!!

Michelle: Do you mean horny?

Mike: Woweeeeeeeeeeeeeeeeee! Okay... Cut them loose and let them free and we will do it.

Michelle: I am on it...... action... go......

Mike: Okay ride on Michelle... Slow trot and building up to a gallop.

Michelle: We could live on love... Southern Comfort... body chocolate... and each other...... WOOOW---eeeeeeeeeeeeee

Mike: I just hope there are no fences to jump over!!!

Michelle: Yes... Mike Turner... you always cheer me up...... no fences... but... plenty of bounce from Michelle

Mike: We should try it... What about the chair!!!

Michelle: So what is this?... you sitting on the chair?

Mike: That is a big fence to jump... Just hang on tight, okay!!! Aintree the chair fence!

Michelle: You make me laugh out loud... I am crazy!!!!... it is official... So are you sitting on the chair... and I am riding?

Mike: Yes, you have chocolate all over your boobs and nipples... I am sitting on the chair, and you are facing me... legs wide apart, and sitting across me...

Michelle: So you can lick the chocolate off my boobs and nipples... as they bounce... MMmmm... interesting, but nice positioning!!

Mike: Wow... 13 font has just grown to 31 font.

Michelle: OMG... Mike... the hot rod has just slipped into my love tunnel... Ouch... font 31... ??? be gentle with me Mike...

Mike: Do not worry it is only the font size not 31 inches... You really are getting greedy Michelle.

Michelle: I would be greedy for your love 24/7

Mike: Have I told you... I LOVE YOU?

Michelle: Could you put up with being sectioned with me for 6 months... locked away with me for 6 months?... no... you haven't told me for ages that you love me

Mike: MMMmmmm... Forgetfulness I think they can do something about this.

Michelle: I need locking away... with you... and every single day of your life... I would tell you... I LOVE YOU

Mike: Yes please... ☺

Michelle: MMMmmmm...... yes please too... ☺

Michelle: I think I should just bury you head first into my chocolate boobs... and I will ride up and down on the new tattoo... up and down... in and out... right out... right back in again...

Mike: Yes go for it... How fast can you ride me?

Michelle: How fast and hard do you like it?

Mike: Try me?

Michelle: Hot... and... horny now!!!!! so fast... and hard... and passionate; we are about to climax...

Mike: OMG Michelle... You are always so sexy...

Michelle: Oh Mike... my world is exploding around me here... you send me into orbit... and I can feel your love juices exploding inside me... Oh wow...

Mike: Sorry I have to go... I will try and download the pictures if I can now and send them to you later... Bye.

Michelle: I hope you can eat your dinner after all of this chocolate? Byeeeee... love you

Mike: I love you too, my sexy passionate cyber wife

---

5 February 2013 ~ Live Interactive Text

Michelle: So I am hear looking for my sexy horny husband... Has he been done yet? or is he still waiting to be done?... Or is he being done right now, and the engineer is reading this!!! OMG... he will get the shock of his life... you may have to gag him after he has read the draft copy of 'our book'... So... Mr Engineer... you may have read `Lady Chatterley`s Lover`... you may have read `Fifty Shades of Grey`... but what do you think to this as a basis for a book? yes... I agree with you... it will be a best seller...... Hey Mr Engineer... how inconsiderate of you... you have stolen my precious time with `MY MIKE`...... couldn't you have come earlier, or later?

Mike: I want to be done, but by YOU!

Michelle: Hello... is that `My Mike`... or the engineer?

Mike: I am the engineer... you are sexy and naughty!

Michelle: Oh... I cannot talk to you then... I want my Mike...

Mike: Anyway it is your cyber husband here now Mike.

Michelle: How can I believe you? You could be anybody? Give me a code word

Mike: "DITTO"

Michelle: Hello my sexy husband... well... I have two things on my mind... can you guess what they are?

Mike: Hot rod and hot spot! ☺

Michelle: 1)... YOU 2) body chocolate and YOU... so I guess you are kind of right

Michelle: Are you all done now darling? Is your computer OK again now?

Mike: I am waiting for you to DO ME!

Michelle: OMG... I would love to do you...

Michelle: I LOVE YOU...... even more than chocolate......

Mike: Woweeeeee... I love you more!

Michelle: What, more than chocolate? Never!!

Mike: Yes, more than chocolate... and you know how much I love chocolate

Michelle: Woooooowweeeeeeeeeeee!! You have made my day!!

Mike: Bye my crazy lover... I am being called, and have to go now

Michelle: Bye darling... mwaaaah

E-mail from: Mike
To: Michelle
Date: 5 February 2013
Subject: Photos of my Michelle

Hi darling

See attached photo`s taken of you today on Skype. I cannot help that there are so many. But, when you kept getting up and dancing around, I could not help but keep pushing that button. Well the top you had on certainly had a nice v neckline, and when you shimmered those boobs at me... As you can see, I had the most fantastic view!!!

MMMmmmm...... Michelle......

Love always... Mike xxx

E-mail from: Michelle
To: Mike
Date: 6 February 2013
Subject: A very boob-a-licious Michelle

Hi my darling

OOOooooo...... EEEeeeee...... naughty 'boob-a-licious' Michelle!!!... What on earth was she up to?... oh yes, showing you one of the new tops she bought for work. Maybe this one is a little 'boob-a-licious' for work!!...

If we ever meet up to spend a day together in bed... I will bring my camera, and you can take some photo's of Michelle's boobs without the top on!!!... I will then e-mail them to you, and you can add those phot's to your collection...

MMMmmmm... how nice would that be!!!

I LOVE YOU...
Michelle Xxx

E-mail from: Michelle
To: Mike
Date: 8 February 2013
Subject: I am feeling sexy and naughty

Hi 'my sexy Mike'

So... It is my day off, and I have the day to myself... I have had my shower and washed my hair... Spoken to you... and yes Mike, you would love to come over and help me here... So... I have only a towel wrapped around my wet hair... a dressing gown on... and nothing underneath it... so one little tug of the belt and the dressing gown would be off... But...

You remove the towel from my hair... rough my hair up, with your fingers... get the hairdryer in one hand, turn it on... and with one hand your fingers are gently combing through my hair, and you are drying it with the hairdryer... MMMmmmm nice!!!... so this takes quite some time, as you keep stopping to give me nice sexy kisses on my lips... MMMmmmm Mike... I am enjoying this...

Then you say, this is dry now Michelle... so I need to check to see if the topiary heart needs drying...... Gently and slowly you undo the belt of my dressing gown, and pull it undone... the dressing gown falls open... and you slip it off my shoulders, it falls down my arms... down my body... and lands on the floor... Now I am naked...!!!

With the hairdryer... you gently, seductively dry the topiary heart... MMMmmmm... your fingers gently skimming over the topiary heart... warm heat from the hairdryer blowing directly onto it... Oh WOW!!!

Now I am feeling, not only naughty, but very sexy!!!... Then you say you have to make sure I am dry all over... and you will test this with your lips... So... you start with a sexy sexy long lingering kiss on my lips... Oh wow... heaven... then kisses all over my face... then down to my neck... nibble all around my neck... OMG Mike I am feeling soooooo sexy now... Your kisses move to my shoulder... and then to the other... little kisses, with little nibbles... OH SO NICE... then to the other shoulder... and then down my arms, one and then the other... Heaven!!!... and then back to my neck... Mike, you are driving me crazy here... Then slowly your kisses move down... right down to one of my boobs, kiss it all over, and then start to suck gently on one nipple... I am definitely going crazy here now... then you repeat this with the other boob... Nipples like American hard gums now... You make me feel so sexy...

Then the kisses move down my tummy... long lingering sexy succulent juicy kisses... OMG Mike... you are good at this... further down your kisses go... right down to the topiary heart... Yes, you say, Michelle I made such a good job of this heart shape, it looks good... but tastes even better... OMG... your tongue is on my hot spot now... Yes Mike Turner... you drive me crazy... I am now feeling, extremely naughty, extremely sexy... and wanting more...

To be continued......

Love always and forever
Michelle xxx

E-mail from: Michelle
To: Mike
Date: 8 February 2013
Subject: Pleasure for you...

MMMMmmm my darling... the pleasure cannot only be for me... so now it is your turn...

I would place such a soft and sexy kiss on your lips... and slowly with gentle fingers, undo the buttons on your shirt... one at a time... one button undone, a kiss on your lips, two buttons undone a really sexy kiss on your lips... three buttons undone, MMMmmmm... more kisses... all buttons undone, and gently, slowly pull the shirt out of your trousers, a very sexy passionate kiss on your lips and my nipples just touching your chest... MMMmmmm we both like this... we like it a lot... you have that very sexy look on your face... My hands gently skim down your chest, gentle little massaging on the way... Undo the belt on your trousers... gently undo the zip on your trousers... let them fall to the floor... Really sexy passionate kisses now... gently slip off your underwear...... now my hands are by your face, so gently, so tenderly I hold onto your face, and kiss you with all my love... How I want you right now... slowly, gently, my little kisses all over your face... down to your neck... succulent kisses all around your neck... all over your shoulders, and my hands skim all over the skin on your back... hands up onto your shoulders again, and then gently run down your chest... down to your tummy... around to your hips, and skim down your hips... down to your knees, hands gently around your knees and fingertips up the inside of your thighs... around the crown jewels, but not touching them... and again I repeat this, warm hands skimming across your tummy, down the outsides of your hips, back up the insides of your thighs, and this time skim all around and around the crown jewels... Oh Mike... sensual... sexy... provocative......

Kisses on your lips again... kisses moving down your chin... kisses moving down your neck... kisses skimming down your chest... sexy, succulent, lingering, loving kisses... moving down onto your tummy... lots of loving kisses here... moving slowly, oh so slowly... downwards... downwards... downwards... down to your pelvis... slowly, seductive, gentle, tender, and oh so loving... down the front of your hips... down to the golden nuggets... gentle caressing of the golden nuggets, with gentle little fingertips... MMMMMMmmmm so, so nice... and then, gentle little kisses on the golden nuggets... Oh Mike... you love this... so plenty of attention here... more gentle caressing of the golden nuggets, as my lips move onto your hot rod... kisses all the way up your hot rod... your tattoo has grown... yes, I can read the whole of the tattoo... Michelle Turner... Mmmmmm... still caressing the golden nuggets...

Yes... My sexy delicious husband... Much pleasure for you today... no quickie here today... just long lingering pleasure for both of us......

To be continued......

How I love you Mike Turner...

With my love
Michelle xxx

E-mail from: Michelle
To: Mike
Date: 8 February 2013
Subject: Sexy... Sex-o-licious... Love making

Oh Mike...

Now we are both feeling very sexy indeed... I know what you would say now... My hot rod is standing to attention, and needs to go into its natural home... But... I would say to you, Mike... we still need to play...

You pull me on top of you, so I am kneeling astride you... you take hold of my nipples, just fingers and thumbs, and play with my very erect nipples... I lean forward, and place one nipple against your lips... Oh.. My... God... you are looking so sexy now... gently you suck on one nipple... then the other... MMMmmmmm... soooo nice... soooo sexy... such love... but your gentle little sucking of my nipples, turns to gentle little biting... you are soooooo ready for some loving...

I take hold of your hot rod, and guide it towards my hot spot, and just with the very tip of your hod rod I touch my hot spot, and make gentle little circular movements... Oh wow... how nice... how sensual... how sexy... and just a tiny amount of love juice seeps from the end of your hot rod... we are both so ready to make love now... I lean down, kiss you on the lips... tell you how much I love you... love your body... how much pleasure you give me... and oh so slowly and gently just guide your hot rod into my love tunnel... then gently back out... more kisses on the lips... oh so passionate now... gently back in my love tunnel I guide your hot rod... this time right in... right in... right in the warm, loving place, just waiting and wanting you... I keep still, and can feel you throbbing inside of me... MMMmmmm... I grip you inside of me... the muscles from my love tunnel doing all the work... and then slowly start to move up and down on you, sliding your hot rod in and out of me... you lean up and suck on my nipples... Oh wow, Mike... this is heaven... and I can hear you saying... Michelle... I can never get enough of you... or your loving... I hug you so tight... Mike Turner... I love you with all my heart... and I am so glad I married you... and then we are kissing... kissing so passionately... holding each other so tight...

So now, I give you the choice, do you want to stay where you are? Or do you want to go on top?... I think I have found my answer, when you pull me tight onto your hot rod again... you are sucking and biting my nipples... your hands around each of my boobs... oh yes... I have found the answer... you want me to stay right where I am... so I move up and down on your hot rod... a little more friction now... grip you tight inside of me... up and down... you bury your face into my boobs... as we both become frantic... and then I hear your groans of delight and pleasure, and I feel your love juice just pumping inside of me... Oh... My... God... this does it for me... and my world explodes around you, as you send me to heaven... Such pleasure... Such wonderful sensual pleasure... your love juice just keeps on coming... and my pleasure goes on and on... I am holding onto your head, as your face is still buried into my boobs... You are still biting and sucking at my skin, my boobs, my nipples... We are both in absolute heaven... nothing else matters... just us... right now we have become one... not your pleasure... not my pleasure... the pleasure is one... with you still inside of me... our bodies completely wrapped around one another, it is hard for either of us to know where our own body ends, and the other starts... We have become one... our hearts beat as one... and it is sensational...

When I try to move away from you a little, you just hold onto me tighter, and say, don't leave me yet Michelle, just hold me... So still with your hot rod inside of my love tunnel, I hold onto your head, and rock to and fro on you... your face still buried in my boobs... I love you Mike Turner... I will always love you... I can feel you so warm, even quite hot... we hold onto each other so tight...

To be continued......

Love Always
Michelle xxx

E-mail from: Michelle
To: Mike
Date: 8 February 2013
Subject: I will love you forever

Oh Mike... my darling Mike...

Wonderful love making with you... I love you so much... Eventually, we lay next to one another... Snuggled up together... With you laying on your back, I snuggle into you... My boobs snuggled onto your chest... Our legs around each other... One of your arms is around me... the other hand is caressing one of my boobs... and I gently lay one hand onto the crown jewels... and we just drift off to sleep...

Happy... Contented... So comfortable... So in love...

I love you Mike Turner...
You are so easy to love...
I will love you forever...

Michelle xxx

E-mail from: Mike
To: Michelle
Date: 9 February 2013
Subject: Re: I am feeling sexy and naughty

Hi my sexy Michelle…

I have just read your first email. So… You are feeling sexy and naughty, eh!… MMMmmmm… I love you when you are like this! I think you are very passionate, raunchy and horny too and I know just what you want! Yes, I know what you want my darling and I have the very `hot rod` waiting and ready for you which will satisfy and cure your wild exotic desires!

Yes, I opened the emails from the bottom up, so that I read them in order… so I thought I should keep to the same process working on you… So yes, your topiary heart first, my fingers stroking it gently and slipping onto your `hot spot` and giving that some nice strokes with my fingers and a nice gentle circular rub. It maybe be wet from you having a shower, but it will certainly get a lot wetter by the time I have finished with you Michelle Turner…

To be continued…

Love… Mike xxx

E-mail from: Mike
To: Michelle
Date: 10 February 2013
Subject: I am feeling sexy and naughty… cont/…

Hi my sexy Michelle…

I have just come to the conclusion why you like me starting at the bottom and working up! So, having started on your topiary heart and having gently give you some nice long brush strokes with my fingers and having found your `hot spot` and given you a gentle massage… I can tell this little pussy loves being stroked and is now purrrrrrrring! OMG… You have now rolled over onto your back with your legs wide apart shouting, I want more and more

Mike! I have not even started on your boobs yet, but you are getting sexcited!

Hey Michelle!!... You have just shut your legs tight and crossed your legs over, but my fingers are still inside there!! You want a tight massage, eh! Your hot spot is now squeezed tight on my fingers and you are shaking, squeezing tight! Wiggle your fingers there!!... Mike, this is sensational!! The purrrrring is now an sexcitable moan tone and you are just loving this.

Now what?... You have now released the tight grip and you have again opened your legs wide apart and you have just parted your topiary and what is staring at me... Yes, your hot spot!!! You are shouting, come on Mike, give this some loving, some kissing and some gentle sucking. I am feeling sexy and naughty!

To be continued...

Love... Mike xxx

E-mail from: Michelle
To: Mike
Date: 12 February 2013
Subject: Re: I am feeling sexy and naughty... cont/...

Hi my darling

You are Seriously... God... Damn... Sexy in these e-mails...

I am very sexcited, and looking forward to the next instalment...

I hope you have ten minutes this weekend to continue??? And... You carry on however you want to my darling... bottom to top... top to bottom... or anything inbetween... because do you know what?... I'm sure I will enjoy it all anyway...

I am sure I will just melt into you... and love you right back.

I will send you your 'job description' next week. You can then decide if you want to take on the job as 'The Bodyguard'?

Loving you always & forever
Michelle
Xxx

14 February 2013 ~ Live Interactive Text

Michelle: "Happy Valentine's Day my darling Mike"... I know you probably could not be here today, so do not know when you will see this... But you will know it was you I was thinking about on Valentine's Day... I love you... I will always love you

Mike: Hi my darling... I have just read your emails and your e-cards... Thank you.

Michelle: Hi darling... and thank you for your card and e-mail today... My romantic, loving husband... Mwaaaaaaaaaaaaaah

Mike: I cannot stop... I just want to say... I love you and Happy Valentin`s Day!

Michelle: We both sent each other Whitney love songs!!

Mike: Thank you... but I have to tell you her songs... and you... will get me certified.

Michelle: MMMmmmm... lock you away, and throw away the key... Me and you together forever... ☺

Mike: I love that thought Michelle... more than you know... ☺

Michelle: MMMmmmm... Me too...

Mike: I must go... Bye and big hugs and cuddles

Michelle: Bye Darling... Even bigger hugs, cuddles, kisses, and LOTS OF LOVING

---

18 February 2013 ~ Live Interactive Text

Michelle: Hi darling... how was your day?

Mike: Hi my Michelle... my day was okay... how was yours?

Michelle: Somebody told me today I am a very 'bouncy' person... what do you think they meant?

Michelle: Bouncy hair? Bouncy personality?

Mike: Bouncy boobs! ☺

Michelle: or... Bouncy boobs?

Mike: Especially with no bra and they are free!

Michelle: Yes... I thought so. I think I really need that bodyguard at work at the moment!! Put your application in for the bodyguard job... I think you may get it...

Mike: MMmmm... I would love to guard that body of yours!! But, I do not want the job part-time, you need 24-hour protection!! I am not working back-to-back with someone and sharing this job.

Michelle: OMG... I love the thought of you guarding my body 24/7... full-time job then? MMMmmmm... we will have to see what we can arrange?

Michelle: Bye for now darling

Mike: Bye for now Michelle

---

21 February 2013 ~ Live Interactive Text

Sometimes when Mike is not at home alone, they video link in silence, so that they can see one another, but type the text... As today!

Michelle: Hello my handsome and horny husband...

Mike: Hi my sexy babe

Michelle: You are soooooooooo sexy

Mike: Stop it, you are making me laugh... How can I do it in silence? I sound like a husky dog.

Michelle: OMG... I have now just read the e-mail you sent at 6.20pm... I have barely been able to concentrate on my work today, thinking about the one you sent this morning... You have had my head in a spin all day today...

Mike: Well... The next chapter will be the closing climax.

Michelle: WOW...... I cannot wait ☺

Mike: So hang on, because I will surely be doing this for sure.

Michelle: Make sure my hands hold onto that tattoo with both hands... and you have put me on top, because you like my boobs bouncing all over you, and so that you can see them in action!!

Mike: Of course there is a motive in my madness.

Michelle: I am loving it... I love all of your words of how we make love.. Tell me what it feels like for you, when you climax... tell me Mike, how it makes you feel...

Mike: I will have blown out the big ends!

Michelle: You make me laugh... you get me all sexcited... and I just love it...

Mike: I think there is also a weak gasket because it leaks out the end

Michelle: I think these e-mails, you are sending me at the moment should all go in 'our book' when it gets published

Mike: Adult reading only!

Michelle: Defo… and… I love your tattoo…

Mike: What about if it ever became a film?

Michelle: Wow… very graphic!!! well… you never know…

Mike: I know you love my tattoo… you cannot get enough of it

Michelle: ☺ Well, this definitely has not been a quickie… this is my kind of loving…

Mike: Well when I finish the last chapter, you will be worn out, and me… I will be hanging on for your life… You are in the driving seat, it just depends how fast you can go through the gears when you are sitting on them.

Michelle: I can go as fast or slow as you want me to…

Mike: Before you blow the head gasket I mean

Michelle: Well… I will just have to bring you to the brink… and stop for a few seconds, so you calm down… .

Mike: Wow… Do not blow the bottom ends out… You know when it comes it cannot stop and I do not want to take the backfire… Anyway, that is teasing.

Michelle: I hope you are not laughing as much as I am here…

Mike: And do not take it out and put your finger over the hole at the top either.

Michelle: I cannot type for laughing now

Mike: I will explode…

Michelle: Well… I will make sure you explode with full enjoyment inside my love tunnel

Mike: Mmmm… Yes I will ensure you have a full tank of love.

Michelle: I think you have got more and more 'sexy' since we got married

Mike: My darling I had better go… Do you know you are so lovely and I love you…

Michelle: I love you Mike Turner… so very much

Mike: I love you Mrs Turner… and when I have finished the last chapter you would have your full names deep inside your love tunnel… and filling you with love.

Michelle: I wish you were here with me now

Mike: I wish that too... I am so glad that we have our cyber world though

Michelle: Me too... Goodnight darling

Mike: Goodnight my Michelle... Sleep tight

Michelle: Mwah

Mike: Mwah

E-mail from: Mike
To: Michelle
Date: 20 February 2013
Subject: I am feeling sexy and naughty... cont/...

Hi Michelle...

Just a brief recap from the last paragraph......

Now what!!!... You have now released the tight grip and you have again opened your legs wide apart and you have just parted your topiary and what is staring at me?... Yes your hot spot!!! You are shouting come on Mike, give this some loving, some kissing and some gentle sucking. I am feeling sexy and naughty!...

To be continued...

So it has been cold today, but your topiary heart looks very snug and warm. Certainly your hot spot is looking really, really hot!!... With my fingers having stroked your pussy and you having wrapped your legs around so tight this has certainly aroused this sexy little kitten and the gates to heaven have now just opened very wide... Your legs are now wide apart and you now have both your legs in the air pointing up to heaven. You are now shouting... OMG... come on Mike get stuck in here!! ☺

Okay... So some loving and some kissing and some gentle sucking to get this little pussy purrrrrring!!... You still have your fingers pulling apart your topiary and that hot spot is just waiting for my tongue to roll over it up and down and from side to side... Mmmmm... Lots of nice tongue movements all over your hot spot. Nice wiggles with the tip of my tongue on your hot spot and this is starting to send you into orbit... MMMmmmm... This little sexy kitten loves these tongue movements and this pussy is now getting sexcited and wet. I think this pussy now needs some nice kisses and a gentle little suck too... Mmmmm... hot-o-licious lips now sucking away on your hot-o-licious hot spot!! You are now shouting, Mike this feels so good. I want your hot rod now!! So with both hands you grab my hot rod. Yes, I did say both hands because you have just shimmered your fingers down the full length of my hot rod shaft and the other hand is playing with the two large ball bearings attached at the bottom. I can see by your sexy blue eyes you cannot wait to have this stuck inside your love tunnel and have me blow my head gasket!!

MMMmmmm... Michelle you are now with both hands starting to work on my hot rod and getting it really cranked up!! The font size and the lettering on the side of my shaft has now grown to maximum size with my tatoo fully expanded showing your name...... M i c h e l l e T u r n e r. Oh!! Oops!!... Mike it looks like you are getting sexcited and a little moisture has just popped out the top of the head. Mmmmmm... Michelle your fault! Mike I don't want your love juices wasted, so put you hot-rod on my hot spot and rub it there to cool it down for me. Mmmmmm... That now feels good too... This little pussy is now purrrrring away like a really sexy naughty, but lovable loving kitten...

To be continued...

I love you Michelle Turner...

Mwah! Mike xxx

E-mail from: Michelle
To: Mike
Date: 21 February 2013
Subject: Re: I am feeling sexy and naughty... cont/...

Hi Mike...

WOW!!!... you have blown me away with these last e-mails!!!... I have not been able to focus on anything else today.

Well, until very recently I would have said I do not like tattoos at all... but this is the exception... I love this tattoo... How sexy you are... and to see the full extent of M i c h e l l e T u r n e r... Oh Wow!!!!... It looks so good I have to trace my finger tip right over each letter... I have known that when people really love someone they may have their name tattooed somewhere... but this is something really special, and I certainly have not heard of this one before... This is a first in my world... How honored I am!

And, there have been occasions you have told me I am greedy... But, Mike... it is not my fault... you are in control of my body here, because I am certainly not... When you sent me an e-mail a long time ago, and told me I could have any orgasm on the chart... I do not remember there being `multi-orgasms`... but, Mike... this is what you are doing to me here... In the e-mail preceding this one, you give me my first orgasm with your expert fingers... and now in this e-mail you have given me the second orgasm with your expert tongue... Oh... My... God... you are driving me absolutely crazy, crazy, crazy!!!!!!......

And, now I am holding onto your 'hot rod' with two hands, guiding it towards the open gates of heaven... where my love tunnel is ready and waiting for you... and OMG so wanting you... Is this going to be the third??? I look forward to you sending `To be continued – part 3`...

Mike, I am telling you... you get more and more sexy since we have been married. I think it agrees with you, being married to me... I think it agrees with me, being married to you... We are a perfect match for one another...

I love you Mike Turner...

With my love, 'your sexy kitten' purrrrrrrrrrrrrrrrrrrr......
Mwah ~X~

E-mail from: Mike
To: Michelle
Date: 21 February 2013
Subject: I am feeling sexy and naughty... cont/...

Hi Michelle

Just a brief recap from the last paragraph…

MMMmmmm… Michelle you are now with both hands starting to work on my hot rod and getting it really cranked up!! The font size and the lettering on the side of my shaft has now grown to maximum size with my tattoo fully expanded showing your name…… M i c h e l l e T u r n e r. Oh!! Oops!!… Mike it looks like you are getting sexcited and a little moisture has just popped out the top of the head. MMMmmmm… Michelle your fault! Mike I don't want your love juices wasted, so put your hot rod on my hot spot and rub it there to cool it down for me. MMMmmmm… That now feels good too… This little pussy is now purrrrring away like a really sexy naughty, but lovable loving kitten…

To be continued…

You really are a sexy naughty sexcited little kitten. This little pussy sure does like being stroked between the legs. You just love it and you are now purrrrrring away like a good'n. Laying on your back, your legs wide apart and your legs still pointing up to heaven. Well I have said this before, but now I am going to `do you` so I guess you know what is coming now, eh!! Yes a hot rod with the name "M i c h e l l e T u r n er" down the side. You are now screaming for joy… Mike give it to me, OMG!… OMG!… get stuck in, I cannot wait!!

Laying in the same position, you take my hot rod and put it to the entrance of your love tunnel. Mike I do not want a quickie, so just pop the head of your hot rod in a little way to start with at first… Oops… Mike!… I have just noticed a little more love juice coming out the top… You are getting so sexcited!! MMMmmmm… Nice and wet it will slip inside me easily. But…OMG!… OMG!… I do not want you coming just yet Mike, you have some sexercise to do here first with me.

Mike… Okay take it inside me a little further and then out again. MMMmmmm… so nice!!… Okay Mike, back inside me again and a little further in this time… I hope you still remember the lessons I gave you gave you Mike!! Well Michelle, this time you have taken half of my hot rod and tattoo inside… Just the "Michelle" lettering part left to give you full deep penetration.

Hey Mike!!... I want to see this now. So get your naked body down here where I am, because I am taking over here. So let me just sit on you Mike and take charge. Okay back with your hot rod and to the entrance of my love tunnel... OMG, OMG... sinking down on it and pushing down... yes... "r e n r u T"... Woweee... Just like having a dipstick to check the levels!!! But Mike, I want the full works now! Yes the "Michelle" letters too, I want them letters so deep inside me now. Only your golden nuggets preventing your hot rod going further and further and deeper. OMG... I really feel hot and sexy now. Those golden nuggets will fill up and explode before long, I want them rattling at the entrance of my love tunnel and then I can really feel you come on with me and fill me with your warm milky juices of love...

To be continued...

Mwah... I love you Michelle... I cannot see the Turner bit now it has just disappeared down a love tunnel!!

Mike xxx

E-mail from: Michelle
To: Mike
Date: 22 February 2013
Subject: Re: I am feeling sexy and naughty... cont/...

Hi Mike...

Wow... this is sex-o-decilious!!!!!... and I am loving every single minute of it... Loving with you Mike Turner is wonderful... I love this tattoo so much, I just have to have one more look at it before it goes into my love tunnel...

So back out it slides... and I gently take hold of your hot rod with both hands once more, and skim my fingers up and down it... MMMMmmm so nice... run one finger gently over the tattoo once more... MMMMmmmm M i c h e l l e T u r n e r and oh so gently place the tip of it back at the entrance to my love tunnel... These blue eyes of mine, looking into those sexy brown eyes of yours... but that is not all that is looking at you, because now it is not my topiary heart, or hot spot looking at you, it is my boobs and nipples... OMG... now they want to feel your lips and tongue... and gently I slide onto your hot rod... yes... halfway... so we can both see now, your hot rod penetrating my love tunnel, and we can also see half of the tattoo... M i c h e l l e... slowly, slowly in it goes... now we can see M i c h e l l... and a little further in... M i c h e... oh darling......

With all the attention you have given me here, I am going to show you just how much I do love you... yes, Mike Turner... I would be whispering here... really really love you... really really love you...... always and forever...... love you...

Michelle
~ X ~
that kiss is......
Mwaaaaaaaaaaaaaaaaaaaaaaaaah... long and sexy and passionate

E-mail from: Mike
To: Michelle
Date: 28 February 2013
Subject: I am feeling sexy and naughty... cont/...

Hi Michelle...

Just a brief recap from the last sentence...... I would just add this is a bit naughty!!... In fact not just a bit naughty, but very, very naughty!!

Mwah!!... I love you Michelle... I cannot see the "T u r n e r" bit now, it has just disappeared down the love tunnel!!

To be continued...

Michelle... You really are a sexy little kitten and I can see this little pussy wants her milk and just desserts. You also want plenty of whipped up cream with it too, eh!! You are so greedy and impatient, but I can see by those sexy blue flashing eyes that you are very playful, sexy and lovable.

You are on top of me and you have now pushed down on my hot rod and taken the initials "e l l", in reverse order of course, three more letters of my tattoo. Slowly and sensually I am slipping inside your love tunnel. Like a certain TV advertisement said, "Calm down, dear". You are so sexcitable, but also so lovable and you will get more than you ever wanted when we have finished making love together, but you know it is not about quickies!! This could give you sexual indigestion taking in too much and too quickly all at once!!

Well I did say I would be working from down up to the top. So the only way is up, baby, you and me now. So you are on top of me with my hot rod tattoo "Michelle Turner" inside your love tunnel. Already disappeared inside are all of the letters "r e n r u T" and you are already down my hot rod dip-stick to include the "e l l", leaving only five letters to go before my two golden nuggets start rattling at the entrance door to your love tunnel. Mmmmm... sex-o-delicious!!!... This must be a record on my part with the longest erection time ever recorded making love to Michelle Turner over several days. This must be worthy of a Guinness Record Book entry!! Okay Michelle!! just do your loving and get stuck in!!... OMG... Mike!!... I am having a vaginal orgasm... MMMmmmm!!!

Okay so you are on top of me with my hot rod still inside your love tunnel and you are pushing down on me and the direction is slowly working up to the top of your love tunnel. I do not want you getting too sexcited, so nice and slow and easy does it. I had better talk you through this slowly okay......

Okay... Ready... Push down on my hot rod again, but only take in the next letter "e"...... OMG!!.. Mike... "e" for "ecstasy"... Yes I love this my darling and then back out again......

Okay... Ready... Push down on my hot rod again, but only take in the next letter "h"...... OMG, OMG!!... Mike... "h" for "heaven". Yes this is like making love in heaven and feels soooo good.

Okay... Ready... Push down on my hot rod again, but only take in the next letter "c"...... OMG, OMG, OMG!!... Mike... "c" for "climax". Yes making love is doing just that to me.

Okay... Ready... Push down on my hot rod again, but only take in the next letter "i"...... OMG, OMG, OMG, OMG!!... Mike... "i" for "intimate" sexual intercourse with my cyber husband.

Okay… Ready… Push down on my hot rod again, but only take in the next letter "M"…… OMG, OMG, OMG, OMG, OMG!!… Mike… "M" for "Mmmmmm"… I just love making love to you.

Now you have full deep penetration "Michelle Turner". Mmmmmmm… Mike I love it when your hot rod is about two inches inside me with the head just teasing its way inside and keeps popping in and out. I could now scream at the top of my voice… give me full fast hard deep penetration. I want all your love because this feels so sexy, sensual and good. Mike I keep having these multiple orgasms with you. I think I could be joining you in the Guinness Book of Records too.

Michelle… You are now getting very sexcited and jumping up and down on me like you are riding a pogo stick!!… OMG… Michelle… I need to hang onto your boobs, yes those lovely movers and shakers or they could swing out of control and knock me out. I love it when it when your C's are in free-fall. You are now happy and purring away and getting faster and faster. I would be your coxs-wain and shout, "In… out… In… out," and shake it all about, but you have already got into a perfect rhythm. Nice full-length strokes all the way in and out again.

Come on Mike, I am going to blow that head gasket on your hot rod in a minute. Michelle I am filling up with love juices and if you keep this pace up I am just going to explode inside your love tunnel and pump you full of warm milky love juices. OMG… Mike give it to me now. Mmmmmm… I think Michelle is having another orgasm!! Oh Michelle… let us both come together… Yeeeeeeeeeeeees!!!… I cannot hold it back any longer and I am exploding my love juices deep inside your love tunnel and you are squeezing your thighs and legs together tight holding me in to maximise the sensual feelings of love. Michelle I really love you and I appreciate this special love that we share together.

Hey Mike!!… What Michelle?… And before I knew it, you have whipped my hot rod out and pushed it in between your boobs. You have placed your hands each side of your boobs and squeezed my hot rod in the middle and now you have started jumping up and down again. You whisper in my ear, feel my hard nipples, whilst I massage your hot rod in between my boobs. I want a little more love juice spurting out the top of your hot rod so I am going to stimulate you in my boobs. Oops!!… Mike here it comes, just another little spurt of love juice again right where Ditto sleeps. Oh… It is now slithering down my boobs. MMMmmmm… Nice and wet and warm and a bit whipped up now like cream. Mike I just knew you had some left in your reserve twin tanks. MMMmmmm… Mike look into my blue eyes because I want every last drop of your love juices. Get that sexy little finger of yours and run it over my hot spot!! Quick Mike save that last little drop of love juice running down my boobs and put it on your finger. Yes moisten my hot spot with it now and give me some nice slow finger strokes on my hot spot. I love you doing this to me with the tip of your one finger gently and slowly stroking and running over my hot spot!! It is mind blowing when you do this to me. MMMmmmm… Mike I am having another orgasm because this gives me so much pleasure. I love your finger technique. It really arouses me and I am almost delirious and shaking with sexcitement. OMG… MMMmmmm… I am now having a heart-pounding clit orgasm and I am really feeling very wet down there… I love the way you stimulate my hot spot. Come on Mike it is time to shower together and go to bed and sleep. Shower and bed!!… Okay let`s do it.

Michelle stop running into the shower naked, because you are bouncing about everywhere and you will do yourself a mischief. Mike… Hang onto my movers and shakers, I know you love my C's. Michelle you can wash me and then you can do me. Hey Michelle stop flashing those blue eyes at me again. Noooooo… Michelle not meaning "DO ME"… OMG… We have just done that!! You are so greedy and sexxxxxxxxy !! Come on you, let's shower and bed now…

You are looking lovely and fresh now Michelle… So jump into bed with me and come into my arms and let me hug, cuddle and love you. I will brush your hair to one side and give you lots of kisses down that lovely neck of yours. MMMmmmm… Mike you just do not know what that does to me!!. Okay… Let me give you lots more kisses the other side of your neck too. So a lot more kisses and then across to those luscious lips… Very passionate kisses and when our lips touch we can taste the love that we share and have for each other now and always. I LOVE YOU… Michelle Turner.

MMMmmmm… Mike cuddle me and hold me tight in your arms. This is such a nice way to complete our day. I think we will both sleep well tonight. Come on Michelle just lay your boobs across my chest and press those lovely hard nipples into me. I will hug and cuddle you tight until the morning…… Good night my darling!!…… I LOVE YOU.

P.S… Okay… Sorry Michelle… I almost forgot you can have the light on, he!, he!, he! Sweet dreams!!

Love always
Mike
xxx

E-mail from: Michelle
To: Mike
Date: 1 March 2013
Subject: I am feeling sexy and naughty… cont/…

OHHHH…… WOOOOOOOOOOW!!! MIKE…

THIS IS SERIOUSLY SEXY!!!! SEDUCTIVE… SENSUAL… RAUNCHY… EROTIC… PASSIONATE… LOVING… AND ABSOLUTELY SENSATIONAL!!!!!

OMG… MIKE TURNER… I LOVE YOU…

My darling Mike… you have excelled yourself with this box set, of four episodes, sexy sexy e-mails… They are well and truly "Simply the best"… as are you darling… Simply the best… Better than all the rest… Better than anyone… Anyone I ever met… Oh yes!!!!

Thank you for all the time you have spent on these e-mails… and all the time you spent making love with me in them… Time very well spent I would say… Mike… How I love you…

You say it was me naughty in them… but I think we have both shown some real loving here, shared love… time taking… very considerate love… such long and lingering love making… such enjoyment for both of us… Oh wow… this is my kind of loving Mike… and I just love you so, so much.

I love that sexy smile of yours… I love those seductive lips of yours… I love those sexy brown eyes… I love that sexpert finger of yours, and what it can do to me… I love that tongue of yours, and what it can do to me… I love that hot rod of yours, especially now with the tattoo, and what it can do to me… I never, ever knew a tattoo could have such entertainment value… and OMG I just love this one so much.

I love being wrapped in your arms to sleep… I love you kissing me… nibbling my neck… teasing my nipples… touching my skin… I guess what I am saying here Mike Turner is I love everything about you… and everything you do to me…

We should do this more often…

MMMMmmmm = I am just loving this…

You are adorable!!!

I will think of you all this weekend now that I have seen you today…

I love you now Mike Turner as much as I always have…

There never could have been a more appropriate record for us…

"I WILL ALWAYS LOVE YOU" … yes always, and always…

My love to you now and always my darling
Michelle
~ X ~

---

5 March 2013 ~ Live Interactive Text

Mike: Seeing your here on Skype today, you are so sexy… You were making eyes at me when you were blowing me those kisses…

Michelle: I always have eyes for you darling

Mike: I could tell you were feeling sexy… Those blue eyes are the tell-tale signs when they flash at me like they did today

Michelle: But I have left some lipstick on you… hang on, I need to wipe it off… so gently with my thumb I will run my over your lips../ and then one finger down your chin… down your neck…

down to that sexy hairy chest...... MMMmmmmm...... I need to go on a treasure hunt here!!

Mike: Treasure hunt?

Michelle: MMMmmmm... no treasure yet...

Michelle: Round and round your chest... OH... I have found two little buttons, but no treasure yet...

Mike: Hey... You know what my single finger can do to you!!

Michelle: And you know what I can do to you with one finger!!... down, down, down to your belly button...

Michelle: Round and round the belly button... no treasure yet...

Michelle: Down, down, down, down, the finger goes... are you talking to me Mike?

Mike: Mesmerized by you Michelle

Michelle: Down, down, down,...... and... oh what is this?

Mike: Tell me?

Michelle: I think I may have found the treasure?

Michelle: Yes... round and round... I have!!!

Michelle: I have found two golden nuggets for a start...

Michelle: Oh wow... they feel real good...

Mike: Precious!

Michelle: They may like two fingers gently skimming over them... gently... gently... gently... oh they are crying out for a gentle little massage... so this is what they will get... so, so gentle... MMMmmmm...

Michelle: And what else have I found here?

Michelle: OMG... it is hot... in-fact, it is the hot rod... Oh wow... standing to attention already...

Mike: With a tattoo down the side, eh!

Michelle: So my one finger needs to skim over this tattoo... slowly... slowly... slowly... outline each of the letters of your tattoo... MMMmmmm. Are you still there Mike?

Mike: I am mesmerized by my Michelle...

Michelle: Yes... I can read it without even looking: Michelle Turner... and run my finger all around the other side... right up to the top... and back down again...

Mike: You're coc-eyed! ☺

Michelle: I might be cock-eyed… but it feels real good from where I am…

Michelle: I have definitely found the treasure here Mike…

Mike: If you keep playing with this you could get a teardrop out the top.

Michelle: Well… I can hear this hot rod saying… I want more than just one finger now…

Mike: Followed with like a full blast canon.

Michelle: But the one finger… goes gently up to the top… and tickles gently right over the end…

Michelle: Just rubbing my one finger, right over the tip, so gently… MMMmmmm…

Mike: You have better do this quicker I have to go now.

Michelle: Do you need to go darling?

Mike: Unfortunately I do… ☹

Michelle: Shame… your hot rod was enjoying me playing with it

Mike: I know…

Michelle: Bye darling

Mike: Bye my Michelle

---

8 March 2013 ~ Live Interactive Text

Mike: Hi my sexy babe

Michelle: Good evening my sexy cyber lover

Mike: You have an evening to yourself… I wish I were right there with you now

Michelle: Come and cuddle me then… come lay on this sofa with me……

Mike: MMMmmmm… You know, if I could I would.

Michelle: Wouldn't it be nice!!!

Mike: Wonderful.

Michelle: MMMmmmm… Yesssssss!!!!

Mike: Just to be with you and not have to look at the clock.

Michelle: I know……

Mike: Or what eyes are looking at us.

Michelle: How lovely would it be just to snuggle up in bed together for the night, and nobody else knowing, asking questions

Mike: April 5 again… us in the Cotswolds!!

Michelle: How I would love to just have you to myself for a few hours… but we both know… we can't

Mike: MMMmmmm… Michelle.

Michelle: But… how lovely to just think of spending a night cuddling you

Mike: Only in our dreams… ☹

Michelle: I know… only in our dreams… ☹

Mike: We do it in our dreams, but then when we wake and you are not there I realise it was just a dream. ☹

Michelle: We do it in e-mails as well… and we both share that…

Mike: Do you know most is virtual, and we express a lot in words, yet I can feel your presence, I can feel your love and that is still a nice feeling to have with you.

Michelle: I love that feeling with you too…

Michelle: At this time of year, I always think about us and the Cotswolds

Mike: Me too and I will always remember this forever.

Michelle: Me too… every year since then I have thought about it… how lovely it was to just lock a front door… lock the world out… and it just be you and me…

Mike: How about… we book in there again and say we want to read what you put in the guest book again. What did you write in there?

Michelle: Something about it was a lovely place to spend our honeymoon

Mike: It was so peaceful at that cottage

Michelle: It was perfect there with you darling, and just snuggle up in bed, and cuddle each other all night

Mike: All day and we were confined to bed…

Michelle: Well we did go out occasionally… it was so lovely to do that with you darling… I will never forget that for as long as I live

Mike: How we planned that and got away with it I do not know!

Mike: I love you… I want to wrap my arms around you now in front of a log fire.

Michelle: Ohhhhh how I would love that darling

Mike: I will put so many logs on you will be so hot!...Off come your clothes and then...

Mike: We make love together.

Michelle: MMMmmmm... yes please...

Mike: I think I am dreaming again.

Michelle: I love that we have been able to talk about all of this again... I love this cyber world with you

Mike: Yes, and sometimes we just talk about nothing yet we are both happy and full of laughter.

Michelle: Always with you my darling... Nobody else has ever made me happier!!

Mike: MMMmmmm... Come and lay them boobs on me and I will cuddle you tight.

Michelle: I would love to darling... and given half the chance I would... I love being with you... I love everything I have ever done with you...

Mike: "DITTO"

Michelle: You are very special to me...

Mike: You are very precious to me...

Michelle: I love all the emails we share now...

Mike: Seeeeexy emails.

Michelle: I love text chat Skype... I love seeing you on Skype...

Mike: Seeeeeexy chat... I love you... you are sexxxxy

Michelle: I love that tattoo of yours... I would like to run my hands over it now... right now... I will just start by running one finger over it...

Michelle: Then one hand... then two hands...

Mike: MMMmmmmm... Michelle, I really want you tonight!!

Michelle: "DITTO"

Mike: Sorry darling, I am going to have to go now

Michelle: Yes, we have been on here quite a long time, I do not want to get you into trouble

Mike: Goodnight my darling... I love you

Michelle: I love you... Goodnight my darling

E-mail from: Michelle
To: Mike
Date: 20 March 2013
Subject: Bodyguard job description
To: Mike Turner

JOB DESCRIPTION

Job title: Personal Bodyguard

Location: As close as possible to Michelle Turner
(within her three feet personal zone)

Roles and responsibilities:

* To be the personal bodyguard to Michelle Turner, to guard her body, protect her from all others, and keep her safe.

* This will be a 24 hour a day task. 7 days per week. 52 weeks of the year.

* To remain by her side at all times, including bath and shower times, help her out here however you feel necessary.

* To sleep by her side at night, and hold her gently/tightly in your arms.

* Holiday entitlement. There will be no holiday entitlement away from Michelle. Therefore all holidays may be taken in the future with Michelle, where your bodyguard responsibilities will remain fully operational.

* Should you wish to only accept this responsibility on a part-time basis please advise accordingly.

Knowledge, skills and experience:

* A knowledge of Michelle's body will be ongoing progress.

* To develop your skills and techniques with Michelle's body, as enjoyed by both of you.

* Experience, you have apparently already demonstrated to Michelle that you have plenty of experience and expertise regarding bodywork. To be continued in this manner.

Your next step:

* To read carefully the above job description. To reply within 48 hours.

* You may discuss any points above before accepting the contract.

* If you decide to accept, this must be done within the next 48 hours.

Should you choose to accept, a starting date will be mutually agreed

---

25 March 2013 ~ Live Interactive Text

Mike: Hi darling… it is cold today… you must need a cuddle?

Michelle: Hello darling… yes cold… yes please to a cuddle to warm me

Mike: It is my duty now as your bodyguard to take care of your body, this includes to keep you warm

Michelle: MMMmmmm… nice, very nice… Your dedication to your work is commendable!!

Mike: So how would you like me to warm you?

Michelle: Our bodies touching… making love…

Mike: I think we could both warm ourselves up, don't you!

Michelle: We certainly could darling…

Mike: Mmmm… Wild, passionate love to keep us both warm.

Michelle: MMMmmmm… nice… how I would love that

Mike: I have said… I would even put up with your nipples digging in me!!

Michelle: Put up with… you would love it… they are all yours… you are now part owner of the C's as my bodyguard

Mike: Yes I think I need a bonus to guard them!! Maybe danger money too, with the way they can swing about at times

Michelle: Well you have to guard all of me…

Mike: Yes I know what a big job this will be, but I am sure it will give me job satisfaction. I will make sure your vital parts are protected and I will do this by the regular checks that I need to do on a daily basis… Just in case!! I will formulate a checklist…

Michelle: How I would love to be safe in your arms where nobody else can touch me... I thought you may bring daily body checks into this

Mike: Boobs... Big C's... check

Mike: Topiary heart... Needs a trim

Michelle: I'll book myself in, bring your equipment

Mike: HOT SPOT... Woweee... No I cannot do this more than once a day... Greedy Michelle!!

Michelle: I promise not to be toooooo greedy!!!! I do not want to wear you out... I need to preserve you... I want to keep you for a very long time

Mike: I have to go my darling... I LOVE YOU

Michelle: Bye darling... I love you

Mike: Bye and just remember I will always love you... Reference the film, very fitting that one day I should become your very own bodyguard

Michelle: Very fitting indeed... 'Our record' from the film `Bodyguard`, and now you are my very own bodyguard

---

E-mail from: Michelle
To: Mike
Date: 25 March 2013
Subject: The Bodyguard

Hi my darling

Well Mike, the job as my bodyguard is yours!!! This seems only right as Whitney's song "I will always love you" is the soundtrack to the film `The Bodyguard`... so how fitting this really is!! As my bodyguard you will need to protect me in every way, keep me safe in your arms, where nobody else can ever touch me again, only you!!! Keep my heart safe alongside yours!! When it is cold, hold me close to you, where we will share our body heat and keep warm. When it is hot, you cover my body with sun lotion, of course my 'movers and shakers' and my nipples are the most vulnerable here, so you will need to give these two coats... MMMmmmm... your hands just sliding all over my boobs and nipples, until you feel plenty has been applied.

As my bodyguard I give you my mind, body and soul to protect, all of which I share with you... Oh dear, is it right to fall in love with your bodyguard?... Too late!!!! this has already happened, long ago... I have loved you for such a very long time... and I will always love you...

Thank you for your e-mail this morning... 'You & I belong'... I completely agree with you... we do... 'We belong'... we have for so long... we always will... How I would love to spend my Easter with you... cuddled up together in bed to keep warm.

Congratulations on your new job... this starts with immediate effect... and will last for as long as we both live... Now you are my husband, my friend, my lover, my bodyguard, my soulmate!!!

My love to you always and forever
Michelle
xxx xxx xxx xxx x

---

26 March 2013 ~ Live Interactive Text

Mike: Hi my Michelle

Michelle: Hi my Mike

Mike: I have read your email this morning regarding the bodyguard job... I fully accept the terms and conditions of employment and all I can say is...... I will be glad when the sun comes out!!

Michelle: Well that is settled then... the job is officially yours now... from this day forward

Mike: I will protect that body of yours 24/7... 365 days of the year.

Michelle: 'Blue eyes' to 'Brown eyes' cam you cam yet?

They video link for half an hour, then revert to text

Mike: It is not fair!!... This is like me having sweet things placed in front of me and however tempting, I cannot have them...

Michelle: You can have me... I am all yours

Mike: I would make sure you get plenty of love, care and attention 24/7

Michelle: Oh this would be my dream come true

Mike: Mine too... we both need to go now darling, look at the time

Michelle: OK darling, so nice to see you, talk to you, thank God for all this technology. Bye darling. Mwah.

Mike: Bye... Mwah

Mike: Hi... Good morning Mrs Turner.

Mike: This is Kevin reporting for duty... So I think I need to do a quick body check, after all this is my job now!!

Mike: MMMmmmm... Well I can see you have just got up and although you still look a bit sleepy, the body on first glance looks to be in good shape.

Mike: Now I had better do a complete check all over. Yes the face looks good and I think I may need to just wake you up with a few kisses here

Mike: Yes down both sides of your neck and then across to those lovely lips... Mwah! This is beginning to wake you up and you have now just opened those sexy blue eyes.

Mike: Okay let me move down and... WOWEE... They are a nice set of assets you have here. Gosh... No bra on yet and those C's definitely need a once over.

Mike: I will just run my hands over them and see the bounce effect... Mmmmm... Bouncy, bouncy and they are in good shape. The nipples look a bit soft so I will just give each one a little tweak!!

Mike: OMG... They are alive and have just sprung into life and now standing up like American hard gums... I think I just need to have a taste on the ends and see what flavour these are. Mmmmm... Very very tasty and there is a Vitamin `C` taste for sure when you get stuck into them and really have a good suck. I think your are really starting to wake up now Michelle and starting to feel little bit raunchy and sexy... I can tell those eyes are saying, come on Mike come inside me!!

Mike: Oh... At last good morning!! You have decided to appear here at last, eh!

Michelle: Morning darling ~ wow you were well early

Mike: You have had a part body check and now you are fully awake my darling.

Michelle: Do I have to call you Kevin or Mike?

Mike: Just call me Mike or I will get confused.

Michelle: So will I… Mike it is then… thank you for waking me up in such a nice manner… you are definitely the right person for this job

Mike: My pleasure Michelle… I love this job!!

Michelle: MMMmmmm… I love you having this job

Mike: You arrived here just in time, I was just getting down to the nitty gritty bits when you became fully awake.

Michelle: Don't let me stop you now then… carry on Mike…

Mike: Your boobs are fine, full bounce and the nipples are now hard. They just wanted a little tweaking on the ends to bring them into life.

Michelle: Good… are they 'up' to expectation now?

Mike: Yes 13 out of 13 scored… They will pass! They are standing up on end now!!

Michelle: Wow… thank you… top score for the movers and shakers!!!

Mike: It's a good job you have me doing this testing early morning.

Michelle: Thank you darling… why did I not give you this job earlier?

Mike: You just do not know what you have missed, so maybe you now have to make up for lost time. Well should I continue this body check and move on down!

Michelle: I am not resisting

Mike: The top half is just fine now having made a few minor adjustments.

Michelle: Ok… continue with your checks…

Mike: Mmmm… Okay. Hey you need a hairdresser's appointment down here Michelle… I cannot see the wood for the trees!!

Michelle: Oh… That bad?… well with your topiary skills maybe you can do a little bush trimming?

Mike: Bush!!!!!… It's more like a rain forest! Just like searching the Amazon jungle.

Michelle: OMG… really?

Mike: Woweeeee… wait what is this… Yes there is a valley here somewhere!!… The Valley of Love.

Michelle: Wow… what are you going to do with that?

Mike: I think I need to investigate and explore further. Yes... Now I have parted the trees there is a valley with a damp like feel to it.

Michelle: Are you going in there? Be careful, you never know what you may find

Mike: It is truly a rainforest down here. I could get lost in there forever...

Michelle: Wow... you may have to stay there forever...

Mike: Wait... At the top there appears to be a heat source... Yes, Yes... A hot spot!!!

Michelle: Oh darling... you are on form this morning

Mike: OMG... I will just rub around that and see what this does.

Michelle: Be careful what happens when you touch that hot spot

Mike: Michelle... My God you are shaking now with sexcitement... I think I have just touched a sensual nerve.

Michelle: Oh... Mike... whereas I have just been lying back and enjoying this you now have me wiggling and squirming everywhere...

Mike: Yes I know you like my finger technique... I think this is why you gave me this job... It turns you on!!!

Michelle: It turns me on big time... I love the things you do to me with your finger

Mike: Now those boobs are big and bouncing now with joy.

Mike: I have to go now my darling... Maybe to be continued another day... I love you..

Michelle: WHAT?... you bring me up to fever pitch, and now you are going?

Mike: Look at the time, we will both be late for work

Michelle: ☺ Bye darling... I loved you waking me up this morning... Mwaaaaaaaah

Mike: Bye... Your ever loving bodyguard... Mike Turner code name... 0013

Michelle: My very own James Bond... 0013

Mike: Bye and have a nice day... You are awake and fully alive now.

Michelle: Tingling from head to toe... Byeeeeeeeeeeeeeeeee

Mike: Bye now and remember I will be like your shadow in this job... Not to walk behind you and not to walk in front of you, but to be by your side always... I am your bodyguard and there to care for you.

Michelle: I love you Mike... this morning you have just melted my heart... ☺

E-mail from: Mike
To: Michelle
Date: 31 March 2013
Subject: Bodyguard

Hi my darling Michelle

I am missing you like crazy! How can I do my job properly without you by my side, 24/7 and 365 days of the year?

I'll always protect you and be here for you, like your shadow, not walking behind you, not waking in front of you, but by your side forever.

I need to do a body check each morning and last thing at night, just to make sure your body is in good shape for both ends of the day. My priority is to guard your two vital assets... Yes your C's because they are not only your natural beauty, but also the home for our son Ditto. I attached some pictures of the `The Bodyguard` film and yes they do sleep together. Looking at those assets... They do catch the eye and yours will need some protecting!!

At night when that bra is cut lose even more so!! When those movers and shakers are in free fall. Mmmm... Michelle just come and lay your boobs on my chest and I will cuddle you in my arms and protect you all night.

In the morning... I will do a full body check like in our Skype conversation.

Mwah!

I will always love you...
Mike 0013
xxx

CHAPTER TWELVE

E-mail from: Michelle
To: Mike
Date: 4 April 2013
Subject: A special treat for us in The Cotswolds

Hi my darling Mike (0013)

Well… as this is the only way this can happen!! In our cyber world, I am going to transport you off to the Cotswolds for a week… the anniversary of all those years ago. So just for one week, we will leave our mud hut, and off to the Cotswolds we go… arriving there early in the evening, let`s go back to the lovely little cottage we once shared… The last time we went there we were simply 'Lovers', this time you are my cyber husband and bodyguard, so much more special.

The sun is setting across the field, we can see spring flowers everywhere, and sheep in that back field, with a phantom lamb on its way… We quickly unpack our suitcase… unpack a box of food and drink… we decide for ease we will have takeaway for our dinner this evening, you can choose it. Because, for the rest of the week I am going to spoil you with my cooking. You can choose the menu each day and I will cook some gastronomic gourmet delights for you.

You order our takeaway, and in the half hour wait for it to be delivered, we make up a real fire… the log burner as been changed to a large open fireplace, and you build us a fire, as now it is getting dark it is getting chilly. Whilst you do this, I fix us both a drink, this has to be our joint favourite 'Southern Comfort and lemonade'... We sit on the sofa opposite the fire, drink our drinks, and watch the fire start to take hold...

We spend our evening just snuggled up on the sofa, drinking Southern Comfort, eat our take-away dinner, and sit kissing, chatting, laughing and drinking... soft music... the fire is crackling... you put your drink down and kiss me on the lips, soft and gentle... you get a flash of these blue eyes... you can see how much I love you, I don't even need to tell you... but I do anyway, and I whisper to you... "I love you Mike Turner... and I am so pleased I married you... and now you are my bodyguard too... I am the luckiest person on the planet"... Your kisses move to my neck... MMMmmmm... I put my glass down now... and your kisses are moving further down my neck as you start to slowly peel my clothes off... Time for a body check, you claim... You run your hands all over me... MMMmmmm nice soft skin Michelle, nice soft curves... Your hands run down my shoulders, down my arms, down my sides, over my hips, down my legs, and back up to the 'movers and shakers'... MMMmmmm Michelle, these lovely soft curvy boobs are a hand-ful... you tweak at my nipples, and in an instant with your touch my nipples turn into American hard gums... You plant kisses all over my lips, all over my neck, and then all over my body... the body you now protect... Before too much longer, we are both naked and laying on the floor in front of the fire, making love... it is slow... it is gentle... it is so tender... it is so loving... it is wonderful... time-taking love... the love that we share is so special...... our appetite for our love making together is insatiable, and when the fire dies right down we decide it is time for bed...

The next morning I wake up early, the dawn is breaking, I can hear the birds singing outside of our window... your arms are around me and you are sound asleep. Mmmmm... I love you so much, and could not be happier!!! Slowly and quietly I creep out of the bed and go off to make us both coffee and bring it back to the bedroom. I put it down beside you, your eyes are still closed but there is a faint little smile on your face, then you whisper, "Where have you been?"... I smile at you and say, "Room Service"... still with your eyes closed your smile turns to a big smile and you say, "Room Service???... MMmmm what kind of service?"... you open your eyes, my god you look so sexy... you reach out of the bed, pull the belt on my dressing gown, and it falls open, then you say, "Yes please Michelle, I will have the full works"... I slip the shoulders of my dressing gown off, and it falls to the floor, now I am standing next to you naked... you pull back the duvet, and pull me into the bed and on top of you... Wow... a lovely good morning kiss takes place. But this turns to tickling and laughing... we drink our coffee before it gets cold, and go off for a shower together... MMMmmmm I remember the shower in the Cotswolds with you Mike... In the shower we make love.

After breakfast, out we go for the day. Explore the beautiful quaint little villages, and admire the wonderful countryside. Back to our cottage we go... I start to prepare our dinner, pop it into the oven, you fix us both a drink, S&L of course, we go outside and sit on the decking, drink our drink and watch the sunset over the field... When the sun has set we go back inside, lay the table, with flowers, candles, crystal glasses etc, this is how I like to eat. We put nice music on, and enjoy our dinner, you have two helpings of the delicious dessert I have made. You top our glasses up again, and we just sit talking and laughing at the table for ages... We have a Celine CD on, you walk around the table, take my hand, stand me up and take me in your arms for a smoochy dance to it, your arms around my waist, my arms around your neck, brown eyes looking into the blue eyes, blue eyes looking into the brown eyes... it's all in the eyes!!!... see the love we share!!! we gently sway to and fro, our bodies pushed close together. Mmmmm...

You say it's time for this game of chess we keep threatening to have, winner chooses the prize!! We open a bottle of Red Cherry wine, and we take to the sofa, in front of the fire, and decide to play the chess game...... what a battle this will be... so we set off playing the game, drinking the wine, both concentrating hard, neither of us want to lose this...... OMG... you are getting me worried here, you are playing pretty well... OH NOoooo... how have I let this happen? You win the game... and like a nutter you start to run around the room, with your arms out, like an airplane, shouting at the top of your voice, "I am the champion"... OMG... I will never hear the end of this... We top our glasses up, and play the best of three... the next game is very pains-taking... each of us taking each move very carefully... I am determined to win this one!!!... and I do!!! Yessssss!!!... One – One, Mike Turner... So we top up our glasses with the last of the red wine... I think we are getting a little drunk now... we are laughing like complete nutters... OK... we decide to up the ante and play for clothes this time, and the overall winner chooses their prize... so, pawns do not count, but for each piece you lose, you lose an item of clothing... We lay on the floor in front of the fire...... Off we go... I lose the first piece, off come my tights... I lose the next piece... Oh dear, off comes my jumper... you are laughing at me already... MMMmmmm bra, skirt and knickers, not much left for me to lose... next you lose your socks... shirt... trousers... Oh I like it, this has evened things up a bit... but next I lose my skirt... Oh dear, only my bra and knickers now... then I lose my next piece... off comes my bra, I hand it to you, flash these blue eyes at you, lay back down on my front, but what a good view of my boobs you must have from where you are!!!... Your eyes are on fire as you are visually devouring my body... we continue with the game... Oh dear Mike, you have just lost another piece, so off come your pants... WOW... now you are naked... your body flawlessly proportioned and as sexy as hell, it makes my mouth water... Concentrate Michelle... In another couple of moves, it happens... I have you in check mate... I AM THE WINNER!!!... You are protesting as you learn across and kiss me... and say I cheated you, because from the minute my bra came off you could not concentrate!!!... Good one Michelle, note to self for another time... I get to choose my prize... I choose... 'YOU' as my prize, to do whatever I want with... MMmmmm... So I push you to the floor, and straddle myself across you sitting up, looking down at you... but you are so naughty you just get hold of one side of my knickers and just rip them off of me!!!... and throw them in mid-air... your hands are running all over my boobs, my body, I lean down and kiss you... kiss you... kiss you... and then that hot rod is inside my love tunnel and we are making loving very passionately... your body is so lustrous, healthy, strong and vigorous. Wow, Mike we are quite drunk here, you are biting at my nipples, my neck, my lips... it is frantic!!! your grip on me possessive and commanding. I climax 13 seconds in front of you... OMG... Wonderful... and then I feel your warm love juices just pumping into me...... OMG HEAVEN!!!! WOW, WOW just heaven... we lay quietly in front of the fire, which has died right down now, and you say it is time for bed... You pick me up, yes I did say pick me up, and carry me into the bedroom... Wooo I am feeling quite light headed and a little bit drunk... Into bed we get...... And then we just cuddle up tight... oh so tight... just like 21 years ago, we completely lock our bodies together......

Goodnight darling... I love you
All my love
Michelle
~ X ~

---

5 April 2013 ~ Live Interactive Text

Mike: Hi Michelle... I cannot believe we have got away with you coming to my office again today!!

Michelle: Hi my darling... is everything OK?

Mike: Thank you for today, it is always nice to see you and even better when I can share my love with you for real and hold you and cuddle you in my arms. Everything is OK.

Michelle: How many times will we get away with me coming to your office? I do not want to cause you any problems, raised eye-brows or anything at work!!

Mike: We need to be careful... maybe we should leave it a while before we do that again? ☹

Michelle: I agree darling... we do not want to give anyone chance to get suspicious! But... OMG... so nice to see you today!!

Mike: For sure darling...... I love you Michelle... just really love you!!

Michelle: Our love is very real Mike... and so lovely to feel you in the flesh...... We don't just have a virtual love... ours is a real love......

Mike: Well just remove little Ditto and get that bra off and place those movers and shakers on me tonight in bed.

Michelle: Tonight I will cuddle you in my dreams

Mike: Can I see you just for a minute on cam... here, now?

Michelle: Why darling?

Mike: I miss you... I want you!!!

Michelle: OK

They video link in silence for a couple of minutes, as Mike is not alone at home. They blow kisses at one another. They each place their hands on the screen to touch……

Michelle: I have to go now darling

Mike: Virtual kiss… but the real kiss was best.

Michelle: I love you darling… so very very much…

Mike: "DITTO"… Enjoy your weekend… You made my day today.

Michelle: Yes the real kiss was better… I love your kisses I love your cuddles…

Mike: I will cuddle you tight tonight like 21 years ago.

Michelle: MMMmmm… Mike…… Bye for now

Mike: Bye darling

E-mail from: Michelle
To: Mike
Date: 9 April 2013
Subject: End of our virtual week in the Cotswolds

Hi my darling

Well, already we have come to the end of our virtual week in the lovely Cotswolds… We have had a wonderful week together, sharing our love, sharing everything together… Having fun… Playing together… Laughing… and loving…

MMMmmm Mike… this is the last chapter of this virtual holiday, so we must end it in bed together… We are cuddled up together naked… my boobs are laying across your chest, just the way with both like it… your arms are around me, just the way we both like it… safe in the arms of my bodyguard… you smell delicious, and I cannot get enough of you… MMMMMmm Mike, I love you…

I plant kisses all over your chest… move up to your face, and kiss those delicious lips of yours, you kiss me deeply, licking into my mouth the way that you do… OMG I think you could give me an orgasm just kissing me… I am going to move down, my warm velvet tongue sliding seductively across your skin… I kiss that

little belly button of yours… delicious… the kisses move lower…
my hand is caressing the golden nuggets, as my lips find the hot
rod…MMMmmmm Mike, delicious… Gently I suck on the hot
rod… OMG it loves this… so I do it some more… and more…
and more… Now I need to check out the tattoo on the hot rod…
Oh Wow… I love this tattoo. each letter means something, as well
as my name…

M = MMMmmm sexy
I = Incredible sensations
C = Climax
H = Heaven
E = Erotic
L = Luscious
L = Lips
E = Enthralling pleasure

T = Tantalizing Michelle
U = Utterly provocative
R = Raunchy
N = Never stop loving me
E = Endless love
R = Real love

How could I ever resist this hot rod?… Never!!!!… my hand
strokes the hot rod… MMMmmmm… Mike you are just loving
this… and then you say, the hot rod wants to find little Ditto's
home… So I move myself around and on top of you… your hands
move onto the movers and shakers… and then you are saying
OMG Michelle, these nipples are like American hard gums
already, your fingers and thumbs are tweaking at my nipples…
MMMmmmm so nice… Your hands cover my boobs now… and
you say, yes Michelle, these C's are a handful… one in each hand,
soft, warm, curvy, squidgy… your boob-a-licious Michelle… all
for you Mike Turner… I move down a little, and with your hot
rod in my hand I place it right in-between my boobs… you push
my boobs together, and the hot rod is trapped there…
MMMmmmm… how sensual for both of us… your hands are
pushing my boobs tighter and tighter to your hot rod… my hand is
back on the golden nuggets, as the hot rod is fully consumed
inbetween my boobs… Now you are hot… so hot… your

temperature has risen at least thirteen degrees... and you are saying OMG I know exactly what little Ditto feels like now when he is trapped in here, no wonder he never wants to come out... I slide my boobs up... and then back down... your hot rod is well and truly gripped in-between them... MMMmmmm Mike!!! ...

We are hot... steamy... sexy... this is so sensual... we are both loving it... then you say, my hands should take over from yours... and so they do... now my hands are holding each of my boobs firming together, with that delicious hot rod of yours well and truly trapped in-between them... I slide up and down... your hot rod is throbbing at the pleasure!!!... my nipples are getting harder and harder, and they are trailing up and down your tummy as they go, OMG there will be indentations here before we have finished... and then you are saying... Michelle, there is going to be a mess here in a minute if you do not stop doing that... Mike... I know you do not want me to stop!!!!... and then your hand finds my hot spot... OMG... this is just heaven!!!... your fingers are working on my hot spot now... OMG I am as hot as you are now!!!... your fingers are being gentle, but they are getting faster... OMG... I squeeze my boobs even harder against your hot rod... both completely captured by the severe intensity. My pulse is raising... my head is spinning... we are both breathing hard and fast... OMG... this is... just... too... much!!! ... I feel guilty as I climax already... the heavenly sensations reverberating right through me, but not for too long, as then I feel your love juices pumping all over my boobs... OH MIKE... I squeeze you even tighter... and just keep on sliding up and down on you...... your face looks as though you are in heaven...... and we each keep on doing what we are doing to each other, as ecstasy just continues to fill both of us... Sexy... Erotic... Sensual... and so enjoyable!!!!!... the sensation is phenomenal... MMMmmmm... eventually we both still, and I just lay on top of you, still your hot rod between my boobs.. Oh my darling... wonderful... sending goosebumps racing over my body...

After a while, you say, we both need a shower now, and off we go together... We pack up our things, and it is time to head off home... but this time, it is not separate homes, it is back to 'our home ~ our mud hut'...

I love you as my virtual husband... I love you as my bodyguard...
I will love you forever...

Michelle

xxx xxx xxx xxx x

E-mail from: Mike
To: Michelle
Date: 9 April 2013
Subject: Re: End of our virtual week in the Cotswolds

Hi my darling

Woweeeeeeeee... You are so sexy!!!... I just love you to bits...
And all your bits!!! You are outrageously flirtatious with me...
And so provocative!! You are a real aphrodisiac to me, that is for
sure... I am intoxicated by you... You certainly get my adrenaline
flowing... Do you know I have been thinking of us too, yes us 21
years ago and our plans to go to the Cotswolds together. Yes it
was Sunday 5 April 1992... Wow! Even typing this it seems like
such a long time ago, but really for me it was just like yesterday
and the memories and the love that we shared that week has never
faded.

I attach a picture of Bourton-on-the-Water. I am sure you
remember this quaint little place. If you remember we held hands
and on the left where the shops started we went into the little
butcher's shop and you purchased some steaks for dinner. Do you
remember further down and towards the latter part of the shops
still on the left we went into a little gift shop? Yes I think you still
have that Swarovski bear that we purchased for your Mum. You
were blessed with lovely parents my darling and although I was a
stranger to them, like with you, I always found a warm loving
welcoming presence in both of them. Even now I cannot get over
the food parcel and the bottle of Southern Comfort that was
packed in the boot of your car. I wish I had only got to know them
both better. What you told me about your parents the other week
was news to me and maybe they had a better understanding about
our situation. All I know is they could not have made me feel
more welcome in what was probably a difficult situation.

Anyway… back to your email. I just want to pick out some points. Well I cannot ever forget the showers we had together and all the body shower lotion!!! On the Monday we had the phantom pregnant sheep to listen too and if you remember it bucketed down with rain non-stop all day, but what better place could we have been than in bed together. I remember you saying to me… what side do you normally sleep!!! I could have replied, do you want to be on top or me!!! OMG… The panic on your face when I turned the light off in the bedroom Sunday night. Well in fact I could not see your face of course, it was so dark you we couldn't see a thing. So yes my baby slept with the light on all night!! I am glad you have a good camera now. It must be much better than taking pictures with your fingers!! Do you remember crossing the road and only you could do this, which was to take a picture of a chocolate box thatched cottage? Do you know I really love you?, I loved you then and I still have that love for you now.

I have missed you so much over the years my darling… I will always love you…

Mike xxx

---

11 April 2013 ~ Live Interactive Text

Michelle: Good evening my sexy cyber lover

Mike: I have just had my shower… Oh… If only you were here to join me.

Michelle: Oh… if only I were…

Mike: Yes please… I would love to shower with you and then… MMMMmmmmmmmm

Michelle: MMMMMmmm… and then… ???

Mike: End of day job… I need to check that lovely body of yours from head to toe and maybe stop off at few places in between. Just check the movers and shakers to see if they are in good shape.

Michelle: Are you checking with your hands or eyes?

Mike: Both!

Michelle: MMMmmmm… nice…

Mike: I must have got a bit sexcited then and hit the wrong button. See what you do to me!!

Michelle: So how about we cuddle up in bed to do this... whilst you do my body check... both of your arms around me...... naked cuddles......

Mike: Are you naked? Can I play with your nipples? Even better, turn your cam on if you are naked!! ☺

Michelle: Naughty, if you were here yes... but no boobs on www!!

Mike: I want to roll my tongue all around those nipples of yours... I bet they are looking lovely... (if only I could see them)

Michelle: You are making them feel good. I need to check out the golden nuggets...... caress them gently, whilst you are playing with my nipples

Mike: You really turn me on Michelle Turner.

Michelle: You also turn me on Mike Turner. I think my boobs want to cuddle that hot rod of yours

Mike: You want to masturbate me again there? Little Ditto will lodge an official complaint if his home gets flooded in love juice again!! He said it was as though a Tsunami had swept through there last time ☺

Michelle: He is asleep in his bed, he will not even know...

Mike: Michelle I have a question

Michelle: Ok... fire away

Mike: If our book ever gets put together as a book... and then it gets published... do you think people will have a mass debate over that?

Michelle: ☺ are we talking mass debate here? Or Masturbate?

Mike: Masturbate!!! ☺ ☺

Michelle: Oh... that is very naughty!!

Mike: I am feeling very naughty... So, I will just slip my hand down in between your legs and feel your topiary heart. Yes... Feels good and a bit moist... I take it that is a good sign of a healthy Michelle. I think at least, I am new at this job.

Michelle: What a good and thorough bodyguard you are... I think I will have to make the job permanent for you...

Mike: Hey you... Do not give this job to anyone else!!

Michelle: OK... you have yourself a deal

Mike: I will just do the one finger test okay.

Michelle: OMG... you know this will do things to me...

Mike: Okay... Let me find the love tunnel and follow upward along the love valley... OMG... what have I found here, I think this is your hot spot.

Michelle: MMMmmm Mike... that one finger of yours is a very powerful finger.. that finger of yours has magic powers... Mike you are driving me crazy here!! I am getting all hot and bothered here

Mike: I think I had better just cool it down and run by tongue over it. Just the tip of my tongue, in place of my finger, licking and parting the sensitive tissue...

Michelle: Oh... my... God... Mike you do drive me crazy

Mike: A rolling tongue MMMmmmm... You like this... I know you do

Michelle: I am on fire now... I love this Mike... get yourself over here right now

Mike: On fire!!! Do I need to put out a fire now? I could cool it down with some love juices. I know you now want my hot rod to replace my tongue over your hot spot, eh!!

Michelle: Let me play with that hot rod of yours, and guide it towards my love tunnel

Mike: Just the tip of my hot rod now running over your hot spot. I think something just spurt out the top of my hot rod then, because you are even more wet down there. It is very slippery down there now!!

Michelle: Come on slide just a little more of that hot rod inside of me

Mike: I think I had better slip it back down that love valley and find the entrance to that love tunnel. Just the head of my hot rod to pop inside and have a check out of your body parts. This is my job remember? I am just doing my job here, and checking everything as a good bodyguard should

Michelle: Darling, you really do make me laugh... come on my baby... I want you inside of me... just come in there and love me...

Mike: Now you are shouting... Search me inside Mike. So, I think I may just invite myself inside and feel my way around.

Michelle: You have made it wet... I am warm...... and very loving... come inside me Mike... I really want you

Mike: I know you are so sexxxxxy!!!

Michelle: You are really sexy tonight my darling...

Mike: I will just ease it slowly in a bit more and then back out. But... Next thrust will be a little further darling. Wow... Yes that slips in easier now... Already up halfway down the tattoo now.

Michelle: I love that tattoo

Mike: Next thrust in could go all the way to the bottom... deep, deep inside of that tight little love tunnel of yours... Michelle... I have told you before that is my golden nuggets rattling at the entrance to your love tunnel and no they cannot go inside too... Greedy Michelle.

Michelle: I can feel them there Mike... just touching on the lips of my love tunnel, rubbing all against me... and your hot rod deep, deep inside of me

Mike: I will just slip my finger down there whilst it is inside you and give that hot spot some caressing... Multi-tasking now, remember this is my job.

Michelle: OMG Mike, that is what I call the full works... this job is yours for keeps

Mike: No... Be patient. The full works is not just yet. Don't worry you will know when the full works comes, it will pump you full of love juices and fill your love tunnel all the way with my love.

Michelle: Ohhhh Mike... I am ready for you to pump that hot rod hard and fast...

Mike: I need to really get into my job now. Working you up inside and outside, I think I am earning a bonus here!! I think we need to speed this up now and go into overdrive, eh!

Michelle: Come on then my baby... let`s go

Mike: So in and out fast and furious and my finger is still over your hot spot and speeding up too. Christ Michelle, it feels so good inside you... I've never been so hard and thick... I am so deep inside you...

Michelle: OMG... crazy!!! Crazy!!!... I am loving this so much... give me all of your love here Mike...

Mike: Okay... My golden nuggets are full to maximum and ready to come... Mmmm... this thrust deep inside will fill you full of my love... Pump... Yessss I have exploded deep inside you... Faster than a bullet it has shot everywhere

Michelle: Feel my love for you Mike... as our love juices combine... you send me to heaven and back... my head is spinning with the orgasm you give me

Mike: I think it was a pump action hot rod… and both barrel have been shot everywhere… I love to fill you with my love juices… It feels real good to me!!

Michelle: I have taken all of your love juices inside of me… and it is the nicest feeling in the world… me full of your love

Mike: You have a full tank of love now for sure, and… I love you… I love watching you come Michelle, the sounds you make, and the way your body quivers.. I remember this so well with you…

Michelle: And I love you darling… truly love you

Mike: I had better go now my darling… Boy how the time goes so quick when I am with you.

Michelle: I know you need to go now darling, so I will let you go… I wish it were this time last week, and I was coming to see you tomorrow

Mike: Do you know it feels the same to me now, like all those years ago. I love you so much darling…

Michelle: It does to me too… I think our love will last forever…

Mike: For eternity and never ending..

Michelle: Cuddle me tight in your dreams tonight… and I will do the same to you…

Mike: MMMmmmm… I will recharge… and we can do it again in our sleep and in our dreams.

Michelle: I love you…

Mike: "DITTO"

Mike: You are precious to me and like a little gem… I will be here to protect you… and be here for you always

Michelle: Can I have a silent movie goodnight kiss before you go?

Mike: What… On cam? You are greedy. ☺ Okay just for 13 sex.

They video link in silence, blow one another goodnight kisses.

Mike: Goodnight my darling

Michelle: Goodnight darling… Mwaah

E-mail from: Michelle
To: Mike
Date: 12 April 2013
Subject: I am in love with my bodyguard

Hi my darling Mike (0013)

When I eventually went to bed at midnight last night, I could not get to sleep... I tossed and turned thinking of you... thinking how lovely it would be just to be snuggled up in your arms... 2:30am I was still not asleep...

I just laid there thinking about last Friday, seeing you... remembering the feel of your arms around me... our bodies so close together... our lips touching... which made our skype feel so real to me last night... last night, I swear, I could almost feel you doing all of the things to me you were describing... oh Mike... I love the way you make me feel...

I love you in a way I love no other... so real... so good... I am so pleased we have found one another again in this way... even today I can feel your love inside of me, warm and tender... a part of my heart will always belong to you darling, always...

I am so in love with you Mike Turner......
and this love is FOREVER AND ALWAYS......

Michelle
xxx xxx xxx xxx x

E-mail from: Michelle
To: Mike
Date: 13 April 2013
Subject: Wanting you...

Hi my darling

Still today I am thinking what a mind-blowing and earth-shattering orgasm you would have given me on Thursday!!!... MMMmmmm Mike... how I love you...

This morning I am all alone, and just had my shower... and as my bare hands skimmed the shower gel all over my body, I was wishing it were your hands doing this to me... and when the water cascaded down my boobs, and dripped off the end of my nipples, I thought how you would have loved to see this...

I am craving your touch... The 13th today... and I want to tell you "I LOVE YOU"

Always and forever
Michelle
xxx xxx xxx xxx x

E-mail from: Mike
To: Michelle
Date: 21 April 2013
Subject: Bodyguard body check

Hi Michelle

Well my darling, I think I should do a quick body check to see if you are in good shape. Otherwise, you will be saying I am not doing my job very well here. Where will start I say to myself?... I think it should be your vital twin assets and after all these are big body parts to check out. Those movers and shakers look to be in good shape, but I need to check and give them a quick once over. I need to just unclasp your bra and let then go into natural free fall... Mmmmm... they sure look good... Mmmmmm... they sure feel good. I will just test the reflexes!!! Left big C boob first, just a gentle lift and gently let down... Yes good reflexes here and a good bounce. Okay now right big C boob and the same again... Yes again good reflexes here too and again this shows plenty of spring and bounce. Definitely your pair of boobs are both looking good and in good shape. I think I had better just do another little check on them to test your reflexes. I think I should undertake a nipple test!! I will just take your left nipple between my finger and thumb and just give it a thirteen second massage manipulation. OMG... a spontaneous response and already proud and hard and standing up on end like a good American hard gum!!! I think I will try the other nipple now, but change tactics and instead of using my finger and thumb I will use my lips and give it a thirteen second massage manipulation. OMG… I have barely go my lips over it and your hard nipple is projecting into my mouth… So tasty, tasty and yummy yummy!!… I can tell you like this little test. So the boobs are fine and just a little rumble together for a final check just to make sure Ditto's home is structurally sound. Those twin assets are in good shape for sure and they have passed the body check.

Well my darling I think I should do another quick body check on you to see if that topiary heart needs a good cut or just a trim. Oh… Michelle have you forgotten to put your knickers on again today. Okay for this you just need to lay down and then?… Yes you know, legs open wide!!! Mmmmm… You know the saying you cannot see the wood for the trees!! Well there is a bit of work required here. I would say there is a forest down here!!! A lot of cutting back is required my darling in order to get this back to a topiary heart shape. Let me think for a moment, do I need a tractor mower!!!… a lawn mower!!!… a hedge strimmer!!! ..a pair of shears or a good pair of scissors!!! I am only equipped with a pair of scissors so these must suffice!!!… I will need to check your reflexes on your hot spot, but first I need to do some trimming back to find it!!! Okay… Yes legs wide apart so I can get stuck in there!!! Michelle stop laughing and let me do my job properly because this may take a bit of time. I can see I will be earning my money doing this job!!! So out come the scissors and snip snip here!!!… snip snip there!!!… snip snip everywhere. Thirteen minutes later and I can begin to see the light of day down there now. Your hot spot is hot enough without wrapping a fur overcoat around it my darling!!! Now for the shape and to carry out some more body checks and reflex tests. One little finger running over your hot spot and let us just see what happens!!! Hey stop screaming with sexcitement Michelle I have not even started yet!!! I need to just part this love valley and run my little finger up the top and try and find your hot spot. Found it!!!… so just a little reflex test okay… Am I running my finger clockwise or anti-clockwise over your hot spot? Michelle you are groaning, just answer the question!!!. Okay… Am I running my finger up and down over your hot spot? Michelle are you talking to me or not!!! Okay… The tongue test next!!!...the tip of my tongue is running all over your hot spot can you feel this?… Michelle talk to me!!!

Okay... faster and faster now... you will talk to me!!! OMG... Michelle there must be a problem here, just tell me what's up!!! You then shout out at the top of your voice, OMG... OMG!!!!... yes in your religious voice, put your hot rod up inside me Mike I am so sexcited I am lost for words...... to be continued...

I love you Michelle Turner... I really miss you!! Mwah!

Mike xxx

E-mail from: Michelle
To: Mike
Date: 23 April 2013
Subject: Bodyguard body check... continued

Hi my sexy bodyguard (0013)

Well, I am so pleased to hear that on your inspection duties all seemed well with Michelle. Nice to hear that the 'movers and shakers' were looking good to you... feeling good... and passed the bounce test!!!! MMMMmmm nice!!! Nipple reaction seemed quite spontaneous... I know these nipples love your touch, the fingers and thumb test, MMmm they like this... but the lips and tongue test MMMmmmm they 'love' this. And you say they tasted so good... MMMmmmm so nice (maybe I will dip them in sugar for you sometime... Oh, how about into Southern Comfort and then sugar). It is also good to know that little Ditto's home is sound with the 'rumble test'...... yes, I love it.

As for the topiary heart, well... I am so relieved to know that a tractor mower was not necessary, or a lawnmower, even a hedge trimmer, and please do not use a strimmer there, it sounds very painful. I like the thought of the very tiny scissors, and you taking your time to do this... I am sure I would just lay back and enjoy all of this attention and treatment. The topiary heart is now looking sexcellent... Oh and Mike, once you have started to run those fingers up and down, round and round, I am loving it... OMG!!! once your tongue becomes involved you drive me crazy... I am very sexcited at the very thought of it...

So I am thinking to myself, today I must be a very 'boob-o-licious' Michelle, with a very well trimmed topiary heart... OMG, I wait with bated breath for the 'to be continued'...

I have missed you like crazy recently... and I love you like crazy......

Michelle
~ X ~

---

26 April 2013 ~ Live Interactive Text

Mike: Hi my sexy Babe

Michelle: Hi darling... how are you today?

Mike: Missing you... other than that alright I guess

Michelle: MMmmmm missing you too... Hey here is a thought... it is raining, yes?

Mike: Yes, it is raining

Michelle: How about meeting me in the woods in 13 minutes... to come and do some naked dancing in the rain...

Mike: What ?

Michelle: It`s raining!!... dancing in the rain!!...... you know... naked dancing in the rain... and then... as we are in the woods... make love naked, in the rain, in the woods

Mike: Pussy will get wet

Michelle: What from? The rain?

Mike: Well outside by rain, but inside by love juices.

Michelle: Wow... I love it...

Mike: What about the ants?

Michelle: We will have to stand up!!

Mike: You mean against a tree?

Michelle: There will be no pants, to get ants in our pants... Yes, make love against a tree

Mike: Will it be a chestnut tree? ☺

Michelle: Chest 'n' nuts... ☺

Mike: Me on your chest and you taking my nuts.

Michelle: You can have the scratchy part of the tree... I will lean on you...... don't worry I am more than happy to hold onto 'your' nuts

Mike: I will just hang onto your boobs... I think they will both be bouncing! Bouncy... bouncy... boob-o-licious Michelle

Michelle: With her bodyguard protecting her

Mike: Bouncy boobs and bouncy nuts... Bonking hard.

Michelle: Hey... darling... don't worry I have got hold of your nuts... I have to take care of these for you, because if a squirrel came along!!!... Well?

Michelle: Sorry if you are laughing darling, because I am chuckling away here

Mike: Shhhhh... I will be heard laughing in a minute, then when she says what were you laughing at, I have to try and invent some e-mail I was laughing at

Michelle: Sorry darling... Shhhhhh... let's do it more quietly... I need to give you plenty of kisses, to keep those lips quiet

Mike: Is the tree shagging... I mean shaking?

Michelle: MMMmmmm... nice treeshagging... Oh, yes I mean, the tree is shaking ☺

Mike: I am working away now.. I sound and look like a woodpecker... Bang, bang, bang...

Michelle: Oh darling... I am crying with laughter now, I hope you are being quiet?

Mike: I am well deep in the hole... and I think they are hot chest-nuts now!!

Michelle: Oh dear... the tears are rolling down my face with laughter

Mike: I am going to have to go, because I am laughing so much, and she will hear me

Michelle: Just call downstairs and tell Cheryl you are busy at the moment, doing some woodwork...

Mike: Doing a tongue and groove... My tongue in your groove will send you crazy!!

Michelle: Wow... I know this for sure...

Mike: Tongue and groove needs to be a good tight fit.

Michelle: Oh this is the perfect tight fit

Mike: The glue can be the love juice to make sure. Does it feel sticky?

Michelle: Mike we could get stuck together forever at this rate…
and in broad daylight, naked in the woods… Ohhh

Mike: OMG darling… I am going to have to go now… I cannot stop
laughing

Michelle: Sorry darling… Shhhhhhh…

Mike: I LOVE YOU x 13

Michelle: MMMMmmmmmm… thank you… love you too… bye

E-mail from: Mike
To: Michelle
Date: 28 April 2013
Subject: BBC exclusive news report

BBC exclusive news report

An ariel photographer flying over spotted a tree violently shaking in a small wooded area. Why this came to the pilot's notice was simply that there were several trees in close proximity of each other, but only this one tree was violently shaking. The pilot circled over the area again to do another cognisance check. Due to the trees having very little leaf coverage it could be seen that two people, a man and a woman, were spotted standing at the base of the tree. At the time it was raining and the couple appeared to be both totally naked. Yes… again it could be seen that the tree was shaking quite violently. It looked like the guy was shagging her against the tree causing the tree to shake!!

This BBC exclusive news report coincided with several reports of someone hearing a lot of groaning that was going on in the same vicinity. Was this a religious group carry out a religious ritual, because chanting of "Oh My God" repeatedly could be clearly heard in the local neighbourhood? One local neighbour called the 999 services to investigate the area, but upon a thorough search of the area nobody was seen.

The crime report showed that the only evidence was a woman's bra and knickers tossed high in the canopy of a chestnut tree… This was exhibit Bouncy Boobs `C`. This evidence was labelled BBC. The only other evidence reported at the scene (see picture attached) was the tree itself. It was also believed that the woman had some sort of bespoke designer heart shape in between her legs. However, it was also reported this heart shape on the tree also looked like a woman's vagina!!! Everyone has become so sexcited about this BBC exclusive news report. Questions are being asked… "What was down in between her legs and would this back up the alleged shouting of stick that hot rod into my heart?". There was no proof that there was any religious ritual or spiritual sacrifice despite the alleged shouting of "Stick it in an out, harder, quicker and faster into the heart" followed by "This is heaven" and shouting repeatedly "OMG" on each occasion.

The conclusion of this case was that a married couple, but not married to each other, were having a naked bonking session against a chestnut tree in the rain. One reporter asked, "Was he fondling with her chest and was she playing with his nuts?" The area has now been cordoned off because everyone is now flocking into the area to visit the so-called "Bonking Tree" which could turn into a "hot spot" attraction for lovers.

The couple have not been identified and are still on the run. If the woman is seen running and wearing no bra, she could be considered to be dangerous and people are warned not to get in her way!!! The man is thought to be her new employee and bodyguard. It was allegedly reported that the unknown couple might soon publish a book about their secret love life together. Everyone is so sexcited about this BBC exclusive news report.

File case and crime report 0013 unsolved, but now considered closed.

Hi Michelle… All I can say is look out everyone because there is a crazy loving couple out there somewhere!! So if there is a spring or the sun comes out, beware!!!

I love you with big hugs and kisses x 13

Mike
Xxx

E-mail from: Michelle
To: Mike
Date: 29 April 2013
Subject: BBC exclusive news report update…

Following on from the recent BBC Exclusive News Report regarding earth tremors and a tree violently shaking in the local area, it has been revealed that a partial identity has been uncovered regarding the 'mystery couple' in question last Friday. A detailed analysis of sound recording taken from the spotter plane has revealed several clues to this.

It has been discovered that the woman's voice said "Mike, I want your hot rod inside of me." It has not yet been established exactly what the hot rod is, but leads investigators to believe the man's name could be Mike. Muffled sounds of the man's voice were also heard, muffled it is believed by kissing sounds, but he is thought to have said "Michelle, you are so greedy." Which leads investigators to believe they could be named Mike & Michelle. It is possible that they could be an American couple, as the man also talked of tasty, delicious, juicy, succulent American hard gums, as they romped. The area is still cordoned off, as people flock to see the 'Bonking Tree', and there is assumption that gold may have been found in the area, as the woman was also heard to say, she had found two golden nuggets!!

There is also thought to be some suggestion that they may be involved in some kind of religious cult, as the woman shouted "Oh My God" on several occasions!!!… And the man was heard to shout, "Jesus… this is so good". It has also been revealed that an earth tremor was recorded at this 'hot spot' measuring 1.3 on the Richter scale. This passionate couple certainly made the earth move on this occasion!!!

It is also believed that the couple may have a 'love child', as once all activity was over the man was heard to say "Come on Son ~ Ditto we are leaving now"… Speculation is the couple have now left the area, with their son, and returned to a remote island in the Seychelles, where allegedly they could live in a mud hut.

Well, whoever you are Mike & Michelle, publish your book. Because if this was a preview trailer of things to come, the world now eagerly awaits in anticipation. Last summer a riveting read was `Fifty Shades of Grey`, a book which went viral globally. It is considered the novel about to be unleashed here could put *Fifty Shades* in the shade. This one short preview has given us a taste for the content of their book, surely to be full of love, steamy erotic sex, and passion… We all wait with bated breath…

****

Hi Mike, maybe… we should be sectioned together… I think we have driven each other mad… Or, are we just insanely in love with each other ? ? ?

I love you (x13) Hugs and cuddles I would like right now (x13) A million kisses (x13)
Michelle… Mwaaaaaaaaaaaaaaaaaaaaaaaaah

E-mail from: Mike
To: Michelle
Date: 29 April 2013
Subject: Re: BBC exclusive news report… update…

Hi Michelle

This really made me laugh… I even have to wait here for a minute now because there is still a wide smile on my face before I can go downstairs.

You truly are Craaaaaaaaaazy!! I just cannot help loving this crazy Michelle.

Mike xxx

---

29 April 2013 ~ Live Interactive Text

Mike: YOU!!!… you are absolutely crazy
Michelle: Oh hello darling… I love the chest… nuts tree
Mike: I love your chest…
Michelle: I love your nuts…
Mike: I can have your boobs and you can have my nuts. At least that way we both have two things to play with.

Michelle: Sounds like a fair 50/50 share to me... come over and play with them whenever you want

Mike: I think I have the bigger things to play with

Michelle: When I play with your nuts all sorts of other things get bigger!!!! so maybe I got the better end of this deal?

Mike: Do you mean my tattoo?

Michelle: Yesssssssss!!! my favourite tattoo of all time.. I love it when it looks like this... M I C H E L L E T U R N E R

Mike: I love it when it puts its head inside your love tunnel. Just has a little look and then the rod follows up through! OMG!!!

Michelle: MMMmmmm... meeeeeee tooooooo...

Mike: I have to go now... I love you... I would love to hold you now and just give you a cuddle...

Michelle: I would love that too... really and truly I would

Mike: Bye for now... mwaaaaaaaaaaaaaaaah

Michelle: BFN... Mwaaaaaaaaaaaaaaaaaaaaaaaaaaaaaah (x13)

---

30 April 2013 ~ Live Interactive Text

Mike: Hi my sexy cyber wife... You are truly crazy!!

Michelle: I think we both are!!!... maybe we should have to take the day off work for this?

Mike: MMmm... Okay we will bonk it off.

Michelle: Ok... maybe we can make the news headlines again...

Mike: Well just make sure you put your knickers and bra on before going to work

Michelle: How can I?... They are stuck up a tree!!

Mike: Are they the only ones you have then?

Michelle: I am just going to have to 'bounce' around all day!!!!

Mike: You will be classified dangerous and could do someone a mischief if you are on the run!!!

Michelle: I may even give myself two black eyes...

Mike: Headline News... Knocked out by two bouncy boobs on the run.

Michelle: My bodyguard will just have to keep these movers and shakers under control, now I have no bra to wear

Mike: I will hand my notice in at work... this has just become a full-time job, with all the overtime I can manage!!

Michelle: Talking of jobs... we both need to go...... Bye darling PS... I LOVE YOU

Mike: PS... I LOVE YOU

Later that day......

Michelle: OMG you were so sexy on this cam today

Mike: I want to feel that heart beating

Michelle: I think you are sending off 'pheromones' today...

Mike: What are pheromones? Is that catching? Can I get cream for it?

Michelle: Pheromones are hormones that attract the opposite sex

Mike: Mmmm... Be careful, the sun is out today and anything could happen!!

Michelle: I could take your clothes off you right now, with my teeth...

Mike: If you do that... I will spring into action for sure!! Wow... Teeth, eh! Be careful when you get to my hot rod...

Michelle: Don't worry... only the lips and tongue would touch your hot rod... but I have to get your clothes off first... OMG... I would have fun with you today... I am feeling SEXXXXXYYY

Mike: You 'are' so sexy and so crazy. But I love you all the same.

Michelle: I need some of your loving

Mike: You would get 113% loving from me all day every day and the forever loving would have no end.

Michelle: Ooooooh WOOOOOOW... I would love this... and in return you would get the same from me... All of my love... 24/7

Mike: In fact you could just run around naked and then it would save time me having to take all your clothes off.

Michelle: What about everyone else seeing me? I don't share my body with everybody!!... or is this at our mud hut?

Mike: No... you can only be naughty with me.

Michelle: I only want to be naughty with you... and I want to be naughty right now

Mike: Yes I would love to feel your heart beat next to mine, two hearts beating as one

Michelle: MMMMmmmm...... I would love that too... place your hand on my heart now, see if you can read its Morse code

Mike: It's says... da da dit dit da.

Michelle: ..---... ----... ----... I think I can feel what it is telling you... it is telling you... it loves you

Mike: No... Wrong............ It is telling you, that I love you

Michelle: Both of our hearts know... we love each other

Mike: Damn it... sorry darling... Cheryl has just come home, I have to go

Michelle: OK darling... Bye

Mike: She comes in and says... Why are you always on that computer when I come home?... and I say, just checking my e-mails dear!!!

Michelle: Go darling... I do not want to get you into trouble

Mike: I love you Michelle

Michelle: "DITTO"

E-mail from: Michelle
To: Mike
Date: 1 May 2013
Subject: Three wishes ~ for my bodyguard

Hi my darling

<u>WARNING: DO NOT READ THIS E-MAIL JUST BEFORE YOU GO TO BED, IT WILL GIVE YOU EROTIC DREAMS ALL NIGHT... AND DO NOT READ IT BEFORE YOU GO TO WORK, YOU WILL FIDGET ALL DAY!!!</u>

A quick re-cap of the bodyguard body check... you have kissed my lips, to check they are supple and pliable, yes they have passed your test... You have removed my bra and checked the bounce of my boobs, MMMMmmm yes, they have passed this test... You have checked my nipples, they were too soft, so you have tweaked them into a better shape, they are now the size and texture of American hard gums... You taste them to make sure... MMMmmmm... nice... they have passed the test... You have trimmed my topiary heart into perfect shape, it is looking and feeling real good now!!! Your fingers and tongue have teased my hot spot... OMG sheer pleasure!!!

Now, you have made me feel real sexy!!!... so after all of the pampering you have given me, I feel like returning the treatment. I have kissed and caressed your body... I have worked my way down to the golden nuggets, licked and gently sucked them... I have worked my way up the hot rod... licked, sucked and nibbled until I have driven you crazy now... the tattoo now looks like this... M... I... C... H... E... L... L... E... T... U... R... N... E... R... MMMmmmm Mike... what to do with you next???

As we are both naked, and you are lying flat on your back... I straddle my legs over you, and sit back on your thighs whilst I decide what to do next. These blue eyes are flashing at you Mike Turner, and the smile on my face must tell you how much I love you... In your gorgeous brown eyes I see this love reflected. Your love for me... My love for you... I reach over a get a bottle of baby lotion... slowly I remove the lid, and pour some into the palm of my hand. I hand you the bottle to put down, then I slowly rub the baby lotion into the palms of both my hands... My eyes do not leave yours. Your eyes are watching my hands... Then I slowly place my hands over my boobs and so, so, slowly massage the oil all over my boobs and nipples... Now you are licking your lips and breathing deeply in anticipation. My hands continue to massage the oil around and around my boobs... then I tell you I am going to grant you three wishes. Your eyes are fixated on my boobs and you put in your first request. The request is... can your hands join in with mine and help to massage the oil into my boobs. Your wish is granted Mike Turner... and your hands join in with mine. The oil slips through our fingers as both of our hands massage around and around... our hands locked together... MMMmmmm... Sensual... I know you are loving this because your hot rod is standing to attention... You take my hands in yours, and manipulate them so we both tug gently at my nipples... OMG 'they are' like American hard gums... I move my hands away and let you continue, my hands slide down my tummy, real slow... my fingers get to my hot spot, and I slowly rub a little of my oily fingers there... Mike, you are just loving this, your hot rod is pulsating now, and your breathing is so deep. I gently take hold of your hot rod and slowly rub my oily hands all over it. You are gasping now, as you say I am driving you crazy!!!...

You put in for your second request of the three wishes... you ask me to part my love tunnel with my fingers and let your hot rod slide its way in... Mike, your wish is granted... I slowly part the lips of my love tunnel with my fingers... your eyes have left my boobs now, and are firmly fixed upon my love tunnel and fingers... I manoeuvre my body over you, and just let the tip of your hot rod touch inside of my love tunnel... just that first inch... MMMmmmm... sexy... sensual... sensational... my fingers swirl around my hot spot, down the valley of love, and come into contact with your hot rod, right there in the entrance of my love tunnel, I swirl my fingers around, I can feel my love tunnel, I can feel your hot rod in there... MMMmmmm this is so sensual... I run my fingers up your tattoo, and then pull you in towards me with my fingers, and let one more inch enter inside there... Mike... so warm in there... so wet, just wanting you in there... MMMmmmm... your fingers are still playing with my nipples, but your eyes do not leave what you are watching ~ your hot rod entering my love tunnel... How sexxxxxxxxxxy!!! My fingers stroke the hot rod, from you, towards me... and gently ease you in, one more inch... this is really a turn on!!! I wiggle my body... and let you slide a little further in... MMMmmmm sooooo goooood...... I pull back, not wanting to rush anything here... Mike, you look so sexy!!!... I love you... I love your body... I love your mind... your hands are caressing my boobs, sliding all over them, around and around with all the softness of the baby oil. My boobs are so full and tender at your touch. My nipples so hard. OMG Mike, the way you make me feel is incredible. How I want you right now... the tip of your hot rod is just touching the entrance of my love tunnel. I slide back down onto it... it goes in a little further this time... inside my love tunnel is rippling around you, squeezing, trembling on the verge of orgasm. I close my eyes, this is heaven. But your hands leave my boobs, slide down my sides and land on the cheeks of my bum, you pull me harder onto you as you say... "Ah, Christ Michelle... I am going to come so hard in you"... my love tunnel opens up fully to you as your hot rod enters inside me. Our body temperatures have risen considerably. I move back up, but lower myself onto you again, immediately taking you into me once more, this time you push in past my limits… OMG, this is so good… you have completely filled my love tunnel now with your hot rod… it is so thick and hard. Our eyes lock on each other, as the pleasure spreads between us. Your hands move around my hips and suddenly your thumbs are outlining my topiary heart… OMG… I am in heaven with you right now Mike Turner… and with your hot rod fully penetrated inside me, one of the pads of one of your thumbs circles my hot spot… this is it… we can hold back no more, I ride up and down on you. Your hands are on my hips now, as you control our rhythm. I am losing my mind here… it is sooooo good… it is too good… my love tunnel tightens and shakes, as my orgasm explodes through me, spasms through the very core of me and radiates out until I am trembling all over… this pushes you over the edge Mike, your head forces back into the pillow, your eyes shut tight, as you groan loudly "Michelle… the things you do to me"… your hot love juice explodes from you and fills me… it is like a volcano… OMG Mike… is this still the same orgasm for me, or yet another, I just fall apart in front of your very eyes… my whole body is quaking!!!!!… but so are you, your entire body judders as you pull me onto you even harder, and still the love juice is pumping into me. I keep up the rhythm, and want every last drop of your love. And when you body starts to calm, I slow the rhythm… you open your eyes, and we smile at one another… still slowly I am moving up and down on your hot rod… MMmmm sheer and utter pleasure for both of us here darling. Still keeping your hot rod inside of me, I lean down and kiss you on the lips… Mike, I just love sharing our love together… I can feel that you do too, this hot rod of yours is not subsiding yet…

And then, you say you want to put in for your third and final wish… the wish is that I slide down the bed, and let your hot rod slide in-between my boobs… your wish is granted Mike. I slide down… and trail my nipples right down your chest… down your tummy… and find your hot rod with them… the hot rod slides between them… you place a hand on each of my boobs and squeeze them tightly together, your hot rod is trapped firmly between them…… MMMmmmm…… we are sexy and so good together… I move my hands down, and my fingers gently find your golden nuggets, I stroke them so tenderly up towards me… they are touching the underneath of my boobs… I lay my head on your chest… continue to gently stroke the golden nuggets into my boobs… your hands still have hold of the sides of my boobs, and your hot rod is nestled and trapped right there in between them… Oh Mike, this has been heaven… and now I am so comfortable, and so are you. I think we could fall asleep like this… We stay as we are, and both drift off to sleep…

Goodnight my darling
I love you…
Always and forever
your loving wife
Michelle
xxx xxx xxx xxx x

---

1 May 2013 ~ Live Interactive Text

Mike: Hi Michelle… Wow… 3 wishes!! I have just read your email. So how do you expect your bodyguard to rest and sleep after this, eh! Seductive and sexy!! OMG… I have the best job in the whole world looking after your body. Body and mind. Yes a sexy body and a very naughty seductive mind. You will… No, you have driven me crazy!!

Michelle: Good evening my darling… SEXXXXXX – OOOOO – LICIOUS email ☺

Mike: I will not be able to sleep tonight now, I will just lay there thinking of you and my three wishes.

Michelle: My bodyguard looks after me so well, how could I ever refuse him anything

Mike: I don't think the last wish will happen and we then fall asleep… In 90 minutes you will be getting your call for someone to be picked up. Maybe you will just say… I am just finishing off the last wish with my bodyguard!!!

Michelle: Did you like the choice of your three wishes? Were they good choices?

Mike: Yes… I like all three and in that order.

Michelle: MMMMmmmm…… me too……

Mike: Well when you masturbated me in between your bouncy boobs I think the golden nuggets had been totally drained and the needle was on empty… But… Oh… My… God…… did I enjoy it… My head is still spinning!!

Michelle: I told you… I am feeling, sexy and seductive today… the golden nuggets were getting a goodnight cuddle too

Mike: I think they sure filled your love tunnel to the full and gave you all my passionate love.

Michelle: I think we shared 'all of our love' there… how I would love to be doing all of that with you right now

Mike: I think all of your sensual areas were fulfilled, and your body filled with my love

Michelle: MMMmmmm…… lots of sharing, lots of loving

Mike: Love tunnel, hot spot, boobs, nipples, now what order turned you on most?

Mike: You are thinking on this eh!!!

Michelle: I don't have any particular order… I just enjoy it as it comes

Michelle: OK maybe I do…

Michelle: I like to start with kisses on the lips (lips of my mouth that is)

Michelle: I like my body touched all over… I am a very tactile person, incase you have never noticed this

Mike: Hummm… I do not know what other lips you may be referring to? ☺

Michelle: I like my boobs caressed, and kissed… my nipples played with and kissed and sucked… I love you touching them… playing with them… kissing them… sucking them… gently nibbling them

Mike: When your nipples are hard at least I have something to hang onto without slipping off.

Michelle: Well there was plenty of baby oil involved in that email, you didn't slid anywhere you didn't want to. Did you like 'me' putting the baby oil on my boobs? Would this turn you on to watch?

Mike: Woweeeee… what do you think? Of course I did… I liked it when you put some down in between your legs to get the loving started too… God you make me horny just thinking about this!!

Michelle: MMMmmmm… I thought you might… I liked that too

Mike: I do not like you boobs too slippery, I like to have a double handful and not keep slipping off or try to do a juggling act with them. I have never been much good at juggling.

Michelle: There wasn't tooooo much… just enough to be sexy and erotic!!! Just enough for an easy, sexy, slide with your hands

Mike: You do not need baby oil to do this my darling.

Michelle: Do you not like baby oil?

Mike: Not too much, I like what is natural.

Michelle: No, not too much… just a little…… it is sexy!!!

Mike: I would not know about these things!!

Michelle: You are deprived…

Mike: Yes, I think so!

Michelle: I would not deprive you

Mike: I know you wouldn't Michelle… Sod it… let's get this book published and disappear together

Michelle: Be careful Mike, last time you said sod it let's do something… we got virtually married!!

Mike: Sod it… let`s do it ☺

Michelle: OK… ☺

Michelle: In the meantime… as your golden nuggets are drained, how would you like to come to bed with me for a nice cuddle… a naked cuddle… our arms and legs wrapped around one another…

Mike: Yes please… Just clear this with you know who?

Michelle: The cat said it is OK…

Mike: I would truly love to spend a night with you, but we both know this will never happen even if we had another 13 wishes.

Michelle: ☹

Mike: ☹ indeed… so sad, and I can only dream of this with you.

Michelle: And me with you… but we can talk about it here

Mike: I think my pillow is going to have a hard time tonight.

Michelle: I would love to just be cuddled up with you now… cuddled right into you… some nice kisses… my boobs on your chest… hear you breathing…

Mike: MMMmmmm… Just to feel you and love you like a long time ago.

Michelle: I would just love to lay next to you, and hear and feel you breathing... so... cuddle me... now on here... tell me how you would cuddle me...

Mike: I would if I could stretch my arms that far... MMMmm I would love to cuddle you and feel you laying with me and we just enjoy the moment.

Michelle: And just snuggle into you... I enjoy all of my moments with you... now... always... and so nice to spend some precious time with you here this evening

Michelle: Always and forever... forever has no end...

Michelle: Are you OK darling?

Mike: I just want you more and more, that's all......

Mike: Have I told you...

Mike: I LOVE YOU...

Michelle: Have I told you...

Mike: No never!!!

Michelle: Hang on... I haven't said what yet

Mike: I just like you to say it again, that is all.

Michelle: I love you, every single time you tell me, it gives me a warm glow inside

Mike: Do you know I have told you a million times that I love you?

Mike: And one... I love you...

Michelle: Mike Turner... you melt my heart at times...

Mike: I want you right now... Michelle Turner and I want you to relive this last e-mail for real.

Michelle: Come on then Mike Turner...... sod it... let`s do it...

Mike: One day Michelle

Michelle: Put that e-mail on the slate... if ever the 'One Day' comes, 'I promise' you can have all of that for real... you would sleep well that night, after I have finished with you

Mike: Yes I am sure I would, but in the morning when I wake with you... Just look out again.

Michelle: Wow...... put that on the slate too please

Mike: You would be saying, put your legs down darling, I would say that is not my legs standing up!! Maybe an inner third leg!!

Michelle: Hang on I will just check that for you...

Mike: Come on if you want a good ride.

Michelle: I will just have to slide my hand under the bed covers, and check this out... OMG... yes this is well and truly ready for action again... MMMmmmm... my bodyguard is an action man too

Mike: So just put your lips over it... What lips you are saying now, eh!

Michelle: Which lips would you like?

Mike: You can choose... as long as they are wet lips...

Michelle: So which would you be going for right now?... both sets are wet now!!!

Mike: I am greedy so I will go for both...

Michelle: I will start with my mouth... kiss your mouth... a little tongue... a little nibble...... would you like me to try this on your hot rod now?

Mike: Well I was thinking this, so yes for sure.

Michelle: Ok... so my lips are just about to touch your hot rod... my tongue first... flicking the end of your hot rod... my lips just gently sucking the tip of your hot rod...

Mike: Are your fingers also running up and down my tattoo?

Michelle: Oh yes... both hands... fingers up and down, feeling the tattoo

Mike: OMG... what speeds are you doing here?

Michelle: Slowly to start with... slow, gentle, but getting firmer... just how you like it... the first inch of that hot rod is in my mouth now. MMMMmmm... yummy... gently little sucking, in and out of my mouth...

Mike: That head seems to like it inside you.

Michelle: I am sucking it quite firmly now, the head just going in and out of my mouth... Both of my hands are firmly running up and down the sides of your tattoo...

Mike: If you keep sucking that head you will find it starting to leak. I have told you it has a weak head gasket.

Michelle: It's OK... I can fix this...

Mike: Hey I do not want you putting your finger over the top when it comes, it will blow my nuts off. ☺

Michelle: Take it out of my mouth... one finger on the very tip... and rub gentle little circles to spread this little leak... round and round... do not panic, I will not plug the hole ☺ I am just teasing it with my finger!!

Mike: I think I want to plug the hole in between your topiary heart now. Because you are getting me so sexcited here... or else what will you do when if touches the back of your throat?

Michelle: More and more in my mouth then... let's see what we can do here... a little massage of the golden nuggets... with my hands... gently, gently does it... these are very delicate, my mouth is sucking your hot rod quite hard here... in and out... in and out... those golden nuggets are rock hard... but again both of my hands take hold of your hot rod... and squeeze it gently tight...

Mike: OMG...... Michelle......... Sensational

Michelle: The entire length of your hot rod being taken inside my mouth now...... my delicious sexy husband... so tasty... I suck you so hard......

Mike: OMG...... I cannot hold on much longer.

Michelle: Plunge you back into my mouth, sucking harder and harder...... here it comes Mike... more of your love juice...... I can feel it spurting hot and fast into my mouth...... and still I continue to suck on you so hard...

Mike: You said this morning you were feeling sexy and naughty and you sure have lived up to this today.

Michelle: I could be sexy and naughty with you every day

Mike: I officially declare that I love you

Michelle: "DITTO" and that is official...

Mike: I had better go my darling... You have made my day complete. I can never really express how much I love you... I think we were made for each other...

Michelle: I think we were too... Am I allowed a silent movie good night kiss... or is this too naughty for you?

Mike: Mmmmm... Okay just a quickie, but no sound

The video link for two minutes.

Mike: Good night and let us relive the same dreams... Bye for now... Signing out 0013 your bodyguard.

Michelle: Goodnight darling... let us relive the email in our dreams...

E-mail from: Michelle
To: Mike
Date: 3 May 2013
Subject: Promissory note

Hi my darling

Well… if you can find 'our slate' add this 'promissory note' to it… if you do this, this promise is yours to keep… yours to redeem, in the real world, when the time is right… The promissory note is… All contents of the e-mail sent to you, from me, on 1st May 2013 are to be fully upheld… I never go back on a promise!

I love you Mike…

I cannot get you out of my head at the moment…

I will always love you…
Michelle
xxx xxx xxx xxx x

---

7 May 2013 ~ Live Interactive Text

Mike: Hi Michelle… I bet your bouncy boobs need some lotion to protect them from the sun… A job for your bodyguard! Mmmmm… Just pour some lotion on my hands and I will gently massage your boobs and get that worked into them. You do not want them looking like fried eggs. I think after a good massage they could be scrambled eggs with hard centres. Where are you Michelle, you have not got up this morning? I have to go now… Miss you my darling.

Later that day…

Michelle: 54,800,485 people online… but I am only looking for my cyber husband

Mike: And two… Us now! So what have you been doing today? Laying around in your garden, topless… sunbathing?

Michelle: So where was my bodyguard with the sun lotion when I needed him?

Mike: Decorating and where were you, I could do with you rolling around in paint. I bet you could slap it on the walls naturally.

Michelle: I checked on the internet at the weekend, of how to go about getting a book published...

Mike: Wow... and what did you discover?

Michelle: It may not be quite so impossible as we first thought.

Mike: I will get Michelle my sexcretary to do it for me.

Michelle: Basically this is how it works... you e-mail them to make contact... then 2nd e-mail is a synopsis of your book, with the first three chapters... then they tell you if they are interested

Mike: It has got to be well presented first time otherwise they will not give it another look. It must be sexciting from the beginning.

Michelle: Our identity will be kept a secret. We could give it a shot, see what happens?

Mike: You are being serious?

Michelle: Yes... why not. What have we to lose?

Mike: Hummmmm... You?

Michelle: If it happened what would you do with your half of the money?

Mike: Spend it.

Michelle: On what?

Mike: Michelle and Mike.

Michelle: Would you?

Mike: MMMmmmm...

Michelle: Would you come on a world cruise with me?... For starters

Mike: Starters and never ending.

Michelle: Well... let`s try and see what happens then...

Mike: We could buy a nice home abroad for the two of us.

Michelle: I'll type something tomorrow... send it to you for approval... then send it to them and see what happens... let's just look into it...... yes? obviously this would be identity protected

Mike: Okay. So what is this book to be called?

Michelle: When we joked about it on the phone the other day we said `Cyber Lovers`... I've even looked on internet to see if there is a book by this title, and there is not

Mike: Yes there are 55,623,610 captive audience here now, even if 13% of them bought it... that is a lot of books

Michelle: Yesssssssssss...... exactly!!!!... this started as a joke... but I think there is a chance it could happen, seriously

Mike: Okay... so watch this space, eh!

Michelle: I have to go now darling, let's look into this

Mike: I am sure it cannot be that easy Michelle

Michelle: Lets just look and see... Bye darling

Mike: Bye Michelle... mwah

---

8 May 2013 ~ Live Interactive Text

Mike: Hi my sex-o-licious Michelle

Michelle: Hi my sexy bodyguard

Mike: I need to do a body check my darling

Michelle: Come on then, come over here now!! ☺

Mike: Let me squeeze my hand down your bra... Those nipples are big and hard and I am not sure I can get my hand by them. Oh... Just managed after a bit of lifting and pushing, there is not much spare room

Michelle: You will get your fingers caught up there... and then you will have to come on my holiday with me... I don't want to leave you for a couple of weeks anyway... I wish I could get away with taking my laptop and texting with you... ☹

Mike: I will miss you darling, but will look forward to when you come back to me... so in the meanwhile I will check you over to make sure you are in good shape to go away... Now I do have a full handful... MMMmmmm... at least a couple of pounders here.

Michelle: How much do you think each of them weigh?

Mike: 2 lb ??

Michelle: One ounce less each... 13oz each? ☺ ☺

Mike: That was a good guesstimate then

Michelle: A very good guesstimation... I would say... you are a sexpert!!!!

Mike: I remember them so well...... I hope you are not laughing, or they will be shaking everywhere!!

Michelle: They do shake when I laugh... but you would know this

Mike: This is why I call them your 'movers and shakers' ☺ Plenty of bounce… I can just bounce them back into shape. Rubber boobs come back to me!!!

Michelle: They are all for you Mike Turner…

Mike: I love it.

Michelle: If we sell our book… you can hold and caress them 24/7

Mike: 365 days a year… and forever!!!

Michelle: Yours forever…

Mike: I will never get bored again.

Michelle: Neither will I…

Mike: I will always have something to play with.

Michelle: I think we would make a very good job of entertaining one another… playing with one another… loving one another

Mike: Bouncy boobs, what could be better?

Michelle: Bouncy golden nuggets to go with them… ☺

Mike: Well when they are both going, it… Like you say the earth will move.

Michelle: We could make the earth move for sure…… If we ever went on a cruise together we will have that cruise ship rocking and rolling

Mike: Yes the Captain will say, full speed ahead and we will go into turbo speed… The hot rod pistons will be working overtime.

Michelle: Oh darling… I am laughing my head off here, I don't know how you keep quiet sometimes. We are good together Mike Turner…

Mike: True… and sometimes I think we have some kind of telepathic link?

Michelle: We are certainly on the same wavelength darling, that is for sure

Mike: I have to go… Bye my darling… I would love to spend some time with you right now and show you how deep my love is for you.

Michelle: MMMmmmm…… me too… so in love with you… Bye darling

Michelle: Hi darling... I am fed up with work today... Simon is getting on my nerves... so I have decided... get this book published... and take off with you... ☺ except I am not joking!!!

Mike: I know what I would like to take off right now!

Michelle: I think we should take the view... if our book got published and we became rich it was meant to be... and we were meant to be together forever more

Mike: We would die rich and happy.

Michelle: I could be very happy with you forever more... I know this

Mike: And Ditto could have a home for himself, we have to take him too

Michelle: My bodyguard by my side forever more...... OMG where would little Ditto want to live? are you moving him out of his home, down in boob valley?

Mike: No I could not do that! He would be devastated to move out of his home.

Michelle: He would be happy to share his home with YOU

Mike: He told me too... He said Daddy this is such a nice home that Mummy has provided for me. I can put up with the movers and shakers rattling around me. I know I may be a bit deaf now, but I can feel my way around my home adequately enough now.

Michelle: I love you darling... we are so on the same wavelength

Mike: I said my son... I like to feel my way around your home too.

Michelle: You will get along very well then...

Mike: Yes... I think we both know a good thing when we feel it.

Michelle: MMMMmmm...... Mike you always make me want you...

Mike: Come on then YOU!

Michelle: I might just do that

Mike: Sorry darling I must go... Love you...

Michelle: and I love you darling...
Mwaaaaaaaaaaaaaaaaaaaaaaaaaaaaaah

Michelle: I LOVE YOU MIKE TURNER... I love you more than I can ever tell you... but I know you feel my love for you, like I feel yours for me... We are so alike... we like the same things... we dislike the same things... we are so good together... you are right, we were made for each other... It was so nice to see you today darling... to touch you, kiss you, feel your arms around me, feel your lips touching mine... OMG... I LOVE YOU... I hope everything in your world is OK after today... my weekend will be spent thinking of you... I love it here on Skype with you... I love your e-mails... but nothing comes close to actually seeing you... and feeling you... cuddled up so close to you... you are the one thing in life I can never get enough of...

Michelle: Hello darling... is everything as it should be?

Mike: Hi Michelle... Thank you for today, it really made my day... YOU!!!!!... Everything is fine. Thank you for coming over today

Michelle: It really made my day too... OK darling... I should not keep you here now...

Mike: No, I cannot stay on here at the moment. You will probably keep me awake tonight but is was worth it... Bye.

Michelle: You will do the same to me... but, I think it is worth it too... Bye darling

Mike: Your perfume lingers on my shirt! I can still smell you and taste you Michelle. Difficult to type now. I have to go darling... Bye

Michelle: MMMmmmm... Mike... I love you so much... Bye

Michelle: Hi Darling... I watched the film `Ghost` last night... It makes me think of you... I have cried over that film every time I have watched it...

Mike: Yes... I know what you mean, and the record in it... `Unchained Melody`.

Michelle: That film has always made me think of you... yes, the words to that record

Mike: Mmmm... I hunger for your love...

Michelle: I need your love... are you still mine?

Mike: Yes

Michelle: I have always thought of you when listening to that song, and watching that film

Mike: I have also seen it a few times and I think if you every time… the word DITTO came from there for us!!

Michelle: I know…

Mike: DITTO always meaning "I LOVE YOU"… and then we named the little lucky charm Ditto too… so you would always remember I love you… These have always stuck in my mind about you.

Michelle: Let's jazz up the introduction for our book… get it underway… get it published, get some money… and evacuate ASAP…

Mike: Evacuate… Disappear off the face of the earth.

Michelle: Evacuate… before the bomb goes off this time…… little Ditto has started packing his suitcase already?

Mike: He only has a box to pack, the one he sleeps in when not with you

Michelle: So what else can we add to our book introduction, any ideas?

Mike: We both need to get our thinking caps on…

Michelle: OK we will do this… send it off, see what happens

Mike: What if we did get this book published? What if it really gave us enough money for a future together? Could you really leave everything else in your life behind?

Michelle: Mike, if we had enough money to buy a home together, and enough money to live on… I would just pack up my clothes, and leave everything!!!!!… to be with you…

Mike: This would be difficult for both of us to do!!

Michelle: We never said it would be easy!!!… But we have agreed we cannot leave Cheryl and Simon with financial worries, so we leave them everything… we just take our clothes…

Mike: What about the emotional side of things? Leaving Simon? Leaving your family?

Michelle: Mike… it will not be easy… but for me I could say, I would just think about a future of being with you… pack up my clothes, and leave everything else behind me… Start a new chapter in my life…… A life I would share with you

Mike: You need to think of this carefully Michelle… giving up everything!!

Michelle: What about you darling… could you walk away from everything? Your family? Your home?

Mike: It would not be easy!!!… But, let`s just wait and see what happens with this book publishing enquiry? Maybe no publishing company would be interested anyway?

Michelle: OK… let's try… lets see what happens?

Mike: OK darling…

Michelle: Sorry darling, I have to go now…

Mike: Me too… DITTO FOREVER

Michelle: DITTO FOREVER

E-mail from: Michelle
To: Mike
Date: 24 May 2013
Subject: My Holiday

My darling Mike

Well, I am ready to do the packing tomorrow… but one thing I do not have to pack, but will take with me for sure, is 'you'… you will be locked in my heart, just where you belong, the love that we share is always there inside of me, it doesn't have to be painful, just a lovely warm glow… I will miss you darling that is also for sure.

I look forward to catching up with you when I return. We can also decide upon my return if we want to take the initial step of 'our book' enquiry? Would it hurt to find out if a publishing company is at all interested? We can then take it from there… You let me know, if you want us to try. And, one final thought on this, if we do send off our introduction, maybe we should send one of our 'raunchy emails' with it too…

I will e-mail you when I return, but this may not be until the Monday morning (17th June)… Please send me an e-mail to come home to.

I love you my darling… truly… love you… forever and always… without end…

XXX XXX XXX XXX X (massive kisses)
With my love
MRS MICHELLE TURNER

E-mail from: Mike
To: Michelle
Date: 24 May 2013
Subject: Your holiday

Hi Michelle

I hope you have a really lovely holiday, and enjoy…… "DITTO"

Spare me a little thought from time to time whilst you are away… "DITTO"

You will be locked in my heart, just where you belong, the love that we share is always there inside of me. I hope you take this on your holiday too… "DITTO"

I will miss you darling that is also for sure…… "DITTO"

I look forward to catching up with you when we you return… "DITTO"

I will miss you darling that is also for sure…… "DITTO"

Find out if a publishing company is at all interested…… "DITTO"

I will e-mail you for when you return… "DITTO"

Take care… Keep safe… and enjoy… "DITTO"

I love you… "DITTO"

Love Mike xxx

WELCOME BACK

Message from Ditto... Hi Mummy...

Welcome back Mummy... I hope you have had a fabulous holiday. Mummy I have missed you... I have been here home alone!! I know you gave me a little goodbye kiss and put me in my box and tucked me up in cotton wool to keep me warm and safe... but Mummy!!... It is just not the same in my cotton wool box. My favourite home is when I am sitting in the middle of your `movers and shakers` When I am in between your boobs, I can feel your body warmth, I can listen to your heart beating when you get sexcited and I also get some free roller coaster rides... Woweeee!!! When I am sunk in between your boobs I get some nice close warm hugs and cuddles. My home always feels nice and fresh and smells fresh with your fragrant perfume that you wear and squirt all over me.

Message from Mike... Hi my darling...

Welcome back Michelle... I hope you have had a wonderful holiday and I hope all is well and you are safely back home... I have missed you my darling... I was thinking of you even though we were a million miles apart on opposite sides of the world. I am looking forward to seeing you on Skype later this week.

Love always...
Ditto & Mike
xxx... xxx... xxx... xxx... x

PS... Both Ditto and I love you and we want to welcome you back home. We have both missed you.

E-mail from: Michelle
To: Mike
Date: 17 June 2013
Subject: I have missed you... I love you

My darling Mike

Thank you for your e-mail, so nice to hear from you. I feel as though I have been away for ages, and it seems forever since I last spoke to you. But, here I am, home safe and sound. Back to the world of Mike & Michelle.

Back to work for me this morning. Not looking forward to it at all. Tired this morning, as only got home at 6:00pm last night, unpacked cases and went to bed. Not quite back in the time zone yet, it feels like the middle of the night to me right at this moment. Looking forward to when I can catch up with you. I've missed you so much... I love you...

Michelle

xxx... xxx... xxx... xxx... x

---

17 June 2013 ~ Live Interactive Text

Michelle: Hello my darling Mike. How are you?

Mike: Hi my Michelle... I hope all is well and you had an enjoyable holiday? I am fine thank you.

Michelle: I missed you

Mike: I missed you... even little Ditto complained, but that was expected.

Michelle: Thank you for his message... and yours

Mike: Did you have a good time?

Michelle: I kind of did...... but......

Mike: But... ?

Michelle: I was not there with the right person... ☹

Mike: Who should have been there with you then? Little Ditto?

Michelle: Our little Ditto...... and you......

Mike: Oh Michelle...... I missed you so much

Michelle: I thought about you every single day I was away ☹

Mike: I wondered every single day what you were doing?

Mike: Are we going over to cam?

They video link for an hour…

Michelle: So nice to see you on here today… to see your smiling face… I really missed you

Mike: Nice to see you again… Really missed you… don't leave me for that long again… I just pine!!! ☹

Michelle: We need to be together 24/7……

Mike: MMMmmmmmm… I wish…

Michelle: I can't function properly without you

Mike: Send me a couple of nice pictures of you on your holiday, I'm sure you must have a few nice ones

Michelle: I will look through and email you a couple

Mike: I think your body needs your bodyguard check.

Michelle: I think it does too…

Mike: Mmmmm… Where should I start first?

Michelle: Where would you like to start?

Mike: Mmmmm… Those lovely lips, so luscious.

Michelle: Taste them… kiss them…

Mike: I think I need some of the lovely neck too, always so soft and tender and tasty.

Michelle: Kisses down my neck… now I am feeling SEXY!!!!!!

Mike: I think you would still feel exhausted after your holiday and the long journey home. You would say I am feeling tired. So only one answer to this, off to bed together!!!

Michelle: MMMmmm… Mike just hold me in your arms, and cuddle me in bed

Mike: I was thinking I may have to remove your clothes too… especially that white bra you have on today

Michelle: How do you know I have a white bra on?

Mike: I could see it through your blouse today when we were on cam ☺

Michelle: No wonder you were smiling so much

Mike: As I told you on video, you have a nice suntan there… but I want to see the white bits!!!

Michelle: MMMmmm... come over and strip me off... you can see them then

Mike: Woweeeeee my naked boob-a-licious Michelle

Michelle: Absolutely naked!!

Mike: I would love a cuddle like this with you.

Michelle: What I would not give for a real cuddle like this with you right now

Mike: Well when our book is published, there will be endless cuddles like this...

Michelle: WOW... if our book gets published this will happen for sure

Mike: We both need to go now darling... see you tomorrow

Michelle: I didn't realise the time... Bye darling, see you tomorrow

---

E-mail from: Michelle
To: Mike
Date: 18 June 2013
Subject: Catching up with my darling

Hi my darling

I really missed you while I was away, and it would be very honest of me to say that I thought of you at some point every single day I was away. It seemed a very long time without contact with you, I didn't like that bit... There was so much on my holiday I would have loved to have shared with you. You would have loved it too, I know you would.

Little Ditto is getting very thoughtful and vocal now he has a Father figure... He sent his Mummy a card on Mother's Day... He sent his Daddy a card on Father's Day, and he welcomed me home... Bless him... he is learning well from you darling.

Just to let you know, a darts night has been arranged for Thursday evening this week, so I can Skype with you in the evening of 20th, so for me any time from 8pm to 11pm suits, I know if you can this will probably be around 9pm? So just let me know darling? I know you cannot say for definite until the time comes, so I will look for you anyway at 9pm. Come and find me there... if you can... if you want to...

How I would love to have a little kiss and cuddle with you right now… sexy little kisses on those lips of yours… long lingering kisses from your lips to mine… my arms around you… your arms around me… and whisper to you, "I love you… always and forever" Always and forever with all my heart.

Michelle

xxx… xxx… xxx… xxx… x

PS… Thank you for the thirteen kisses, wow… cannot wait to collect all of these!!!

---

20 June 2013 ~ Live Interactive Text

Mike: Good evening my sexy gorgeous Michelle

Michelle: Good evening my sex-o-licious bodyguard… woweeee… an evening to myself, as Simon has gone out or a couple of hours to play darts

Mike: So do you want to play darts with me? I will try and pocket in one!

Michelle: OK… I will play darts with you… just let me polish the balls first… I need to do lots of gentle polishing of the balls

Mike: Can I polish my cue in little Ditto's home? Hey, do not put that blue chalk on the tip of my cue ☺

Michelle: So do you want the cue polished in Ditto's home, at the same time I am polishing the balls with my gentle hands?

Mike: No… I want to go straight for the pocket!!

Michelle: Shhhh darling… I am really laughing, so I expect you are too, Cheryl will up there in a minute to see what you are doing

Mike: I am trying not to laugh out aloud… my hand is over my mouth

Michelle: So should I polish the cue with my hands then?

Mike: I think you need a two-handed grip hold.

Michelle: Two hands is OK with me… a nice firm grip… lots of nice polishing to do here… long strokes right up to the top… then right down to the bottom

Mike: But do not get the cue end wet!

Michelle: Wow… Mike your temperature has risen already… and that is not all…

Mike: Yes for sure. I think you need to sit on my lap and feel what I have waiting for you... The cue is ready!!

Michelle: WOW... sit on your lap... which way round am I going to be facing, towards you?

Mike: It could even be a canon shot... or go in off my two balls. Pocket in one!!

Michelle: Let's see if we can pocket the cue then... so I am going to lower myself gently down onto your cue...

Mike: Are you with your back to me or facing me?

Michelle: Which way round do you want me... I aim to please!

Mike: Are we playing doggy games?

Michelle: You choose... do you like doggy games?

Mike: You will have to explain the game to me first.

Michelle: Well if my back is to you... then when I land on the cue, you get two massive handfuls of my boobs with your arms around me... or

Mike: Yes I like the sound of this game.

Michelle: Or... if I am facing you, you get to play with my boobs, and my nipples trail all over your chest as well... so the choice is yours darling...

Mike: We can try both and see which we like the best... Okay... Your back to me first. I can then put my arms around you and hang onto your boobs whilst the cue finds the pocket.

Michelle: Ok... so my back to you... and I am going to slide down onto your cue... but you need to steer me, with your hands on my boobs and nipples

Mike: No problem... This cue is straight and long, and heading straight for the pocket

Michelle: MMMmmmm...... then I am going to slide gently onto it, if it is that hard and stiff, I don't want to do myself a damage... so slowly, slowly does it... just put the tip in the pocket first...

Mike: The tip of the head is in... Do you want to jump up and down with sexcitement. Yes I am surely hanging on in here. Slide down that cue a bit more...

Michelle: But, it was 'an in-off shot' back out it has come...

Mike: Oh... What do you mean I have mis-cued? I need more practice!!

Michelle: No I moved back up... but I am back on there again now... hold on tight to my boobs... I am loving the feel of your cue inside this pocket... so I am going to move up and down a bit faster now. Maybe one of your hands wants to move down and find my hot spot...

Mike: This is a deep pot, so do I need to put on an extension to the cue.

Michelle: The cue feels really good to me... I think the extension must already be in place...

Mike: Yes... It was screwed and fixed on. I think if need to line it up with some in and out movements.

Michelle: Wow... Mike... I am liking this... I am going to have to move faster... almost right out... right back in... all the way in... MMMmmmmm

Mike: You mean faster, faster and faster. Mmmmmm... I love it... My balls are rattling away now just on the outside of the pocket

Michelle: You are going to squash your balls if you keep pulling me so hard back down onto your cue...

Mike: Hang on... Wait a moment... phone

Michelle: OK you talk on the phone... I will type... you can read... I hope it doesn't put you off your phone call... I can feel little drops of love juice popping their way into this pocket... so I am moving faster, faster, harder, harder... MMMmmmm Mike... your cue is right inside my pocket... and it is just about to explode... I can feel it filling up with your love juices... Mike... come on I can't wait any longer... you are just about to tip me over the edge here... Sorry I could wait no longer... Multi orgasms going on here for me... and your love juice is pumping too now...

Mike: I'm back...

Michelle: Well... you missed the best bit... love juice everywhere now...

Mike: How inconsiderate, I get interrupted when we got to this point. I must say something about this... Right in the middle of the performance and then we get an interruption.

Michelle: I think I will turn around now, and give you a cuddle, and some nice kisses, sexy passionate kisses, and this cue is still in the hot rod position, so maybe I will just let it slip back into the pocket this way round... you should complain, turn this cam on I will put in the complaint for you. So you wanted both ways... now I am facing you... your cue is back in the pocket... and my nipples and boobs are cuddling you too now

Mike: Woweee… Those movers and shakers are now very dangerous. I am going to have to suck them hard… Re-cue and try to pot another one from this angle…

Michelle: Oh nice… I am sliding up and down this cue again… right to the top… right to the bottom… right out… right back in…

Mike: Just keep bouncing and bonking.. Bouncy bonking all the way again. I am just about to pot another one… But first, I am going to slip it out and rub it over your hot spot, I know how much you like it when I do that… Sensual…

Michelle: Yessss… for sure, you know I love it when you do that…

Mike: OMG… here goes Michelle… the cue is back in the pocket… here comes both balls at once… Yessssssssssssssssssssssssss… landed…

Michelle: You set me on fire Mike Turner

Mike: I will run the tip over it and cool it down for you.

Michelle: How I would love to just cuddle up with you now my darling

Mike: Yes just to lay here with you, hold you, cuddle you, kiss you and feel your lovely body next to mine… MMMmmmm

Michelle: MMMmmmm… I would love that

Mike: MMMmmmm… Michelle… …

Michelle: One day!!!

Mike: You will always be loved forever by me and forever has no end.

Michelle: "DITTO" you always make me love you just that little bit more…

Michelle: I know that you need to go really darling… I have another hour or so, but I know that you do not…

Mike: I should go really… but I would rather stay here with you

Michelle: MMMmmm… I love you so much… go darling before you get into trouble… Goodnight my darling

Mike: Goodnight darling… love you always…

Hi my darling

Happy Birthday husband... this is the first year I have been able to say this... My darling husband... Happy Birthday... MMMmmmmm... what a lovely thought!!!

So tomorrow is your birthday, and what would I have in store for you... Now, I know you do not like a fuss in public... So, my birthday treat for you, would be just the two of us... I would give you 24 hours of pampering... and you can choose whatever you want...

I cannot help but think the movers and shakers would be involved, so I have attached four photos taken 'just for you', so you can see exactly what you would be in for... so, you are thinking, "Who took these photos?"... Well... was it naughty little Ditto? or did I just put my camera on the side and set it to take photos on auto? ... It was the auto pilot......

Now, looking at these photo`s I can see you would want to play with these nipples to make them like the American hard gums you love so much... so some tweaking from your expert fingers to start with... and then some sucking and nibbling with that expert tongue and lips of yours... Oh yes, you would have them standing to attention in no time at all... and then, I would trail them all over your chest... some lovely kisses on your lips... tell you how much I love you... I want to love you, love you, and love you a little bit more for your birthday... the nipples want to trail all over your golden nuggets... see how much my nipples love your golden nuggets... and then up your hot rod... MMMMmmmm Mike, the fun we could have!!!... I would be leaning all over you, you can just lay back and enjoy all this treatment... Now, I am thinking your hot rod would love to be squeezed inbetween these boobs... So... I slip your hot rod right in-between them, and rub my boobs up and down that hot rod... sliding with all these soapy bubbles!!... Wow... it is loving this, it is growing and growing... and the look on your face shows me, you are in heaven...... You place your hands either side of my boobs and squeeze them together tightly… and you push your hot rod up in-between them… so tight… MMMMMmmmmmmm Mike!!! This is what you call 'Boob-a-delicious TLC treatment'… I kiss your lips… I kiss all over your face… I kiss your neck… My delicious, adorable husband… How I could love you like this…

Now, you have a choice… would you like to stay where you are? or put that hot rod in my love tunnel?… I think you would say, "Michelle, do not move away from me, I love just what you are doing to me now"… So, I carry on… sliding my boobs up and down… you are pushing your hot rod so tight in-between my boobs, it is really having to squeeze its way through…… as I am typing this, my hot spot is throbbing and getting a little wet, it wants your touch (this is true)… OMG… I would love to do this with you for real… Loving my husband… We would take our time with this, and I would just keep on massaging you in this way until… the hot rod explodes!!!… Love juice all over my boobs…… MMMmmmm… and then, some very sexy passionate kisses… lips on lips… tongues swirling around tongues… MMMmmmm… and then slide down into the nice warm water and warm bubbles, and just cuddle up for a while… When the water starts to get cold, we would get out, and dry each other with nice big fluffy towels, a nice rub down of each other's body, until we are both dry.

So now I would take you off to bed, pull off the quilt, throw it on the floor, lay down with you on a nice clean cotton sheet and pillows, and we would explore every part of one another's body with our fingers, hands, lips, and tongues… and once we are very sexcited again we would make love… slow… slow… gentle… savouring every moment… no rushing here, we have all the time in the world… just you and me, to enjoy making love, in whatever way you wanted to… it is your day of choosing!!! We will give each other endless pleasure, and I will love you more than you have ever known…

Then we will just cuddle up together, naked, no covers over us, just our warm bodies together, your arms around me, my boobs laying on your chest, my fingers gently playing with your golden nuggets… and drift in and out of consciousness, but fully aware of one another and our bodies... our bodies entwined together as one, our minds locked into one another as one, where nothing else, and nobody else matters... just you and me... MMMmmmm... Heaven!!!... And when we are ready we make love again... over and over... I can never get enough of you...

I love you Mike Turner... love you more than you could ever know... I have told you many times before, and I told you this more than twenty years ago "I WILL ALWAYS LOVE YOU" and by now you know I mean every word of this for sure. The Whitney record "I will always love you" is very special to us... and more so now than ever, because in our cyber world, we danced to this barefoot on the beach the night we got married. And, here we are again, loving each other so very much. I truly, truly love you... more than I love anything... or anyone else... in the world... and I will love you in this way 'FOREVER', and as you have told me before, forever has no end... and my love for you has no end... I could be very greedy with you Mike Turner, and want all of your love, and share you with nobody else... just you and me... but I know it is very naughty of me to even think this, let alone say it... But, no better time than your birthday to tell you I love you with all my heart... Nobody could ever love you more than I do... My love for you is deeprooted, strong, endless and timeless... With the love that we share we could achieve anything, and overcome anything... And, I could love you for the rest of my days in this way...

I have sent this to you the night before your birthday, so hopefully you see this, and go to bed the night before your birthday thinking of this e-mail... enjoy your birthday... and the night of your birthday, you still go to bed thinking of this e-mail... thinking of 'YOU & ME'...

I WILL ALWAYS LOVE YOU...
All my love
Michelle
xxx xxx xxx xxx x

PS... This goes without saying really, make sure these photos do not end up anywhere other than in this e-mail address. Don't download them onto your computer anywhere else... or the kidnapping will take place sooner, rather than later... Oh... and did I tell you?... I LOVE YOU...

E-mail from: Mike
To: Michelle
Date: 28 June 2013
Subject: WOW... THANK YOU

Hi my darling

Wow!!!... This is the best birthday treat ever... Photos of you topless in the bath.

Thank you and you know your pictures are always safe with me. I love them!!

Little Ditto... I wanted to thank you and to let you know Mummy sent me your two pictures of you asleep in your bed. You were all snug down inside the valley between her twin peaks and I could just see your cheeky little smile. This was a lovely thought and Daddy's birthday treat!!! Then I think Mummy must have sent you off to your other bed and put you in your cotton wool box... But then...

Yes... but then, Mummy sent me some more pictures for Daddy's birthday treat. Mummy was taking a bubble bath and in the first picture your home in the valley between the twin peaks was covered all over with lots of bubbles. You could not have been there because you would have died. I know you sometimes cannot breathe down there normally, but in this instance my son you could have drowned down there. Maybe one day Mummy will give us both swimming lessons and we can join her in the water. Anyway back to the pictures my son and Daddy's birthday treat because there are another three pictures. Mummy wanted to show me your home for my birthday treat so she gave me a home tour. In these pictures there had been a bubble landslide from off the top of the two twin peaks and this now fully revealed your lovely beautiful natural home. You must know what I mean because even you slip and slide and get knocked about down there between those movers and shakers... My son you are such lucky little sod!!

MMMmmmm… You have a lovely looking beautiful stunning home and the twin peaks where like high mountain snow white peaks with an American hard gum sitting on the top of each one!! When you are at home in that valley it must be like being in heaven. What a wonderful outlook, what lovely views, simply out of this world. This was a picture tour for my birthday treat, so sorry my son I did not get around to puffing up your pillows. Mummy is lovely and we both love her and want to share her love.

Mummy… This was truly a wonderful birthday treat and big thank you to you "DITTO" my son and Mummy for sharing our love together. It made my birthday complete.

I love you and I will always love you…
Mike
xx xxx xxx xxx x

CHAPTER THIRTEEN

3 July 2013 ~ Live Interactive Text

Mike: Morning my sexy Michelle

Michelle: Morning darling

Mike: What are you wearing this morning?

Michelle: Just a skimpy little blue nighty, with little spaghetti string straps that tie up on my shoulders, one tug and it's gone... no bra and knickers

Mike: Wow... I would love to open up this gift wrapped sexy Michelle Turner and reveal the contents.

Michelle: Well, I am just about to go for my shower... would you like to join me?

Mike: OMG... Would I... I remember the showers with you when we lived together for that week in the Cotswolds

Michelle: I remember that so well too... I would love a shower with you now. You could wash me from head to toe and I could do the same to you

Mike: Would we use a whole tub of shower gel like we did before?

Michelle: Yessss... soap bubbles sliding all down our bodies... nice warm water cascading all over us... and... hands everywhere...

Mike: Yes I can remember! Your hands all over my body, and you rubbing your body up against mine

Michelle: I would wash every single little nock and cranny of your body with my bare hands covered in shower gel, and cover you in soap bubbles...

Mike: I would grab hold of your bum, and hook you up in the air, slide you onto my hot rod, put your legs around my middle, and your arms around the back of my neck and give you the ride of your life…

Michelle: I would hold on for dear life, kiss you passionately, and ride on that hot rod of yours…

Mike: I would pin you to the wall…… and make love to you passionately…

Michelle: OMG… we would both be frantic, wild and sexy!!

Mike: Wow… Michelle… I want to do this with you right now

Michelle: Me too……

Mike: We have made ourselves late for work here

Michelle: I don't care…… but we need to go… I love you

Mike: DITTO…… Bye for now darling

Michelle: Bye darling… mwaaaaaaaaah

E-mail from: Michelle
To: Mike
Date: 13 July 2013
Subject: "Happy Anniversary"

My darling Mike

Happy Virtual First Wedding Anniversary. One year ago today, on Friday 13th July 2012, we married one another, barefoot on the beach in the Seychelles, with little Ditto as our only witness… MMMmmmm Mike, what a lovely thought… Together forever in our hearts.

I wish I could spend this weekend with you, in the sunshine… We both love the warm weather and sunshine…… We would both need plenty of sun lotion on before going outside… So… obvs I do yours… and you do mine!!!! MMmmmm Mike, you had better watch out, because if my wish on my wish lantern comes true you could be in for the ride of your life…… and I will be your life jacket……

I love you Mike Turner...
Love always and forever
Mrs Michelle Turner
xxx xxx xxx xxx x

E-mail from: Mike
To: Michelle
Date: 13 July 2013
Subject: "Happy Anniversary"

Hi My Michelle

Yes time goes so quickly which is why we must live every day to the full and be happy and enjoy life. We both know lost time can never be relived and we both know our lives can change so quickly without notice. For all of us, tomorrow is never promised. They say love is blind and if that is true, I can still feel this love when I am with you.

We may not be together, but we will never be apart in our cyber lover's world which we call home and where we share our love together. Our happy times together can never be lost because those memories will always stay in our minds and live in our hearts forever and forever has no end.

"Happy Anniversary"... I love you...

Mike
xxx xxx xxx xxx x

---

16 July 2013 ~ Live Interactive Text

Michelle: So here I am looking for MY SEXY CYBER LOVER.. MY GORGEOUS CYBER HUSBAND... all rolled into one this is 'YOU' my irresistible Mike Turner... Just for you, I have had a shower, in nice coconut shower cream, and I smell and taste just like coconut, and you will too when I have rubbed my body all over yours. And, now I am laying on my bed, just in my bra and knickers waiting for you, with the ceiling fan gently blowing on me, to keep me cool... and keep you cool too when you arrive...

with a nice tall glass full of mango juice with lots of ice cubes… to share with you… ice cubes to play with..!!!!

Michelle: And Mike… I think we should have a sign, just in case the internet police arrive over your shoulder again, if they do, just type this "…………………………" and I will not type anything again until you do, so that no messages pop up on your screen if you need to minimize me.

Mike: Hi darling… Wow… OMG… Yes I can see you have a lovely pair of coconuts… It is difficult for me to type here, so I cannot be long.

Michelle: Shhhhhh… only type a few words, and I will cool you down…… by……

Michelle: Slowly removing your clothes…: laying you down on this bed with me……

Mike: What!!! You make me hot!!!

Michelle: Planting kisses all over your lips…… sexy… juicy… kisses

Mike: I love those luscious lips!

Michelle: MMMmmmm… I love yours too… sexy and inviting

Michelle: Lay you down… and then… still with my bra a knickers on, straddle my knees either side of your hips…… slowly remove my bra… have a little drink of the mango juice… take an ice cube in my mouth… and then…

Michelle: Take the ice cube out of my mouth, hold it in my finger and thumb, and then run the ice cube over my lips… down my chin… down my neck…

Michelle: Down my chest bone… down to one nipple and circle my nipple with the ice cube!!! Now what do you think is happening to my nipple?

Mike: It is getting hard and long. Like my crown jewels!!

Michelle: Very… just for you, and you will have a good view from where you are lying, underneath me… then over to my other nipple… and circle that one… now both of my nipples are standing to attention… and Mike they have been tingling all day…

Mike: Maybe because I was wanting them all day. Telepathy does funny things when we are in love.

Michelle: So with another ice cube… I take it from my mouth… and suck it a little, and a little drip of cold water lands on your tummy…… MMMMmmmm… in love with you

Michelle: And then I run the ice cube all over your tummy... and chest... keep still... stop screaming it is cold... this is to cool you down...

Mike: I am getting hotter!

Michelle: I need more ice then... so the next cube, into my mouth... let the water drip onto you... lean over and give you another kiss...

Mike: You are hot sexy stuff!!

Michelle: I am feeling soooooooooooooo sexy today!!! I am really ready for some loving with you

Mike: You are seducing me!

Michelle: Seducing you for sure!! Do you like it?

Mike: I love it... Seduce me anytime my darling... I am yours!!

Michelle: MMMMmmmm...... tonight you are mine... and I am yours...... we share with no one

Michelle: The next ice cube is on your tummy now... but... I need to cool you down some more... so down a little lower it goes... wow... is that cold?

Mike: I am getting even hotter now... phew!!!

Michelle: I need to cool you off some more then my darling... this ice cube is going to skim the crown jewels... but not for too long... followed by my fingers... because I do not want anything to freeze

Mike: My nuts (coconuts) are filling up with milk.

Michelle: Wow... yes... I can feel them getting bigger...

Mike: Freeze... Look I am stiff.

Michelle: Yes, I have noticed this...

Mike: You had better get those knickers off quick.

Michelle: I still have my knickers on at the moment

Michelle: Wow... we did it again? Exactly at the same time!!

Mike: We are on the same page that is why...

Michelle: These knickers are white, lacy and a bit stretchy... so... I am going to pop an ice cube down the front of them... so you can retrieve it...

Mike: What are you saying... make love with them on? You do not need knickers to be acting like a condom!!

Michelle: Well... slip your hand inside them... see how stretchy they are...... I think you could pull them down a little, and let your hot rod slip inside them too… there is room for you inside my knickers with me… try and see or you could just rip them off?

Mike: They could end up strangling me!!!

Michelle: No they wouldn't… just let me pull them down a little, take hold of your hot rod in my hand……

Mike: Both hands?

Michelle: MMMmmmm… give this hot rod a nice little stroke… yes, with both hands…

Mike: It likes the head stroked.

Michelle: In fact quite a firm stroke… with both hands…… OK… I am stroking the head… but do not let it explode just yet

Mike: I will try and hold on..

Michelle: And then… I am still stroking it… but now the tip is just stroking up and down the valley of love… and these blue eyes are flashing at you Mike Turner…

Mike: Loving this my darling.

Michelle: A little smile on my face… because I am thinking how much I love you… and still stroking you… up to my hot spot, and circle that…

Mike: Look at the head it has a smiley face too now.

Michelle: Smiley… and glistening… I think maybe it has already found some of my love juice, and loving it…

Mike: That is not tears coming out, just sexcitement, love juice looking for you

Michelle: So are you liking it inside my knickers with me?

Mike: MMMmmmm… yes, there is room for my hot rod in here with you…

Michelle: So do your golden nuggets want to come inside my knickers too?

Mike: The head, the shaft, and the golden nuggets if there is room?

Michelle: There is room for you… come on right inside of them… I would love you inside my knickers with me…

Mike: Wow… I am getting wet now. I think you need to get wet and take me inside you.

Michelle: So still I have hold of your hot rod… and very gently place it at the entrance of my love tunnel… which is well and truly wet, and wanting you inside of it… so gently… just the head inside of my love tunnel... wow... these blue eyes are really flashing at you now...

Mike: Can I follow through now?

Michelle: Come on then Mike... more of your hot rod, just sliding inside of me now...

Mike: Okay... All the way job now.

Michelle: MMMmmmm... SO NICE!! All the way in Mike... Deep inside of me... Deep, deep inside of me...

Mike: Dark hot inside and steamy!!!

Michelle: My sexy gorgeous husband... deep inside of my love tunnel

Mike: Everything is misting up now. Moisture and heat... Friction too.

Michelle: Let`s let you back out then... but... straight back in... is that better?

Mike: Much better. I can see where I am going now... OMG it feels so good in here

Michelle: Just sliding myself up and down on you... on your hot rod...... you have pushed inexorably into me, the heavy surge of your penis inside me is intoxicating

Mike: This is a piston type job!

Michelle: Lets see if this piston is firing on all cylinders... wow an eight-cylinder hot rod!!

Mike: A gasket is going to blow any minute.

Michelle: Ok Mike... so faster and faster now... plunging deep inside with every stroke

Mike: They will explode soon.

Michelle: Come on then... we will explode together... let our love juices flow... and mingle...

Mike: Yesssssssssssssssssssss Speed 130... and my head gasket has just blown!!!

Michelle: You are filling me with your love juices... and it is blowing my mind here... I orgasm with you... and our love juices mix together... the orgasm rolling through me like a crashing wave, filling me completely with a warm rush of pleasure

Mike: MMMmmmm Michelle...

Mike: ....

Mike: Sorry darling the internet police are on patrol, I have to go ☹

Michelle: OK darling… good night darling…

Mike: I love you so much Michelle……

Michelle: "DITTO"

Mike: Good night my darling… see you soon

E-mail from: Michelle
To: Mike
Date: 16 July 2013
Subject: Blue Eyes

Hi Mike

These 'blue eyes' would be flashing at you tonight for sure!!!

They would be smiling at you… They would be twinkling at you… I enjoyed my time with you this evening, shame about the timing of the internet police. I was going to turn my cam on and show you, I was lying on my bed, just in my underwear…

I love you… Always and forever
Michelle
xxx xxx xxx xxx x

E-mail from: Mike
To: Michelle
Date: 17 July 2013
Subject: Re: Blue Eyes

Hi My Michelle

I love your `blue eyes`… I love your `blonde hair`… in fact I love everything about you.

I just love you to bits…

Mike
xxx xxx xxx xxx x

Mike: I LOVE YOU... You know better than chocolate and even better than sliced bread... I could just eat you right now.

Michelle: WOW... thank you... better than chocolate, and that is your favourite thing in the whole wide world

Mike: I would like a little nibble on the nipple, never mind the chocolate when I have you

Michelle: MMMMmmmmm... I would like that too... my nipples are quite hard... but the rest of me is tender, succulent, and very tasty

Mike: I wish I could taste you right now... taste your lips... that delicious flavour of my Michelle mixed with your perfume

Michelle: I wish that too darling... to taste you... to touch you...

Mike: I am missing you Michelle, missing that we cannot Skype so much at the moment ☹

Michelle: Me too... ☹ Missing you so much... I need more of you

Mike: Let's start putting all of our text together and e-mails, see if we can turn it into that book

Michelle: It will be a very sexy and raunchy book, that is for sure!!

Mike: Well, let's start doing it then... we can copy and paste, put into a Word document and see what it starts to look like... Sod it... let`s try

Michelle: OK darling, let's give it a whirl...

Mike: I have got a memory stick, I will store it on that...

Michelle: OMG darling, once we have loads of our e-mails and text on that, do not lose it, or drop it anywhere!!!

Mike: NOooo... if anyone found it.. it would be the `Turner-gate Affair`

Michelle: Darling you are so funny, always so witty!!!

Mike: SOD IT... let`s go for it...

Michelle: OK... deal...

Mike: Have to go darling... mwah... see you soon

Michelle: Bye darling... mwah

Michelle: Where are you my sexy lover?... It is currently 32 degrees, and all I have on is a wet T-shirt and white lacy knickers!!!!...... now the T-shirt is see-through, and yes my nipples are standing to attention like soldiers!... but the water has dripped down from my T-shirt all over my knickers and they are see-through as well now!!!

Mike: Hi darling... Do you want some nice ice cold water over you chesticles to keep you cool? OMG a wet T-shirt!!!

Michelle: MMMmmmm... yes please... now my nipples are like the biggest American hard gums you have ever seen!!!

Mike: That hot spot will be at boiling point. I need to rub my nice cool wet body all over yours to cool you down

Michelle: Maybe you would like me to run ice cubes all over your body to cool you off too?... The hot rod needs some of my attention

Mike: Look... Just take my hot rod and play with it, I am sure whatever it will give us both pleasure

Michelle: With both hands Mike Turner...... it would be my pleasure... to give you pleasure

Mike: You are so hot and sexxxxxxxxxxxxy

Michelle: We need to play with ice cubes then... to cool us down

Mike: With how hot you are, and ice cubes, there will be steam everywhere!!

Michelle: You are `sex-o-licious`

Mike: I would love to hold you tight and close in my arms... Just one problem... Your boobs and your nipples will press into me... Don't worry I can take it.

Michelle: I would love to press my body close up to yours... and press my boobs and nipples into your bare chest... MMMmmmm...

Mike: MMMmmmm... Micheeeeeeeeeeeeelle...

Michelle: MMMmmmm... Mike ...

Mike: I think I may just unclip the back of your bra and slip those straps off your shoulders and throw your bra across the room and see if I can get them over the door handle.

Michelle: OK... try it... I am all yours this evening, I would love a naked cuddle with you right now

Mike: Come on them... I will start on your movers and shakers. They are now in free fall.

Michelle: So my bra has gone... and now my movers and shakers need a cuddle from you

Mike: Yes my hands are better than any bra you may have.

Michelle: MMMmmmm... I remember your tender touch... I think my boobs are a perfect handful for you

Mike: MMMmmmm... I will try not to get your nipples trapped in between my fingers.

Michelle: Yes, I remember this too...

Mike: But that occasion you had your bra on. I really thought my hand was stuck down there and I was having to call out a locksmith.

Michelle: You do amuse me darling

Mike: Oh yes... A roll of finger and thumb of the nipples... they will get hard and long darling if I do this to you... and that is not all... it makes my hot rod stand to attention

Michelle: MMMmmmm... I love it when you play with my boobs and nipples... it makes me feel reeeeeeeal sexxxxxxxxxxxxxy

Mike: Seduce me darling I cannot wait now... I want you... I am yours for the taking.

Michelle: I'll take you then... all of you!!!

Mike: What if you got fed up with me if you had me 24/7?

Michelle: Never!!!!... I will always want you as much as I do right at this moment.. But maybe you will get fed up with me... maybe I will want too much of your loving all the time?

Mike: I will never get fed up with you Michelle... You can have all of me... and all of my loving 24/7 for eternity!!

Michelle: Oh Mike... I would love this for sure... Do you think this day will ever come for us?

Mike: I don't know darling... we are putting our book together, we have to wait and see what happens with it... see if we have enough money to have a life together?

Michelle: If we are meant to be... surely our book will happen!!

Mike: I hope so Michelle... you will be mine... I will be yours...

Michelle: Forever more!!!

Mike: I just love you... I love all of you... Every single little bit of you.

Michelle: "DITTO"

Michelle: I need to go now darling... Take me to bed with you tonight, and cuddle me in your dreams...

Mike: I will darling... Good night... do you know what... We have the same minds, like the same things and love each other. The peeeeerfect combination for a couple in love.

Michelle: Just Purrrrrrrrrrrrrrrrrrrrrrrrrrrrrrrrrrrrrrrrrrrr-fect

Mike: Exactly... Just made for each other

Michelle: So in love... but cannot be together... ☹

Mike: I know... ☹

Michelle: Goodnight Mike... Mwaaah

Mike: Goodnight darling... love you always... Mwaah

Michelle: You always captivate me Mike Turner... always have

Mike: Likewise!!!!...... Goodnight... and... DITTO

---

12 August 2013 ~ Live Interactive Text

Mike: Hi Michelle... Soon you will be a birthday girl. I will send an email to you later tonight, but just to say have a great birthday and have a wonderful day. Lots of love and very best wishes. Mwah! and lots of big hugs and cuddles...

Michelle: Hello my darling... Just come in and checked my e-mails... OMG... I am suddenly VERY SEXCITED about my birthday!!!... This could be the best birthday I ever had???... I love you Mr Turner... REALLY, REALLY LOVE YOU...

Mike: So you say all you want for your birthday is my naked body eh?

Michelle: MMMmmmm... nothing else I would rather have

Mike: Well, I will have to see what I can do

Michelle: WOW... I am VERY SEXCITED now about my birthday this could be the best birthday present I ever had

Mike: You have seen me naked before

Michelle: I know... How do you think I would ever forget this? I love you naked...

Mike: I have the same problem with you.

Michelle: MMMmmmm... so in love with you...

Mike: Michelle, at times you turn me inside out and upside down. I had better go, I will email you tonight.

Michelle: OK darling... nice to find you here... missing you... loving you... always and forever... Kisses for all over your naked body... and those delicious lips...

Mike: MMMmmmm... Michelle...... Bye

E-mail from: Mike
To: Michelle
Date: 12 August 2013
Subject: "Happy Birthday"

My Michelle

Well I had my shower and walked naked into the cam and it took three pictures... Mmmmm.. I am sending you two out of the three, but the third!!... what they would say is the full monty. I think what a photographer would describe as `over-exposed`... He, he, he!! OMG... It is bad!!!

Happy Birthday for tomorrow my darling... I know you will have a lovely day and be spoilt, but you deserve this... I wish I could spend your birthday with you... But, know this, I will be thinking of you, and hopefully we can Skype text tomorrow at some point.

Love you...

Mike

xxx xxx xxx xxx x

---

13 August 2013 ~ Live Interactive Text

Michelle: Morning 'MY SEX-O-LICIOUS HUSBAND'... Woweeeee... I want to spend my day NAKED with you now!!! MMMMMmmmmmmmm Mike Turner, you are still as delicious as you ever were!!!!!...... Wow... just as well we don't live together, I would never be able to keep my hands off of you...

Mike: Happy Birthday darling... Wish I could spend the day with you just in our birthday suits

Michelle: Thank you for the pictures you sent me for my birthday...
OMG... how I would love to rub my naked body all over yours!!
My nipples want to press into that lovely hairy chest of yours. My
boobs want a cuddle from you

Mike: Well two out the three pictures. The third like I say was the
full monty! I nearly did send it under the `Sod it` attitude, but
then I thought better of it.

Michelle: Maybe you will say, "Sod it", and send it one day?

Mike: It was what you would term in photography terms being
over-exposed... it would have borered on PORN!!!

Michelle: Send it... and I will let you know... press your naked
body up against mine, and cuddle me tight... and give me some
of your delicious kisses

Mike: I would if I could and you know this.

Michelle: COME ON THEN............

Mike: Oh... Sod it!!!... Be there in 13 mins.

Michelle: I do love you, you know!!... you always make me laugh
and smile

Mike: You never tell me this!! ☹

Michelle: OK... I will tell you now, listen carefully... I LOVE YOU,
SO VERY MUCH

Mike: Michelle... today on your birthday I will tell you... I love
you... and I will always love you......

Michelle: Mike... Really nice pictures... you are sooooo sexy!!!! I
love that sexy body of yours... as well as that playful brain of
yours... you are always so loving and witty with me

Mike: I was thinking how I could take them but this was the only
option, the cam, it was a good job the neighbours could only see
the top half of me standing at the window.

Michelle: Thank you for those pictures, I love them

Mike: Go and enjoy your birthday darling... I wish I could spend it
with you

Michelle: Maybe one day we will... see what happens to our book
in the next year

Mike: Our fate is in the hands of others...

Michelle: If it is meant to be... it will happen

Mike: I hope it does...... Byeeeeeeeeeeee

Michelle: Me too... Byeeeeeeeeeee I can never get enough of you

Mike: You are always on my mind… and I can never get enough of you either

---

E-mail from: Michelle
To: Mike
Date: 14 August 2013
Subject: Re: "Happy Birthday"

Hi my darling Mike

Thank you so much for all the lovely birthday treats you sent me… you send me hearts & flowers… you send me hugs and kisses, you send me a birthday cake, you send me your love… You are soooo Romantic at times, I love all of this in you!!!

And darling, I absolutely love the two pictures you have sent me… 'You naked'… OMG… I love your naked body. How I remember so well, when we used to cuddle up together naked… I have never forgotten this, I will never forget this… How I would love to cuddle up naked together today, and just enjoy one another's naked bodies!!!!… MMMmmmm Mike, what a wonderful thought… How I would love to skim my hands all over that delicious body of yours… How I would love to plant kisses all over that naked body of yours… How I would love it to be my hands covering your crown jewels in that photo, not yours. MMMmmmm darling, the things I would love to do with you!!!

Mike Turner… I LOVE YOU… I want you……

I hope you are enjoying your time off work, and your decorating and other jobs are ticking along. How I would even love to be decorating with you. So, now three days to myself…… Chilling and relaxing… How I would love to do this with you too.

Hope to catch up with you soon… Missing you… Wanting you……

Loving you always my darling
Michelle
xxx xxx xxx xxx x

Hi my darling

Just got my Skype turned on to see if you were able to come on there. Don't even know if your computer is working now or not. Maybe you have disconnected it all by now, to do your decorating.

But I just wanted to tell you something… For the very first time in my entire life, I saw a shooting star last night. As we were leaving the place we went for my birthday meal, in the car park saying all our goodnights to all the others, talking about the meteorite showers currently taking place over the UK. Whilst I am busy telling everybody I have never seen a shooting star… low and behold, there it was… shot across the sky and was gone in a second… But, I saw it… my daughter saw it… and her sister-in-law saw it… everyone was shouting 'MAKE A WISH'… So for the first time in all my years I made a wish on a shooting star!!!

I used this wish VERY WISELY!!!… so watch out!!!

I love you Mr Turner

Always and forever
Michelle
xxx xxx xxx xxx x

Hi my darling

I hope you had a lovely special day for your birthday celebrations. A special day for a very special person… My lovely Michelle!

Really, so you have never seen a shooting star before? I have seen several, perhaps I am just a stargazer!! I have never made any wishes after seeing them, so perhaps I should start now. I assume it is never too late to start.

I have not started my computer room yet, but I will put my computer in a spare bedroom and run the telephone extension across the landing so I can still use it.

Miss you... Mwah!

Love you...

Mike
xxx xxx xxx xxx x

---

3 September 2013 ~ Live Interactive Text

Michelle: Hello darling... I am feeling real sexy and seductive this evening, and here I am looking for 'YOU'... and while I am waiting for you I have got us a nice drink to share, a large Southern Comfort and lemonade, not too strong, with lots of ice

Mike: Wow... Fancy meeting you here Michelle Turner. One drink, with two straws!!!

Michelle: Two straws... one glass... for us to share... and because I have been looking forward to meeting you here all day, I need to give you some lovely little kisses

Mike: Or what about we share each side of the glass and meet up in the middle?...

Michelle: OK, we will meet in the middle... and you know the little kisses I mean... the little butterfly kisses... the ones where your lips just about touch... but they make your head spin

Mike: Sounds good to me... and bet you are looking sexy and good... and smell good too

Michelle: I smell, and taste, of Georgio Armani

Mike: MMMmmmm... I love the smell and taste of you... So you may have to describe those little butterfly kisses to me

Michelle: Gentle... little seductive kisses... lips just about touching

Mike: MMMmmmm... seductive and full of promise!!!

Michelle: Slowly undo the buttons on your shirt... all the buttons...... run my fingers down your chest

Mike: Mind the claws!... I like you in my shirt, no bra and looking sexy!!

Michelle: I loved wearing your shirt...

Michelle: Undo the buckle of your belt... undo the button on your trousers... undo the zip... whoops, my fingers have just brushed against your hot rod whilst I have done this

Mike: That is precious! Handle with care!

Michelle: I will take care of it for you... and handle with the greatest of care...

Mike: I know they are in safe hands!

Michelle: So onto the bed you go, and I will pass you the drink... and you can lay back and enjoy watching me get undressed for you...

Mike: Wow... I am getting sexcited now.

Michelle: I thought you might like that

Mike: Love it.

Michelle: So off with my top... but still have my bra on... unzip my skirt... a little wiggle and it falls to the floor... so just my bra and knickers now...

Mike: Mmmm... More sexciting!

Michelle: A little twirl for you... a very sexy little twirl... turn my back to you, and look at you over one shoulder, and let you see me undo the clasp on my bra... flick it over my shoulder, and my bra lands on you... what colour is it?

Mike: More and more sexciting. I cannot see, it is covering my eyes! Blackout!!!

Michelle: OK... it`s blue to match my eyes...

Mike: Woweeeeee... Love it...

Michelle: Maybe you want to remove it so you don't miss anything... because... now I am going to turn around and face you...

Mike: Yes I think I should remove them, I cannot see a thing with blinkers fitted.

Michelle: So a little sexy wiggle and a giggle, and heading towards you on that bed... now all I have on are the sexy little blue lacy knickers that match that bra...

Mike: More than tension and suspense is building up now.

Michelle: And the lovely blue ear-rings you bought me... and the Georgio Armani perfume

Mike: MMMmmmm... So seductive!!!

Michelle: So gently I am going to climb onto the bed, and kneel astride you... lean forward, take the glass of drink from you, and have a little sip, take an ice cube out with my fingers, and let you have the drink back... now... with this ice cube, I am going to circle it all around and over one of my nipples!!!!!

Mike: My ever-sexxxxxxxxxxxxxy Michelle

Michelle: The ice cube has melted a little all over my nipple... so I am going to move up the bed, now you have to keep very still, because I am going to position this nipple 13 inches above your mouth, and the melted ice is going to drip into your mouth

Mike: OMG... You are teasing me now.

Michelle: So still with this same ice cube... I run it all over the other nipple... now this nipple is very erect... I am going to lean back over you... and... now you can lick and suck the melted ice off of this one if you want to

Mike: At last... Yummy, yummy... So tasty and scrummy

Michelle: Next I am going to take what is left of this ice cube, and run it right down in between my boobs...... down my tummy... whoops... I have dropped the ice cube down my knickers, can you get it out for me?

Mike: I am not sure... The hot and cold meeting together has created a lot of steam down there. You know what I mean, all this ice dripping onto your hot spot

Michelle: OMG... I am really laughing at that one

Mike: Put out the fire!

Michelle: I think I need you to 'rip' my knickers off...

Mike: With my teeth? Okay... Let me move just in case you swing your boobs around... Health and Safety and all that stuff..

Michelle: These knickers have the little tie-up bits on the sides, so you just have to tug at the laces, and they undo, and off come my knickers...

Mike: Like opening Pandora's box... I will do this with my teeth...

Michelle: So off they come... exactly......

Mike: You just never know what you will find inside.

Michelle: With the little piece of ice cube that is left... down it goes, with my fingers, and circles my hot spot... my little topiary heart that wants to play with you...

Mike: You're after my crown jewels.

Michelle: A gentle tiny little skim over the hot rod... down to the golden nuggets... for a little play with the golden nuggets...

Mike: Mind now it could spit out at you... so sexcited.

Michelle: I am glad you are feeling so sexcited... because I am too...

Mike: You should not skim over it because it will raise its head more.

Michelle: Another gentle little skim right over your hot rod... gentle fingers only... all the way from the bottom to the top...

Mike: Both hands Michelle... Do you mean two hands to cover it... hold it tight with both hands wrapped around it?...

Michelle: I know... you like two hands... so two hands it will be... and a little tighter... right up... right back down...

Mike: You could be in trouble doing this.

Michelle: Should I stop then?

Mike: Well... I think you should put it in your pussy because that wants some warm milk. It must be feeding time for the pussy.

Michelle: Well... I could do that... or... first of all... still holding onto your hot rod... rub the tip of it around one of my nipples?

Mike: Mmmmm... OMG you know I love that... I love your nipples, and to have the head of my hot rod rubbed against them...... Wowsa!!! Heaven. Oopppps... I think they may get a drop of moisture on them now.

Michelle: Whoops you are right... so this little bead of love juice, must not be wasted, so... I am going to wipe it off with one finger, and lick it off my finger!!!!!!!

Mike: MMMmmmm...

Michelle: And then continue to rub that head around and around the other nipple because it is feeling left out... is that OK with you?

Mike: I am sure that is okay with me... Do you hear me complaining?

Michelle: No... I didn't think you would...

Mike: Noooooooooooooooo way!

Michelle: Next you have another choice...

Mike: OMG... One hour we have been here, and I am making another choice... you are teasing me

Michelle: I warned you this would not be a quickie... does your hot rod want to go into my love tunnel right now?... or... does it want a little cuddle right in between my boobs first?

Mike: OMG... I love your boobs and you know this.

Michelle: So a nice little cuddle between my boobs first then... I have put it right down the middle of them... and I think you need to push my boobs together for a nice tight cuddle...

Mike: It going to explode if you do this?... But you know how I love this... But will little Ditto complain about his home being messed up again with another flood?

Michelle: He won't even know, he is in his box asleep

Mike: I can hear a little pussy crying because she wants some nice warm milk...

Michelle: My pussy is longing for you...

Mike: Yes... Come let's move on up baby

Michelle: OK... still holding onto your hot rod... I will move up your body, sit astride you again, and rub your hot rod, around and around my hot spot... how is that?

Mike: MMmmm... very nice... Feels pretty good to me... and to you.

Michelle: Very nice... I am loving it......

Mike: I LOVE YOU

Michelle: I LOVE YOU so very much

Mike: Take my love inside you and let us share our love now together.

Michelle: Come on then darling, let's slide you inside of me... let that hot rod, just slide right in...

Mike: All the way first time... (I am being called... I just said won't be long, just need to finish something off) ☺

Michelle: Do you need to go darling...

Mike: Are you kidding me? 'Go'... I am just about to 'Come'

Michelle: With you deep, deep inside of me... let me slide up and down on your hot rod... slowly at first... slowly almost all the way out... but right back in... all the way in

Mike: MMMmmmm... it is sexy... seductive... and sensual...

Michelle: Now you are right deep inside of me... and I am loving it...

Mike: Mmmm... I would love you to bits.

Michelle: MMMMmmmmm... I woud love you to bits too... always

Michelle: Your hot rod is pulsating inside of me...... fill me with your love juice

Mike: The piston rod is doing overtime... hard and fast... ready to explode

Michelle: Come on then darling... lets explode together

Mike: OMG... it is happening... gallons of love juice because you have worked me up so much here... I am filling you with gallons

Michelle: MMMmmm... yessssssssssssssss... I can feel it, and my whole being is just falling apart at the pleasure you give me, as our love juice mixes inside of me

Mike: I like you riding me.

Michelle: Take me to bed with you tonight...

Mike: Okay... not far to go, it is right behind me. Computer moved to this bedroom where I sleep.

Michelle: Wow... put me in your bed then... I want to spend the night in there with you... think of that later when you climb in there... I will be there waiting for you...

Mike: Okay... You know how I want you... You in my arms and your boobs laying across me and me holding you and cuddling you tight.

Michelle: That is exactly what we will do... all night

Mike: Deal... I will never let you out of my arms.

Michelle: I would love to be in your arms always... I know you need to go darling. So I will say Good night... I love you...

Mike: Good night... Nice wet dreams..... I love you...

---

13 September 2013 ~ Live Interactive Text

Mike: Hi my darling... All okay and no problems. Thank you for today, thank you for the chocolate, thank you for sharing your love with me.

Michelle: So nice to come over and see you today, Friday 13th, always our special day... I love to share my love with you...... There is nobody else quite like you in the whole wide world

Mike: Dare I ask this... If we went over to cam... I cannot talk of course, but say I just cough and you can test if you can hear me or not? I will then know if my cam sound is okay or not. Just a quickie!!!

Michelle: MMMmmmm...... really?

Mike: I just want to see you for two minutes... I miss you...

Michelle: Darling this is so risky for you, as you are not at home alone.

Mike: Pleeeeeeeeeeeeeeeeeeeeeeeease!!! Just a silent quickie.

Michelle: OK

They video link and type, can see one another, but so sound.

Mike: Like silent movies again... you look really sexy today my Michelle

Michelle: You are soooo god damn sexxxxxxxxxxxxxxxxxxxxy yourself...

Michelle: Blowing you lots of sexy little kisses

Mike: Mwaaaaaaaaaaaaaaaaaaaaaaaaaaaaaaaaaah a long seductive kiss for you, just like the ones in my office today

Michelle: So lovely to feel your arms around me today, and kiss your lips

Mike: Promise not to tell the world, well at least not until our book is out, I love you

Michelle: MMMmmmm... I love you so much

Mike: Bye and have a nice weekend... Be good and if you cannot be good only be naughty with me.

Michelle: When you go to bed tonight, I will be in that duvet cover, just waiting to cuddle you all night

Mike: Hugs, kisses and cuddles... I had all this today on Friday 13th.

Michelle: I had this on Friday 13th with my very favourite person

Mike: Do you think we could ever get away with spending a whole day together? Like we did all those years ago? Both say we are going to work... meet up and spend the day in bed together in a hotel somewhere?

Michelle: I would love to do that with you darling... very risky for both of us... but OMG so tempting... I would love it... ???

Mike: We could make love all day... I could kiss all over your body... set that hot spot of yours on fire with my tongue...then slip my hot rod into your love tunnel and give you pleasure for hours... I can still taste you on my lips from today, I want to taste more of you!!!

Michelle: OMG... MIKE... what are you trying to do to me here?

Mike: Love you Michelle... Just love you... think on this, we can arrange something if you would like us to? When we have made love all day, we will save an hour to shower together before we go home

Michelle: OK darling... we will both think about this... maybe we will do it?

Mike: Bye and have a nice weekend.

Michelle: Bye darling

Mike: I LOVE YOU

Michelle: "DITTO"

---

18 September 2013 ~ Live Interactive Text

Mike: Sometimes in life, you find a special friend. Someone who changes your life just by being part of it. Someone who makes you laugh until you can't stop. Someone who makes you believe that there really is good in the world. Someone who convinces you that there really is an unlocked door just waiting for you to open it. This is forever friendship. When you're down and the world seems dark and empty, your forever friend lifts you up in spirit and makes that dark and empty world suddenly seem bright and full. Your forever friend gets you through the hard times, the sad times and the confused times. If you turn and walk away, your forever friend follows. If you lose your way, your forever friend guides you and cheers you on. Your forever friend holds your hand and tells you that everything is going to be okay. And if you find such a friend, you feel happy and complete because you need not worry. You have a forever friend, and forever has no end... I will always love you.

Michelle: Hi darling... Thank you, that is so nice

Mike: You are my forever friend Michelle, my friend, my lover, my cyber wife

Michelle: "DITTO"

Mike: I have to go now... see you soon

Michelle: Bye darling

Mike: Thank you for sending me that picture… you stunning 16 year old!!!!!

Michelle: I thought it may give you a grin

Mike: Good job I did not know you then, I would have stolen you and never given you back.

Michelle: WOW..!!!!! if only I had met you then… neither of us married

Mike: If we had met then… would you have married me in the real world?

Michelle: Would you have asked me?

Mike: I am asking you

Michelle: Yes, I would

Mike: MMMmmmm…… Michelle… if only!!

Michelle: If only…

Mike: I LOVE YOU…

Michelle: I LOVE YOU… who knows what will happen in the future if our book gets published and does well… but Mike… we are married now, virtually married in our cyber world

Mike: Married in our hearts and in our heads. We are doing well with putting our book together, it is sexy and seductive like you

Michelle: MMMmmm…… Only with you…… I have to go darling… Bye and see you soon

Mike: Bye Michelle… Take care, because I care

---

21 September 2013

Michelle & Mike have planned on the telephone what they hope will be water-tight alibis… they meet up for the day. They meet at the agreed hotel, early morning, as if they had each gone to work for the day… Mike takes a bottle of champagne… Michelle takes a punnet of raspberries… they spend the most wonderful day together in bed… Making love… Playing… Talking… Dreaming of a life together. Talking of what they would do if their book is ever published… They end their afternoon, taking a shower together… and both return home, at what would be the end of their working days… They each return home with their hearts in their mouths in case they are found out… But… They get away with it…

Michelle: Good morning 'MY VERY SEXY YOUNG MAN'… I would love a kiss right now, with those very tasty and sexy lips of yours… Calvin Klein and Mike Turner flavoured lips…… MMMmmmm…… Soooooooooooooooooooo TASTY………… My favourite kisses of all time. This is a long… passionate… and very sexxxxxxxxxxxxxxxxxxxxxxy kiss

Mike: Morning gorgeous… Wow thank you… and here is one in return for you… MMMmmmm… so tasty my Michelle and her perfume… my head is spinning

Michelle: That should set us both up for the day… I cannot wait to get to work, get home and continue with the part of 'our book' that I am doing

Mike: Yes… the part I am currently doing is coming on well… then we put them together… MMMmmmm…… like we want to put ourselves together

Michelle: It makes me want you, when I am on my own and reading all the text we have typed to one another

Mike: I know what you mean, sometimes I take my memory stick to work, and do some there!!!!

Michelle: OMG… do not lose that memory stick!!! `Turner-gate Affair`

Mike: I love you more and more…

Michelle: MMMmmmm… here is another sexy kiss… and I would look into your eyes… and whisper to you, "I love you, more and more too"…

Michelle: We both need to get ready for work darling… Bye for now

Mike: Bye darling… Take care going to work in the rain

Mike: Hi my darling... it is getting colder at nights now... I need you as my love blanket

Michelle: Hi darling... MMMmmmm... sounds good, but can you tell me what a love blanket does exactly?

Mike: Well you go to bed with it for starters.

Michelle: Well... I like the sound of that

Mike: Then it covers you all over and feels sensual and warm.

Michelle: I am liking the sound of one of these

Mike: You can then wrap it around your body to wherever you want to feel the love from your love blanket.

Michelle: Sounds heavenly...

Mike: You can puff it up... Just like your `C` sized boobs and cuddle into it.

Michelle: Sounds wonderful...

Mike: You can put it between your legs and run it up and down there slow or fast.

Michelle: Wow... I was not expecting that

Mike: You can also put the end in your mouth and give it a nice suck.

Michelle: Woweeeeee... I like to do this

Mike: Gets wet... But reminds me of a certain hot spot and little pussy I know

Michelle: MMMmmmm... I need one of these... Where do I get one from?

Mike: You can also toss it on top.

Michelle: Can it go on the top... or on the bottom?

Mike: Your love blanket is versatile so either way, bottom or top.

Michelle: Wow... you know I like variety

Mike: Yes I know only too well.

Michelle: Does it keep you warm in the winter?

Mike: Sure... Just like your boobs and you can tuck it around you.

Michelle: Does it snuggle you tight if there is a thunderstorm?

Mike: Sure it does... It would always protect you and keep you safe

Michelle: Would you like to be my love blanket?

Mike: Please... Love it, love you.

Michelle: Can I be your love blanket?

Mike: Anytime... I would love you as my love blanket

Michelle: OK... it is a deal... you will be mine... and I will be yours...

Mike: Together as one.

Michelle: What a lovely thought...

Mike: Joined... In body and soul.

Michelle: I really want to be your love blanket... Joined body and soul is good... we have ourselves a deal here

Mike: Where do you think we should be joined in body?

Michelle: Lips...... hearts...... belly buttons... hot rod to hot spot... oh and boobs

Mike: Stuck together with love juices..

Michelle: That sounds a fantastic way to get stuck together... our blankets will never be able to be separated again

Mike: We will have to see what happens with our book? Maybe our love blankets will be together after all?

Michelle: MMMmmmm... Mike, do you think this could ever really happen?

Mike: I don't know darling, we will just have to wait and see.

Michelle: All my fingers and toes are crossed... Bye darling, we need to go

Mike: Bye Michelle... cuddle me tonight as your love blanket

---

8 October 2013 ~ Live Interactive Text

Mike: Hi my darling... You are at work today so mind how you go, it is foggy. You covered me with your love my love blanket all night... I would love you as my love blanket covering my naked body... You kept me warm all night.. Mmmm... I can feel your love right now burning into me... So nice, so warm, so loving... I LOVE YOU...

Michelle: I could feel you last night as my love blanket...... I snuggled right into you and cuddled you all night...... I LOVE YOU

Michelle: And, I dreamed about you last night... I went to bed (on my own) snuggled down into my quilt, thought about you as my love blanket, and went off to sleep very happy, cuddling the quilt all around me... then I dreamed that you were in my bed, kissing and cuddling me... we were laughing and giggling, and I told you to be quiet because Simon would hear you in the next room. But you said you didn't care... because it was you in my bed, not him!!!!...

Mike: MMMmmmm... Michelle... Oh well I am typing and Cheryl is still asleep in the other bedroom. Come here in my bed and we will relive your dream.

Michelle: MMMMmmmmm... I'm on my way...

Mike: Shhhhh... Be quiet when you come up the stairs!!

Michelle: OK... I will tiptoe... and we won't make quite as much noise as in my dream... I would love to come in that bed with you right now... I am just out of the shower... and smell delicious!!

Mike: I have a spare double bed... with a firm mattress if you prefer in the other bedroom?

Michelle: No, I like the sound of your single bed... more cosy for the two of us!!

Mike: Yes, I bet you smell delicious and look boob-a-licious.

Michelle: Boob-a-licious for sure...... you would love the taste of them this morning... Cherry flavoured shower gel...... MMMmmmm...... Yummy

Mike: Woweee... I love the cherries on the top...

Michelle: Cherry flavoured nipples! you would need nothing else for breakfast, after you have feasted on this boob-a-licious Michelle

Mike: Love them darling... very plump and ripe!! I would love to feast on them right now

Michelle: One day darling... One day!!!

Mike: I so look forward to that day!!!... but, for now we have to go to work

Michelle: Bye for now darling

Mike: BFN darling...... I love you

Michelle: "DITTO"

E-mail from: Mike
To: Michelle
Date: 22 October 2013
Subject: Our love blanket

Hi Michelle…

I would love to be your love blanket tonight and sleep with you naked. I will hug and cuddle you gently tight and yes I will cuddle right up into your lovely soft boobs and nipples. Once I wrap my arms around you and hold your boobs in my hands you will feel my love and your nipples will pop up to greet me. I will then give your hard nipples some nice butterfly kisses with my tongue just shimmering over the ends… MMMmmmm… Tasty, tasty… Let me suck them a bit harder so they get longer and harder with the tip of my tongue lapping all over them.

I am going to cover you… Yes cover you with my love, and make love to you… You are feeling hot now darling, yes getting really hot now that my hand has slipped down off your boobs and has slipped down in between your legs… MMMmmmm… You are feeling sexy and already your pussy is feeling warm and wet. I will just place my finger up on your hot spot and give you a feel in that sensual area. I know you like me doing this to you. A nice figure of eight with the tip of my finger around and around we go!!. Oh… You have just crossed your legs tight on my finger now, you must like my finger squeezed in there hard and tight whilst I am doing this to you… Hey… Stop sighing and groaning, I do not want you having an orgasm just yet!!! Okay… With that you kick your legs wide apart and release my finger… You then grab my crown jewels and you start on me… Straight away you take my hot rod and kiss the tip… Then you suck my hot rod and you take it straight back inside your mouth and start sucking me hard and fast… Your fingers working down the side of my hard shaft whilst you suck me hard… Hey… I will explode if you keep doing this to me. Come on we want to make love together here and now. I think we are both ready and hungry for love.

To be continued…

Mike
xxx xxx xxx xxx x

466

E-mail from: Michelle
To: Mike
Date: 23 October 2013
Subject: Re: Our love blanket

Hi Mike

Wow... I have never had a love blanket before... So you need to tell me just how it works... I am loving the sound of this love blanket. Now just let me recap!!...

You have covered me with your love blanket. You have kissed and caressed my nipples, until they have stood up on end for you... MMMmm very nice!! Then you have run your hand down, and placed it between my legs. With circles of eight you work wonders on my hot spot... OMG... circles of eight... Wowsa!!!! I am loving this... No wonder, I have then reached out and taken hold of your hot rod. With my lips, I have gently kissed the very tip. With both hands at once I have caressed the shaft. Then my kisses have turned to licking and sucking. My hands have become firmer, both hands rubbing up and down quite firmly now. My sucking hard and fast... MMMmm... you are tasting delicious tonight... But, if I carry on like this, it will be over too soon. And then I hear you say...

"My Poor Michelle... You have had one heck of a three days of work so far this week... just lay back there for a minute... I need to calm myself down, before it is too late." Gently you climb back on top of me. Your kisses run all around my neck... then your lips are once again sucking one nipple, and then the other... the kisses and sucking moves right down the centre of my tummy, until you come to my hot spot. With both of your hands, you part my topiary heart, and then plunge your tongue right onto my hot spot... OMG... I groan loudly with absolute pleasure!!!... And then the thing you were doing earlier with your finger, you do with your tongue... The circling of the figure eight around my hot spot... OMG... Mike... You are going to make me have an orgasm if you keep doing that, and then you will say I am greedy!! Oh... Mike... now you have starting sucking my hot spot... and... it is too late now... my entire body shudders with the pleasure you give me... and I am completely lost in the sensual sensations of the orgasm you are giving me... On and on it goes, as your sucking turns to flicking your tongue all around my hot spot again and again... My head is spinning and I am lost in this sheer pleasure you give me.

But, then you move your mouth away... And, that has brought me back to earth... Mike I want you... I want you inside of me... I want you to fill my love tunnel... I see you smiling as you crawl up the bed, and I hear you say... "Yes, Michelle you are well and truly ready for this hot rod now."

Mike... Fill me with your hot rod... fill me with your love... cover me completely with your love blanket... pin me to this bed... and make love to me...

To be continued...

Michelle
xxx xxx xxx xxx x

---

23 October 2013 ~ Live Interactive Text

Michelle: Good evening my sexy cyber husband MMMmmmm... some precious time with my own, very special, love blanket

Mike: Mmmm... I have just read your email my sexy darling.

Michelle: Come and cuddle me... cover me with your love blanket

Mike: I have just felt under the blanket and I have found two hard nipples... Try typing with them and give that keyboard a proper hard bashing.

Michelle: OK here goes... come and love me... kiss me... play with me

Mike: Okay... Just one problem, you have no cat flap for me to get in.

Michelle: I will open the door for you.. let you in 'my bedroom'.. whilst Simon is out... so you have to keep quiet when he comes home... no laughing, or making any grunting noises

Mike: Oh... I thought I was staying for the night and not for just a quickie...

Michelle: You are staying all night... I will give you a lift to work in the morning...

Mike: I will give you a lift all night long...

Michelle: MMMmmmm... how I would like that... come and snuggle with me... cover me all over with my love blanket

Mike: You would be so hot, you would be kicking this love blanket off.

Michelle: I will cuddle into it all night long,,,, I will press my boobs and nipples right into it... I will wrap my legs around it... I will stroke it with my fingers... I will kiss it...

Mike: MMMmmmm... I would have a nice couple of soft spots to cuddle into with you.

Michelle: I will cuddle all of you... get right underneath you... and just love you.. I will be cuddled up so close to you... you won't know where you end and I begin... we will be as one!!

Mike: One Love... two hearts together beating as one... I would love to spend the night with you...

Michelle: So would I with you......

Michelle: Sorry darling, I have to go............ Bye

Mike: Bye darling Mwaaaaaaaaaaaaaaaah

---

25 October 2013 ~ Live Interactive Text

Michelle: Morning my darling... Well if you come here this morning you are going to read, I have got up, packed Simon off to work, made myself a coffee, and come back to bed... Here I am in my big bed, all on my own, no clothes on at all... So, on this dark and miserable morning all I need now is my 'love blanket'...

Mike: It really is dark this morning... What no clothes on at all? Can we cam?

Michelle: Morning my darling... absolutely NAKED!!!!!... but I know you cannot use your cam this morning, because you know who is there

Michelle: Come and be my love blanket for the day... I have the day off work

Mike: Come on... give them movers and shakers a cam to cam.

Michelle: You are so naughty!!

Mike: I will fit the wide-angle lens on so I can get them in shaking and bouncing about.

Michelle: You are naughty... but tempting

Mike: Come on then... Dare you!!!... Dare you!!!

Michelle: But Mike...... for you I would... but the www? And what if Cheryl suddenly appeared behind you?

Mike: Only me can see not the whole wide world.

Michelle: But what if they can?

Mike: They can't.

Michelle: Hummmmmm... I'm tempted I can tell you...

Mike: No bouncy bouncy boobs for Mike then?

Michelle: If you were here no problem... I would be happy to do a little shimmy for you... but I can't quite bring myself to on here... maybe one day ??

Mike: ☹

Michelle: What if I ended up on You Tube? Oh don't make a sad face, you know I will give into you, I know what your puppy dog eyes do to me when they are sad

Mike: Good... Come on then.

Michelle: Go and get ready for work darling... before I do something I might regret...

Mike: Damn... Cheryl is out of the shower!!!... I need to go now... One little peep? Pleeeeeeeeeeeeeeeeeeeeeeese!!

Michelle: Darling, she could walk into that room at any minute... at least when you are texting you can quickly minimize the screen... I do not want my boobs squashed and minimized...

Mike: You tell me no... but you still make me laugh... I love you... and you are right, I have to go now... Mwaaaaaaaaaaaah. Phone me later, at work if you get the chance.

Michelle: OK darling... speak to you later... Mwah

Mike: Mwah... Mwah... one for each nipple ☺ ☺

E-mail from: Mike
To: Michelle
Date: 25 October 2013
Subject: Re: Our love blanket

Hi Michelle

I need to just do a recap here, if only to get my mind focused and back on the job in hand. So you are totally stark raving naked like the day you were born, eh! Well not quite of course. You have had some very sexy curvy developments taken place since then and these have been added to your bits and pieces that make you the Michelle Turner that I met twenty years ago that I still know today OMG… What can I say?… But when it came to your time for sharing and dishing out what size boobs and nipples you would have later in life, they must have given you a couple of extra big portions. Talking of extra big portions and taking into account the job in hand, they need both my hands to support your big lovely delicious boobs. I am just waiting and getting ready to catch them and hang on with both hands. I see you standing here naked and both boobs looking in their natural state of free fall. I need to keep an eye on them, but what an eye-ful.

When we were talking with me the other day on the phone and you asked me what I have got for packed lunch. I replied, I have a nice fresh fruit selection with some melons, raspberries and banana. When I said banana, I could read your thoughts, because I know you often like a bit of nana! I certainly like melons with raspberries sitting on top. My thoughts were the lovely melons and the raspberries on top being gently squeezed in between my finger and thumb and my lips gently sucking and licking them! Mmmm… This reminded me of when I would gently suck and lick my tongue all over your nipples and play with them just like this in between my finger and thumb. A little squeeze and a gentle tug your nipples would go solid and get so long when I twiddled with them like this. So hard and you could really get the bit between your teeth when hanging on them. These juicy raspberries must nearly be the size of your nipples. They are huge and really taste yummy. You said were they like a raspberry ripple? I said I much prefer a raspberry nipple because they are much firmer and harder than a raspberry ripple. All I can say is that the raspberries were soft and juicy, but when I gently suck your nipples they soon get big, hard and erect with lots of little bumps around the edges. They look just like a raspberry nipple or should that be raspberry ripple?

Back to the business end of things… We have both got rather sexcited caressing each other's sensual body parts and ready to make love, but no quickies here! This is going to be a slow and easy right from the start and then work up to a final climax with

feelings of wild passionate, sexy love for each other. MMmmm…
you always look so sexy naked and so good with those lovely
movers and shakers in natural free fall. Come and jump in bed
now darling and let us get down to business. Oppps… Be careful,
don't jump or those boobs could bounce anywhere and do you a
mischief. Let me hang onto your boobs with both hands and ease
them into bed on top of me. OMG… They are two big handfuls to
handle! Come and cuddle your naked body into me and lay those
lovely boobs across my chest. I will wrap my arms around you
and hold you close and tight to me like we would always do…
MMMmmmm… lovely big boobs keeping me warm just like a
love blanket. You give me all the comfort and all the feelings of
love when you cuddle up to me like this. I can feel your excited
heart beat getting faster and I can feel your love and warmth
coming through into my body. Your legs are crossed over me…
OMG… We are almost gift-wrapped here together! What a very
special present, but no wrapping paper to undo because we are
both naked. I want to run my fingers through your long blonde
hair and just stare into your lovely blue eyes, holding you,
hugging you and cuddling you into my arms. MMMmmmm…
this feels so nice to have you again.

MMMmmmm… your soft boobs are pressing and squeezing into
me and I can feel your big nipples are getting harder. You start to
move a little and I can feel your boobs slipping down my body
and your hard nipples shimmering over me and almost dragging
over my skin. You are making the hairs on the back of my neck
stand up on end and that won't be the only thing standing up in a
moment if you keep doing this to me. Your body movements are
now becoming very seductive and I can feel you are wanting for
love. Yes a love that we have always had for each other and
shared for such a long time. Oh… you have now slipped on top of
me. You like to have control on top of me, eh! Having you this
way I can see we will both come to no harm with me taking
control over your boobs when you make love and they start
bouncing up and down and start rocking from side to side. Once
you get started there will be no stopping you. You are like a
bonking bronco making love on my pogo stick… my hot rod! I
just wonder how many times you can bounce up and down on my
pogo stick before you topple off. I will hang onto your bouncy,

bouncy boobs, but you are still top-heavy. My hot rod is hard, firm and rigid to prevent you falling off, but you can put this to the test later. Your legs are wide apart and straddled across my hips and you are sitting upright with a sexy smile on your face. Then you come forward towards me dragging your hard nipples over my body again and kiss me. Mmmm... very passionate kisses and little butterfly kisses! Mike your hot rod is getting hard and digging into my skin... We are both ready for love!

You wrap your fingers around my hot rod and take me down to your topiary heart where you part the walls of your love valley and take me straight up to your hot spot. MMMmmmm Mike... I like that figure of eight movement, so let me try this with the tip of your hot rod. You lift your body a little above me and almost suspended in mid-air you rub me in a circle of eight over your hot spot. Mmmm... you are so seeeeeeeeeexy darling. Oh... Mike you know I love a bit of nana?... You then take my hot rod out, pull back hard the foreskin and you start sucking me. Hey!... Michelle be careful or you will start to choke with that much nana inside your mouth all at once!... You just look at me with those sexy blue eyes and just keep sucking away getting much harder and faster with your fingers running up and down the shaft of my hot rod like you were playing a violin. I am shouting, Michelle stop it or you will know what will happen in a minute. Save all these love juices for where they naturally belong. You sit upright and take me back to your hot spot and you just give yourself a few more caressing hard strokes pressing the tip of my hot rod hard into you. Mmmm... I am ready for your love now Mike Turner...

To be continued...

Love you always...

Mike
Xxx xxx xxx xxx x

E-mail from: Michelle
To: Mike
Date: 28 October 2013
Subject: Re: Our love blanket

Hi my sexy, sensual, seductive 'cyber lover'

Well this has well and truly developed into a gastronomic delight of a feast, and I am loving it. Oh darling, all weekend I have thought about being laid cuddled up to you in this way. You running your fingers softly though my hair, looking into my blue eyes, that for sure will be sparkling at you. Your arms around me, holding me gently tight, just the way that you used to. My legs wrapped over yours, my boobs pressed firmly into your chest... The best cuddles I have ever known, and I remember these so well with you darling. So, this is how we have been all weekend... and you have lingered in my mind the whole weekend

Now, I am thinking it must be time for some breakfast... there are still some raspberries left, and I need to feed them to you!!!... So, I sit up... straddle my legs over you once more. My knees resting either side of your hips... Wow Mike... look at the view you have, my topiary heart is hovering over your hot rod... My boobs are in freefall looking down on you laying with your head on the pillow... my nipples are firm, long, and so hard... I take one raspberry, pop it into your mouth with my fingers ~ you eat it but say although it is nice, the flavour is not quite right... I know what the problem is here, you have a taste for 'raspberry nipple' now... So with one hand I roll the next raspberry around in my fingers, to make the whole inside of it nice and big... with my other hand, I roll a couple of fingers and my thumb around and around one nipple... OK let's put the end cap on now... I am watching your eyes light up, as I place the raspberry right over my nipple as I attach it like an end cap. MMMmm... this looks good, and you were right... the perfect fit... So I take another raspberry and do the same all over again, and place it on the other nipple... MMMMmmmmm... a matching pair now!!!!... You are licking your lips, so only one thing to do now, carefully (so that the raspberries do not fall off) I lean over you, and my nipples come to your mouth... Gently you suck one of the raspberries off... and you are smiling with delight as you eat it... I move over a little,

474

and hover the other raspberry nipple over your lips… but this time, you take so much of my boob into your mouth, and groan with delight, as you suck hard, and the raspberry is vacuumed into your mouth… Once you have eaten this one, your mouth is sucking hard at one nipple and then the other, you say to make sure you have got all the juice as well… But, next you say you need to fit these end caps on yourself… so this is just what you do, taking your time, enjoying the sensual feelings… I can tell just how much you are enjoying this, because your hot rod keeps touching my valley of love, and trying to push its way in there… but, you are distracted by the raspberry nipples… Now, you are laughing, you have that naughty monkey little look in your sparkling eyes… and say… "Michelle, I have to capture this moment to keep for eternity… yes Michelle, you know just what I mean"… Out comes the camera, and you are pushing the button, taking pictures of 'My raspberry ripple nipples'… You zoom out, wide-angle lens, and photograph both boobs in full…then you zoom in… one boob at a time… then zoom right in, and just take the raspberry end-caps!!!!…Wow, you are getting very sexcited now… this hot rod is well and truly standing to attention and brushing itself along my valley of love…… OK… it cannot ignore the hot rod any longer… your big beautiful penis has a mind all of its own…

I move back a little… take hold of your hot rod in both of my hands… all of my fingers caress up and down each side of your lovely hot rod and tattoo… this is as hard as a rock… thick and long… Oh my word, you have enjoyed taking these pictures, I can tell… I run my fingers right up the shaft of your pulsating hot rod once more, right to the head… then gently I roll back the foreskin, as far as it will go… MMMmmmm… the head of your hot rod is shiny and looks ready to blow… A little drop of love juice just slides out of the tip… With one finger I run it right over the tip, and wipe the love juice onto this finger… MMMmmmm… looks delicious… my sparkling blue eyes lock into your sexy smouldering brown eyes… I am smiling at you… and seductively place this finger into my mouth, and very slowly suck the love juice right off of this finger… MMMMMmmmmmm sex-o-liciously delicious…

And, with this you move… you say, "Enough playtime Michelle ~ my hot rod is ready to blow like a volcano"… you roll me over and onto the bed… lay me on my back… with your legs you part mine, first one… and then the other… you have parted them far apart… Now, it is you hovering over me… looking wild and sexy… and with that you say, "Michelle… you are going to get it now… with a vengeance… I am going to pump you so hard and fast you will not even know what day of the week it is by the time I have finished"…

To be continued…

Loving you always
Michelle
xxx xxx xxx xxx x

E-mail from: Mike
To: Michelle
Date: 2 November 2013
Subject: Re: Our love blanket

Hi Michelle

MMMmmmm… So you are really feeling sexy, raunchy and ready for love. I am feeling very horny now, so let us both get down to the business end and give you all my love. My hot rod cannot wait to get inside your love tunnel to give you pleasure and fulfil all your sexual desires and sensual feelings. So here you are lying on your back with your legs wide apart. Your blue flashing eyes are telling me, take my body and give me everything you have got down there in between your legs. Just fill me up with your warm milky love juices. With that you put your two fingers either side of your love tunnel and pull your valley lips apart to reveal a really wet entrance to a very inviting passage leading all the way down inside your love tunnel. OMG… Now you have pulled everything wide apart down there and you have stretched your valley of love even wider apart to reveal your hot spot. Everything is fully exposed and is looking ready for some real loving.

You then take my hard erect long hot rod with both hands and place it at the entrance to your love tunnel. Just when I think you are going to pop it straight inside, you then decide to take me the full length of your love valley up to your hot spot and you start rubbing the tip of my hot rod firmly over your hot spot. You are so sexy Michelle Turner. Mmmm… Now you are taking it back to the entrance of your love tunnel and then back up to your hot spot again and you keep repeating this in a very rhythmic way. That is so nice Mike and I am getting very sexcited and wet down there now, just a few more strokes of your hot rod like this and then you can come inside me. Michelle let us change positions, I much prefer you on top and then I can take charge of your movers and shakers. Neither of us wish to come to any harm once your boobs really get going. They will start rotating and shaking around like a whirlwind once you start making love.

OMG… You are hungry for love and already you have jumped on top of me. Your legs again straddled over my hips and wide apart and ready for love. With both hands on my hot rod you sit very upright and pull my hot rod in a vertical position to the entrance of your love tunnel. Slowly and gently you then lower your body on the tip of my hot rod and I can see the head just starting to disappear inside you. I can feel you are very wet and slippery and gradually the long hard shaft gradually starts sinking and disappears inside you. Mmmm… Mike you are so hard and horny I just need to adjust my body to take the full length of you inside me. You have a little shimmy wiggle and you say, that feels better. I can now see you smiling with just grin of sheer satisfaction, pleasure and enjoyment. You are now getting into a rhythm and you are starting to jump up and down, like you are on a pogo stick. OMG… You have now arched backwards and I can see and feel you really pulling and stretching my hot rod back with you. Michelle you are giving that plenty of welly now and you are getting into a top overdrive position moving faster and faster. Hey… watch out, your boobs are going everywhere and I had better just sit up a little to grab a big breast in each hand. You need to be careful with those long hard nipples because they could dig me in the eye. You must be so sexually sexcited to beable to get your nipples that hard and that long. Then you just lift both arms in the air and brush your fingers through your long blonde hair and you say… This is what I want, really really want, you making love to me in this way. I give each nipple a gentle little suck and then I start to roll my tongue over the ends. They are so long and hard it is like having a bit between your teeth. You can really suck hard and get your teeth stuck into them, Michelle your nipples are so long and hard. I love you Mike Turner caressing my boobs and I know you like long hard nipples. With that you push me right back, still with my hot rod all the way inside you. You then lean forward and take my hot rod back the other way towards me again and you lower your body on top of me and drop your boobs on my stomach and then you start to drag your hard nipples across me. You are not only making the hairs on the back of my neck stand up on end, but just look at the hairs on my body standing up on end when you do this to me. You drag your boobs and nipples right up to the top of me and then you plant a kiss on my lips and then you slowly in reverse drag your nipples across me again. MMMmmmm… Michelle that feels so good, do that again for me. So back you come and what a sensual feeling, this is like no other with my hot rod all the way inside you and you pulling me the other way whilst you drag your nipples across my body once again. This is sheer ecstasy!!

Michelle I can feel my golden nuggets filling up with love juice and you need to go all the way now and ride me out. I am just going to lay back and watch you and enjoy this. You sit back upright again and you raise your body a little so you can get the full feel of my hard shaft going in and out of your love tunnel. Wow… What a lovely body movement up and down in and out, in and out and getting harder and faster. Now you are starting to do a little body twist action like you want it screwed right up inside you. There is no control over those big boobs now; they are going in all directions. Come on Michelle ride me, ride me. You put one hand in the air like you are riding a bucking bronco. Ride me high darling and give me all you have. Then you start crouching down and you are getting lower and lower with every stroke of my hot rod all the way inside you and your hips and thighs start to tighten up and I can feel myself starting to come. Michelle come with me and let's have a final climax ride together. Okay Mike I am going to keep riding you hard and you say just tell me when you are ready to explode. I will know when you are coming anyway because if will feel your hard long shaft pumping all of your warm wet love juices inside me... OMG... Michelle it is coming now, but do not stop, I want you pumping me hard to extract all my love juices and fill you up with my love. You then start shouting that you are about to have an orgasm right at the same time. Come for me Michelle, I need to see you come riding my cock... reaching down between your own legs, you rub your clit with the pads of your fingers, hastening towards your own sweat climax. I throw back my head into the pillows as my panting breaths cried out, "When you are ready to come, your cunt gets so tight... so hot... so greedy" These words push you over the edge, I feel your orgasm ripple throughout your body, spasming all around my pulsating, pumping cock... with one last almighty pump I thrust into you.. and growl out your name through my hissing teeth, my hot liquid fills you... the sensation phenomenal...

Slowly you start to slow down and to get your breath back once again. I am not sure what sort of cocktail we have just mixed up there inside of you, but one thing for sure it was juicy, sexy and hot. You come forward on me and lay your boobs on my chest and I can feel your heart pounding against me. Mike that was a good workout and I think I gave you a good ride and certainly rode you out all the way. I bet there is no love juice even left in your reserve tanks.

With that you take my hot rod out and rub it between your fingers and squeeze it real tight. Oh Mike... I am just going to see if I can manage to get a little spurt of love juice out by squeezing you really tight and bringing my fingers right along the full length of your shaft to the top. Oh... yes! A little spurt has just popped out the head of your hot rod. MMMmmmm... Let me push that foreskin right back and keep it back and take that right into the back of my mouth to finish off this last little drop... MMmmm... yummy, yummy and so tasty. Mike you know sharing is caring. I look at Michelle and she has that sexy cheeky look again on her face. Then she pulls her boob right up to her mouth and dribbles some white frothy juice out of her mouth and places it onto the end of her nipple. Mike this is a well stirred and shaken cocktail of combined love. Come and lick this off and share it with me. MMMmmmm... yummy, yummy and so tasty. A cocktail full of our combined love. My tongue rolling, sucking and tugging at your nipples sending waves of pleasure right through you… your body igniting with the sheer need for more… so with my tongue and lips I suck your nipples so hard… you hug my head into you… and rock your body still with my cock inside you…

This has been so wonderful Mike. Let us just lay here and kiss and cuddle each other and give ourselves a bit of time to recover. Then we can do this all over again, but you can do the work next time! This is the love we shared just a few short weeks ago, our love making wild and passionate. We don't just fuck Michelle, we make love… But our love is not only the lust and need for one another's body, it is the irrefutable love deep within each of our hearts.

Loving you always
Mike
Xxx xxx xxx xxx x

E-mail from: Michelle
To: Mike
Date: 3 November 2013
Subject: Re: Our love blanket

Hi Mike

OMG!!! WOWSA!!!

I need my love blanket… My bed is cold and lonely on my own…

Wow… this is one heck of an e-mail you have sent to me…

I absolutely love my love blanket 113%

Loving you always with all my heart
Michelle
xxx xxx xxx xxx x

E-mail from: Mike
To: Michelle
Date: 7 November 2013
Subject: Cyber relationships

My darling Michelle

In our new modern technology world many relationships are being maintained over mobile phone calls, texting, emailing and video chat. Many couples are using these modern means of communicating and changing to a greater sense of intimacy that is making affairs of the heart grow fonder. Many couples that live apart are finding they have a stronger love and more meaningful love interactions with stronger bonds than those who see each other every day.

Some are in long-distance relationships, some are in relationships outside of their marriage, and others are seeking new relationships. Indeed with interactive marriages throughout the world our cultures are changing and so are our means of communication. In our modern technological world communication and day-to-day conversation are changing and are no longer physically face-to-face. Typical communication using modern technology is finding that in so many ways people can now share their experiences with more intimacy and feel a close bond with each other. Couples are now finding they try harder to communicate and express their love and affection for each other in a modern cyber world.

This is our cyber world that we call home and this cyber lover's book is filled with messages that express the feeling and meaning of love that are shared between two people. With sensual love and passion our cyber world opens our minds and our hearts. These emails and text messages captures the fun-filled love that be have both shared. In our cyber world messages express fun, love, lust, romance, seduction, raunchy, passionate, erotic and explicit sex. A beautiful love that when you read it is not just confined to words, but you can feel it. Sense it and taste it. A love that shows a way and new beginning about sharing love in a modern cyber world.

Love always…

Mike
Xxx xxx xxx xxx x

---

13 November 2013 ~ Live Interactive Text

Mike: Hi my sexy 'cyber lover'

Michelle: Hi my even sexier 'cyber lover'

Mike: This is a good title for 'our book'

Michelle: Yes, I think so too… Any person who is indulging in a cyber love affair, this title will capture their attention, and hopefully they will want to read this book

Mike: Maybe even other lovers in the real world… Shenanigans going on everywhere

Michelle: So we have now put all of our text and emails together, and they sure do tell our love story… I don't think anyone could write a story quite like this on their own… This book is a synergy created by the two of us, the interaction of the two of us… it tells the story from the female and male perspective

Mike: It sure is darling… more than twenty years now, our love has spanned, and I think if this book ever gets published people will relate to this… Although I am not sure that many of them would have had such a love for this long? Our story is from both sides of the love that we share… But, people will think we are really old!!

Michelle: Hey, we were only in our mid-twenties when we met… We are not that old yet ☺

Mike: Not too old for some hot loving, eh? ☺

Michelle: We will never be too old for that darling… ☺

Mike: I hope not… ☺

Michelle: So we are now ready to send our draft manuscript off to see if anyone is interested in publishing it… But how do we really end the book? Is this where we type "THE END" ?

Mike: Darling, this will not be the end… If this book is published… It could be our new beginning?…

Michelle: If we make enough money… we buy a home together… And take off in the real world?

Mike: Yes my Michelle… You will be all mine then… And I will be all yours!!!

Michelle: We never thought we would find a way for this to happen... Mike, you have a warm heart and a sharp mind, and I love both of them

Mike: And you do too Michelle, this is why we go together so well... We were made for each other... and, No we could never see a way to be able to afford to do this... But... Maybe this will provide a way?

Michelle: So, if people are reading this book, they should tell their family and friends to buy it too... then we may make enough money to just be together

Mike: If people are reading this... they may hope we are together somewhere... Maybe we will even write a sequel book to tell them all what happens next?

Michelle: So, this is not the end... But a new beginning

Mike: We have wanted to be together for so long darling... I hope this provides us with a way... We just pack a bag of clothes each... Take our passports... The money from our book... Leave everything else behind us... And go...

Michelle: Oh darling, do you every really think this could really happen?

Mike: I hope so Michelle... I have loved you for so long. I want you to be mine 24/7... You are a lovely person inside and out. I wish now that we had taken the risk and done it all those years ago, but we cannot turn back time. We can only move forward. You and I belong together... Let's hope this is our time. I want you Michelle. I want us to be together for the rest of our lives. And, I know that is what you want too.

Michelle: Mike... I love you so much... I could never love anyone more than I love you right at this moment... I want this too... and I will always love you, whatever happens.

Mike: "DITTO"...

* * * * * * * * * * * * *